The Writings of Owen Wister

NEIGHBORS HENCEFORTH

The Writings of Owen Wister

RED MEN AND WHITE

LIN McLEAN

HANK'S WOMAN

THE VIRGINIAN

MEMBERS OF THE FAMILY

WHEN WEST WAS WEST

LADY BALTIMORE

SAFE IN THE ARMS OF CROESUS

U. S. GRANT AND THE SEVEN AGES
OF WASHINGTON

THE PENTECOST OF CALAMITY AND
THE STRAIGHT DEAL

NEIGHBORS HENCEFORTH

The Writings of Owen Wister

of The American Academy of Arts and Letters
Membre Correspondant de la Société
des Gens de Lettres
Honorary Fellow of the Royal Society of Literature

Neighbors Henceforth

NEW YORK
The Macmillan Company
1928

PRINTED IN THE UNITED STATES OF AMERICA BY
R. R. DONNELLEY & SONS CO., AT THE LAKESIDE PRESS, CHICAGO

PREFACE—*A Piece of Extravagance*

BAD business again, this autobiography about things seen, heard, said, and thought, in-doors and out, in England and France, while Woodrow Wilson was there, and after that. The critics received it cordially in Paris, London, and at home; but the public—! It bought something else.

What is the life of a man?—three-score-and-ten, we're told; and what the life of a book—not Homer or Horace —but the wares we scribblers of to-day mostly produce? Isn't it a lucky book that lives ten years? Shouldn't any that survives its author dance and sing? Don't most of us witness the passing of our own works? I have outlived this one, anyhow. Published in 1922, it immediately expired.

My fault. No writer has any more call to curse the public than to bless them: his debt is to himself. I chose an unpopular subject. Though we're no longer free to drink what we like, we're still allowed to read what we like—and *write* what we like, taking the consequences!

In this case, I would take them again: the two years of dedication, the two journeys to Europe, the friends made there, the golden hours of speech with great English and great French, the laughter, the sadness, the inspiration of emotions which when set vibrating can toll instead of merely tinkle—all this is an adventure I would live over for its own sake: as I turn the pages and recall the days from which they grew, would it were possible!

Almost I am tempted, as I re-read the chapter entitled "The Cook and the Doughboy," to slip in a new chapter just there, one that I began, but abandoned. Its facts, and the feelings which they aroused, were all compressed into just two remarks.

Upon returning from a journey to Verdun, St. Mihiel,

and the Argonne under military escort, I called upon our
officers in Paris, 37 rue de Bassano, to thank them for the
constant courtesy and hospitality which I had met; and to
say good bye. Return to America was imperative.

They urged that I remain; material for a hundred books
lay thick over the face of the desolate earth; all should be
shown, if I would but delay and see it; the very next day
I could be sent to Cologne. Without a visit to us, and the
French, and English, in Germany, my explorations would
be incomplete. A week there was offered. It could not be.

"Yet in a way," I said to the officer, "I feel as if I had
seen all I can bear. For among the ruins I have met our
congressmen."

He flung up both hands—

"I know what you mean!" he exclaimed.

The chapter was given up, because it seemed too much
of a digression. And I remembered that in 1916 I had met
a Congressman who could both read and write. And I
felt sure there must be others.

But the general understood what I meant.

OWEN WISTER.

Long House, Bryn Mawr, 1928.

THE plight of France, the deed of Germany, and inevitable path ahead of the United States, are the main themes of this volume, which closes a series of three, begun with *The Pentecost of Calamity*, followed by *A Straight Deal*.

Philadelphia, Decoration Day, 1922.

TABLE OF CONTENTS

PART FIRST

IN THE FOOTSTEPS OF THE HUN

xi

Contents

PART SECOND

AFTER TWO YEARS

NEIGHBORS
HENCEFORTH

I

FACES AND A SCAR

AS we went along the straight road, I began to see
what was not there, while what was there dis-
solved slowly away from my open eyes. The
April night, full of sounds and storm, had
dropped upon the hills one last thin veil of snow, and this
still stretched its gleamy film over their ridges. Below, it
was gone from the wide flat lands, where blossoms ex-
panded beneath the sun of the April day. These came by
like white clouds caught in the twigs of the fruit trees.
Along the road as we went, they showed above the tops
of the high French walls, they shone mistily across the flat
French distance. Among the taller trees, in the heights of
the poplars and the willows, hung like a breath the
faintly tinted web that betokened sap stirring, life awakening, leaves invisible but soon to come. Every early deli-
cate hue of field and garden and wood beamed through
skein upon skein of weaving exhalations. On either side
the constantly straight road, I watched between the trunks
of the poplars acres upon acres, where wet new grass
glinted, brooks ran full, and far-off tufts of spring color,
like puffs of smoke, seemed enmeshed in the tangle of the
copses.

How unlike was this to England, the England I had just
seen! Yes, but one strange, deep likeness there was. I

1

had not walked for five minutes in England after setting
foot on shore—I had not walked for two—before I was
aware of the changed English face. Once aware of it, it
was something I should never forget. In the trains, in the
streets, in the houses, in the churches—especially in the
churches—you could read that the English face had looked
upon something, and was changed. When they were talking, even when they were laughing, it did not quite go, this
change in look; and it always wholly returned. Soldiers
had it, and civilians, men and women; not all the children,
but even some of them. It corresponded to nothing that
they ever said. Their talk was usual, cheerful, and they
referred to sad things lightly, and they joked and enjoyed
your joke. The one thing that they never said was the
thing which their faces said for them. Did they know this?
Could I ask them? Never. People of old that saw
Medusa's head were turned to stone. I thought of this
myth and its marvellous symbol often in the first days;
but it was not Medusa's head that had been looked upon.
The English were farther away from being stone than ever
I had seen them. Turn to old photographs of Northerners
and Southerners in our Civil War, and in the faces of
those dedicated boys, and of their fathers and mothers,
you will find the counterpart of what I saw in the English
face. Compared with those of our Civil War, the general
American face of today is an empty countenance. Then,
on coming from England to France, the same thing had
been visible at once. Those who examined our passports
on the quay, those who opened our baggage, the porters
who then carried it, the woman from whom I bought coffee
and bread at the station, and the woman at the bookstall
on the platform—in the faces of them all, whether they
talked, smiled, or were silent, was what I had seen in
England, what I had not seen at home. The Parisians had
it, too, in the hotels, the shops, the cafés. I ceased to see
the kilometre stones as we passed them on this April forenoon, or the blossoms, or the fields; my memory showed
me only the French faces, of women or of men, belonging

to every class. The look they wore was like a sort of language which did not need to be spoken, which needed no translation. It was a common language to both French and English, and they all understood it.

Suddenly, in the green field by which we were passing on that long straight road, an object broke my reverie. It was a charred, half-roasted aeroplane, lying there like a great dead black bat. It was a symbol, like Medusa's head. The Huns had never been able to walk as near Paris as this, but they had sailed here through the air, dropping flames and death during four hideous years. To my fancy now, as we went along that straight highway, the trees with their blossoms, the hills with their snow, the flat country veiled with the tender heralding hues of spring, all nature, seemed to wear the look of the English and French faces.

II

AGAIN for a while I watched it, this avenue between the high poplars, broad where we were, narrowing to a line far ahead in the April haze. There was no breeze. The air lay limp after the night's long turbulence, but our speed brought a sharp wind against the face. I watched the houses and villages. La Chapelle-en-Serval came and was gone, and Pontarmé; after which we went through some lean woods. These were empty, so were the fields, so was everything. France was here—but where were the French? That crumpled aeroplane, far behind us now, gave the answer. It was rare to see man or woman dotting the flat spaces. So little motion of human beings there was, that each occurrence of it caught the eye. Even the village streets stared somewhat blankly because they were so nearly bare of people. Paris streets had swarmed. Every pavement had been a jungle of men and women. The crowd seemed to obscure the very architecture. One stood a long while waiting for a vacant seat to dine, and the trains underground were congested thick with passengers. There, in Paris, one had met the aeroplane in various symbolic guises. By the window in the bank where I got my money, stood a young messenger with one eye sunk in blankness, and black gloves upon his artificial hands. Walking about in the room, or seated, were figures with crutches, and empty sleeves, and limping mechanical gaits. Nothing had seemed the matter with the smiling fellow who answered my bell, took my clothes, knocked on my door at the appointed hour, until his charming cheerfulness and succulent pronunciation led me one day to say:

"You're from the South, I can hear it."

"Yes, monsieur. From Toulouse. Monsieur should make

4

us a visit. It is not France here, we are more amiable than these Parisians. Paris is not amiable."

"You're very far from home."

"Yes, indeed, monsieur. One must do what one can. Oh, I shall go back."

Then I learned of his three wounds and that one of these was still a living pain. But as the days passed this pain was growing less, he was going to be quite well and strong. He told me, too, that once for twenty-four hours he had been buried with some comrades by the bursting of a shell. "We thought that was the finish, but they dug us out in time. I shall be able to do heavier work as soon as this gets all right"—and he touched his body lightly. If in his valiant smiling spirit there was a sore spot, he never revealed it.

In Paris, it needed but to fall into friendly talk like this with almost any man at all, except the very old, and you learned that he had paid his toll of blood. He had paid it in nineteen-fourteen, or fifteen, or sixteen, seventeen, eighteen—sometimes in several of these years; and often he had brothers who had paid the final toll. Now and then his women had paid women's toll, and not infrequently his house and village, like his brothers, were come to dust. To you who read this, how can I impart what hearing it was like, face to face with those who had lived what they told? It cannot be done. I cannot make you hear them any more than I can make you see that crumpled aeroplane, lying like a scar on the clean fields. It was the first broken refuse, the first dead ember of war that I met; and all the mounds and miles of extinction that I was presently to look at and remember for ever, have not obliterated this stark evil image, this plague-spot upon the face of spring.

Senlis came and went. War signs were here more plentiful, yet not enough to jog me back to the sights of the road. We passed Villeneuve-sur-Verberie. These names I heard, and for a moment saw the places, but remember nothing of their aspect. I was travelling forty-nine years away; I was sailing up the Rhine that day in 1870 when that war began; I was seeing Bismarck's locomotives puffing by, linked for mobilization; I was hearing that hysterical shout of false alarm from a man in the skiff on the river:

"Die Französen sind zu Bingen!"

Thus this frightened German had raved as he stood swinging his arms in the middle of the Rhine to warn our steamer back. It had raised amongst the passengers a flutter and a suspense, all pleasure to me. The events that followed upon this day during many months had been all pleasure to me, because I understood the significance of none of them: our boat's unhindered passage up the Rhine, near which, in that war, no French ever came; our stay at Mainz; our thwarted plan for Oberammergau; our flight from Munich to Lindau upon a long, crowded train of travellers likewise seeking in haste a neutral country; our crossing of the lake to Romanshorn; then Switzerland; and soon for me the boarding-school of Hofwyl, near Berne. Of less importance to me then than my studies and my home-sickness was the public news. Older people spoke of Gravelotte and Sedan. I did not connect these names with Bismarck's locomotives. Those were a picture, while names of distant battles and surrenders had no reality for me. Reality of the locomotive sort came next with another set of pictures at that Hofwyl school. Our long stone house wherein we both lived and studied faced west, and the setting sun blinked upon it through a grove of trees. Eastward at our back the open land sloped slowly down for about a mile to a lake, itself about a mile long and half as wide. Flanking our right was the gymnasium in a big sort of granary, slightly in advance of the front line of the house. In this I know not how many French soldiers came to be barracked. They had fled across the border, from Belfort if I remember, into Switzerland, and here they had been interned. They were drilled each day. They used to be drawn up in front of the granary, and we would go and watch them and

hear them answer to the roll-call. Their faces were grave,
unhappy, little washed, little shaved, their uniforms dingy,
their voices, as they responded, rather wild and strange.
They were a little piece of the rags of Napoleon III's
Empire. Bismarck's locomotives had torn it and these
lives to shreds—though this I took in not then, but long
after. What I then took in was just the pictures, the daily
scenes; the white snow, the black trees, the red sparks of
setting sun; the long gaunt lines of the schoolhouse and
granary; we boys in our uniforms staring at the drill; the
dingy unhappy interned, their hairy faces, their strange
voices, their winter breath; and then, one day, we boys
running to the east side of the house, where we watched
one of the interned French trying to escape. He was a dot
on the frozen lake, other dots were on the land, and puffs
of smoke behind him came from the guns, as he struggled
to get away—and he did not succeed. You may say that
Bismarck's locomotives caught him, after all.

Well, well. Thus near the beginning of my days and
thus again near their end, I had seen the symbols of
Germany's murdering, mangling plunge: puffing engines,
victorious then, the bones of a wrecked aeroplane just
now. A Germany truculent, but as yet unpoisoned in
1870, a malign, putrescent Germany this time. Was she
now cured of her evil dream? Was the world henceforth
to be able to breathe naturally? I saw a stream and a
broken bridge; by the side of this we crossed a make-shift
bridge, got out for a noon meal, and after it set forth back
across the river to walk into the streets of the town.

III

HOW suddenly it came! What must the noise of shells be? On the ninth day of the siege of Verdun I have been told that almost every soldier was crying. That is what noise can do. During four months there—four months, one hundred and twenty changeless days—ten thousand shells each day—eight-inch shells and upward—fell upon the Verdun fortresses, Vaux and Douamont. One hundred and eleven days of this shattering noise were still ahead of those French soldiers who were crying on the ninth day—still ahead, that is, for such as lived it out. I stared at the mute wreck which the shells had made in Compiègne. Since November war had been silenced, noise was dead, the deafening years that France had heard, and through which she had been able to keep her heart undaunted and her head clear, were behind her, while before her was—what? In the death of noise silence was born. This silence I had begun to enter on the way from Paris; here at Compiègne it deepened. I felt it deepening as you feel the change when the thermometer is falling. In the days that were to follow I waked and slept and lived in this huge silence that spread everywhere, cloaked the country and the towns, enveloped trees and ruins and people and houses and graves and trenches and barbed wire, and was like an element. As fish swim in the sea, so did we move in this silence.

Something, some intimation, had impelled my friend and me to separate and walk apart. Each of us saw Compiègne alone, and met again after the first experience was over. We did not say much about it. All the large joys, loves, griefs, horrors, amazements, lie outside the realm of speech: the man who makes words in their presence lives too close to himself for true understanding or sharing.

8

The hand of the Hun had been laid upon Compiègne, and Compiègne was withered. Its blight was not complete. All its inhabitants were not dead or gone away, all the houses were not gutted, life stirred in the streets, goods and wares were for sale in some shop windows, the French soldier, bright in his blue, starred the prevailing darkness of civilian garments:—but then you turned some corner and all this was ended. Ruin like a barrier stopped you. Through gaping windows you looked beyond to more gaping windows, it was dangerous to climb and peer, signs warned you off, and decency bade you avert your eyes. One turned away from peeping through this keyhole at naked, slaughtered France.

People at home have often asked:

"But when you have seen Compiègne, have you not seen everything? Is not one ruin just like another?"

One ruin in a Sunday paper is like another and you look at it spread upon your lap. Mile upon mile of ruin in France, travelled over, paused at, dwelt on, compared, its particular story listened to—this has no monotony, this fills your knowledge fuller and ever more full each day; compared to Sunday papers, it is like seeing Niagara, the Rocky Mountains, the Grand Cañon, after looking at a map of the United States.

Compiègne was now behind us, and to our right the Oise, brimful, pouring swiftly along, as we went on the road to the town of Noyon. That was twenty kilometres ahead. The words in my diary of this unearthly stretch are few and almost illegible, scrawled at the finish, in Noyon.

Very abrupt in France are the transitions from ground and dwellings untouched by shells to fields that are all gashed and houses that are mere scorched husks. The houses here were worse than the fields. The comparison seems desecrating, yet I know of none better than to say that every house along this road was like a painted house in a play. As each came into view you thought, "This one is all right." In the next instant the illusion was blasted.

Distant walls and chimneys of pomp, suggesting grand
pianos and family portraits within, turned out as we
passed them close to be stark, roofless shelters of the void,
hollow squares, enclosing charred beams, rank weeds, and
twisted iron. From haughtiest to humblest, all were dead.

"Of 1914, that one," explained our chauffeur. It had
evidently been a residence of comfort.

How did he know the year when its ruin was wrought?
Had he been there?

"No, monsieur. One knows easily from the moss and
vines. Those have been growing already a long while
without any disturbance."

It was real yet unreal. The sense of the theatre haunted
the whole of those twenty unearthly kilometres that first
day between Compiègne and Noyon. Later, as one's initiation deepened and grew steeped in the terrific until the
terrific became the usual, it was then that the usual itself
began to look far off and unreal. All the way to Noyon,
the invariable repetition of ruin failed to stop appearances from deceiving me. A little farm would come in
sight, its walls looking so solid and the tall trees about it
so serene, that I would exclaim:

"At least these people have their home safe!"

A few seconds more and we were passing another husk,
and where were the people whose home the husk had been?
Yet still I continued to watch for an exception along this
road, all the way to Noyon.

Here the silence let down another veil between us and
the natural world. Rain was now falling. Through it I
saw what was neighboring to Noyon—barbed wire,
trenches under a hill topped by a ruined wood, shell holes,
dead trees, ruins of brick, gas-tank ruins; and amid all
this various death, the dingy green forms of German prisoners, and the constant sound of explosions in the fields.
The prisoners were at work around Noyon, setting off
bombs by wire, and pillars of smoke rose slowly upward
in the rain.

"They are victims, too," I said to the chauffeur.

"Yes, monsieur."

Victims they were, and their plight was bad, though it was as nothing beside the plight of France, their victim. While their chance lasted they had done to her all that I was seeing and to see, and they would be doing it still, had their tide not turned.

They were at work in Noyon as well as around it. Here were no shops, every house I saw was dead, many fallen walls piled the streets high, there was no passing, not even any walking, save in the few cleared spaces. Lumps lay about, lumps made of houses burst and spattered over their crushed gardens; roofs belonging nowhere, yet still almost whole, tilted like kites tumbled from the air. Doorways stood alone, leading to vacancy. Cellars yawned wide. Into these fell the rain and in some of them people seemed to be living. Walls still erect masked dislocated interiors, and the placard *Verifié* was on several. This meant that the interior had been visited and that nothing there would fall upon you or explode, should you choose it for a lodging. Older placards were on other walls, announcing *Cave abri 50 personnes,* which meant that fifty could hide down in there when bombs were falling upon Noyon. I had seen beauty lying dead at Compiègne, arches, pillars, carved stones. More was here. The church was a shambles of murdered architecture. Black, cawing birds sailed and slanted in and out of its windows. Its tower stood, and its outer walls, but within its dismembered entrance everything had been struck by the blow of hate and toppled in one mass of broken aisle and choir and crucifix and tomb. Through the shrivelled dial of its clock on a tower a shell had made its way. They had done to it the worst they could; yet its beauty was not all killed. What of it was left stood there, ancient, serene, sanctified by centuries of human souls at prayer, still delivering to Noyon its message of love divine. From its steps I looked across at the wreck of a sweet old house, beautiful even in its fragments; above the shattered walls of what had been the garden, a little fruit tree lifted its head. Amid the aching stillness, the crumbling, the death, it stood up, alive and growing. Its cluster of pink buds would be blossoms by tomorrow. The sight of it, so fresh, so young, so futile, was very pitiful. A verse from Exodus came to me unsought: "Draw not nigh hither: put off thy shoes from off thy feet, for the place whereon thou standest is holy ground."

Between me and the little blossoming fruit tree, three women veiled in black walked into sight. They stopped at the foot of the church steps. After a short silence, two of them went on slowly, whilst the third, who remained, fixed her grave eyes upon me.

I came down the steps with my hat in my hand.

"Madame," I said, "this is my first day among all this."

"Yes, monsieur, one must get used to it. I was from Noyon. I live at Nevers now."

"Nevers is a long way from Noyon, madame."

"Others have gone farther. I am here today to look for my house."

She turned away from the steps of the church. In a little while, as I walked back to where our car was waiting, I saw her with her companions in a street impassable except by climbing over the stones of toppled residences. The three black figures were pointing out and consulting amid a waste of featureless débris, the rain streaming heavily down upon them.

Throughout this day each aspect that April can wear had its turn. Nothing of the snow veil, or the gleam, or the hazy gentleness of the forenoon accompanied our journey from Noyon to Roye. The sky bulged low with swollen, restless clouds. We passed the kilometre stones in a pelting shower sometimes, and sometimes in the grey of a light that betokened further showers along the kilometres which lay ahead. For a while our way was accompanied by the noise of explosions and their smoke. Stooping women were in the fields, their faces down, their arms moving at some work. I thought they were sowing seed, but the chauffeur told us that it was the shell holes they were filling. These spotted the earth far and near, and seemed thick to us on this first sight of them; before the land could be fitly farmed they had to be filled by those stooping women.

Somewhere along this road we saw for the first time a war railway, a light narrow-gauge affair, vacant and idle now, laid in haste upon no secure ballast. Over its unsettled bed it tilted and curved through this bit of country, its disused rails reddened with rust. A year ago it had been full of business, plying the Huns with means to deal this silence to the slain earth. No trains were here now, and nothing to load them with, had they been here. The poplars bordering our road had been felled, we ran along between their severed stumps, and here for the first time we saw in some of the farms the murdered fruit trees. There would be the house, shattered, and the out-buildings, shattered, sunk in various angles of wreck, and beyond these the symmetrically amputated orchard, dead, on its knees, so to speak, as if it had prayed its destroyers to spare the other orchards' lives. Since this land was not to be the invader's booty, as much of it as could be killed should die.

Upon the walls and doors of Noyon we had read the placards announcing shelter from bombs. These were French, in the language of the victims. The language of the invaders met us at some cross-roads half-way to Roye. The single word *zur* was on a sign-post, the rest broken off. Zur: To——. The name of the place was splintered away, and the place itself was no more to be seen. Shell holes and dead trees lay between us and its stones. We might turn right or left—shell holes and dead trees and the stones of little places would be all that there was to see. *Zur*. Three letters of the alphabet put together. The wrecks of homes and fields were the Huns' work, but this was their speech. They had intended that German should be spoken here in the future.

We read the next Hun words on a head-board over a grave at the edge of Rove:

"Hier ruht in Gott Fahrer Ph. Rihr Mag. F. Kel. 188
Gefallen beim Vormarsch 30 Marz, 1918."

"Here rests in God" . . .

In what God, in whose God, was he reposing?

No man can say. It was neither he, nor such as he, upon
whose soul lay the guilt of all this. From his cradle he
had been schooled for it by those who had drilled him,
mind and spirit. The guilt was theirs. This soldier, had
he lived to see the Fatherland again, would have been
with millions of other Germans an uncertain quantity for
the rest of us. Would disaster have cured him, or would it
have merely made him wish to bide his time and come
again? He was a victim, too, like the living ones I had
seen as prisoners at Compiègne. His dust was more tragic
than that of the dead French or English that slept in the
battlefields of Picardy and Flanders. Their countries rose
to sacrifice, his country fell. That is why Germany's
tragedy, from the time I saw it clear in the first months
of the war, has seemed to me always the greatest tragedy
of all.

Just thirteen months ago this soldier had fallen at an
hour when it seemed as if he and his hordes were at last
to overrun and rule these shell-shocked fields. In that case
our turn was to come, our homes and orchards were to look
like this. We did not know it then, we went to war not
to defend them but to save a cause. We learned later
that "Paris in three weeks, London in three months, New
York in three years," had been the plan in full.

The very ground to which our road was leading us today was sacred to the memory of our dead also, had seen
the stain of our long neutrality wiped away with the grit
of our onset, the blood of our dead, the tears of our bereft.
Montdidier was ahead, where our 1st Division had been
rushed this week a year ago, and one month later it had
taken Cantigny with a swift and splendid sweep.

Through Roye our road twisted like an S, by an extinct
church on the left and on the right a half ruin, wherein
butchers were at work and whereon was advertised horse

meat of the first quality. Half ruins and whole ruins surrounded a square, the Place d'Armes, and over what was left of the door of a more important ruin on this square was the sign of the Hun: *Stadt Kommandant*. Along the seventeen kilometres to Montdidier the ravages of war continued unchanged, and war's other leavings increased and thickened. So far, trenches and excavations had not been close to the road we had come. Line upon line of them now furrowed the face of the land like huge sentences scrawled across a huge page in some ancient alphabet. Dug-outs lined the road, cellared the higher banks in rows, like the suburban operations of contractors. Immense piles of obus, never fired, still alive, littered the bare and muddy fields. From an aeroplane one could have looked down upon these slabs and blocks of unexploded shells as if they were the fragments of some dislocated town. A grey lattice-work of camouflage three metres high still shielded the road, its material torn and hanging in strips, but much of it as it had been in the days when it concealed the passing troops and trains of munitions and provisions. Squads of men were at work removing and effacing all this. Camions lurched by, or stood in the mud. Winter had but lately left this region and the labor seemed but just to have begun; for all the change it had made as yet to the eye, war and the Huns might have gone away last week. No house seemed whole at Montdidier. Between the houses and everywhere around them the ground looked like a paste of mud irredeemable. You have seen places where floods have swept all shapes to a general shapelessness. The valley here was something like that. In the mud labored the squads of men, small objects in the large obliteration.

We did not take the road through Cantigny, but that on the west bank of the river, along a ridge, to which we mounted as we left Montdidier. From this high ground I was able presently to look across the lower territory over which our 1st Division had made its attack. Straw still covered the wet floors of the dug-outs, their steps

were slippery, telephone wires stretched and dangled between them, they were still concealed by the disguising
bushes and the burlap lattice-work of camouflage. The
footprints of war seemed very fresh. You could have
picked up from the floors and shelves of the dug-outs more
tokens than you could have carried away.

Quite different from Compiègne or Noyon or Roye was
the aspect of Moreuil; quite different, too, from the
smaller clusters of dwellings, the *petit pays*, the assembled group of the French farm. Those had been generally
grey, built of brittle stone, and when their walls were
struck they crumbled partly or entirely, and their ancient
beauty vanished never to be made again. Moreuil was of
brick and did not fall when shells bored through it. Its
gutted walls enclosed nothing, they stood up like masks, or
a bad dream. They were of today, their like could easily
be built again. We looked down upon them from the road
along the ridge, with the sun shining upon their spread
of ruin, out of which stuck high into the air one chimney
that the shells had missed. Beside the road a family had
built a hovel of tar paper and slats, and in the mud the
children were laying a brick porch in front of its door.
Five thousand people had lived in Moreuil, five hundred
were able to live there today; in what and on what I did
not see.

Soon after this the signs of war began to dwindle away
as we went along the valley; houses that were whole increased in number; the town of Boves was much less
damaged than any in the fifty miles since Compiègne. In
Amiens, at a hotel I had known for a long while, I ended
this day.

IV

GAUNT renovations, raw partitions of wood, newly set up and still awaiting paint, met my sight. They gave to this place, so familiar and once so upholstered and cheerful, where I had eaten and slept in other days, the appearance of a friend whom one is allowed to see for the first time after a wasting and perilous illness.

"Yes," said the landlord, "we were bombed, as you see. We began again in January."

"But the cathedral?"

"We have it, we shall have it. Only hit seven times. You will see."

"And the stork?" I now asked him.

"Ah, you have been here before, then?"

"Many times. And the last time, in July 1914, I watched from my bedroom window the stork walking with a sea-gull in his domain beneath; and I went down into that domain of lawn and garden which the wings of the hotel enclosed. But the stork turned away from my advances."

"He is dead," said the landlord. "When the bombs came, an English officer quartered here was going on leave, and he offered to take him to a place of safety. The stork went to London, where he died."

The hotel was chill as a cave, few guests seemed to be lodging in it, and but a few of these were civilians. Of travellers such as we there seemed to be none except ourselves. The mere sight-seer was still debarred. He would swarm later, when roads and roofs and meals and all facilities were more ready and less scant than they were today.

Daylight still lingered, the dinner hour was not imminent, so I walked out of the cold hotel into the cold, damp

17

streets and turned my steps to the cathedral. This town,
larger than Compiègne, was like Compiègne and like no
other through which our road had lain during this day of
desolation, until our fleeting sight of Boves. As I went
along the streets, a curious sensation of reassurance increased within me, and I grew aware that this had begun
in Boves. There I had noticed the first houses which looked
like usual houses, with roofs and doors and windows with
people looking out of them, and I had seen people walking
about or crossing the street, like usual people. Here was
more of it. Shop windows had usual things for sale in
them, cheeses and books and hats; people stood in the
shop doors, women put parcels into baskets, men bought
newspapers and struck matches to light cigarettes; I saw
children, dogs, and a cat recumbent, sleek, licking her fur
as if there had never been a bomb in the world. As a man
who has been deep in a dreadful dream where nothing
happens but the monstrous, faintly begins to feel that it
is not true, and then suddenly knows that he is in his bed
and safe, so I walked in Amiens, released from the haunting day by these natural sights. The real world still
existed. The haunting day seemed not of this time, but
something long ago: those cities of dug-outs and tilted
zigzag trenches, those slabs of piled ammunition, those
toppled clumps of masonry, those stooping women over
the shell holes, might all have been a piece of legend, woven
in some great stiff faded fabric hanging in some castle
where cold airs blow from turrets and corridors unseen.

"We began again in January."

The Hôtel du Rhin had been bombed, its landlord's business had been smashed and shattered, emptied of all profit,
guestless, even the pet bird obliterated; but one year ago
the destroyer had been shaking these gates; and here were
we guests, fed, bedded, paying bills. I rejected the sombre
prophecy of a great Belgian lady, made to one of our
soldiers: "There will be no recovery." These French would
recover. There was that cat, licking her comfortable fur.
She, too, was a mute parable. France was not dead, was

not going to die. Even amid the spread of the war-desert were areas of life. Between Maubeuge and Landrecies it was said that the Hun had not ravaged. Other spots than this had been left alive, and the dead places would be raised from the dead. Smoke would come again some day out of that lone chimney at Moreuil. Smoke would come again from the dead chimneys of Lille. Machinery would clank again in the dead factories and drowned mines. Wheat and fruit would ripen again where I had seen the shell holes. Later eyes than mine would never see those stooping women. Later eyes than mine would see the farmer back upon his farm, the exile restored to his dwelling; travellers coming after me might stand on the steps of Noyon church and hear singing within. I verily believe that nothing I saw in Amiens streets on my way to the cathedral this evening gave me more of reassurance and more brought me back out of the world where I had been into a possible world than that quiet cat, licking her fur!

V

AN INN OF THE SOUL

I WENT along the street of the cat and the people and the little shops where little purchases were being made, bidding a new welcome to each new humble sign that I saw of home life being lived. The very humblest were the very best. I can remember stopping to watch a stream of soapy water flowing from some outlet; I had never thought to feel thankful for such a sight. Little in the world is more awful than the first visit to familiar places after some eternal change has passed over them, or over oneself. I went on and reached a street so well remembered that for a moment time shut flat, and all my bygone sauntering here became present; it was unbelievable that round the corner I should not meet those who had walked there with me once. Then I turned the corner and with this step was in the silence again. My own personal memories vanished as they had come, like ghosts. My own silences were swallowed in this great silence of France. I had thought it distant for a while, out there, out beyond Boves, out among the barbed wire and the holes and the stooping women. It was here. It filled like a presence the narrower street I had entered. Sills and doors were heavy with it. It set its weight upon the very paving-stones. The small bustle of life behind me was merely a hole in its vastness. I cannot remember what ruin I passed in this street, what roofs or walls were bomb-broken, perhaps there were none; I remember the silence alone, its sweeping return upon me, the hush in which it steeped my thoughts.

Were the life and motion in the other street nothing but a raft from a great wreck, floating upon this waste, never to reach shore, in a little while to be engulfed? Did those people sell and buy their small wares and cook their sup-

pers merely as men with sudden, mortal wounds sometimes
go onward for a while, unaware that they have been severed from existence?

The landlord's word came back to me.

What had they begun again in January? The first steps
of a long climb back to health, or the last lap before the
null and the void? Was our whole era mortally wounded?
Had we all been severed from existence, were we all on the
last lap? Other days and civilizations that were long ago
came into my head; great, crumbled, prone cities, whose
names conjure up the mounded desert, and pillars lying
about, and wide stone stairways with lions prowling upon
them. Were the yellow sands of Asia presently to have
their turn and to sweep over and bury us all?

I looked up; I had come in my slow walk to the
cathedral.

If thoughts can stop, the sight of it stopped mine. So
does a shutter thrown open in the morning pour the room
full of light. There is music, very little, which to hear
makes one feel that it happened of itself, that it came
out of space like a wind. There are lines of poetry, very
few, that do not seem to have been written, unless by the
elements. No poetry that I have read, no music that I
have heard, so lift one up into that region of marvelling
which lies beyond the powers of speech, as does this church
of Amiens. Its two great sisters of Reims and Chartres
do this also: no others in the world: no buildings made
by man at any time in Italy or Greece or anywhere so
strike self to nothing and leave only wordless wonder,
wordless awe, motionless delight. Out of Eastern sands
rise monuments as august, but they are unfriendly. The
only sights surpassing the befriending glory of these
churches are of the water and of the earth and the air,
and what nature does at morning and evening. To be able
to look at them unmoved must be to have no soul at all.
They are endless like nature; one does not tire of them,
and to return to them is to find them greater than one's
memory.

My thoughts began again, whilst that miracle in stone shone down upon me and into me. How had men made it? It looked as if beings from another place had come through the sky, bearing it among them, and had set it down here and gone away. It was greater than the silence. It rose symmetric into a realm of august tranquillity far above the voiceless, shapeless hell which I had begun to enter at Compiègne. Then I heard myself saying aloud:

"....magic casements opening on the foam
Of perilous seas, in fairy lands forlorn."

I looked about the square, the place was empty, I had it to myself. Forlorn? Yes, forlorn indeed, but not fairy lands. Noyon and Roye and Montdidier and Moreuil were not fairy lands. I thought again of those in whose company I had gazed at these magic casements in other years. I was glad that they were gone, glad that none of them had lived to know what men can do to this earth: villages dead and those who had lived in them, fields extinct and those who had plowed in them, churches in dust and those who had prayed in them, tombs burst open and the bones that slept in them, toys in ashes and those who had played with them. These casements had opened on the foam of many mortal lives, on seven hundred years of men. They were two centuries old when Columbus was born. Men and women in how many fashions of dress had knelt beneath the vast arches within, while the stained light streamed down upon their heads. In how many languages had "Our Father who art in Heaven" been whispered here?

The words of one of those companions who once had stood at this corner with me, looking up as I was looking now, came back to me:

"You are so beautiful with the promise and the consolation which you speak without words," she had said, addressing the great church, "that you set one praying before one enters you. Surely, just to see you would open in every one the vault where his childhood's prayers had been shut, no matter how long it had been locked!" She walked away from me and went into the church.

No vault was unlocked in me while I stood remembering this, yet none the less was I drawn by memory and by the power of the great church. I wished to go inside by that door where my friend had entered, and sit down for a while and think quietly of her, and of those others for whose death I was glad, because they had not known what man can do to this earth.

A soldier came out of the door and behind him a verger, who locked it and departed. The church was shut till morning.

Dusk was advancing but light was by no means yet gone, it would be slow in going. I did not wish to leave until I must; I moved beneath the spell. The power of the church seemed something which not the spirit alone but even the body could feel. I stepped slowly back from it to see as much of its majestic length and height as I could. Then I grew aware of the first figure that had come out of the door. I had hardly noticed him while the official was locking it. I had seen that he was a soldier with a broad hat and had thought no more about him. He was an American, an officer. Something more than his uniform betokened his race, something apart from whatever features he might have, something young, ages and generations younger than the official who had locked the door. He was still standing near it, with his back to me. He was too close to the church to be able to see anything of it, except the door and the temporary scaffolding surrounding it. He stood motionless, graceful, intent, and I wondered what it was that he found to absorb him so deeply.

A young soldier from America, standing in antique Picardy, staring curiously at the cathedral of Amiens: the latest war-clad figure in the pageant of wars which had wet every one of that cathedral's seven centuries with blood: behind these seven, ere ever its first stone had been

laid, other centuries wet with blood, back to the bringing
of Christianity to this antique Picardy, sixteen hundred
years ago: and then still back until the records die away
and the pageant of wars fades into the years unrecorded
and unknown. Roman blood, Norman blood, English
blood, Spanish blood, French blood, had drenched this
soil; and now, as if the veins of the Old World had been
opened too often and too long, and were running dry,
time had tapped fresh reservoirs, and had drawn the
blood of the New World to drench this ancient soil.

The young soldier stood so still that, had he not raised
his hand once and passed it over his forehead, he might
have been inanimate; his form had the quietness of the
cathedral itself. Did this American close to that Gothic
portal which had been a portal long before Columbus was
born know on what ground he was standing? Had he ever
learned the name by which Amiens town was known to
Julius Cæsar when he made it the centre of his wars
against the Belgians? Was he of the sort that cares about
such things? Roman emperors had dwelt here, and after
them Peter the Hermit; Geoffrey Chaucer may have passed
this way on his errands for his Plantagenet king. This
great church was begun before St. Louis, King of France,
went on his first Crusade. Did this latest crusader, this
soldier from the New World, who had left his own land
and crossed three thousand miles of sea to save Christian
shrines and homes from pagan desecration, know any of
this? Six hundred years ago, the invaders whose weapons
had been cloth yard shafts had come here. Again and
again Amiens had been wrenched by one violent hand from
another. The ancient glass of these magic casements had
been shattered in the French Revolution. They had looked
down upon the Prussians, entering victorious from
Villers-Bretonneux in November 1870. They had seen the
Prussians again in August 1914. One year ago Prussia
was reaching very close to wrench off Amiens from France.
But France had it safe and America had helped France.
Was the boy thinking of this, was he saying some sort of

prayer as he stood facing this house of God? I should never have known, for I would never have trespassed upon the mood that held him so still; but he moved abruptly, wheeled from the door, and began to walk away. In a few steps he stumbled and I saw from his manner of walking that it was difficult for him and cost him pain.

I approached him and asked, had he ever seen this before?

"No," he answered without turning his head.

"Don't you find it very beautiful?" I inquired.

"I suppose I do." His voice was low, and gruff and defiant.

"I care for it more every time I come back to it," I said. "Just for its sake alone, I almost think I would cross the ocean."

"You American?" Still he looked away from me as I answered.

He remained silent; only his intention changed. It had been plain before this that he wished to go his way, and without my company; but now he walked with me.

"I am going round to see the west front," I explained.

He went along by my side, stumbling a second time.

We walked very slowly, and, as he did not say a word, I spoke of the famous carving. I mentioned some of the groups which I remembered; Kings of France, a figure of Christ, the apostles, the resurrection of the dead. Then we came to the west front and there was no carving to see; piles of sand bags wholly concealed the glorious company of figures to keep these master-works of a lost art from the bombs of the Huns.

"They're piled like that inside, too," said my companion. "Where the choir is. The man said the choir was a great thing."

"It's a great thing, indeed," I said. "Nothing like it could happen today. Today nothing like any of this could happen—and it happened only in France. You will find nothing in England to stand with it, and Germany made a gigantic failure at Cologne." I could not be sure that

he heard me, nor yet could I stop. "Men are still trying
to do what these old builders did. They fail. They measure
and study and copy exactly, and they fail. They have
tried to reproduce the Day of Judgment group that is
behind those sand bags. They have built perfectly correct
Gothic churches in many modern towns and every one
of them is as cold and dead as a door-nail."

The soldier was looking up at the towers. Now and
then he nodded as I continued my comments and my facts.
He was a captain and his age I could not guess; different
ages seemed to meet in him. He was tall, full six feet, his
hands shapely and of powerful mould, the nails large and
smooth. The lines of his body were boyish; the lines of
nineteen, twenty, perhaps, a year or two more at the most;
and his face was boyish in shape; but in his voice a
seasoned maturity sounded; boyhood does not speak in
such tones. The scant words he had thus far vouchsafed
me were serried in their utterance, and matched by a
silence equally compact. Yet he was not being rude. His
manner conveyed some sort of wish for companionship.
Something was going on beneath his taciturnity. He was
holding himself in. I remembered his stumbling, and
thought that he had better sit down on the steps, but I
hung back from making the suggestion.

He turned from the towers, and, for the first time,
looked full at me. His eyes burned with a sullen fire. In
his face I saw, too, what I had seen in the general English
and French faces, and as yet in no face that was American: this boy, also, had seen that which had let him into
a knowledge he would not get over, though he might
grow used to it: young his flesh was, young his spirit
would never be again.

"That is as dead as a door-nail too."

This declaration he accompanied with a flinging gesture
of his arm at the cathedral.

I looked at him, what he meant not yet quite dawning
upon me.

"As for your Day of Judgment"—he snapped his

fingers at the piled sand bags—"that will never happen
at all. Never. Because only one person would be judged
that day. I'm not afraid of any Day of Judgment. Are
you? Nobody need be afraid, except God for making a
world like this. So He'll be careful not to let it happen."

Again he looked at the cathedral. His voice was change-
lessly quiet with something in it implacable.

"Dead as a door-nail," he repeated. "Just as dead as
any temple to Jupiter in ancient Rome."

"What? When people have been getting strength and
comfort from it since the thirteenth century?"

"What did these people know?"

"Do you remember who some of them were, and what
they did?"

"I don't care who they were or what they did."

"England, France, Europe, America, you and I, everything we see, are partly the result of their doings and
their thoughts."

"Sure they were grown up as to all that. Children about
religion, though. Swallowed the whole thing. Got blessed
in there by some guy with candles and millinery and then
came out and behaved worse than I ever would. And
I'm no saint." He paused a moment, and took it up anew.
"Why one of those kings that they say built up this
French nation used to pray to leaden images in his hat."

"People need images still. Some always will. Where's
the harm? It's what's back of the image."

He did not seem to have heard me. "I swallowed it all
too, once. Never again. What's back of the image?
Nothing."

Young people find much pleasure in assuring themselves
that they are infidels, and still more pleasure in assuring
other people of this. The case before me was not of that
kind. No callow intellectual snobbism was prompting this
young soldier to show off for my benefit. Showing off
there was none. True war was raging in his soul. Not
from spiritual shallowness, but from spiritual depth, did
his eyes burn and his voice quietly ring with bitterness.

Each sentence was evenly spoken and every word fell like a blow dealt by implacable disillusion. I think that he had never said any of it before; that he might never have said any of it at all, but for my crossing his path, and his learning that I was a fellow-countryman at a moment when the mighty power of the cathedral had collided with whatever mighty anguish was within him. I think, too, that he would have said it to no one but an entire stranger.

Having begun, he did not stop. "If a man started sinning the first day he was old enough to be able to sin, and kept on every day of every year of his life till he died, would he deserve eternal damnation?" This question he answered for himself. "Not even the Kaiser deserves hell-without-end. The one who ought to be punished—if there was any such thing as 'ought' in this game—is the one who made a world with love and death in it; the one who could have made a world where good health was contagious instead of disease, and didn't do it. I don't think I'd look down on millions in suffering and tell them I'd make it up to them some other time in some other place. I'd get to work making it up to them sooner than that—that is, if I was the kind of God they claim He is. It's much easier for me to believe a devil made this world —let you catch a sight of joy just to make you know all the better what pain is. Of course I don't believe that either."

"Then the world made itself?" I asked.

"Oh, I've been round and round all that. You can't think about it. You can't think about space, or the stars, or how anything began. If you try to pour infinity into a finite brain, smash goes your brain. But I have a reasoning power and I'm not going to believe a thing my reasoning power denies."

I quoted to him from a great Frenchman: "The heart has reasons which reason does not understand."

He was dogged. "If the sweet-bye-and-bye business is good enough for you, it's not for me."

Of his own move he now walked to the steps and sat

down. "Friends are coming for me here," he explained.

Of what blood was he, of what tradition? Only New England could produce just this, I thought; yet in his aspect the senses gleamed untamed. The Greeks would not have imagined fauns in the woods, had there not been Greeks whose features and whose ways put this into their heads. Now and then in these days, a face will make one think of this. The ears of this boy, close set to his head, ran up to slight points, his brows slanted down to each other, almost meeting, and beneath them the wide set of his eyes brought woodlands and myths into the mind, and nymphs fleeting and hoping to be caught. I watched him as he sat on the cathedral steps, brooding, a nature-woven Pagan and Christian, like all the best of our human texture.

"Count me among the children as to this," I said, and as he looked blank, "as to this church," I explained, "that towers behind us with its tremendous assertion. I do not need leaden images, and to me that stands for the greatest thing in life. I, too, have been round and round. It is what that stands for that makes this world sensible instead of senseless to me."

To this he seemed to pay no attention. He lounged on the steps, looking at nothing, his body as motionless as his eyes.

"When the *Lusitania* happened," he said, "I was about through school. But my father insisted I must stay at home and go to college. I wouldn't go, though; I told father I was going to France. I was with the French from August 1916 till we came in. Then I transferred." He made one of his pauses here. "So I have seen it."

I said nothing.

"Yes. I have seen it," he resumed. His voice sank and once more he said, "I've seen it." After a little while, he added: "I am glad I didn't know beforehand. I don't believe I'd have gone in."

"I believe you would."

What had made him shake his father off and go, what had plunged him into revolt when he came into the serene presence of this church, was just what had built this church seven hundred years ago; what long before Christ had made a great man say in Asia: "Do not unto others what you would not have them do unto you." The same light that lived in the heart of the Oriental teacher, of the cathedral at Amiens, lived in the heart of this boy from the New World. His denials, his fury, and the horror that caused his voice to sink came from the eternal religion in the heart of man. How had it come there, why did it persist? Logic gives no answer, nothing but a far-fetched guess. Logic proves in three steps that a brook cannot flow; that all motion is impossible. Try to make logic fit anything that moves, like life or water, try to make it fit anything except what is stationary, like the multiplication-table, and you will speedily reach false-hood.

"Why, I was innocent!" exclaimed the boy on the steps. "America is innocent—except those who saw it."

"I understand. I've seen its work today. You saw it at work. But you mustn't be one of those whose survival depends on never knowing man's full wickedness and life's whole horror. Very few ever do come to know it, and it would kill many of them if they did. But you mustn't let it kill you."

He got up. "It's damp," he said, and began to walk a few steps one way, and back again, stumbling occasionally.

"What good have all their cathedrals done?" he demanded. "You say this one has been here since the thirteenth century. How many years of peace has it seen? How many years since Christ lived have been years of peace? And there are your sand bags piled up to keep your Christ and your apostles and your Day of Judgment from being smashed to powder by the worst and latest war of the lot. Everything that heathen savages ever did has been done again and more knowingly, and new things have been done that savages didn't know how to do; more kinds of killing, more kinds of victims, more kinds of torture, more brains crazed, more tatters of human flesh, more ashes of human bones, more holes where houses and cradles were, than were ever in the world before; war on land, war in the air, war under the sea. Science is alive and kicking; but where's your 'Peace on earth, good will to men'?" In these last words he came near to losing the controlled level of his voice.

"Yes; the worst war of the lot," I assented. "All your words are true but the last. Good will to men is not dead. Never was it alive so much. Against the worst war of the lot has been raised the greatest, deepest, widest outcry that ever the world has heard. No outcry used to be raised at all. Slaughter of the defenceless, burning, pillaging, torturing, were held the soldier's perquisite and duty, and priests blessed his performance of it. No protest came from anywhere. Today these monstrous deeds break the rule. When these very stones were laid, where was your Red Cross, where your trained nurse, where your dozens and scores of organizations for relief work? What nation sent help to Belgium when the Duke of Alva ground down the Netherlands? And so these stones, these stones sacred to Christ, have seen all that mercy happen in the name and for the sake of Christ. Yes, today your Hun breaks the rule. What rule? The rule of pity. What is it that is new, what is it that has grown, slowly grown, through the red and smoking centuries? Pity, mercy, care for the weak, hospitals, homes for the old, homes for the child, for the cripple, the deaf and blind, protection even for animals: Pity. The glimmer of light that shone in those words 'do not unto others what you would not have them do unto you' has come down the ages, through Asia, through Greece, through Rome, through Christ, who enlarged it, sometimes a bare spark, but never wholly extinguished, until today it glows in millions and millions of breasts. It makes apostles of tenderness and healing out of doctors whose reason denies God, yet who give their lives in acting out the word of God. The simple-minded—those whom you have called children—have always needed and always will need revelation, miracle, mythology, the *not-true*, the thing in that cathedral which you decline ever to swallow again. But you'll not need to swallow it. Use your spirit as well as your reason. Tear off the mythology from any belief—Greek, Asiatic, Latin, Christian—and you will find beneath those very various rags something abiding, something noble, true, something that all the beliefs have held in common: the mysterious, nameless thing which the Greeks had their phrase for, and the Latins had theirs, and the French have theirs, the thing that makes what we Americans call a 'white man.' Let it go at that. Oh, I, too, have been round and round—and years before ever you began it! No more than you, do I attempt to grapple with space; and I don't attempt to grapple with God. I don't see why the conclusions of the head and those of the heart should so often deny each other. I don't see why reason should often so overwhelmingly destroy belief, and emotion—the spirit—the heart—often so overwhelmingly affirm it. But will you tell me why we should accord more validity to the conclusions of the head than to those of the heart? I believe that the head's reasoning fits stationary things, while the heart's fits life. I believe that the cathedral holds the truth. Look at it, inside and out. Don't let the mythological rags which help children to see the truth blind you to the truth. I believe that Christianity is the latest and greatest sign of something greater even than itself; the same thing that all preceding temples of any race and any age had something of, only not so much as this cathedral holds. All along from his infancy, man has built these inns for the soul. After a while the soul moves on to be rid of the rags of mythology which have begun to stifle it. Truth says forever to man, 'I exist; but dare to utter me, and I will turn to a lie upon your lips.' But today, you and I hold one thing at least which both the head and the heart can unite upon: Pity. Pity has come into the world and grown great, while wickedness is no larger than at the beginning; it only has more tools to do its work with. Why do we value good men most of all, miss them most of all when they leave the world? Because the heart loves goodness best and goodness comes from somewhere."

I stopped. I had been surprised into this. It was almost as if it had said itself for me or in spite of me. I now became aware that the boy had ceased walking back and forth and was standing quite still, his untamed eyes fixed upon me.

"I believe you have said something," he slowly muttered. "If head and heart could get together on anything——"

He stared at the cathedral once again. "That might make one serene," he added.

A car came with two young French officers, one of whom hailed him in friendly English and quickly gave him help as he tried to pull himself in. As they started he said to me gruffly:

"I am glad we met."

Yes, we had met. He had not asked my name nor I his. Neither knew where the other lived. We were without clue or context to each other. It was not that we expressly forbore from the usual questions, but that from first to last we never came to the surface where usual questions are exchanged.

VI

WASTED beyond hope of repair would have been our next day, but for some members of the British Army. These came to our help when we were floundering like a ship without a rudder or compass at what seemed to me then, and still seems to me as I look back, the uncharted edge of the world. Our chauffeur had known his way and the lay of the land through which we had come so far. In the cold little room with its frozen piano at the Hôtel du Rhin he followed my finger as I ran it over the route I had laid out for us; and he assented intelligently, with readiness, even with eagerness, when I asked him at each point could we do this, and this; would the whole journey be too long for one day, if we started early? Not at all, he answered. I cast up the sum of the various distances for him, I consulted with him about lunch—in short, I collaborated every step and every hour with him.

I had to choose, steering my proposed course closely by the map and by what I had learned in Paris from army officers. The chauffeur saw, heard, ratified each one of my points with that lucid, comprehending diction which is native to France and envied by the rest of us. How should I know beforehand that beneath that fluent courtesy he was a forlorn imbecile?

Our start was prompt. The sky threatened, but not yet imminently. Thank fortune I took with me my maps. Former journeys had made me familiar with the fact that taking the right turn as one goes through the French country is not at all the puzzle which even a village of ten or a dozen clustering cottages can present. In these little knots one is frequently tangled and emerges in a wrong direction. But I was not worried yet as we made our way

out of Amiens. I was not even yet worried by our
chauffeur's stopping two or three times while we were
still in the town to inquire the road. What I had forgotten
was the fact, made equally familiar by former journeys,
that any French peasant who knows the road farther
than ten kilometres beyond his manure pile is a prodigy
of travelled experience. To be sure, the townsfolk of
Amiens were not quite peasants—but the town of Doullens
was our first point, and Doullens was distant twenty-seven
kilometres. This stretch proved too wide for the knowledge
of such townsfolk of Amiens as pointed the way to our
chauffeur.

My map was spread out. So I had learned to keep it,
not alone against going wrong, but to herald approaching
little places as well. I looked out for Poulainville. It
didn't come. I supposed that we had passed it. I wondered
if we should see Coisy. We didn't. I concluded it lay too
far to the right to be seen. But I was rather surprised
at getting no sight of Villers-Bocage. Presently our road
struck me as being narrower than the road to Doullens
looked on the map. I spoke a word to our chauffeur. He
reassured me with true French competence. I believed
him abjectly, but, when I read upon a corner wall the
name Contay and there was no Contay on the map of the
road behind us or before us, nothing at all like that all the
way to Doullens, I spoke another word to the chauffeur.
You who know the history of the war, know well many
reasons for my wishing to see Doullens. Near that place
the Huns had knowingly bombed a hospital full of
wounded Canadians and their nurses. Papers upon the
aviator captured afterwards proved this: the hospital was
marked conspicuously upon these with a cross: so his
bombs were accurately dropped upon the sick-beds and
turned them to death-beds. But this was not my chief
reason. I had one, and it would have been enough without
the others. Here at this place Doullens, in a garden,
General Pershing had said some momentous words at the
close of a momentous conclave. That was a spot I wished

to see. This time the chauffeur was less successful with
his reassuring French competence. He reiterated that we
were going quite the right way, quite the best possible
way, but I held to it that we were not going the way to
Doullens.

"Oh, no, monsieur," said the chauffeur, in a surprise
as perfect as if the word Doullens had never been uttered
between us. "But we are going to Arras much straighter
than one goes by way of Doullens. The road by Doullens
is destroyed, monsieur. That is well known."

Then, when had it become well known to him? And why
had he never told me so till now? But why ask him such
a question? Why ask a Frenchman why he is French?
Or why, for that matter, ask why the good qualities should
be dealt out scatteringly among the nations, and nobody
hold all the trumps?

"Go on," I requested him resignedly; "go on to Arras."

After all, if no road went to Doullens at present, at
present one couldn't go there. Without it our day would
still be crowded with the deepest interest. I settled back
into calm—partial calm. Certainly we were headed towards Arras upon a way straighter than if we had curved
to it westward through Doullens. My calm was but partial,
because upon the map our present road looked a slight
thing, a narrow line of red, while a broad important red
stripe represented the road to Doullens. How singular
to indicate a destroyed highway thus! But a rag of faith
in our chauffeur was still left me.

We went through some more little places, or what had
been little places once, and before long my rag of faith
began to tear. In the chauffeur's back I seemed to discover
a less assured expression. The appearance of our road
was growing less and less the sort of thing that keeps up
a man's heart, our speed was growing more and more
cautious, and the bumps had ceased to be occasional. Rain
began to fall, mud began to deepen, stones and holes became the floor of this thoroughfare. We crawled up a hill
and through a village street, evidently of some grace and

symmetry once, now battered featureless, and at perhaps
the end of a mile reached a ridge, went on for a few
wallowing yards, and came to a halt. You might have
been at anchor on the top of a wave of mud struck still,
in a mud ocean struck still. What wonder? We were at
the Sucrerie beyond Mailly-Maillet, Beaumont Hamel was
at our right, scarce a mile off. A waste of motionless,
featureless undulations lay ahead, and in these our road
died away, sank to nothing.

As well as I can remember, the chauffeur sat mute and
stationary, like the obliterated landscape. Big heaps of
shell stood about. Barbed wire lay everywhere, ragged or
rolled into rusty coils. It straggled amid deep mud, ruins,
and stones. The rain was now pouring. A crumpled single-
track railway crossed what had been the road. A camion
stood near by. Some English soldiers were guarding some
German prisoners. These worked stolidly, gathering the
shells. It was now eleven o'clock, we had been travelling
slowly and more slow, and had made about thirty kilometres, instead of sixty or seventy, when help from the
British Army came to us at this point for the first time
this day.

I looked out of our car, and my look brought a young
officer up to it.

"We were trying to get to Arras," I said.

"You have come too far. You must go back a bit and
turn west at Hedauville, and go round by Acheux. This
road used to go to Arras, but it's quite gone wrong itself,
you see."

"Oh, yes, I do see! How long will it take us by Acheux?"

He considered for a moment. "You might do it in two
hours and a half."

At this my heart sank indeed. Two hours and a half
to Arras, and it was eleven already! We were to have
been at Lille by twelve-thirty, at Lille we were to have
lunched, and Lille was twenty-five or thirty miles beyond
Arras. I saw my whole plan of the day fall to nothing.
We were to lose not Doullens alone, but Arras, Vimy

Ridge, Lens, Lille, and the whole returning part as well,
Douai, Arteux, Cambrai, every precious point that I had
chosen for this day of pilgrimage.

"Where do you come from?" asked the young officer.

"Amiens."

"You should have gone by Doullens. Why didn't you?"

"We were going, but they told our chauffeur that was
all torn up still."

"Well, I know that's not true, because I happen to have
rebuilt it myself."

What was there to do but laugh? I looked at the mud
and I looked at my map. Lille had been the point where
food was sure. In every direction about us here the only
thing we could be sure of was ruins. Yesterday, when
there was no need for it, we had provisions with us; today
our cheese and crackers and chocolate were reposing in
our rooms at the Hôtel du Rhin. We might decide to go
without refreshment and push on into space, but how
about the chauffeur? After all, his fault had been to believe the word of his fellow-countrymen in preference to
my map and me. Well, we must turn round, anyhow; that
was the first thing to do. Our plight had gathered a little
group of starers and listeners. Our chauffeur couldn't
budge the stuck car. A young German prisoner sprang
forward to help push it so that it might be backed and
turned. He was natural, friendly, anxious to be of use.
He looked less than twenty. Many of his comrades
seemed as young. Many had amiable, fresh, and even
handsome faces. Our young German, who pushed us out
of our sticking-place so willingly and capably, spoke English. He added to our information about the country and
the state of the roads. Go back to Amiens? Not if desperation could prevent. If we could not see what we
had set out to see, let us at least try to see something else.
I discovered that I had with me a few forgotten pieces of
chocolate, nothing to keep ourselves and the chauffeur
going all day, but enough to put off emptiness when this
should begin. Again I looked at my map and there found
inspiration: Albert was not far off—not far, that is, in

ordinary times. Yes, Albert was accessible. The young officer gave directions to us; our collapsed expedition had appealed to him, and he entered into our anxiety to save some fragments of our broken day. He did not address our chauffeur at all; he had taken the measure of this moral paralytic and as the hours wore on this measure was repeatedly verified. In the various moments of stress through which we were destined still to pass, this chauffeur displayed the enterprise of a stale poultice.

We thanked the member of the British Army who had appeared to us in the nick of time—the first nick of our time—and our car slowly waded out of that huge pie of mud, away from the ridge, the camion, the prisoners and the soldiers, and down that sluggish rise up which we had so vainly toiled.

Back we went into an alarmingly small lane which tried but did not upset our faith in the British officer. This led us to a biggish road (*bon pavé*, said the map) and so quite soon to Albert.

To see this place, known to all the world by its Virgin that hung from the shattered church tower so long in mid-air, was to save something at least to show for our day. Were we to save anything more? It did not look so just then. The sky was black, the rain poured thick, the wind shook our car as it stood. Outside lay dismantled Albert, dumb and prone. Bleak streams of water spouted from holes and slants of blind fragments. We had been told to expect no food here. We could see no sign of life, only ruins and mud; but through the violence of the wind again the great silence of France was perceptible. I first became aware of it here, and then remembered its presence all along our road since leaving Amiens. We had re-entered it but a little way outside the town. A few soldiers appeared. To one who passed near I said, "Was there a crumb of food anywhere within reach?" And now stepped in the British Army and saved us and our day the second time. At my words, "a crumb of food," the face of the soldier changed from indifference to brotherhood.

"Come with us," he said, "we're just going to mess."

He called another soldier and to his care committed our car and our lump of a chauffeur. We walked along with him through the ravaged street.

He conducted us through puddles and across fallen walls in the pelting rain to a little house built out of ruins by German prisoners; a little hollow of shelter and comfort, set in the midst of the haggard débris. To step into such a box of snugness from such a wild and disordered outside once again took one into that same unearthly region of marvel, or of dream, through which our stunned minds had been moving yesterday: gaunt, shrivelled, wasted France—and then, suddenly, in the heart of it, this warm little hole full of England!

Inside the hole were three of our guide's comrades: Tommies all, and every one so friendly, so human, so simply and plainly glad to make us welcome and share with us whatever they had! They had a fireplace and a fire; none before this had we seen in France. One of the Tommies was a Scotch boy, I think, and one the very marrow of English England; blond, blue-eyed, illimitably and unfathomably humorous. I never learned, but I suspected him to be city-bred. So developed a philosophy, so mature a sophistication, such a readiness of both words and wit, could hardly have ripened in the hedges. He made himself the spokesman for the party.

We seldom measure how cold we are until we have come from chill into a place of warmth. Our hosts poured out Scotch whisky liberally for us, and I took a long, stiff, reviving drink of it.

The fire burned, civilizing the atmosphere; books were there, a few; and a few pictures, newspaper and other, tempered the walls. A piano was also present, escaped partially alive from the Huns. Behind the room opened a tiny kitchen from which our food was now carried in. Over the table at which we sat hung an empty brass shell case. This was the Tommies' dinner bell. Meat and potatoes were served, and tea in cups of great size. Cheese there was, and sugar for the tea instead of the usual saccharine.

The blond Tommy talked along, his comrades evidently liking to listen to him as much as we did. He relished it, too, without a particle of vainglory, but simply because his thoughts came of themselves and surprised and delighted him. He had attained a philosophy. No school books had helped him to this. If education had fallen to his lot, I think he could have made his mark. Perhaps he would make it anyhow. I doubt his being over twenty-five. Life, as it had come along, had day by day written copiously and clearly upon his alert mind; and this war, this gigantic adventure, through which he had come alive, had evidently set free in him every power of observation and reflection that he possessed.

"She hung on through a good bit of it," he said, "but she went at last."

It was of the Virgin that he spoke. Pictures of her have taught her appearance to us all; the upright figure with the unusual stretching aloft of her child; and then, after the bomb had struck her, the horizontal form in the air at right angles to the tower.

Albert had been dragged from hand to hand and dragged back. It was when they had let it go for the last time that the Huns smashed it to pieces, as they smashed every French thing that they had time to break and which they had meant to keep. Albert had numbered thirteen thousand inhabitants. Of these three hundred now lived here, in cellars.

The Tommy had been four years in the war and four times at Albert. Against whatever he had been dashed to his temporary hurt by the tides of destruction, he had not sunk amid the back and forth of their churning; he had floated out like a cork, buoyant and sound.

"What would you do to the Kaiser?" he asked us. "Or would you let him go?"

We had reached the Kaiser, inevitably. The Kaiser, in the spring of 1919, was reached more often than he is reached today. The voices of the world were then still busy propounding various dooms for him; and various dooms were forthwith propounded at our lunch table. Everyone had his idea as to what would be good and fitting for the Kaiser. None were barbarous, as I remember, but all were what you would call thorough. The Tommy was clever enough to hit my own with his first shot.

"I have my plan for him," I said.

"You would have 'im 'anged in front of 'is palace at Potsdam."

"Right," I answered.

"Right it would be. But don't ye know not one of 'em 'll ever do a thing to 'im?"

"Well," I said, "things have been done to people."

"They'll do nothing to 'im."

"They didn't let Napoleon go scot-free."

"Ow," said the Tommy, with a look that no words can reproduce, " 'ee wasn't related to any of 'em."

This unexpected generalization was presently followed by another. It was after they had been telling me the history of Albert, as known to themselves since 1914, the destitution of its people, and the obliteration of the very sites of where their homes had stood, that I told him about the lady at Noyon, the lady who came back from Nevers, and whom I had last seen searching for her house. This set going at once the blond Tommy's philosophizing.

"I wouldn't come back," he stated.

"You mean to find your house?" I asked him.

"I wouldn't do that. The French are sentimental. They say we English 'ave no sentiment. I think we 'ave just as much as the French. But——"

"But you don't mention it?" I ventured to put in.

All the Tommies gave a barely visible nod, and he continued:

"We'd not come back to our 'ouse, with it looking like that. We'd keep away from it, an' live somewhere else."

It was not for me to comment or philosophize any more than I had dared to do in that single remark which I had interpolated. It had fared well, and I would not risk spoiling it by another which might fare ill. I longed for the leisure of a day or two in which to exchange as many confidences—private, public, and international—with these Tommies as they would permit. Apart from their desire to help us out they were really glad to see us. What wonder? We made a break in their gruesome task at Albert. This task was *disinterment*. Upon the hill and over the hill lay the dead, not by the hundred, but by many thousands.

"It 'elps their folks at 'ome a lot to have 'em cared for," the Tommy explained.

"Are you able to know them *all?*" I asked.

"About 'arf of 'em can be identified," he said.

These British soldiers did not do the actual digging, they were too few. They were in charge of some forty "Chinks," we learned from them. And among these "Chinks" they had found three women in disguise.

The blond Tommy made a final generalization to me. Our meal was ended, our chauffeur waiting somewhere for us with the car, our plan of pilgrimage laid out for us, and the Tommy and I climbing in the rain together over some heaps that had been houses. I spoke to him of the pitiful destruction of old architecture in France which no modern builder would ever make again.

"Yes," he said, "the French 'ave a great idea of the beautiful. And a very poor one of sanitytion."

I wish I were to know his career henceforth, but that is not likely. He stood in need of but few books. His brain was awake and open and the war had educated it to a point not commonly reached upon the benches of our schools.

Between Albert and Bapaume an appalling stage of eighteen kilometres, the strokes of war had scourged the face of the earth to a blind pulp. On either side of the road the land was a mere featureless confluence of bruises and welts. Close at hand, near enough for the eye to see and count each different kind of rubbish and scar, and seam, and pock-mark, one noted rusty cans, rusty wire,

rusty shards of metal, holes and mounds, graves alone, and
by twos and threes, arranged and unarranged, scattered
and continuous, their pale crosses sticking up along the
road and outward from it until their slim, incessant pattern faded into a distance, where lay pieces of tanks, and
the dead trees pointed crookedly up like jagged fingers
of bone. From time to time came by the little towns—
Becordel, Pozières, Le Sars, lying upon the dead land like
dead leaves. Far away upon each side of us the welts and
bruises blurred indistinguishably, merging into a wide,
blank, strange-colored, mangy waste. Upon this tremendous desolation the rain descended from a sombre sky. I
thought of certain bad lands in our West. Their aspect,
with its hues suggesting some sickness of the soil, some
sterility brought on by a curse, was like this lost look
of the earth between Albert and Bapaume. But beneath
the resemblance was a difference that went to the bottom
of things. The Western bad lands were of nature's doing,
boiled or baked, and so cooked to their strange chemical
look when our continent was shaping and before man
was there. These bad lands of France had once waved
with grain, rustled with leaves, smelt of fruit blossoms and
gardens. Their present leprosy had been dealt them by the
hand of man. This explained suddenly to me the secret of
the French silence, why it held all motion and all noise in
a hollow that was like a great, cold, dead hand. In the
overhanging silence of our bad lands there is that which
may well fill the perceiving spirit with solemnity, even
sometimes possibly with awe; but that silence speaks of
the mystery of the universe, while this French silence
spoke of the mystery of evil.

Through the continuing tempest we came to Bapaume,
another town dashed to empty fragments. It was smaller
than Albert, numbering thirty-five hundred in its days of
prosperity; two hundred of them were then living here,
as the three hundred of Albert were living, in cellars.
Twice in the grasp of the Huns, like Albert, they had
given it the same fate, squeezing it to death when they

found that they had to drop it from their grasp. The crushed beams of machinery toppled like trees leaning together after a hurricane. Not a house stood whole. Disabled tanks sprawled, dripping, along the streets. The rain fell now so furiously that we were glad to descry another shelter. It held no comforts like that of the Tommies at Albert, but no rain came through the corrugated arch of iron which formed its roof, and beneath this we sat dry in the company of some French workmen. The wind reverberated through torn sheets of metal while we huddled round a brazier with them and they told us of themselves. They were friendly, and in their own lucid French way, philosophic. They were at work upon some wooden barracks to furnish better lodging, I suppose, for those who were now eating and sleeping in cellars. They spoke, as I say, lucidly and quietly about their country, but not happily. It was not what had befallen her in the war, but her present state and her future, and what was befalling her in the peace, over which they shook their dishevelled, thoughtful heads.

"France is ill-organized," said one.

"Look, monsieur," said another. "In the matter of tobacco. This is a part of our supplies which they bring us to keep us going. Three ounces in three weeks!" He made a gesture. That had been all the smoking supplied to him. He fed a little charcoal to the brazier with his thin, discolored fingers.

In the matter of tobacco my companion was better organized than France, and he left them all that he had brought for the day. We stopped with them a little while longer, talking of France and of themselves, while our chauffeur finished repairing a puncture. We left them looking after us from their iron hut.

Devastation encompassed us, we had been in its midst for many hours, we were to be there for many more. Never did it abate, never did we pass a spot which it had not blighted, never a house which was not a ruin, nor a field unswept by death. Death lay upon the surface, death lay beneath. There is an awful line spoken in *Lear*: "The worst is not so long as we can say 'This is the Worst.'" Between Albert and Bapaume we had said, "this is the worst." Now, during the nineteen kilometres between Bapaume and Péronne, we said it again. The strokes of annihilation to our eyes seemed here to cut deeper: more little places—Beaulencourt, La Transloy, Raucourt—lay like dead leaves along the way, the pale crosses stretched outward each side beyond sight, little distinct groups of them making a sort of thin mist, in which one could fancy that the spirits of the dead were hovering. Strewed also over the earth as far as one could see were the old broken shells, the old wire, the cans, a ceaseless layer of rusty, littered refuse. Northward and eastward this spread on farther than we could see or were going to see, beyond Cambrai, and Le Cateau and Ypres, away over the frontier, sheeting whole counties and departments with this extinct deposit of war.

It was between Bapaume and Péronne that we first saw shell holes in their fullest, thickest mass. We stood upon the edge of wide spaces, acres upon acres, which once had been smooth, healthy fields, where now not one blade of grass was to be seen. As pestilence can pit and discolor a human face, until it is rough with holes like a colander, so this land was pitted. The fertile surface wherein seeds and roots can flourish was gone, baked, charred, cooked to an ashen compound, into which the bombs by bursting had plowed up and kneaded the sterile, chalky undersoil. There it lay, like some mass of horrible contagion. Had you tried to cross it, every step you made would have been from edge to edge of the holes. They touched each other, broke into each other. Some were wide and deep, some looked as if one might jump across them. Into their slop and slime the rain poured steadily. Sometimes one could look across and see where they ended, and sometimes one could not. Had one tried to make a way over them I do not think one would have arrived. Where they were, life had been—pastures, groves, crops, cattle walking and grazing, the voices of grandchildren playing, the voices of grandmothers calling to them. I looked upon the ghost of a land. As it spread out under the dark sky I did not think that the storm made it worse. In the light of the sun it would be no better. It did not seem as if summer or winter could make any difference to it. It looked as if the four seasons which we know would never pay their visits to it again, but that a changeless season of its own was always here, beneath whose lightless day it would stretch in all the years to come.

As at Noyon, so at Péronne were the returning dwellers to be seen, clinging to their old places, seeking out their hearths, unearthing possessions which they had buried before they took flight. Like Albert and Bapaume, the Huns battered it down when they could not keep it as their booty. The message which the destroyers had left behind them still placarded the ruined front of the town-hall—a board nailed up, with these parting words of advice to the homeless French of Péronne:

Nicht ärgern nur wundern—
Not anger but wonder.

How could there be either anger or wonder after four years' experience of their acts?

Other messages in other places whence they were flying to save their skins had been left behind—messages without words: in Soissons the hidden bombs had killed many returning people in 1917. In 1918, south of Cambrai, when the destroyers were fleeing before the British, they had concealed one of these bombs and above it in plain sight had nailed a live kitten. They were right in their guess. When some British Tommies saw and heard the kitten, they rushed to help it and were blown to atoms.

"How you must hate us," said a captured Prussian officer to a British sailor on a ship, and was assured that there was no hate. Surprised, he repeated his remark, and received the same answer.

"It is impossible that you should not hate us," he heavily insisted, "when we have done you so much damage."

"Oh, no," said the sailor, "we don't 'ate yer. We just
looks at you like scum or vomit or some other narsty mess
to be swabbed up."

Through this region of the Somme, this grave of human
flesh and of homes and towns, all lying silent together, we
continued upon our way. Marquaix, Roisel, Hargicourt,
each alike was quiet and dismembered; just a broken spot
along the road, with the pale, thin crosses and the crooked
skeleton trees and the jagged bits of houses sticking up
among the mounds and shell holes, mile after mile. At
some point during this stage of our journey, the sun
shone a little and I saw that its light cheered nothing. It
showed more plainly the mists made by the crosses and the
distant clots of barbed wire. You have seen some autumn
hillside where the brambles dried by frost spread upon the
open land like rusty clouds; thus, far off, the barbed wire
blurred the slopes. At Hargicourt, though my map showed
the way, we halted at the sight of a living man to ask
him the road to Bellicourt. He was an American, a "Y"
man, and answered us right. He was seeing after the welfare of several hundred "Chinks," he told us.

We were very glad to see Bellicourt, to pause and get out
of the car and climb up and down by the steep entrance of
that canal tunnel. We were treading the exact earth of
the Hindenburg Line. Seven months ago almost to a day
—September 29th—October 1st, 1918,—our second corps,
the 27th and 30th Divisions, had so battled here, together
with the Australians, as to win a word of high praise from
the British General under whom they served. The rain
that had sluiced us at Hargicourt was now holding up.
We made our way about in the mud through which our
men had struggled. Here were still the shell craters and
the labyrinth of trenches. We looked down the abrupt
slope to the tunnel wherein the Huns had so elaborately
and for so long made their electric-lighted nest, and out
of which we had helped to eject them on those gallant
days. No church was here in which to give thanks for our
participation in the capture of this position and to think

upon my dead and living countrymen who fought over this desperate ground. I gave my thanks wordlessly, in the open air. In my mind I saw the cathedral of Amiens, lofty, tranquil, pensive, living; and I tore away a piece of a poster which must have been pasted up at Bellicourt soon after its re-taking by the Allies. It requested the men to deal with the people round about considerately, like men, not like Prussians. It was wet then from the rain and much stained. Today it is stiff. I put it away with a little bullet from a garden at Péronne, whence the householder returned from exile was digging his silver, his china, the small treasures of domesticity that he had buried.

Along the thirteen kilometres of road to St. Quentin there was sometimes more sunlight, as I remember it, but never a change in the gloomy scene. We skirted one shell crater not yet filled in, wide and jagged and deep like a quarry; it was the largest cavity we had seen so far, and a road had been made around it. Not far off to our right lay the remains of a little place with a name whose beauty tinkles like a silver bell: Bellinglise. All France is musical with names; names sonorous that chant like legends, or gay, that trip like the dances of old *jongleurs;* names full of overtones, where the vowels and syllables fall into cadences so melodious, that to read them aloud is like a song. Bellinglise! The mere syllables drew a poem from Alan Seeger. That is all I know of Bellinglise, except that its wreck lay there by the Hindenburg Line.

In a way St. Quentin was the worst sight of all among the ruined towns which we had thus far passed. There was much more of it to be ruined than at Albert or Péronne, and the whole of it seemed to be destroyed. It lay not prone upon the ground, it stood up, it presented as one drew near to it, a vertical aspect; there was the illusion of its being mostly safe and sound. But above it gaped the hulk of the cathedral, splintered, shattered, sky showing through its holes; and once we were among the streets we saw the truth. Here again in this town came the sense

of scenery painted for a play of disaster. Walls that
looked steady and inhabited from a short distance, turned
sham at close quarters, like wings or the back drop on a
stage. In the many streets that we went through never a
house did we pass that was not gutted: behind the mask
of each front, ceilings slumped to floors, stairs sagged to
cellars, beams blackened and gnawed by fire stuck through
holes in tilted roofs, mirrors and bureaus, unscathed,
perched alone upon ledges of landing over gulfs of broken
plaster.

By the time that we reached here, we had become judges
of ruins. We had learned to name their kind at sight, and
approximately to gauge their maturity. These vintages of
destruction fell into a number of classes. There was the
farm or the village which had happened to be in the way
where a battle was going on. It may have fallen at the
hands of its friends as readily as at those of the enemy;
but whether hit by French, British, or German shells, its
pushing down would be lateral, from the missiles passing
horizontally through it. There was the dynamited dwelling, the work of mere disappointed greed and malice. Its
walls might often still be upright, or but a little caving
in, or bulging out. No shell holes would be in such walls,
no lateral rents. The earthquake would be up and down,
within the walls, and it would be the floors and ceilings
and crushed things between that marked this class. There
was the dwelling that had been mined. This somewhat
resembled the dynamited sort. The difference would be
seen chiefly in the clots of soil which had been heaved into
the air and had fallen upon the top of beams or lodged in
high crevices. There was the dwelling that had been
burned by the pastilles invented by the skilful German
chemist, Otswald. In these there would be no shaking down
or up, no slanting, no sign of lateral or vertical shock.
Everything would be simply and quietly gone that fire
could burn, leaving the stones or the melted metal. One
entire village had been left behind thus by the retreating

Huns. The presence of plants and weeds growing about upon various elevations of a ruin marked it as being of the earlier war days.

Despite the state of St. Quentin, plenty of people were to be met in the streets. I suppose that these, too, were living in cellars. Of one of them we inquired the way. I do not see now what else we could have done. My map could not show us how to thread our way clean through from one side of the town to the other and strike the right turning. It could and did show us our general direction, more or less parallel to the river, and near enough to be in sight of it at first, I imagined; and this I explained to the chauffeur. We were to keep southwest, I said, and we should cross a railroad in about two kilometres. But I made no objection when he stopped and asked of an inhabitant the right road to Jussy, I merely remembered Doullens uneasily. We were told at once, without pause to meditate, the right way to Jussy, and I could see by the chauffeur's back that this word from a fellow Frenchman meant more to him than anything I and my map could say. We crossed the railroad remarkably soon, it seemed to me, quite within the city limits, and I saw nothing of the river. A good way out in the country, after nothing was as I expected it to be, I forced the reluctant chauffeur to stop, when I called to a man driving a wagon with two wheels, how far we were from Jussy? He did not seem to know the name. He was from Origny, four kilometres onward. Origny? I sought my map. There was no such place on the road to Jussy. Origny? I found it. We had been set on the highway to Guise. It was as if, being at Chicago, you had asked the way to Omaha and had been carefully headed for Pittsburgh.

"Henceforth," I detonated to the chauffeur, "you will do exactly as I say and nothing that anybody else says. To the seventy-nine kilometres that we had still to go, you have added about twenty-eight more. Turn round. Go straight back."

I spread the map upon my knees and there I kept it.

"Left," I said to him as we reached the rim of St. Quentin.

"Right," I presently ordered; and in due time we came to Jussy.

Here, with imperishable instinct, he was taking the wrong turn, but I hailed him.

"Right," I commanded; "and cross the railroad, and go to Ham."

He bleated something about Chauny. A sign pointed thither by the road he had tried to take.

"Do what I say and do it at once," I returned. "Do you want to take us round by Noyon and Roye that we saw yesterday, and add twenty or thirty kilometres more when hours are growing as precious as diamonds?"

The sun was now showing itself more often than during the stages over which we had so far travelled, but we had fallen seriously behind time; it was a westering sun that shone, and our journey was become a race with the ebbing day. At the points where we had been especially told to stop, Ham, Nesle, Chaulnes, Villers-Bretonneux, there could be no stopping. We must rest content with a glance at each as we passed through it with the careful and abated pace which bad stretches of road enforced upon us; it was doubtful if the light would last to our journey's end. This seemed so uncertain that I resolved to forego even the attempt to see Villers-Bretonneux, and decided upon what looked upon the map like a shorter cut to Amiens by Rosières.

Perhaps through our lateness we gained another knowledge of the desolation. We saw the day leave it, as we made the best speed we could over the disordered kilometres. Furthermore, many parts of our road now lay along the line of rail over which fast, expensive trains used to run direct from Calais to Bâle and Lucerne and the Alps. Thus, having seen the tatters of towns and houses, we had a good view of this uprooted railroad, alongside of which we frequently drove, and over which we frequently

crossed. I retain in mind particularly one blown-up spot
at which there seemed to have been important and large
machinery and but few houses. The machinery had been
spilled and splashed over the railway station and the
houses and the railroad itself. All lay lumped and stirred
together, like a gigantic petrified stew. Sidings stuck
forth from beneath heaps of cranks and wheels, vats lay
bottom side up between detached doors and bushes and
pieces of chimney, and one steam whistle severed at the
neck had evidently flown through the air and now sat
lonely upon a truck which had been dashed from the rails.

Ham we passed, and were glad to put it behind us. Its
name rang with memories; it was strange to be glad that
we had passed it, instead of sorry that we could not stop.
Yet, even so, there was the silence with us always; and
here also wa the river with the name that must forever
be an awful name to many, the river Somme. Nesle followed Ham fairly soon. We made those nine kilometres
evenly, and again I was glad to count them off. I was
watching the daylight rather than what more it showed us
of destruction, and I was watching the road. On my knees
lay the map open, and the chauffeur had at length been reduced to believing what I said. I had by now delivered a
number of directions to him, all of which had come true.
At every cross-roads, or fork, or turn, he would submis-
sively slow down and listen, and then obey me as I barked
to him, "Right" or "Left" or "Straight on." The light
waned and I looked at it and at my watch and at the map
wherever I could see the kilometres of devastation which
lay ahead of us still. I could read which turns we were to
take, but the time was coming very soon when I should
be able to read them no longer. I wondered what we
should all do in the dark. Many ridges and descents and
roads unknown lay between us and Amiens. We had
nothing with us in the way of food or covering, and no
desert could promise less of either than this silent land of
the Somme. The last sight that we saw clearly was the
motionless sadness of Chaulnes. The grey dusk was

coming down upon its fragments. We could make them
out, thin shapes rising from a blur of mounds and under-
growth, and behind and among them, grey, stark trees, all
dead. More trees rose beyond, a wood of them, crooked,
splintered and dead. No sight that day had conveyed so
much the immovable chill of extinction.

We left grey, quiet Chaulnes behind us, and came to a
fork which might be so important that I made the chauffeur stop. Coming towards us along a smooth-looking way
for which I yearned, was a camion. In my hesitation, my
faith wavered, and I asked the driver how to go to Amiens.
To the right, he answered, and was gone. It was wrong.
The way he had come, to the left, was the one.

Dark was now treading on our heels. We crossed without due circumspection a single railroad track that jutted
rather high and abrupt, bounced with a forlorn inward
clink of snapping, and stood still. Various urgings and
motions made by the chauffeur brought no response from
the impassive car. He got down and opened it. Something
was broken. He told me its French name. Was it fatal?
I asked him, and he assured me that in time he could mend
it. I did not in the least believe him; why should I? It
is better in such cases to assume the worst and see what
else can be done. My friend and I walked about while the
figure of the stooping chauffeur grew more dim in the
departing light. We did not seem to be anywhere, there
did not seem to be anything to do. We had come to
grief exactly beside a little estaminet, dark and closed,
the glass gone from its window and blind boards there
instead. It stood where the road and the railway crossed
each other. I paced several times in front of its silent
door and pictured us all breaking into it presently when
the night should have completely fallen and the chauffeur
completely failed to restore the engine to life. Even if it
should prove entirely empty, the floor of it would be larger
to sleep in than the car, and smaller than the wide world.
What difference would it make, anyhow, such a small
mishap in the presence of such great calamity? Then I

heard a sound inside, and spoke to the sound appealingly
and reassuringly. The door was opened with caution and
there stood a woman. Her face was pleasant and it was
with a pleasant and gentle voice that she greeted me. I
could not tell her age, she had seen war: young and old
who have gazed understandingly upon the full countenance of war become of like age. A gash, recent and not
half healed, crossed her forehead. She glanced at us and
our car, took in the mishap, and bade us enter with words
of very sweet apology:

"You see how we are installed."

The light of one dull lamp was quite enough to disclose
the state of this home. I suppose that there had been a fire
in something, for she must have cooked somewhere, but I
saw none. The room was damp and cold. Beside the
boarded window which I had seen in front were others
with neither boards nor glass in them, open holes into the
night. Still, the place had a roof, and it was the first edifice of any kind which we had during many hours an opportunity to see that was not a total wreck.

"We have just come back to it," she said.

Who "we" were I did not ask her, but presently learned
without any asking. She and her husband had come back
from Normandy where they had been for a year in refuge.
She had lost everything. She told us of her fortunes
simply and sweetly and every syllable was full of perfect,
unforced courage. They would get on; the estaminet was
on the road where people passed and they would be passing more and more as times revived. While she told us
of her prospects, heavy coughing broke out somewhere.

"Your husband?" I asked her.

"Yes."

"I hope that he is not ill?"

"But not at all, monsieur. It is nothing. He went out
with friends today, and there it is. It's but that."

"I hope he doesn't do it often?"

"Oh, no!" she assured me with a gay smile as I looked
at the gash in her forehead.

Directly he coughed violently and she hastened to him
in some hole behind the room. Some turn that I now made
disclosed to me that what I had taken for a huddle of
bedding lying across some article of furniture was a
perambulator with a baby asleep in it.

"He'll be better now," said the mother, coming back to
us from the father. Then she showed her placid child to us.

She had a loaf of coarse bread and some butter which
made our dinner; she wanted but "six sous" for it. We
took the chauffeur's share outside to him, where he labored at the engine. It was now entirely dark. She had a
bed and we could have stayed there, but as we were considering this the chauffeur came in to ask for water
and told us that the car would go. She had water there in
a bucket which she gave him. No water was near the
estaminet, the nearest was at about a kilometre's distance,
whence she fetched it each day. We gave her some francs
for the water, and some others in the name of the child in
the perambulator. She did not wish to take them. She
protested. There was nothing in her face or voice of hard
luck. She seemed strangely refined for that estaminet,
her smile rode over her adversity, she was a French
woman, perfectly game in the true French way.

Our misadventures in wrong roads might have discouraged my asking any more directions from the local-minded
natives, had there been any other choice save to go blindly
on. The camion driver had sent us off the broad plain way
into a perfect nest of local lanes which my map showed
now by the light of the smoky lamp. We were close to
a little place called Harbonnières, in sight of it, really,
had there been anything now to see except the darkness.
But whether to go forward or back, and which turns to
take if we did either one or the other, who of us could
say? Least of all that chauffeur. To go blindly on with
him and a mended car did not appeal to me, and so once
more I inquired the way of a native.

"Go through the *pays*," she said (the *pays* was the little
village of Harbonnières) "and at the church turn to the

right, and go two kilometres, and turn to the left on the *grande route* to Amiens." Today I know that it is from the women, not the men, that you will be directed right.

Thus we left her, and her estaminet, and her sleeping baby, and her husband who had spent the day with friends, while she fetched the water from Harbonnières.

There was no map any more. Its work was done. We sat back in the car and heard its noise as we went along. We could see nothing of the land, but when objects came close we could make out their general shapes. We went through the dark ruins of village after village. Here and there some window would dimly shine and pass. Along the road we met a two-wheeled cart now and then, and sometimes some soldiers. We did not know Villers-Bretonneux when we came to it, or any other place, but we knew when we had passed out of the slaughtered region. Once more the signs of natural existence looked strange. Soon after these began we entered Amiens, and at a quarter past ten we got out at the Hôtel du Rhin.

This day did not merely double the knowledge which had begun at Compiègne yesterday; it changed what I knew from what had been like a plane into something that was like a cube. In its depths were the French and the British soul, shining like the battlements of light against the powers of darkness. Its surface was the stricken fields of France, fields of life five years ago, fields of the great silence now: The fallen shapes of towns, the disembowelled soil, the shells and the wire where the wheat had been, the crosses everywhere to the horizon, the exiled French groping for their cellars, the strange languages and races swarming upon the French earth, our jaunty doughboys, the British Tommies, the German prisoners, and the Chinese coolies digging up the rotting dead; amid this, the tranquil, unharmed cathedral at Amiens, and far away across more distances of the great silence, the battered cathedral at Reims, both rising high above this wide, sad grave of men and things

VII

HAD gone out of the beaten way to listen to a comic opera, an old comic opera that had been young in the days of my own youth. I had dined early and sought the *Trianon Lyrique* in time for a good seat in the second row, and for all the preliminaries. I like to see the musicians file in one by one from the hole under the stage, and take their places, and turn up the lights over their desks, and spread out their sheets of music, and put their respective instruments to their chins or their lips or between their knees, and get in tune and begin tootling over little scraps of what is coming, until the whole hive of fiddles and flutes and curving tubes is buzzing. Well, they hadn't appeared when I sat down; nor had the public. A few early birds like myself, quiet French birds with very quiet plumage, dotted the spaces. It was a "family theatre," the *ouvreuse* reminded me, where innocence could come with its father and mother, and sustain no harm. I gave the *ouvreuse* a whole franc for telling me this and showing me my seat and trying to take charge of my overcoat. I felt suddenly relaxed and happy to have escaped from the present into this sanctuary of the past, safe from the noises of the restless hour, far from the discords of peace. The *Trianon Lyrique* stood in a backwater, a little bay of true Paris, untroubled by the chop-sea of soldiers, envoys, correspondents, negotiators, diplomats, experts, intriguers, prime ministers, philanthropists, and flags and rags of all nations, which the hurricanes of negotiation had driven to toss and beat upon the wider spaces of the city. Thus I sat waiting placidly, and held a little conference, a true Peace Conference, with myself and my memories. These jostled and needed arranging.

Amiens and the Somme lay behind me, with the remainder of my pilgrimage to desolation still ahead. Between them was this Parisian parenthesis. At dinner the last night at Amiens, an officer, a major in the British service, had sat with us and told us that he had seen women flying from village to village with dead babies and household chattels huddled under their arms; and had seen a child whose hands the Huns had compelled its own father to cut off. I was glad to have the Paris parenthesis, to see the shops, the streets, the living life, and to hear the home voices of our soldiers. These were everywhere in the streets and shops of Paris in April and May, 1919; Paris with a jungle of captured German guns, thickly lacing the Place de la Concorde, bordering the wide way from it to the Arc de Triomphe; Paris with American cars and American soldier chauffeurs clotting the space in front of the transfigured Hôtel de Crillon, waiting the pleasure of the envoys, experts, philanthropists, and secretaries who sat within and seethed without; and Paris, this chop-sea of spying, distrusting sharks swum hither from all waters, afloat with the American soldier. You could look nowhere and not see him. He swarmed above the ground on the tops of omnibuses, on the ground in shops and along the Rue de Rivoli, and underground in the trains of the Metro. The sharks swam in waters congenial; not he. I have heard a verse about him:

> Although he was on pleasure bent,
>   He had no frugal mind;
> He did not care how much he spent,
>   He was not in his element,
> And he was very innocent,
>   And very much too kind.

Whatever rioting he made it was a drop in the bucket of his decency. Saint he never pretended to be, though he was commendably nearer to it before than after the loosening influence of the Armistice. Yet no matter how he spent his Paris nights, he was a clean, irrelevant creature for Paris to entertain; a spirit how uncooked amid this

spiced stew of the jaded Old World! Uprooted by a convulsion, not of nature but of human nature, and flung into
a soil and climate where nothing like him grew, he stuck
out strangely from the general mess; and his figure will
remain with me, buoyant, youthful, detached, the most
far-fetched apparition I have ever seen thrust into a
human picture.

He felt this. He knew it. Those of him who had come
over too late to kill Huns, felt it doubly. Generally he
hated the French, generally he wanted to go home, and
generally—whenever I rubbed shoulders with him in
streets or shops or trains long enough for any conversation—I reasoned with him. Two sentences from an enlisted man at Fort Oglethorpe sum up what our army felt.
He was a young master-carpenter who had left his work,
his wife, and two children.

"You'll be anxious to get back?"

"Not till it's over. Then home as quick as I can get."

That is why they went: to see it through, to kill Huns, to
stop the world crime; not for the sake of any academic
generalizations about democracy. Our own danger had not
dawned upon them.

I did not want our soldiers to go home hating the
French. Without the light that France has thrown round
the world, how dim the world would be! But nothing of
this would go far to placate the sore and home-sick doughboy. It would be "highbrow stuff" to him. He had his
reasons for hating the French, and they were good ones,
too. The flaws in the French character were the very
flaws to displease him. The French set too little store by
the mechanical conveniences of life, such as plumbing and
electric lights; he set too much. He had too little respect
for thrift and tradition; the French had too much. He
could be gay and sociable, evening after evening, exclusively in men's company. The French astonishment at this
estranged him whenever he happened to find it out. He
continually washed and shaved himself clean; he spent his
money lavishly. These were less frequent habits in the

land whence he had helped to expel the Huns. And now these French, after flinging their arms around him while the Huns were walking on to Paris, were asking him when he was going home. He made his English plain, too plain for print sometimes. As if he wanted to stay in their damned, dirty, stingy country of robbers! These small-change frogs called Americans "dollar-chasers." Why the whole of Europe was chasing dollars with its tongue hanging out of its mouth. Only, when it caught one it held on. When an American "treated," they called him vulgar. Well, no frog was guilty of that vulgarity, anyhow.

The doughboy needed no official voices, French or English, to tell him what he had done. He might be foolish and boast, or he might not; but quite independent of recognition from on high, or tinkling symbols pinned on his chest, he knew in his heart that in the darkest hour of 1918 he had tipped the scales to victory; that without his presence upon the fields allotted to him, the British could not have made their magnificent advance over the fields allotted to them; that without his presence in France, the Huns would still be present in France. He knew all this because our American mind, if raw, is clear and just. And now they were anxious to get rid of him, which was natural; and letting him know it, which was not *très gentil.* "Tray jontee" was the phrase employed in this connection by one ironic doughboy, who, being obviously a charmer, had also made substantial conquests among the French idioms. "Stinking" was the word given it by another doughboy, plainer spoken.

"How many words of French do you know?" This was my usual device for entering upon talk with them.

"About six," was their not unusual answer. They would turn at my question, and look at me with an American's grin for a brother American.

Sometimes in shops I computed, at their own request, the sum of their purchases, and the change properly due. The doughboy who had said "stinking" had walked out of a photograph shop with me and opened his heart to me along under the arcades of the Rue de Rivoli. Concerning the French, he knew his mind in his American way, down to the ground.

"Do you think," he demanded, " if they had come over and saved New York and Bridgeport and New Haven for us, we'd be showing them the door like they're showing it to us?"

"They saved New York and Bridgeport without coming over," I answered.

"So they've told me more than once, since the Armistice. I'll call it a good guess. Maybe they did. But they saved us in their own country, kind of unconsciously. On the side, as it were. There's a difference, don't you think? About three thousand miles' difference, according to the lowest figure I can make it."

"You must make allowances——" I began, rather feebly; for I saw his side of it full as well as he did.

"Allowances! I've allowed all the allowances my mind will allow me to allow. Good night! If they were sitting around in New Jersey and Connecticut after an armistice fixed up at Hoboken, do you think we'd be trying to push 'em into the Atlantic, or do you think we'd be setting up the drinks?"

"We're different," I said. I was still feeble.

"Well, I guess we are different. And if it comes to politeness, give me the American brand yesterday, today, and for ever. Too much dictionary about the French article and not enough goods delivered. All froth and no kick to it. Tray biang apray voo mais wee certaynmong meel pardong meel remaircimong. Oh, hell! And say—if your house was afire, and you pretty nearly all in fighting it, and your neighbor saw it and came across the fields and jumped in and helped you put it out, you'd be likely to send him a bill for a pitcher he'd broken and some corn he'd trod down, wouldn't you?"

"Come and eat lunch with me," I said. "It's one o'clock."

He stood pondering. In the course of our talk we had

reached and gone some distance along the Rue Boissy d'Anglas, in the direction of my hotel.

"I guess I can eat something now." As he came out with this, he looked me in the eyes with a confessing smile.

"Too much joy last night?" I asked, smiling also.

"Yep."

"No breakfast yet?"

"No." He gave an expressive shudder.

At the café I chose (where he tried his best to pay for something) I laid before him the French case. I preached to him the good old doctrine of *bear and forbear*. I was growing practiced; he listened. He was just another perfect instance of the American mind, clear and just, once the facts are laid before it honestly. I did not completely bring him round, but he was going to reach conclusions after we had parted which would be more lenient than those he held when we met.

"All the same," he said, "once I get back to Danbury— *never again!*" That was his final word.

Certain things I withheld from him as I did from all of them: worse things that few of them knew. These needed much *bear and forbear*—more than I was up to at times myself. This weather-cock business was not confined to the classes with whom the soldiers mixed. There was a change of wind higher up. The warm blasts which had greeted our entrance into the war and our landing upon French soil had begun instantly to veer and chill after the Armistice. We Americans were no longer Mayflowers and Lafayettes come back to our dear old home. Upon the laurels which they had piled somewhat too thick around our brows when first we stepped ashore, more mud was being cast as each elapsing month pushed Château-Thierry farther back into the safe past. From certain quarters of authority the word had gone forth to tone down our contribution to victory now that the trick was done. A little adroit French phrase had been picked out and passed around from inner circles outward: we had given the Allies a *coup d'épaule*. "Leg up" is the English for that. Papa Joffre, who staunchly insisted that "leg up" fell somewhat short of describing our part at Château-Thierry and Champagne and St. Mihiel and the Argonne, and two million men come three thousand miles, and successful fighting that extended from early summer to the 11th of November—Papa Joffre, who stuck out for it that this represented something more than a "leg up," had been officially "canned," as our doughboys would have put it. I reflected upon this, and upon the fact that the French, with the same breath that they called us a "leg up," were anxious that we should bind ourselves to come over and boost them again, if ever the Germans again started up. I had discerned in some persons a subtle disappointment at our proving ourselves not too proud to fight; it compelled them to seek something else to fling. I had noticed that certain English jeers at our neutrality had shifted to jealousy of our participation; a cold glaze had filled certain English eyes at the lightest reference to our battles. To a friend of mine one English lady had complained that just as the Allies were on the threshold of winning we had come over and robbed them of the full glory of victory. Were such undercurrents to direct the great stream of History? Or would the brag upon our part die away beside the vast fight and suffering of France and England, and their sneers vanish in the realization that in joining them we had wrenched ourselves from one of the deepest-rooted articles of our faith, and asked nothing?

Meanwhile, these countries were teaching full as much of forbearance to me as they could learn from mine. At moments it came hard, but I held to it, even when I heard that we had come to make the world safe for hypocrisy; reaction inevitable and petulant must be met philosophically. Only, not all of our doughboys were philosophers; my next effort at persuasion was not crowned with visible success.

It began in the Metro. A crowd filled the car, and I was glad to feel pretty sure that the remarks which some of my fellow-countrymen were making fell upon ears that did not understand them. The noise of the train in the tunnel led me to move nearer to hear the whole instead of parts of what was being said, as the chief word which reached me was, as usual, "frogs." But as I made my way, over my shoulder came the muttered phrase, "ces sales Américains." Some Frenchman was present who did at any rate understand what frogs meant and he was returning the compliment; and not much league of nations was occurring here.

It was four doughboys comparing recent Parisian experiences together quite placidly, and planning experiences to come. They were not complaining, as I had supposed at first; indeed, their adventures had been wholly to their satisfaction, and to these they referred with a frankness based upon the assumption that nobody else knew English.

"Made me think of one night in Tucson," said one.

"Naw, they're not the same," said another. "Mexican girls can really love you."

"Oh, say, boys," said a third, "he's learned what true love is!" and they all laughed joyously.

"Say, we got to change at Concorde!" exclaimed the second, with sudden alarm.

"Well, tell us something we don't know," said Tucson. "More about true love."

"Well, we don't want to pass Concorde."

"I'll not let you," said I. "I'm changing there myself."

In Paris it seemed invariably to startle them slightly when anybody who wasn't a doughboy wasn't French.

"Is the hotel St. Xavier still the best in Tucson?" I inquired.

They began to grin, especially a tall one, and one with black hair. Tucson was short and slim, with a merry eye.

"I expect," I pursued, "that the right man could find true love in Deming, Lordsburg, Benson, Maricopa, Phoenix and Tempe, even Yuma, just as well as in Tucson."

My "even Yuma" was an enormous success; they drove

their elbows into each other, although two of them had blushed deeply at being overheard. By the time we were getting out at Concorde, blushes had been recovered from, they had learned that I had ridden over Arizona and New Mexico before they were born, and I had learned that the hotel St. Xavier was no longer the best in Tucson. When I asked young Tucson if the big wild cat I had seen in Maricopa in 1910 was still there, he began, I think, to feel as if I must be something in the way of a long-lost uncle; he had seen that cat when he was a boy.

"Mr. Williams owned it," said he. "Acrosst over the track. We lived on Salt River then. Excuse me, sir, but I'd never take you for an American."

"I'll try to excuse you. I should always know you were one. Let me congratulate you on your division's athletic fame."

"We fought some too, sir."

"Oh, all good Americans are proud of that. Where are you getting out?"

"Marbœf. Gosh, I wish we could get out of this country."

"Marbœf's mine." It was not, I had been getting out at Alma, but his exclamation had put the missionary spirit in me. Time happened to be nothing, and we had begun well.

"Why call them frogs?" I asked.

"Do you like them?" This was Black Hair, after we had come up from below and were walking along.

"I like them very much."

They were silent.

"I guess we don't, sir," said Tucson, after a few steps by my side.

"I can give very good reasons for liking them," said I.

One of the two in front of us turned around.

"We have very good reasons for not," said he. This was Tall One.

Somehow it was slightly portentous. They all stopped and faced me, and there stood the five of us in an argument on the wide walk of the Champs Elysées. They appealed, they confided, as to a friend, but every face had grown hard as a flint; they took up their tale in cold anger and grew hot over it at the end.

"You know the St. Mihiel country?" This was Black Hair.

"Not yet."

"Well, that's where our big kick comes in."

"You know we were there last September?" This was Tall One.

"Oh, yes."

"Well, that's where we didn't pay for the privilege," said Tall One.

"Privilege of fighting for France," said Black Hair.

"We'll fight for Germany next time. We know the Germans now. They're the folks to treat a man well."

"Very well," amplified Tucson. "Very, very well. And they're clean. Why, look here. About St. Mihiel. We had orders to dig in at a place there. Second day."

"Never mind the day. We were just starting to dig in."

"Lots of companies were advancing," continued Tucson, "the shells were coming our way right then."

"German shells, you understand. Coming heavy," said Black Hair.

"When up runs the farmer," said Tucson, "and says to our captain we can't go on till we've paid for his land. Then some argument, and then some excitement, but our captain talks quiet."

"Our captain he's a gentleman." This was the fourth, who had been a solemn listener until now.

"Yes. A gentleman," affirmed Tall One. "When you meet a commissioned officer you don't always meet a gentleman."

"Even so!" said Fourth One, still solemn.

"Well, and so the farmer got more excited and the captain got more quiet, and away goes the farmer and back he comes with a French officer. 'You must pay,' says the officer. We all heard him."

"Even so!" said the fourth. "Yea, yea."

"Shut up, Elmer, for God's sake."

"The gentleman doesn't mind. He's been a sport. Yea, yea." And Fourth One suddenly gave a youp that must have come from the cattle range. I now perceived that either his last night was not finished or his next was already begun.

"Consider yourselves, consider my grey hairs, consider the Champs Elysées," I begged him.

For a moment their eyes grew merry, and then hardened, and Tall One took it up.

"The Frenchman told the captain we must pay the farmer for spoiling his land. The shells were coming livelier all the time, so the captain told us to keep on digging and I guess he told the French captain it was his busy day. Anyhow, Froggy said 'biang, biang,' and he pulled out a paper."

"He pulls out a paper," said Fourth One.

"Wrote on it and handed it to the captain," said Black Hair. "Wanted the captain to sign that we'd pay for the land afterwards."

"How about that, sir?" said Tucson.

"But the captain," said Tall One, "handed that paper back to the French officer."

"He handed it back. Yea, yea!"

"And he told him," Tall One continued, taking no notice, "that he had no orders to sign anything; he was here to push the Huns off the land, not to pay for it. 'If you give me any trouble,' he said——"

"Frog had threatened to bring his men over and they'd get more good manners shot into them in a fraction of a second than they might otherwise acquire in a lifetime," said Tucson. They finished their tale in short turns, almost talking at once.

"The French officer said——"

"We didn't get it all, but he and his men were going to come over and——"

"To make us pay or quit digging."

"He and the farmer went away over to where the French were digging, but they never came back."

"Come back yourself, sir, to God's country. Now that the Armistice is signed these French will be glad to tell you good-bye."

Tucson said that, and now I took my turn.

"That French officer," I began, "had paid that farmer for the injury to the land his own soldiers were doing."

Their eyes never left my face. This was a good sign, but a bad one went with it. They never once asked me a question. I must have talked three or four minutes steadily to them as we stood in the Champs Elysées, explaining to them the predicament of the French peasants and the method of meeting it which I understood that the French Government had been forced to adopt, and then I came to an end with dead silence for an answer.

"Better go back to God's country, sir," repeated Tucson, smiling.

"Even so," said Fourth One.

We parted, amicably disagreeing. No arguments, only time and reflection, and perhaps not even these, would change their minds.

Waiting in the *Trianon Lyrique* with my overcoat on—heavens, how cold that theatre was!—I thought over these talks with our doughboys and took out my notes of them. Should I cut them out at home? Should I cut out the *coup d'épaule* and everything else disagreeable? If I did would home believe the agreeable things I should tell? With the cause of France hung our own, and our future welfare, and our enlightened participation in the welfare of the world.

VIII

THE drop-curtain and decorations of the *Trianon Lyrique* well befitted a "family theatre"; innocence with its father and mother could gaze at these also without injury. I blessed them. They ministered to my Peace Conference, perhaps they caused it: Aurora in her chariot, golden rays her background, winged boys her companions, festooning garlands at either hand, the head of Pegasus below, like a trophy of the chase, and that drop-curtain—really a dividing curtain —quiet with colors like a faded oriental rug that had been used and walked on and not cleaned lately. I blessed it as I would a rest-cure, my reasoning rose serene out of the chop-sea in which I, too, had been tossing. The French audience gathered, French undisguised, not on exhibition for the benefit of Americans any more than the opera, quiet domestic parties, out for an evening's highly economical entertainment. I was enjoying the sight of them when the seat next mine was filled by a spectator more exotic in that dingy atmosphere than even myself. A woman, a lady—she made me an exactly right bow for disturbing me; a lady plainly by her expression, by her lines, by the way she sat, and by her perfectly admirable and perfectly quiet clothes. We began at once to study each other in that imperceptible way which is invariably perceived by both parties. She was handsome. All of forty-five (you will be disappointed), probably nearer fifty. She had style and missed elegance. Obviously forcible. Somebody. A look of giving orders and having it done. Too much so. Had probably been in war-work. Yes, probably the head of something she supported with a large bank account. I would bet she had secretaries. Oh, yes; one of the chop-sea philanthropists with a mission. Phi-

70

lanthropists are unmistakable even when they are ladies.
I had seen her type down-stairs and up at the Hôtel de
Crillon but nothing equal to her. American. New York?
I felt so. Why did she make me angry? The fiddlers were
coming out of the hole now. And here she was, by herself. Of course she was American. And if any man pre-
sumed and spoke to her—why he'd get it! In my mind
was no such presumption. Silence was what I had come
here for, and isolation.

"We might as well chat," she said to me, in English.
"Don't you think so?" Deep, assured, entirely civilized
voice. Eyebrows too heavy.

"I'll say anything you like," I responded amiably.

"You'll say nothing I don't."

"I was sure that you appreciated me," I murmured.

She turned this over before she was quite satisfied
with it; then she inquired, "Have you been here long?"

I took out my watch. "Sixteen minutes, I think."

"You know perfectly well that I mean, have you been
in Paris long?"

"Perfectly well. My coming is quite recent." From
the gentleness of my voice any old friend would have
known that I was going to be detestable.

"I wonder if I know your name?" she said next.

"Quite unlikely. I'm not from New York."

This she also turned over. "I can't seem to place you."

"Ah, don't try!"

"I came here to get away from—well, from all that
you are probably mistaking for the true France," she
now explained to me.

"So did I!" I exclaimed. "Well, that is spoiled for
both of us. We must just console each other."

"I am apt to hear of people," she stated, considering
me. "You're certainly not Red Cross. You can't be in
the Reconstruction? Or Neuilly? I know them all there.
You're surely not a member of Congress? One can tell
them as far as one can see them."

"Really and truly I'm not a spy. Give me up!"

"Well, it makes no difference. I hope you have realized that Paris is by no means France ?"

Of course I had. I had realized that about forty years ago. Why shouldn't she perceive that I knew something about France myself? How had I found my way here, far from the areas of Paris got up for strangers, and the spangled shows sung and danced for Americans? Her importance blocked her observation. She took herself for granted too much, and me too little. You will not think highly of me. I fell apart, and my lower nature spoke for me, separately. If I was to have no isolation she should have no satisfaction.

"Do tell me about that," I said.

"You see," she forcibly expounded, "Paris, through being a great centre, draws and develops all the worst elements."

"Oh, I see. Like New York."

"And Americans live here for months perfectly ignorant of the true France. I hope you intend to visit the devastated regions before you go home?"

"Should I find true France there?"

"It's everywhere, of course, in a way. But in provincial France—where the devastated regions are, you understand —you get straight at it, while here you have to sift it out, and that takes familiarity with the language."

"I'll certainly go, if I can."

"It requires authorization, of course." She stopped and considered me again. "One obtains that in various ways. American ignorance of Europe is simply appalling."

"Worse than theirs of us?" I inquired.

"There is much less of us to know. Our importance is great, but it's simple. Knowing Europe would be of incalculable advantage to us. Europe is very complicated. Each nation has things it does better than we do them, and we're so ignorant we don't know it. And then, life here! Why life here compared to American life is like a wedding-cake compared to dry toast."

That last was rather good. Why did I know that she had tried it on others before she bestowed it on me?

"The doctors pronounce too much wedding-cake indigestible," I said.

She looked at me suddenly. "I wonder if you're writing for *The Saturday Evening Post?*"

"How are you ever going to instruct me if you keep on guessing so hard?"

But she now said, "Ssh. People may want to listen." And she settled herself.

I was very glad to listen to the slender, sprightly overture, in which each tune was an old friend.

"That is the true France," she informed me when it was over. "But only the surface. Americans suppose it is the whole. Do you know what the war has cost France?"

She couldn't tell me then, because the curtain had divided and they were singing the opening chorus. But she would tell me between the acts. She was only half listening to the opera. She was busy over me. Whatever her mission was, I had become a part of it while she had the chance. I realized that she was a mine of explosive information, that her zealous days were spent in some large, good work, that she hooked everybody, every likely person, every passing listener of the slightest promise. Thus she scattered the seed of her cause. It so filled her that no place was unpropitious, no time untimely, each new contact caused her statistics to burst out of her. Would she bring herself in? I wondered. The act went on. The little bride was torn from the little bridegroom directly after their wedding ceremony, and hurried away to a convent, while he was forced to continue his education with his two tutors. All in the costume of a bygone Watteau age, to graceful bygone melodies and rhythms.

"Paris cherishes these little gems," she informed me as the curtain closed. "They are extinct with us, because the audience that used to understand them is extinct. They demand on the part of their hearers the rudiments of both education and civilization. They would be Greek to

Hebrew Broadway. Not even Big Bertha stopped the theatres. The actors showed that they were as true sons of France as the *poilus*."

She was going to hammer me with facts like a pile-driver; that I saw in a flash. It would go on through the whole intermission; and intermissions in Paris are long. When they have bought seats for the theatre, the economic French put out the lamps and the fire at home, and feel entitled to lodging at the play until near midnight. That was another good sentence about Greek to Hebrew Broadway.

"I have read about the brave patriotism of the French actors," I said.

You could seldom tell whether she was listening to you or not. Whatever she had been in her youth, she now belonged to that class of important people who hear nothing you say except what happens to strike the key-note of their own preoccupation.

"Everything is needed here," she now declared. "Everywhere you turn, need is what you see."

I sat tight. It was coming. She had got it ready like concentrated essence of beef, or a hypodermic charge of serum.

"The French children have been five years without school. We must get the school teachers back to them. Only think what a loss of five school years would mean to the generation of American voters that is growing up."

"It would be a loss you couldn't see with the naked eye," I said. "You have not been following American education as closely as French."

I know she didn't listen to that.

"France has lost one entire fifth of her taxes. Twenty per cent. of her taxes were paid by the devastated regions."

"Yes, I have read about that, too. Lens, Lille, the coal, the manufacturing section. Yes, I have read that."

"Books without travel are bricks without straw," she said.

That was an awfully good one! I doubt if it was her own. She probably collected lines like this and salted her public speeches with them. I had now become sure that she addressed audiences. I hoped the audiences were not wounded soldiers in bed.

"The whole region north of the Aisne was scientifically destroyed," she continued. "Before the war France normally spent two billions a year on construction. Twenty billions are needed now to put her buildings back where they were. And who is to do this? Of French males between the ages of 18 and 34, 57 per cent. are dead. They can barely cope with the *déblayage*. The farmers that survive are willing to live in holes to carry on, but what are they to do without agricultural machinery?"

She paused. I sat battered and dumb. Had I known the answer I could not have given it. But she did not want it. Her pause was for rhetoric, not for information or for breath. Her breath never failed. It was like an endless chain of prayer.

"What is necessary to a nation?" she now demanded directly of me.

"Why—I should say——" but my mind stopped.

"What, I mean to say, does any nation have to have, or lapse into barbarism?"

I wondered if I could last through this intermission without turning upon her. I decided that I could certainly not bear the next. Perhaps I was being punished for the activity of my lower nature at the outset of my talk. But of this I am by no means certain. I believe that she was one of those who are so driven by the steam of the facts they have amassed, that they plow ahead, telling you what they know, wholly indifferent to whether you know it or not.

"Is not a nation like an individual? If you and I to retain our position among civilized people, not only require a roof over our heads, clothes on our backs, food in our stomachs, but must also have health and strength and education and money to support art, literature, science, and to pay our way in an increasingly expensive and competitive world—is it not plain what France needs? Do you know that tuberculosis is unfitting men and women to be parents, and is waiting for the new born? The percentage of tuberculosis in France——"

My mind ceased to retain any more. In the whirl of statistics which continued, I sat like a man overtaken upon a mountain by thick snow, until the opening of the curtain came to my relief. Truly, if you are in a mood to be let alone, keep well away from persons with a mission, women especially. The music was not able to distract me. I prepared some remarks for her benefit, and rehearsed them all through the act.

"With everything that you have said," I was going to tell her, "I perfectly agree. Most of it I knew already. I am seeing France exactly as you advised. Tomorrow I go to Château-Thierry and Reims, later to Verdun, under the kind and courteous auspices of our officers at 37, Rue de Bassano. So far, I have been under the equally kind auspices of the British, at 30, Avenue Marceau. At 5, Rue François Premier, the courteous French officers were ready to place their services at my disposal and take me to all places in their jurisdiction. I have been urged to accept a week in Germany, beginning at Coblenz; and General Pershing of his own accord has personally bidden me to ask him for anything that he can cause to be done for me, and it shall be done."

But I said none of it. It would have come from my lower nature, although it would have all been true.

After all, the formidable lady who had loaded me so heavily with advice and instruction was not thinking of herself, but of her cause. I had wondered if she would bring herself in, would dilate upon her own exploits in benevolence; but she never did. And her facts and figures were all too true. But I could not, I really could not, trust my lower nature through another intermission.

"I am going to bid you good-night," I said, as the curtain closed again.

It was a blow, I could see that. "Oh, stay it out!" she said. "We can talk some more."

"Awfully sorry. It has been ever so interesting and helpful. I have an early start tomorrow—and the third act isn't much."

"You leave Paris tomorrow!" She thought rapidly and produced this final, compact parcel of tuition:

"You must make allowances for Paris. If you find the hotels and the taxi-drivers and the police officials when you go for your card of identification, rude, remember the four years they have been through. Think how it must exasperate their nerves to be unable to settle down now, to be still overwhelmed with strangers like this. Do make allowances."

"I've been doing nothing else!" I returned, levelling each word straight at her. "And I have been beseeching our soldiers to do nothing else. French manners have always been better outside Paris, as American manners are outside New York. And now the hotels and taxis and police officials here are simply beyond belief--democracy at its dregs."

Directly I spoke of our soldiers, she fixed me with concentrated scrutiny, every word that had followed missing her entirely.

"I know!" she cried. "You're on some vice mission."

"We're finding it up-hill work," retorted my lower self. "Young Frenchmen hold chastity a provincialism they've got beyond, young Americans hold it a virtue they haven't reached. Que voulez-vous?"

She probably took in but little of that, such was her satisfaction in having finally placed me; and with that I had risen from my seat and was gone. Once again a few days later I came face to face with her as we went up together in the elevator at the Hôtel de Crillon, but she did not know me from Adam. It was a great relief.

IX

NOT yet were my conversations over for this day. I emerged from the *Trianon Lyrique* upon pools of water spread in so many places that my short walk to the Metro station was materially lengthened through avoiding them. The floods of rain which had evidently been pouring down while I was being given French lessons, had left the air bleaker and damper even than when I had entered the theatre. In the almost empty train I smiled at myself for so resenting the French lessons. But it is only superior persons who don't mind being told what they ought to know, and very superior persons indeed who don't mind being told what they know already. The right-minded reader will say that I should be ashamed of my conduct to this instructive female. So I should—and am not. The lady had really added to my knowledge; be that said for her. She had given me figures and summaries that I had not known before, which I later found to be accurate, and which made a solid frame, so to speak, for the picture of devastation upon which I had been gazing during my pilgrimage. Albert, Bapaume, Péronne, which I had seen, and the withered soil, and all the rest, were the visible, physical destruction that spelt the twenty per cent. destruction of taxes. The lady was another figure in the iridescent horde that ran and twinkled over the surface of Paris; a wingèd ant, busied upon errands of good; and with all her too-bristling energy, she fitted in well with what I had said to the gloomy, beclouded boy at the cathedral of Amiens.

From the Metro I ascended to the surface of the earth at the Place du Havre. It was between times: the small French cafés and the shops were long closed, the theatres not yet out, and the St. Lazare station had mostly ceased

78

to suck in or to disgorge travellers. In this lull of the hurrying ants, taxis and omnibuses were few, and wide wet expanses of asphalt visible; and there, on one of those islands that make a refuge for street crossers during the crowded hours, stood a tall American soldier. My plans had been for a little diary and a great deal of bed, but I changed them, and walked over to the island.

"Can you guess my nationality in this light?" said I.

His teeth were visible during the smile that began his answer.

"There are parts of Paris that are livelier than this," I continued.

"I'm from Kansas, but I've found that out," he returned. "Oh, yes; there's a heap doing here when a fellow feels like doing it."

"Don't you ever feel like that?"

"Oh, yes, sometimes. I've been around this city some. It's worth seeing, day and night."

"It certainly is," I agreed.

"I guess this isn't your first visit," said he.

"I came here when I was twelve and I've been lucky enough to come again, more than once. I lived here once for more than a year. Of course I travelled, too, during that time."

"Been in other parts of Europe, too?" he asked.

"Several. But I'm American, you know, first, last, and all the time."

He was thoughtful for a moment. "Travel would make me more American all the time."

"Then you're as anxious to get home as all the others are?"

"Oh, I'll be glad to get home. But there's some been over here longer than I have, and it's only fair their turn should come first."

He shifted forth and back slowly from one foot to another, his head two or three inches taller than mine.

"If I am keeping you——" I said.

"Oh, no, I'm on duty here for a while yet."

He was of the American Military Police, and he stood here during certain of the night hours for the benefit of such American soldiers as might need either direction or discipline. Here was Kansas upon an island in the Place du Havre, policing New Jersey and Michigan and California and all the rest of us! Never throughout this whole journey did my mind adjust itself to this stirring of America into the sour broth of Europe.

"I often wonder how my own town would rub its eyes if it saw a French soldier policing French soldiers in the middle of the street."

"Well," he answered judicially, "I know my town would quit after the first rub or two, and start jacking up the prices, same as the French have. You from New York?"

"Oh, no. New York never rubs its eyes at anything. I'm from Philadelphia."

"H'm. Newton is my town. Newton, Kansas."

Nothing could be plainer in the tone of this announcement than his quiet and permanent satisfaction with Newton, Kansas. If the staple product of that town was Americans like this, I hoped that its population would double each year. In his observant, poised self-reliance, he justified our whole theory. And all of six-foot-one.

"So you think jacking up the prices is not a monopoly of the French?" I asked.

"It's human nature," he stated. Patience and toleration pervaded his voice.

"Where we were lately——"

He was interrupted. A night-faring doughboy had come up, and asked him some question. He walked a few steps with the inquirer to the other side of the island, and there evidently gave him some detailed directions, pointing once or twice with a slow and most graceful gesture. But this had not diverted his thoughts.

"Where we were lately," he resumed—"have you ever tasted French champagne made for our express benefit?"

"I don't think so. Not over here in France, anyhow."

"Well, don't you do it." He gave me this piece of advice after a hair's breadth of hesitation and a puzzled

glance, for which I could not account. "I haven't had a
very wide experience in champagne myself," he continued.
"But you knew this was put up for Americans just after
your first swallow of it. No, I'm wrong: just before."
Again I caught the gleam of his teeth as he smiled before
he proceeded. "They had the two flags crossed on the label.
Ours and theirs, you understand, most affectionate. Some
Portuguese were there, too. Well, when a Portuguese
called for a bottle, they charged him seven francs. Americans were charged thirty-five. The captain closed up the
shop when he found that out. Down came the price to the
Portuguese level."

"The French are different from us," I said.

"Different! Yes, we all have found that out. The captain was going to drain a cesspool and put it in some other
place more sanitary. The French farmer was very hot
at the captain and claimed ten thousand francs damages
for his manure pile. The French are certainly different,
and they think we are certainly different, and I think that
the less we see of each other the better we're liable to like
each other. The Lafayette affair was a good while ago,
and I'm not as grateful to him as I was before I met his
posterity."

"But you certainly think the two nations should be
friends!" I exclaimed in a pressing manner. "They don't
expect you to pay the first price they ask. They're used to
bargaining. It's part of the game with them."

"We play poker in Kansas, but we're not used to playing it for a hen's egg with old ladies in caps. Oh, I know!
We slapped our money down first go and it was bigger
money than they'd ever seen, and they hadn't been seeing
much anyhow for four years. We all go down when temp-
tation's strong enough, and I don't hold that against
them."

"Why hold anything against them?"

He reflected. "I don't know as I do. Not more'n I hold
against everybody—including myself!" He gave a joyous
chuckle at this.

A couple of American soldiers passed near with a

couple of girls. The girls were keeping very close indeed to the soldiers. The young men did not have the look of being entirely captivated by the companions whom they had secured—or who had secured them. My Kansas friend followed them for a moment with his eye, which then once more rested, oddly interrogative, upon me.

"Let me tell you," I said, "something you may not have thought of—though you have thought of more things than any enlisted man I've yet talked to—and I've done quite a little preaching to them in this city."

A change, as of resignation, passed over his figure; it seemed to settle.

"Well, preaching can be good," he said. "I'll stay."

"Here's my sermon to you. I've given it to a lot of others—and they've listened. For hundreds of years these French have had to be fighting their neighbors and paying taxes to meet it. We've had no neighbors to fight. We've only had five wars before this, and free farms for every-body, generation after generation. No such thing in France. They've had to look close at their pennies, while we've been throwing gold pieces to western bar-tenders for a drink—and never missing it. But that's not all. The fathers of these same French who are overcharging you saw the Prussians overrun their homes, and rout their armies, and capture their emperor, and make them pay the bill. It was a big bill. Your father never knew the ex-perience of having to dive down into his jeans to help pay an indemnity to a foreign conqueror. That was less than fifty years ago. The old ladies in caps you mention were young wives then, and they saw their men go to the front, and didn't always see them come back. And they had to save and save their coppers and their poor little pieces of silver to meet that huge bill of Germany's. That's what they were doing while we were spreading westward to free farms at our ease. If our fathers had known the bitter experience of these French, don't you think it likely they would have taught their children to close their hands over coin rather than to open them, and don't you think the children would be interested in charging as high for an egg as anybody was fool enough to be willing to pay?"

He had watched me very steadily while I spoke, and, as seemed his custom, waited before answering.

"You have pointed out another way to look at it. History is something I don't know much about. I don't know, if I *had* known, that I'd have put their history alongside of ours and drawn conclusions that way. Yes, sir, I shouldn't wonder if that was so." He indulged himself with a moment of rumination. "I'll mention that. I have talked to some of the boys who are sore at the prices."

"In 1780 the French were sore at ours," said I. "You spoke about Lafayette just now?"

"Well, I learned about him at school. Couldn't tell you the story of his life, though."

"Neither could I. There were several well-known Frenchmen came over to help us. Rochambeau, and a young fellow named de Fersen. He wrote home about us, and he said—well, it will sound quite familiar to you. He said almost exactly these words: 'They fleece us pitilessly, the price of everything is exorbitant.' And then he went on to say that in our dealings with the French we treated them more like enemies than friends. That our cupidity was unequalled; money was our god. There was more that he said. He had met some very fine people, quite a number of them, but he thought the people in general were a set of robbers. Now, you see, this young Frenchman had come over to help Washington win the war."

"Do you mind saying those first words over again?" said Kansas.

"About fleecing us?"

"Yes."

" 'They fleece us pitilessly, the price of everything is exorbitant.' "

"Thank you, I'll tell that to the boys. It sounds natural."

His duty had caused him to turn and inspect the Place du Havre, lest his services or his authority should be needed. More people were beginning to pass and cross, a more crowded hour had just set in. He found nothing, however, to divert his attention. He turned back to me and took it up.

"But I don't need any points for myself. Before I came over here I was a year on the Mexican border. The El Paso barbers didn't sit down on any prices for us soldiers. Nobody did, barber or grocer or tobacco shop or anybody. Let a soldier walk in any place and the prices went up like —like putting your thermometer out in that Rio Grande sun. Well, if my own people do that to me, my own people," he repeated with emphasis, "what call have I to blame these French? Blame them for that, I mean. For I do say that no American that I ever saw to *know* would charge his rescuers rent for the trenches they rescued him in."

"They charged themselves," I said.

"I don't call that an answer," he retorted.

"Land holdings here are often so small that a trench cuts a big slice of what was available for crops. The farmer had to raise food for France. France paid him damages to help him carry on."

"And we got shot to help France carry on."

"I don't say it wasn't clumsy."

"Clumsy!" he chuckled. "I've another word for it."

"Listen! German propaganda twisted another fact so as to hurt France with us. The heavy timber and iron field revetments and all the tools and material to build them cost money. It's like fixtures in a house. Any regiment moving into a trench that another regiment was vacating signed rough inventories of trench stores they were taking over. No money passed between English regiments, it was more for discipline, but money did pass between us and the French. That was made to look like rent by German propaganda."

"All right. Any more?"

"Yes. Wait for all the facts before you jump. English regiments have drunk from French wells. The next regi-

ments that marched by found the pump handles wrenched
off and had to pay for water. It didn't look well to thirsty
men. But French wells are often shallow. They would
have been drained dry, and it was all the water the peasants had."

"Say, brother, you know these French more than I have
had a chance to. What do you make of them?"

"Look at this splendid city of theirs," I replied. "Look
at the fight they put up."

"Yes, that's all so. Yes. But say, take the way they lie.
Why, they don't lie on the American plan at all. We don't
lie just to be pleasant. Got to have a stronger reason.
And morals. Why, decent girls are not allowed to go for a
walk with a young man. Why, boys come back from the
leave areas and tell me that French parents were astonished that their daughters could be trusted alone
with us."

"Europe is different," I said. "But we might learn a lot
of good things from the French."

"Well, give me America. I've heard what you say
several times. A man stood here the other night, and told
me what a splendid thing it was going to be for America
to be filled with young men bringing home such a heap
of knowledge they never could have got at home. Well,
America will not be filled. Those who have seen the leave
areas are going to think France is a better country than
those who never saw any of it but the war regions. Of
course that's so. But you have got to be educated before
you can get education—the foreign kind that he meant.
About the only education that most of the boys will take
home is more varieties of——"

He stopped himself short, and for the third time I was
aware of his interrogative glance at me. I had known
what he was about to say well enough. He had decided,
for some reason that his glance represented but did not
disclose, not to say it. I decided to say it. While I was
meditating just how, for I wished to be neither pharisaical
on the one hand nor coarse on the other, meditation was

spared me and a spontaneous way provided. Paris was coming alive again for its midnight existence. The theatres were out, late suburban trains were ready in St. Lazare, the Metro exits were spouting passengers into the Place du Havre. The number of our doughboys on pleasure bent increased, they were passing by in couples and fours, the bloom of the New World still rich and unworn upon their young faces, and about their buoyant figures—and hanging upon their arms with practised clutch, the Old World in a skirt. No bloom left there, without or within. Female, but feminine no longer. The tragic moulting of a wounded bird of prey.

"See them!" I murmured aloud, after one couple that had crossed close on the island and gone upon their way.

"What's that?" inquired the member of the military police.

"Did you notice him?" I asked. "Did you notice her?"

"Oh, yes."

"I would have no sermon for him," I continued. "None for any of them. They're human. And away from home. But I'd like to say, 'Won't you stop a minute? Won't you just stop and look at her for one minute?' "

"They couldn't see them," returned the soldier—"not before morning. I've been blind myself at this time of night." He looked me up and down with a new eye, and it was in a new voice that he said: "Why, I figured you were one of those social-evil guys taking longer than usual to reach your point."

"I knew you were long-suffering," I returned; "but I didn't know how long."

"Oh, they mean well, they mean well. Better than they get treated. But you know history—natural history, too."

I took out my watch. "I intended to be in bed an hour ago," I said.

He held out his hand. "Come round again when I'm here."

Yes, decidedly I wished great increase to the population of Newton, Kansas, were he of its daily breed. If the plain people were everywhere such as he, faith in them would be more than justified. Like the blond Tommy at Albert, he had also his philosophy, attained and steady: less highly wrought than the Tommy's because Kansas is less highly wrought than London. But it would serve. France did not appeal to him. He had been made in America. That set limits to his grasp of Europe. These both barred his benefiting and shielded his suffering from the complexities of the ancient Latin race. He would have use neither for their exquisite mental subtlety, nor their exquisite moral duplicity. I hoped that he might go home as soon as was fair to our Allies; I hoped that all our doughboys might. He was shrewdly correct in his judgment that most of them would extend the area of their permanent knowledge by but little except chromatic sensuality. In the seething, iridescent ant-hill that Paris was in the spring of 1919, they were truly out of the picture, and home was the right place for them. Their work was over. They had fought a good fight when necessary, they had been charming with children, and respectful to decent women between whiles. In my opinion the New World had no apologies whatever to offer the Old. Such were some of my thoughts as I went to bed and, as I recalled the slight jar dealt me at the end of each conversation that I had held this night, the last strand of coherence which crossed my mind before sleep overtook me was, "Can I be getting to look like a philanthropist?"

X

VERY much do I wish that it had come in my way to see and to speak with the French *poilu* at length and at leisure, as it had been my luck to do with the British Tommy and the American doughboy. More talk with the Tommy would have enabled me to say with a measure of certainty more about him and his wonderful character: that hour at Albert left me with the never-to-be-granted wish that I might then and there have had days in his friendly company under conditions so favoring to intimacy. A glimpse, even slighter, of the *poilu* which I had upon the morning after my confidences exchanged with my fellow-countryman in the Place du Havre, also left me regretful that it was so brief. Something I had taken with me and something I had gathered of understanding about the American soldier; and in the same way, something, though less, of the British; of the French but very little at first-hand, and even this to be set down here with diffidence; of the Italian, nothing whatever at first-hand. Of him I can only repeat what everybody knows—that he is of the land which from centuries before Julius Cæsar down through Dante, Columbus, Michelangelo, Palestrina, Galileo, to Marconi, has produced more genius than any other two countries of the world put together; that his race continues a noble, beautiful, adequate race; that he fought with fierce and gallant bravery on the steep sides of mountains; and that his country is doing better today than some of her Allies. From politicians and newspapers it is that hindrance to true international understanding chiefly comes—the politician can utter a few public sentences that will estrange two peoples, one editor can write a paragraph which will have the same effect.

The *poilu* that I saw for a while this next morning got into our car soon after it had passed the Eastern Railway station and out of the Pantin gate. He stood by the roadside, made us a sign, and asked for a lift as far as Claye. Claye, interesting because the Huns got as close to Paris as this in 1914, was not very far, little more than half-way to Meaux, and this afforded but a brief chance to lead the *poilu* to any opening of his nature. Could I have said to him, "How beautiful is the corner of your village where the old bridge crosses the river!" or any other word of intimate admiration for his *petit pays,* his inch of France, where grew his ancestral roots, that would have gone at once all the way to his heart. A Frenchman's patriotism is very concrete. He loves with passion his own place, his own acre, his little spadeful of France. He wishes to live and if possible to die on the actual piece of earth which has been tilled by his forefathers, tilled by himself, whereon centuries of his kin have quickened, lived, and passed. We Americans do not fold our tents like the Arab and as silently steal away, but we are the latest version of the nomad. We transfer our never-rooted lives from Fort Worth to Spokane, or from Albany to San Diego, about as readily as we cross the street. We have emptied the word "home" of all its hoarded meaning and sanctity. Against whatever benefits this may bring, it has wrought incalculable harm to the national soul. I had been no nearer the *poilu's* country than the line between Lyons and Modane—he was from near Grenoble—and the best I could do by way of establishing some bond between us was to praise the renown of Grenoble as a seat of learning and exclaim:

"How beautiful are the mountains of Dauphiné!"

"Then monsieur knows them?" he responded at once—and became less shy, or reserved, or respectful, or whatever it was that his own nature and the presence of an American captain who was with us caused this enlisted man to be. He was going back to them, his mountains. In all the little that he said, the emotion of return brooded

behind his words. He was existing to *go back;* that was it.
Going *back* and going *on*—these were his two vital motives. We have only one of them—going on. The soldier
on the island might yearn for Newton, Kansas; the other
fellow, the one from Danbury, had said that once back
there, "never again." But if the one could better his lot
by moving from Newton to the apple country of Oregon,
and the other by leaving Danbury for the plum belt in
California, or the oil belt in Texas, or any other belt
where material profit beckoned, why the betting is at least
ninety-nine to one that the lure of betterment would snap
the tie of home and that they would go in a minute. Not
so was it with this Frenchman. To him his *petit pays* was
forever better than any betterment.

"Then monsieur knows them?"

In those four wistful words was not only a longing for
the sight of his mountains, but a love of their looks. You
will remember the words of the Tommy at Albert: "The
French 'ave a great idea of the beautiful, and a very poor
one of sanitytion." Kansas on the island could not have
said just that. He was not ripe enough for that particular
kind of generalization. He was quite capable of apprais-
ing and loathing the villainous plumbing and the villainous absence of plumbing in France; but there he stopped.
Westminster Abbey—or a thousand other sights—
had made ready the Tommy's natural ready eye to see
the excellences of French architecture. No Westminster
Abbeys are in Kansas so far. Once a chauffeur, whom I
had engaged at Reims for a long journey and informed
that we should sleep at Orleans the next night, said immediately:

"Then I shall see if their statue of Joan of Arc is as
good a one as ours."

Imagine a chauffeur whom you were engaging in Philadelphia to go to Chicago, saying immediately:

"Then I shall see if St. Gaudens' Lincoln beats our
statue in Fairmount Park."

A sense of beauty and of art, and a daily-bread use of

beauty and art—that is one gift of the European continent to its plain people, which Kansas cannot give, nor
Massachusetts, nor any state in our New World. In talking with any Frenchman, high or low, it will help our
understanding of him to remember this. It will partially,
though not totally, explain that fourth dimension of his
character which answers to nothing in ours. Art, symmetry, has a hand in almost all he thinks and does, including his immoralities.

The *poilu*, then, was not like Kansas on the island nor
yet was he like the Tommy at Albert, who had said that
he believed he had sentiment, but that this would take the
shape of keeping him away from, rather than taking him
back to, a home in ruins. There he was of closer kin to
Kansas than to the *poilu*. This home near Grenoble was
not in ruins, but had it been so, this would have made no
difference to him, I am perfectly sure; no more than it had
made to the lady who had come back from Nevers to see
if she could find her house beneath the rubbish piles of
Noyon; nor to the woman with the gash who had returned
to a half annihilated estaminet in a wholly annihilated
region, and had given me a loaf of bread, and had talked
cheerfully of her future. *Going back* and *going on:* in
her also these had been the two vital motives. Through
these I connected her with the Noyon lady, with this *poilu,*
and with one other who had been a *poilu*. The cheerful
and communicative valet at my hotel in Paris, he who had
been buried for a day and three times wounded, who told
me that I should visit the South where they were more
amiable than in Paris—he was looking forward to taking
up heavier work at Toulouse, his home, as soon as he
should be well enough. Going back and going on! It was
the unspoken watchword of the people of France.

The *poilu* was a grave personality, of few words, unlike
the valet from Toulouse, who was of many words. Both
were peasants, and both somewhere along in their thirties,
I should say. I don't know whether their taciturnity and
loquacity were individual or of race, and it matters

nothing. Various races inhabit the different parts of
France, some silent, some not at all so, some more open-
handed, some less; and they vary in their dialects as
widely as they do in their characteristics—as widely as
a citizen of Vermont from a citizen of Louisiana. It is
the traits they all hold in common that mean France, that
have built her thought, her art, her literature, her law,
her religion; it is these, too, which have made her spring
from the ashes of herself under which she with the rest
of the world believed she was expiring, and become, far
more truly than the Prussian who coined the phrase, a
figure in shining armor; and it is these traits finally which,
in the great emergency of peace, will prevent the hideous
wound which Germany dealt her from being a mortal
wound. Through their spiritual passion for the earth of
France, backed by their power of infinite thrift, her people
will save her, unless prevented by the tragedy of errors
which began with the Armistice and has been played by
the Allies ever since.

At his little place near Grenoble, the *poilu* had carried
on some sort of trade in leather before he took up arms,
and this he was planning to resume. In his blood flowed
the whole education of his forefathers' deep-rooted and
coherent past, and to this had been added the education
of the war. I told him what of his wounded land I had
been visiting, and what of it I was now upon my way to
visit. All his response was, "Oui, monsieur," but this
was no mere dull assent. It was part of the same pattern
conveyed by the quiet words of the lady at Noyon, "Others
have gone farther": understanding acceptance of irrep-
arable loss and outrage, understanding resolve that the
dead past must not kill the living present, or the future.
Such was its depths, the French state of spirit as I
found it and felt it everywhere; a state as noble and adequate for the emergency of peace as their state of spirit
in war-time had been noble and adequate for that emergency.

At Claye we drew up for the *poilu* to get out; and there

he thanked us and went his way, leaving me with increased perception of his race. The threads of this perception, gathered—some of them—forty years ago and along the years since, but gathered never so attentively as now in the stress of what had befallen the world and what the world was going to do about it, these threads spun a rich texture of reassurance. In that damp street leading to the cathedral at Amiens, my none too cock-sure optimism had been chilled to the bone. So had it been chilled at times along the roads of desolation, and was to be again, along more such roads. But always it was to be warmed up by the rich texture of reassurance. The twin supports of our civilization were England and France, and neither was likely to fall. You could kill Frenchmen by the million, French houses by the hundred thousand, French fields by the square mile, you could disintegrate machinery and drown mines and amputate orchards; France herself you could not kill: not at any rate by the atrocities of war, and probably not even by the imbecilities of peace. Reassurance spun a vision of many *poilus* returning all over France to their little trades in leather, their little tillage of the vine, to all their little, careful industries; and many women resurrecting the little commerce of their estaminets, turning their deft, courageous hands to many kinds of resurrection; and everybody practising that masterly thrift which leads to well-being, just as surely as our American wastefulness leads away from it.

XI

I REGRETTED that Claye should have come so soon and cut me off from further contact with the *poilu;* and yet perhaps I had got as much of him as there was, at least for my purposes of observation. His more personal opinions and adventures, had he during the course of the day become moved to impart them, might or might not have been worth hearing. On the other hand, the coming hours would have been more than likely to shut him up tight. We were headed for the fields where our own soldiers had revealed their quality, and by so doing had also revealed to Foch that he now held in his hand everything which he needed for victory. The cup of the Allies' vitality, drained horribly and repeatedly, and repeatedly filled during the years that we were not there, when we did come had been filled the last few inches that it lacked, had been filled, indeed, over the brim. It could have been re-filled, too, as often as needed. America, by the time of the Germans' Aisne offensive, was at last prepared. After those unforgettable months of extravagant and heartbreaking delay and incompetence, America was ready to pour millions after millions into Europe. She was ready to erupt armies on a scale more gigantic than history had ever witnessed. It smote the Prussian like the tolling of a knell. He did his best to lie to his duped and docile Germany, to belittle our preparation. But in his heart he knew better, and upon his hopes the lights burned blue and went out. More, I believe, than the good blows we struck, did the knowledge that we were there deaden the Hun and quicken the Allies. Our apparition at the Marne was like an instant change of weather. The French *moral* came up visibly, like a parched crop beneath the rain.

"Where are you going?" asked the jaded *poilus* of our jaunty doughboys, as they passed each other, the ones coming back exhausted, to rest, the others going forward, fresh and untested, to fight.

"We're going to stop the Huns," was the cheerful reply.

"You're going to hell," retorted the *poilus*.

Do any of them remember it now, I wonder, and the day on which they said it? Orders for the evacuation of Paris were printed and ready.

Yes, we were on our way eastward through Meaux, and up the Marne, and across the Marne at Trilport, and so through La Ferté-sous-Jouarre to Château-Thierry. Name after name vibrated for me with memories both personal and patriotic. Personal, because I had seen this river and these fields and woods at the last moment of their and my unsuspecting innocence. I had enjoyed them in the company of two beloved friends, both dead before the war ended. On July 1st, 1914, we had passed through this exact region, loving its fertile tranquillity. On that day we had seen Reims, Laon, Soissons; and looked through beautiful gates of country places, sequestered, embowered; had laughed as we went along the roads at certain names on sign-posts right and left—Lizy, Billy, Charly, Missy, Silly; had laughed more at going to the wrong La Ferté in search of the Hôtel del l'Epée—La Ferté Milon;—and had after some thirty or forty kilometres of further tranquil loveliness, successfully found a delicious omelet and a desirable bed at the Hôtel de l'Epée in the right La Ferté. Much ruin now scarred La Ferté-sous-Juarre. We did not pass the Hôtel de l'Epée. Some one during the war sent me a photograph of the street, showing the hotel portal and a swollen dead horse lying in front of it.

We were nearing now the very site and ground of the second battle of the Marne, where the New World saved the Old World and where at the first battle of the Marne, September 6th–12th, 1914, the Old World had saved the New. On May the 27th, 1918, the mailed fist was lifted for what proved its last blow. In March it came near to striking Amiens down. On a day during those weeks when the Hun was sweeping westward, the British soldiers had been told by their general that they were fighting with their backs to the wall. Russia had gone to the perdition that she is still in.

"It is a very black hour," said a lady to me at dinner in Boston, during that time.

"The darkest hour is before the dawn," was all that I could find to reply.

Hope was very faint all over the Allied World. News spread daily at which the heart stood still.

We came to that point where you do not speak of what you and all whom you meet are thinking. I remember trying to turn my mind away from what June seemed likely to bring us. One shrank from the thought of June; and through June the deadly footsteps stalked nearer and nearer. Indeed, hope was very faint. The eye of the Hun was looking at Paris. Our general gave Foch every man he could. The 3rd Division, new-trained to war, was brought in haste to the Marne. Part of it, the motorized machine-gun battalion, able to make greater haste, came first. On June 4th, at the bridgehead opposite Château-Thierry, it was successful. A French *ingénieur* had blown up the first part of the bridge, but the Germans could still cross, and our boys finished the work. From Montdidier the 2nd Division followed, transported by every quick vehicle available to help block the Paris road. It made good. On June 3rd it took Bouresches from the enemy and held his best Guards off, on June 26th Belleau Wood followed. In their race for honor those glorious Marines, with the equally glorious brigade of Regulars under General Lewis, struck the word "stop" from their dictionary, fighting forward ceaselessly until July 10th. Before this 2nd Division was relieved it had taken Vaux. Half of our Second Corps was brought from the British area, and two of the five divisions were added to those already standing between the enemy and Paris.

We at home were too far away to feel clearly the significance of these bright preludes during June, and our hope
did not yet revive. The dark hour still spread over us. But
all the while our troops were pouring thicker and thicker
into Europe, and those in command there knew what this
meant; knew that they had an endless stream of young
blood to use—young blood which, if untried, was also
untired. That was the great fundamental magic of the
touch our hand laid upon the Allies; the touch of fresh-
ness upon weariness. In mid-July parts of the 42nd Division, facing the Germans east of Reims, blocked them
there, while four companies of the 28th Division on the
right flank of this offensive opposed the on-coming invaders. Look at the map of the Marne between Château-
Thierry and Dormans. That is where the invaders succeeded in crossing the river—a farthest fling or splash
of the tide rising to engulf Paris, a sort of Pickett's charge
at Gettysburg. Just east of Château-Thierry, the very
first name on the south bank of the stream is Chierry.
From this little spot run a finger up the river and round
its bend there to Mézy, and then beyond, opposite Jaulgonne. Between these three little places it was that the
3rd Division held the south bank of the Marne. The ponderous power of the advancing Hun was pressed and
driven against this line;—his infantry in formidable
number, supported by artillery and screened by smoke.
Here one regiment of that 3rd Division, though flanked
on both wings by Huns who had got over, stopped them
in front. These Americans met attacks from three directions, tangled up two German divisions, and took six
hundred prisoners. This was a day that had to be saved;
they saved it with their sweat, with their blood, with their
death. Then in the weeks following, our soldiers turned to
spirits of wild battle, flung clothes off, gleamed among
the hills, attacked, pursued, beat flat the Huns like rattle-
snakes. "The Terribles" is the name that a French officer
gave our 32nd Division, as he watched it taking Juvigny.
    This Aisne offensive, launched by the Germans on the

27th of May, by mid-July bulged deeply into the invaded
ground. It was the third pocket dug in the Allies' front
by Ludendorff that spring. First had come the centre
pocket of the Somme, dug to Amiens in March and April;
next the right flank pocket of the Lys, dug to the north
in April, towards Calais; and now this last, the beginning
of the end, at the Marne, dug towards Paris. The change
came between July 15th, when the 42nd, 28th, and 3rd
Divisions were engaged, and July 20th. After that, while
the 3rd Division was pushing the enemy away from the
Marne, and he was falling back beyond the Château-
Thierry-Soissons road before the attack of the 1st Corps;
and while the 42nd Division was fighting through the
Forêt-de-Fère on its way to the Ourcq;—in fact, during
the last ten days of July and first days of August that
saw these divisions of ours help the French crowd the
enemy back from their bulge, back from the Marne to the
Vesle and the Aisne, the change before the dawn grew
into the dawn itself.

In celebrating, and most fitly celebrating our own part
in this, let us take great care lest we forget that we did
not do it alone. It is such forgetting that has done us
injury in the hearts of the English and French. Books
have been written, mere vulgar yelps of brag, from which
you might think that we alone had been there at that
second battle of the Marne. The French had six or seven
divisions to our five during the fifteen days when the
Hun armies of von Mudra and von Boehm were squeezed
out of their Marne pocket.

For me, July the 18th will always seem the day when
the change passed like a spell over our country. That is
the day, too, when, as I see it, the decisive operation in
moral surgery took place. In January, in a great hospital
near Washington, I had sat listening to wounded officers
in bed tell of that day, and of the night of rain preceding
it. Some of them would never be whole again, and they
knew it. All were young and none complained. Two en-

listed men complained to me out of all that I saw—and
these two had never been to France.

"We have friends in Chicago," said one of the officers,
jokingly of himself and a comrade in the next bed. "We
are going to get two street corners. I'm to sell papers,
and he'll sell shoestrings and pencils."

As we played cards, or in other ways killed time, they
told me of the road they came through the Forêt-de-
Villers-Cotterêts; of the great rain and thunder; of the
mud; of the five parallel tides of traffic going one way or
the other along the road; of the heavy trucks lurching
and sticking in the slanted, mushy sides of the road; of
the vast silence before the guns opened, when the rain had
ceased and its drops from the leaves sounded in the forest.

In company with chosen French divisions and the splendid Black Watch (for in those first days of our initiation
it was not yet known by any one how well we were going
to fight) our 1st and 2nd Divisions were picked out for
the work of the Soissons drive. Then through the five
days that we know, the 1st Division went on, not to hell,
but through it, to the heights above Soissons and the
village of Berzy-le-Sec, which it took. The 2nd Division,
quick at its work, in two days was in front of Tigny.
Together they had captured 7,000 prisoners and more
than 100 pieces of artillery. Meanwhile, our 26th Division,
with the 167th French Division, formed a pivot between
Château-Thierry and Bouresches, until the crooked had
been made straight in the battle-line farther towards
Soissons. Then they became the marching right flank of
a greatly stretched-out movement, pivoting near Vaux-
bain, by Soissons, and by the month's end the Huns had
been pushed back, and their bulge chopped short.

And what of the *poilus* who had said that word about
going to hell? They never said it again. At the critical
moment, when hope was sinking very low, when Parisians
were to be told to pack up and fly, the New World appeared at hope's bedside, and gave to the patient its

strong, young, healthy blood. The transfusion was successful. Hope's ebbing life came back and again flowed strong and steadfast. So immediate was the rebound to convalescence, that the patient has sometimes forgotten how dangerous the illness was.

The good deed of our American divisions will glow through the pages of history, and our children in the years to come will say the names of Château-Thierry, Soissons, Reims, as we were saying them in our streets through those summer days of 1918.

Here is the tale of the "Event," of the transfusion, told from the mouths of Frenchmen. They called our coming in the "Event" in those days. On the 4th of June while darkness still spread over our world, Clemenceau thus spoke the grim truth aloud: "Exhaustion has set in, enormous with incredible losses for the English army, and formidable and perilous for the French. Our available forces are spent, but the Americans are coming in for the deciding stroke. . . . It remains for the living to carry out the splendid work of the dead." On the 8th of August General Pétain said to his troops: "The invader falls back. His *moral* totters. Yesterday I told you, 'Abnegation, patience, your comrades are coming.' I tell you today, 'Doggedness, boldness, and you will force victory.' " Between these two dates the comrades had come, the "Event" had happened, the great transfusion had taken place. Throughout that month of August, transfusion continued; each day 13,000 more Americans set foot upon French soil, and by autumn we numbered almost two million.

XII

LUDENDORFF'S POCKET

AT La Ferté-sous-Jouarre we left the river, not to
see it again until dusk, when we came to it at Dormans through Ville-en-Tardenois from Reims. This
was a day between rivers: the Marne, the Ourcq,
the Vesle, the Aisne. They have been flowing through
great events these many centuries. Great events have been
added to them; soldiers' feet from Michigan and Pennsylvania and all our states have trodden earth where Charles
the Bold and Louis the Eleventh and Joan of Arc walked
once. As we went to Belleau Wood I forgot to look at
anything for a while. Pride in our Marines who wrenched
it from the pick of the German troops, and reminiscence,
and surmise, all made such a blend in my thoughts that
I recall nothing clearly of what was said, or how the
villages looked, or the fields, until we came to Belleau
Wood.

Here we got out and walked the ground over, and
listened to the words of the young captain who had been
detailed at 37, Rue de Bassano to be our escort. He had
fought here himself, and he showed us the positions and
told us the course of the action. Following where his
finger pointed, I looked across a valley from the ridge we
stood on to another ridge, where he was saying the enemy
had been at a certain stage. We were at the edge of some
not very thick groves which stretched along it; below were
meadows, green, and a small brook, and beyond these,
up the opposite ridge, more thin groves; and the sun
was shining pleasantly.

"It makes me think of the Huntington Valley a little,"
I mused, half aloud.

"So it does," said the young officer.

"Then you have seen that country near Philadelphia?"

101

"Yes."

Blue flowers were growing about among the thickets where we explored. War had been raging when they last grew here. Spring was now coming fast, had made visible advance since that first day when we had passed the roasted aeroplane in the field and first entered the great silence. But neither spring nor the hand of man had done much yet to cover or remove the traces of war. Among the blue flowers minenwerfer baskets were lying. They were empty of their missiles, and most of the hands that had hurled them were knobs and knuckles of bone now. The dead lay about here so thick in Belleau Wood that they could not be buried. Bits of rotted leather jutted out or lay flat among the flowers, and cartridges unused, quite plentifully, and pieces of firearms. Now and then our officer would pick up one of these objects out of the scrap-basket of the battle, and identify it for us as being American or German. He had had his turn in hospital, and once had gone twenty-eight days without removing his clothes. As we peered and stooped through the thickets, human bones among the new flowers and the old last year's matted leaves would stir and twitch like dead branches, disturbed by our tread. In a pair of old shoes in one muddy place, the bony feet still stuck, German feet; our captain knew them by the make of the shoe.

"It's the young generation at home who ought to know about all this," I exclaimed. "Can the old profit by its meaning? They're trying to forget the war, and Belgium, and everything, already. Just as most adult Germans will die under the influence of forty years of Prussian poison, believing Germany was invaded and fought a war of defence, so most Americans over forty will die drilled in the myth that the United States is a law unto itself, like a comet in space, and can live in a weather of its own, unaffected by the storms in the rest of the world. That's an idea which will send us shortly to a back seat, if we don't get rid of it. At least," I concluded, "I can tell

the boys at St. Paul's School something about this devastated region."

"Are you a St. Paul's boy?" said the captain. "I went
there too."

Though I had heard his name, of course, when he had
been introduced to us in the Rue de Bassano, this had
not then suggested his identity. I asked it now. His
father had come from my town, he had gone to my school,
I knew most members of his family, one of my particular
friends was his favorite aunt. None of these things had
made us known to each other. We old St. Paul's boys
met first beside a couple of German feet sticking in the
mud, in Belleau Wood, in the land of the Marne, and the
Ourcq, and the Vesle, and the Aisne; not so far from
where Joan of Arc crowned the Dauphin in 1429; not so
far from where a synod compelled Abélard to burn his
books in 1121; not so far, either, from where they had
chased Attila and his Huns away in 451. His Pennsylvania feet had been chasing another Attila and his Huns
away in 1918; and here were the feet of a Hun that hadn't
been able to run off.

And so to Château-Thierry down the hill, and up the
hill through Verdille, Epieds, Beauvardes, grazing the
Forêt de Fère, through which our 26th Division, not a year
ago, had fought its way to the Ourcq. By that time, July
24th to 27th, those boys had learned the trick of bird-
nesting for machine guns.

"Kamerad!"

Thus had a German non-com addressed the captain in
a wood, just after killing most of his men, and just before
perceiving that he himself was going to be sent after them.

"I thought 'Kamerad' was too easy to say then," explained our captain. By that remark we understood the
fate of the non-com.

It is said that our men after Seicheprey, where first
they took German prisoners, behaved to them much as
they might behave to curiosities, to wild things caught

alive when hunting, almost as something to play with. Later, they saw some of their own comrades whom the Germans had captured and sent back with mutilations made in Germany expressly for America. After that they did not play with their prisoners.

Soon after the Forêt de Fère, we came to Fère-en Tardenois, and I began to mark my map with a cross against each place that was in ruins. Today patterns of crosses wind over it, east and west and north and south, tracing the kilometres of ruin that we saw beneath the great silence. Once amid all this, and only once that I remember, a train of trucks standing by some litter left by battles, served as a sign that we were not the only living beings who surveyed this valley of extinction. Smoke rose quietly from the engine, a little stream that must have been the Ourcq, or some tributary, flowed placidly near by.

I was curious about Laon, and anxious to see that cathedral with my own eyes. Had it suffered? Did it still exist? Soissons had suffered greatly. Our papers had referred to that, but about Laon I had never seen a word in them. It lay north beyond the Chemin des Dames, on a high ridge, above its steep town, visible from a great way off, very defenceless. It had been a Hun headquarters. Fierce fighting had gone on not far from it in the days of the Chemin des Dames, and the Hindenburg Line, when the Huns were retiring. Indeed, fighting had never ceased in this neighborhood.

Laon was a gem among cathedrals, a little masterpiece by itself, touched by the hand of Italy, with a Virgilian charm and grace shining among its exquisite aisles. We went on therefore to Laon, after seeing Soissons and the Chemin des Dames near Malmaison. The town was intact, and so, save for one now well-known injury, was the beautiful church. How had it come to escape?

Before Laon was hurt, save for the one tower, the Germans striding southwestward from Charleroi during the late days of August 1914, took it, and it remained

theirs, and became a headquarters. Naturally they spared
it. Within the new map of a Greater Germany, represent-
ing that empire after a German peace, Laon was included.
In the fall of 1918 the Germans had to abandon the city,
and their leave-taking was hasty. They had insufficient
time to blow it up, as they had blown up Péronne and its
fellow-victims, and thus retard France's commercial re-
cuperation by one more piece of wanton and scientific
destruction. But they left agents behind, and bombs and
mines, and unluckily for German hopes, the French came
into Laon and found the agents with the bombs not as
yet set off. On the 13th of October, General Mangin, who
through the three preceding days had been crashing forward to the north, first across the Aisne at Œuilly, and
next across the Chemin des Dames and the dominating
tableland of Craonne into actual sight of Laon, entered
that town at half-past three in the afternoon. He was
borne up its steep hill by a crowd, not of traitors or
agents, but of Frenchmen, the tears of joy on their cheeks,
the strains of the Marseillaise upon their lips. The tri-
color had been floating from the cathedral since eleven.
After four years of exile, the great church with its clustering town at its feet had come back to its own.

We descended its hill and soon were again out of the
zone of life and within the zone of death. Through the
forenoon, our journey had been along a part of the bottom
and west seam of the pocket which Ludendorff had begun
on the 27th of May, 1918, to dig to the Marne, with the
mirage of Paris in his eyes. Now for a while we followed
the east seam of the pocket. The high plain of Craonne
through centuries of war had been a key unlocking doors
of communication between adjacent territories of France.
Here, after he had been pushed back in 1914 at the first
battle of the Marne, the German had created his Siegfried
position. Deep dips in the land and the wooded undulations had been wrought into a bulwark dense with underground communications and thick-planted guns. And here
the Crown Prince with his two armies of von Boehm and

von Below had started his share of the enterprise at one in the morning with all the shells and gases and poisons that German invention had placed at his disposal. At one o'clock that morning of May 27th, had begun that bad news which we had to read for so many days. It was only eleven months ago. On the map I looked at the names of the places that were coming on our road, or that lay near to it on one side or the other: Juvincourt on the little river Miette—we should presently cross between it and La Ville-aux-Bois. We went through Corbeny: Craonne was just off to our right. At eleven-twenty that morning eleven months ago, the delighted Kaiser had arrived at a convenient high place, close to where we were now, to watch in the splendid sunny weather the armies of his boys Fritz and William, and all his other armies, battering their way southward, even across the Aisne, digging the pocket which was to reach the Marne.

"William," he telegraphed to William's mother, "has today attacked the British and French. . . . Fritz was one of the first to reach the Aisne. . . . God has granted us a splendid victory and will help further."

"My soul is torn," he had written his Cousin Austria early in the war, "but everything must be delivered to fire and blood, men, women, children, and the old must be killed, not a tree nor a house must be left standing."

He had written that to Francis Joseph at a time when the general American mind still disbelieved that such things as it was reading daily in the newspapers could be. On August 16th, 1914, as Foch with the 9th Army was facing the advance upon Rethel by von Hausen and his army, a German cyclist upset himself in the street of Gué d'Ossus. Immediately, recorded an officer of the 178th Saxon Regiment, in his diary:

"We burned the village and drove the inhabitants into the flames."

As we went over the seven kilometres from Corbeny to Berry-au-Bac, the land changed from being a skeleton into being the dust of skeletons. It lay dead, chalk-white,

blasted and stark; not a blade of grass, nothing but extinction. Along the west seam of the pocket we had seen
many poppies. These red flowers hid the truth that was
behind them: human flesh; then crows in black swarms;
then red poppies—this had been the rotation of war-crops
on the Aisne. Here along the east seam we saw not even
poppies, but only the white sterile chalk. Over this ground
on May 27th, 1918, the German offensive had broken like
a flood from a dam. It had rolled down from the highland
and reached the Aisne, artillery following infantry.
Nothing had withstood it. The German officers whistled
as they walked with their canes in their hands. During
the afternoon it had been the same on the west side. Three
French battalions had been surrounded and engulfed in
the Forêt de Pinon. Carrier pigeons brought the last
message from them, sent about two o'clock the next morning:

"The three last men of the three battalions have just
surrendered."

Whilst these had been holding out, the flood poured
on: five divisions against one French, the 61st; ten against
the 22nd; six against the 21st; from the Kaiser's post to
Berry-au-Bac, eight against two. That is the way it came.
The outnumbered French and the tired English, still un-
rested from their exhaustion of the earlier weeks, gave
way hour after hour. They lost not the Aisne only, they
were pushed beyond the Vesle this first day. The next
was like it. Fismes went. The Germans came up on the
wide land of Tardenois. Soissons burned and went down.
Fère-en-Tardenois followed it. By the 30th the Germans
had dug to the Marne at Jaulgonne. Here our 2nd Division came into it. Over all France wires trembled with
messages. Our Americans at their Jonchery munition
depot did not keep the holiday on Decoration Day for
which they had made ready; men who had gone to Chau-
mont to celebrate it were called back. A message to Jonchery set them making ready instead for a train of trucks
hastening here from Dijon. These arrived and were loaded

all through the night. The electric lights shone upon the warehouses and by their gleam the shells were lifted into the trucks backed up close to the warehouses. Then some fifty started west in a long winding train on the road to Meaux.

Bad news still darkened our world; not many could have then perceived the dangerous thing that Ludendorff was doing, hypnotically lured by the mirage of Paris. In digging his pocket he had gone in through a gate, so to speak, and the gate-posts were still standing, and not in his possession. To the west was the Forêt-de-Villers-Cotterêts, to the east, the Montagne de Reims. He tried desperately, a little later, to envelop these by two offensives. Both failed. Then the squeezing out began. But before that had set in, and before any of us here could know about and understand the significance of those gate-posts, we heard of peasants flying; of towns abandoned; of more Germans on the Marne below Château-Thierry and Verneuil. It was on June the 4th that the force of the flood at length had spent itself. The Kaiser never sent any more telegrams like that he had sent on the 27th of May. For ourselves, as I remember it, the news of the victory at the bridge of Château-Thierry on that 4th of June was the brightest we had heard for a long while—and not so very bright at that: only a spark in the night, but a spark struck by that splendid action of the 7th Machine Gun Battalion of our 3rd Division, which arrived after twenty-four hours on the road and thirty-six without sleep, and made the name of Château-Thierry as immortal for us as Concord and Lexington. Clemenceau spoke on that day:

"Our available forces are spent, but the Americans are coming in for the deciding stroke. . . . It remains for the living to carry out the splendid work of the dead."

The dead! Almost as thick and deep along this road from Laon to Reims as along our road in the terrible land of the Somme, must the dead have been heaped. It was written all over the face of the region. It was to be read not alone through the sight of a great cemetery which we

saw to our right; to look at the mere earth itself was
enough. The earth here had died in torment. I can evoke
the vision of its twisted corpse today. White, dislocated,
crumbled, distorted, it was fearful to see, even for us who
had seen so much. I stared up at a sort of hill. I had
passed this very way on the 1st of July, 1914. I could no
more have recognized the spot than you could recognize
a dead man who had been lying out in the open for a year.
Him you have to identify by something he wore or carried;
a ring, a knife, or his teeth. Well, I suppose that I could
have stood here, studied the canal, or the river, or the
relation of one to the other, and then asked: "Is it
possible this can be Berry-au-Bac?" Of the town
there was nothing left at all. Of the charming country
all along this way, the quiet fields, the groups of trees
I remembered, nothing was left. This ancient doorway
between the Ardennes and the Isle de France was a shrivelled, gaping mouth. The pastures, once so calm, were
flung up into shapes white and wild, like a herd of scream-
ing ghosts petrified to silence suddenly as they crouched
and gesticulated. The hill at which I stared may have been
there before, or it may have been heaved up by the mine
explosion that engulfed many lives here and left a crater
which looked more like the work of natural convulsion
than the handicraft of man. White clay now seemed to
form the substance of this hill, steep, brittle, rough, corrugated by violence, like every foot of the surrounding
country. Nothing was growing there then, and it is one of
the regions where nothing is growing yet. Beneath its
surface, among the dust and bones, lie the bulb roots of
death, the unexploded shells. These are sown in all the
battle-grounds of France. Until they are gone, no farmer
ploughing his field can be sure that he will reach the end
of any furrow alive.

After Berry-au-Bac we went on through the waste that
continued for eight miles or so, and ceased shortly before
we came to Reims.

XIII

ON this May evening of 1919, we had to thread our way through Reims as through a labyrinth where all roads but one led to nothing. A wrong turn right or left in this place, where more than one hundred thousand had lived five years ago, would have brought us to a stop among the stony heaps of their houses. The streets into which these houses had been flung and piled were slits in the silence. In that other German war, the war of 1870, Reims had been made the seat of a German governor-general, and had paid many heavy tolls to its invaders. I looked upon the toll it had paid now, as slowly and carefully we made our way to the cathedral. For this sight I was ready—as ready, that is, as many pictures and descriptions can make one. We all know the particular spite that was hurled at this monument, and why it was so hurled. We know the denial of its bombardment by the ninety-three German professors. They signed a denial of this and the other crimes committed by Germany up to that time. These professors had the choice of doing this, or of losing their positions and having their careers broken and their daily bread cut off. They were at the mercy of one man's word, their emperor's. We pay a high price, a very high price, for democracy; but it is not quite so high as that which Germany paid for her magnificent material order and well-being.

When the Germans found that their purely wanton destruction of what was France's holiest building had turned against them many hearts that had hitherto been neutral or in doubt, they did what they always do in such cases. It happened several times during the war that the effect of their actions upon the outside world had not been anticipated by them and took them by surprise. Their

education had never led them to suspect that their own
standards were behind those of the civilized world. Therefore their battering of the great church of Reims, which
struck the civilized world as being what Attila might
have done when he put Reims to fire and sword in the
5th Century, had to be justified in haste. We know the
pretext that they put forward a trifle too late. It was explained as a military necessity. It was pretended that
the French were using the cathedral to signal from. It
was overlooked that they used aeroplanes for this. We
know, too, the self-contradicting remarks of German officers upon which this excuse was based. We know the
kind of shell that was found embedded in the walls—needlessly heavy for the alleged purpose. The world knows
today that the Germans meant to pound the cathedral of
Reims to dust if they could, because it had been, since Joan
of Arc had the Dauphin crowned there in 1429, the central
shrine, the place of prayer, pilgrimage and patriotism,
the spot of all most sacred and dear to France: her Independence Hall, her Mount Vernon, her Liberty Bell, made
holy, not through one century like ours, but through seven.
It had seen the same seven centuries that Amiens had seen,
often drenched with blood. From 1328 to 1830, almost
every King of France had been crowned here. Its great
bell, weighing more than eleven tons, had been ringing for
festivals and rites before the existence of our continent
was known. At my last visit, the figure of Joan of Arc
had sat on her horse in front of the church. I looked for
her, but the gallant statue was gone and its place was
vacant. She had been taken for safety elsewhere.

No, they had not smashed Reims to dust. It was here
to be seen, and would be seen for long years to come. It
would be proudly standing when those who had aimed
at its fall were dust themselves. It was a wreck, its roof
was gone, its eyes, the glorious windows of stained glass,
were blind; you could see through into its broken interior,
you could note upon its western front the ravage of flame
and shell: the carvings, the maimed and incinerated army

of saints and kings that had been one of the glories of the world, bore witness to the intention and the effort of the Hun.

In the third chapter of his account of Germany, the chapter entitled *From Kant to Hegel*, Heinrich Heine made a prophecy, and this is a part of it:

"But the most frightful of all will be the philosophers of materialism. . . . The philosophy of materialism will be terrible in that it taps the elemental force of the earth, conjures the latent powers of tradition, those of the entire Germanic pantheism, in which it arouses that lust of war that we find among the ancient Germans, the lust of combat. . . . for combat's sake.

"To a certain extent Christianity has mollified this brutal battle lust of the Germans; to destroy it, it has not availed. When the Cross, that talisman which holds it now in curb, comes to break, then the ancient warriors' ferocity will surge afresh, that mad Berserker frenzy which the Norse minstrels are today still singing. Then—and the day will come, alas!—the old war gods will get up from their fabled tombs and rub the dust of centuries from their eyes. Thor will stand erect in his might and with his giant hammer will smash the gothic cathedrals. . . . When you hear the tumult and the shouting, be on your guard, dear neighbors of France. . . ."

Soon after the bombing of Reims cathedral, his passage began to be remembered and quoted. The rest of the prophecy is equally remarkable, and I add it here. Heine continues:

"Do not smile at this advice even though it is given by a dreamer . . . do not smile at a fantastic poet who expects the same revolution in the world of facts that has occurred in the intellectual world. Thought precedes action as lightning does thunder. Thunder in Germany is quite German: it is not very lively, but comes rolling slowly. But come it will; and when you hear a crash like no crash ever heard before in the history of the world, then you will know that the German thunder has culminated at last. At this noise eagles will fall dead from the high air and the

lions in their remotest African deserts will cringe and
slink away into their royal lairs."

At about that time Richard Wagner, the last Norse
minstrel, was singing, not yet of mad Berserker frenzy,
but of the Flying Dutchman, having been led to this
partly by certain other pages written by Heinrich Heine.
People then alive lived to see this same minstrel singing
a triumphal march to that conqueror of France in 1870,
that Hohenzollern whom Bismarck then made Emperor of
Germany; the minstrel was also writing a coarse extrava-
ganza, a Berserker insult to prostrate France, entitled
A Capitulation; he had also reached the middle of his
opera *Siegfried,* in which the old gods were brought out
of their fabled tombs and sang to us on the stage. Wotan,
Brünhilde, Siegfried, were names given by Hindenburg
and his Berserkers to certain of their defense lines of
1914–18, when the philosophers of materialism had completed their work, when the talisman of Christianity had
broken and no longer curbed the ancient German battle
lust, when the creed of blood and iron had been systematically and scientifically substituted for the creed of the
Cross, and when German children had been during forty
years educated backward to be Berserkers. When Thor
in 1914 smashed Reims with his giant hammer, Henry
Heine had been fifty-eight years in his grave, Richard
Wagner had been in his for thirty-one. Heine had made
his prophecy seventy-nine years before the event.

With Heine and Wagner and Hindenburg in mind, I
looked at the smashed glories of Reims. What, I wondered, did those remarkably righteous persons, who were
already assuring us that Germany was a tender and mis-
represented creature, make of these facts? I thought of
another poet also, an American, Louise Driscoll by name,
who sang her noble lament over the cathedral:

> Men planned and wrought
> And set fair towers against a flower-blue sky.
> There is no power in the world like thought,
> And beauty wrought with prayer can never die.

What's lost with Reims?
'Tis Germany—a land we used to know
A pleasant land of songs and fairy tales . . .
    Where did they go?

What's lost with Reims?
The soul of a great people, blind, betrayed.
No roaring guns tore flesh from flesh and made
A desert of their gardens, yet we see
The desert of the world in Germany!

Théodore Botrel, the poet of the *poilus,* wrote a sort of
Litany of the ruins:

> Jeune bon Dieu, dans la crèche
> Rajeunis ton éternité,
> Toi, dont la tendre loi ne prêche
> Que l'amour et la charité.
>
> Doux Roi du plus doux des Royaumes
> C'est toi que nous invoquons,
> Et non les vieux dieux des Guillaumes,
> Des Attilas et des Nérons.
>
> Par Louvain, par Senlis croulantes,
> Et par Reims qui, près de mourir,
> Tends vers toi ses tours suppliantes
> Comme les moignons d'un martyr;
>
> Par notre farouche Endurance;
> Par nos ôtages en exil;
> Jeune bon Dieu, rends la France
> Justice et Gloire! Ainsi soit il!*

*"God merciful and young in thy manger make young
again thine eternity, Thou whose tender law doth preach but
love and charity. Gentle King of Kingdom gentlest, Thee
it is we invoke, not the old gods of Kaisers, Attilas, and
Neros. By crumbling Louvain and Senlis, and by Reims,
who dying lifts to Thee her suppliant towers like a martyr's
stumps, by our endurance fierce and exiled hostages, God
merciful and young give France justice and glory. Amen.''

"They are evacuating Reims," wrote a young Frenchman, a boy of twenty-three, to his godmother on the 7th
of April, 1917; "it is very, very sad to see. Tonight ten
conflagrations were throwing whirlwinds of reddened
smoke two hundred metres high, and the profiles of the
two solemn towers were cast darkly against the flaming
heavens. Sad vehicles defiled beneath me, generally automobiles; women and children, little boys in their black
aprons as if they were coming from school; furniture. The
town burned in a sort of calm, as in submission to an
inevitable and foreseen phenomenon. And the towers,
with a look of eternity, of indestructibility, seemed to
watch. And all this on a fine night, placidly lustrous beneath the Pascal moon."

> "There is no power in the world like thought,
> And beauty wrought with prayer can never die."

That is what the towers saw; Thor could not smash it.
It was in the soul and mind of that boy as he wrote to his
godmother, nine days before his death on the battlefield.
He wrote other letters, there is a little volume of them,
letters to his father and mother, to certain other elders, and
to intimate comrades of his own young generation. With
his soul and mind he was a piece of that France essential to
us and civilization, the ultimate France of the spirit that
should keep our respect and affection. He was the modern
consequence of the ancient cathedral. The same race had
built them both. He was a piece of beauty wrought with
prayer—that form of prayer which is constant, noble
impulse translated constantly into noble action; and as I
think somehow of him and Reims as belonging spiritually
to each other, I place here, not in the order of their writing, some few sentences from his letters, because they are
full of that thing which Thor with his hammer cannot
smash.

He is speaking of two fellow-soldiers:
"If you could only see the strange life we lead, six yards

underground. . . . D is a peasant. X has not the dashing
patriotism of D, but he has his rectitude and loyalty and
courage. He supplements D's intellectual patriotism with
the dignity of a free man, who declines to accept the tres-
passing of an outsider upon his own concerns. He likes to
be master in his house and he is master of himself. He does
not like fighting but goes to it whole-souled from self-
respect. He has supremely the sense of honor. He is the
peasant aristocrat."

The boy was a student of medicine with four terms to
his credit when he entered upon his first term of military
service. This the outbreak of the war cut short. He got
leave to go to the front in the ranks, and not as a hospital
aid. He fought from Charleroi to the Marne, where he
was wounded. He writes of himself:

"Don't imagine that any thought of winning distinction
entered my mind when I took the step I was predestined
to take. Once more, the place of a Frenchman twenty-two
years old is under fire, or with those who are going there.
As it was in 1870 and has been for ever, our business is to
boot the enemy out of France. I took my part at the
Marne. My place now is with those who carry on. It's the
task of my generation. You'll say doctors are needed
as much behind as at the front. I don't want to be that
kind, nor the kind in the hospital trains; some of us are
needed *in it*. I couldn't shake hands with G. or N., or
look at my friends in the eye. I'm ill at ease among
fathers some of whom have sons at the front. . . . I want to
escape any danger purely to learn how better to face the
next. The living must be worthy of the dead, our life
mustn't give their deaths the lie. One has done nothing
so long as anything's left to be done. . . .

"We must win. There's no question of knowing if we
can or can not, or if we shall succeed or shall not. We
must, that's all. It is the man who shall have willed
victory who will vanquish. This determination, deep, un-
conquerable, intimate, this will to vanquish, each of us
must have it, no matter what his place and duty. . . . But

this will to vanquish that I should like to root in every
French heart, in order to be useful must stick to defined
aims, else it will be merely a vague and vain aspiration.
. . . Work, that is the word. Work, that is what the
enemy has been doing since 1871; it is against his work
that our dash and our fine courage are bruising themselves. France isn't working hard enough."

He writes from hospital to a friend:

"The German is alien to our mentality . . . his materialism (he calls it *Deutschland über alles*) stamps everything, stifles every noble generous instinct, everything that
antiquity, the Renaissance, our 17th and 18th Centuries
planted in us of altruistic, humane, disciplined impulses,
the whole higher moral level that distinguishes us from the
ancestral brute . . . have you any time for reading? I'm
going to send you your favorite Musset anyhow. You'll
always find a minute to read over the *May Night*. It's not
very war-like, but beauty in no matter what form is a tonic
for the soul and lifts the heart. . . ."

He writes his mother:

"I'll keep your letter as my guide through the unfore-
seen, and try to show myself worthy of what you think of
me, and to become worthy of what I would exact from
myself. . . . For the triumph of justice and right (though
these may be merely illusions) and for the chastisement
of the greatest collective crime of history, many tears,
many drops of blood must fall . . . the generation of
1914-15-16 will have won moral grandeur, the thing for
which it is worth while to live life. . . .

"What a beautiful walk I took yesterday! I followed
an infinity of different paths and thus greatly heightened
the effect of emerging upon a straight road that cuts
through the moist and mystic heart of the forest to a new
horizon. . . . I'm sure that to enrich one's inner life one
must intensify one's external life. You must, so to speak,
gather sensations to nourish thought during those hours
when external sensations fail. I don't suppose you know
how a dynamo works? Very simply. For one day a

powerful steam-engine spins the dynamo and thus generates the electricity which is stored. Next day it may be the other way round, if you choose. The stored electric energy can run the steam-engine. Very well. It's quite the same with the dynamo we carry within. If we desire that it shall in our dark hours illuminate our life, we must store up light when the sun shines. I doubt if I could have seen any beauty in the landscape yesterday if I had never been in Switzerland. I'm deeply sure this applies to everything, and especially to the things of the heart. But if I start on that I'll never stop. . . . Fool that I am! I was going to forget to tell you that in two days, very likely, they will discharge me from the infirmary and let me go back to the trenches. . . . The joy of meditation, of philosophizing, is a terrible siren who breaks careers and parches strength. She must be merely an episode. Otherwise the man is lost. . . ."

In hospital, where he has time for much reading and re-reading—Shakespeare, Plutarch, Voltaire, La Fontaine, the Bible, make but a portion of it—he writes his intimate friend:

"Dismiss your idea that war is over for me. My cure will take long, but the war longer still. I've sent you Stendhal. I read *L'Amour* in order to talk it over with a young Irish girl (but alas! those things, when one is doing them one doesn't discuss them, and when one discusses them one doesn't do them, oh, thrice alas!). When shall we be able after having sacrificed to Mars to return to the temple of Venus? When can we resume, dear old Maurice, our good confidences, our dreamings by the Marne, all our friendship of yesteryear? . . . As to my foot, doctors disagree. Some counsel another operation, others disbelieve in it. I wish I could at least rejoin my headquarters . . . or else be in the zone of the armies. Think of having to make war here at Vichy! It's a heart-break. . . . At any rate I've been of some use here, day and night now, these eight months. For eight days I had charge of 120 patients, all by myself. . . . There's my life. I blush for it. . . ."

To his father he writes:

"I don't know what monstrous aberration of modesty, what imbecile timidity causes one to open his heart to strangers only. . . . A son ought to treat his father as something different from a preceptor. . . . Many feel a devoted love for him . . . respect, gratitude; few, I believe, think of making their father their friend. Why? False shyness, and then, children have no such notion . . . they seek pleasure comrades rather than thought comrades. On the other hand, if the notion of such a friendship sometimes makes a father wistful, it isn't for him to begin, he would have to trespass on youth's privacy; such a friendship isn't possible unless it springs of its own accord from the wishes of the child. Dear father, I ask you to be my friend. We are so absolutely made to get on together. Between us, right in the family circle, simple and united, nevertheless twenty centuries of convention, of fashion, of controlling tradition, had piled obstacles between two hearts and their natural expansion. We've never talked openly as two young people sometimes talk together, shrouded in the dimness of a room or in the inviting quietness of a beautiful night. At such a time trust is stirred and intimacy follows it. One is surprised the next morning, sometimes, at what one has been moved by certain influences to reveal to a companion. That's because next morning the ice has formed again, the ice that for a moment was broken, melted by the warm breath of friendship, and the conventional chill re-assumes its rights. . . . And since it is to my stay in hospital that I owe this inspiration about a change in our relations, I bless my illness. . . ." (Here for three pages as wonderful as ever came from the pen and heart of a son just twenty-three, he tells his father of what he has read—from Shakespeare to Anatole France, from Montaigne to Loti—during these months in hospital, he tells him of his thoughts, of his character and what it has lacked and how he hopes it has developed, and then he continues):

"And so I mean, dear father, to open an immense conversation with you, guards down, in which I'll make a

clean breast to you of my dreams and my enthusiasms.
I'll reveal my aspirations, my moral and my worldly ambitions, my still halting conceptions about the huge questions I've not yet thought enough about. We'll talk of men
and acquaintances, of life and death, of God and women,
or rather of the gods and Woman, of art and politics, of
history and the wooded slopes of the Vosges, of medicine
and war, of everything that's within the domain of
thought. You'll correct my inaccuracies, I'll revive your
illusions. I'll gain weight, you'll regain youth, and so
you'll really be my father.   ."

This French boy was not quite twenty-one when he entered the war at its outbreak. During three years he
seems to have been in almost every part of it, the Somme,
the Marne, Champagne, the Argonne, and to have seen
almost all the sights of war and felt almost all its sensations, except despondency. If ever he felt that he never
allows it to appear.

To the father of a comrade killed at Douaumont and
dearly loved, he writes, after two pages:

"Listen, sir, this letter is too painful for you to read.
I'll cut it short. But I must all the same tell you that the
sacrifice of your son is not wasted. My first feeling was
one of discouragement, of disgust at the folly of slaughter
which froths over the earth. But soon, as often before,
the lesson of sacrifice rose out of it for me. We need the
Scriptures no longer, the story of Christ teaches nothing
actually, now: to learn the beauty and to understand the
necessity of immolation we need but look around us. Such
examples as André has given put the flabby and the timid
to shame and uplift and strengthen the brave. . . . The
battle goes forward . . . and those not yet fallen must look
ahead and still ahead, until their turn shall come. . . ."

On New Year's Eve of the year that his turn was to
come, he gave a supper.

"My party was a grand success. I had sixteen guests,
and later two who arrived at 11:30. . . . They proved
charming and greatly enlivened the dawn of the present

year with their songs and monologues. . . Pâté de fois
gras, roast fowls, green peas, salad, hot chocolate, plum
pudding, a litre of white wine apiece, decent champagne,
coffee, cigars. I was able to get some rum—not so easy!—
just enough for lighting the plum-pudding. A little before
midnight I had the lights put out. Then as the clock struck
twelve, the pudding was brought in, garlanded with blue
flame, while corks popped and greetings were exchanged.
The *Marseillaise* started by itself. Very characteristic. If
any one at any other time had started the national song,
the *poilus* would have booed him down; but they felt a certain solemnity in the moment, in spite of everything, and
sang the hymn out freely and joyfully. . . . This morning I got to bed satisfied at having done something for
cheerfulness and merriment. . . . That's an imperative
human obligation in war-time. . . ."

Within four months the turn came for this boy. He was
warned not to keep so near some comrades he stood ready
to care for should they be hit. Bullets were falling thick.
"No fear," said he, "bullets are used to me." A few steps
more and he fell without a sound or a sigh, shot through
the heart.

Not quite twenty-one when he wrote his first war letters,
not yet twenty-four when he wrote the last, he had explored the realms of duty, of thought, of emotion and of
action very far. He was a piece of the true France,
and his spirit came from the same world whence, seven
centuries before him, had proceeded the cathedral of
Reims. That world is a place which the hammer of Thor
cannot smash.

XIV

THE TOWERS IN THE NIGHT

AS at Amiens, so now at Reims, day was sinking while I gazed up at the towers of the cathedral. In the square below the towers were *poilus*, standing and moving. I looked at these soldiers of France, over whose spirits the breath of war had passed. What had it done to them? Any one could answer that question who had seen the *poilu* as I had seen him often, and had seen him last in July 1914. In those other days he had been a very different figure. His clothes hung upon him without dignity, his walk and bearing slouched, his face had been trivial, the whole man seemed to fall short of manhood. Today these *poilus* were grave, upstanding, their carriage erect, giving forth a sense of power and accomplishment in full measure. In truth they were a visible part of the majesty of France. Tourgueneff said once: "War makes more men than it kills." The breath of war had blasted the cathedral and had blown the boy away to lie under one of the crosses that scattered the land of France like fallen stars. Yet, as from that first immolation upon the Cross, so from these others, as the boy wrote to the bereaved father of his friend, spiritual resurrection had come. These *poilus* walking beneath the towers, now, had been ready: and the readiness is all. The martyred cathedral of Reims still stretched its towers to God, and they were still suppliant. Why? The boy had written: "Do not weep for us, but continue us." Continuing was what confronted the *poilus*, France, and our whole civilization. Sometimes continuing comes very hard. We rise to meet death, but meeting life is a longer act. When exaltation has performed its task and sunk away, what then remains to carry us through, if we still live? Some things there were that Thor had smashed with his hammer:

122

homes, hearts, bodies. These broken things needed the
supplication of those towers. They that were to continue
must seek help in whatever house of whatever God their
spirits knew. Some would pray in churches, some without
words under the sky, some would pray through action,
through sacrifice, like the boy who saw the sacred worth of
immolation. All would be answered. But voids there would
be when no answer seemed to come. For broken, unhappy
men in these voids, I could fancy that Reims stretched
its suppliant towers to God.

Like that at Amiens, I had known this cathedral well.
To come upon it as it was now, with my memory of it as
it had been, unprepared, would have overwhelmed me.
But the expected sight was so full of unexpected grandeur, that the pain of its disfigurement was lost in new
admiration. It stood up like a sort of proclamation of
faith. More than ever it seemed living; too great to notice
what had been done to it; above all temporal suffering; the
France of seven hundred years, and the France of the
years to come.

Day grew more dim. In its waning light I looked across
the square to see what was left of the little inn, the Lion
d'Or, where I had eaten and drunk and laughed so many
times. From my bedroom windows there, I had always
taken a good-night look at the cathedral before blowing
out the candle. Down in its court had grown a vine,
trained to make a screening arbor, and my last supper
here, June 30th, 1914, had been curtained by its leaves. No
windows faced the cathedral any more. No court was
there and no wine. The Lion d'Or was down on the ground,
and where it had been were pieces of plaster and heaps
of stones.

The tide of dusk rose a little higher. We got back
into our car and began our return southwest through the
brooding silence of the ruins. There were no hours left in
which to include the one thing more that I should have liked
to do this day—swing south by the Montagne de Reims
and thence eastward, forty kilometres, across the

Champagne from Pompelle to Massiges. Then we should have gone over those denuded clay-white plains upon which Ludendorff on the 15th of July had launched that other attempt to retrieve the peril of his Marne pocket. He had enveloped the eastern gate-post no more than the west. He never attained the old Roman road in front of the French lines. General Gouraud stopped him. The Montagne de Reims remained safe and Châlons-on-the-Marne was not reached. Still the Marne pocket was left as it had been dug, defenceless on both sides, a very dangerous success, won beneath the misleading hypnotism that the mirage of Paris cast over his mind. By afternoon of that 15th of July, Ludendorff and his emperor saw from Blanc Mont that they had failed. West of Reims von Mudra did better on that day, pushing eleven French and three American divisions back, and extending the pockets; while still more to the west von Boehm was winning the south bank of the Marne between Dormans and Château-Thierry. But upon the day following, the tempest of thunder and rain in which they came within ten miles of Epernay, was a bad omen for them. They crawled forward on the 16th of July here and there, but the crawling back began also. They gnawed vainly at the flanks of the Montagne de Reims, and along their whole line of eighty kilometres ran a slackening of their impetus. July 17th saw the quiver of the horde on the turn, and by the next dawn, in the thunder and rain of Villers-Cotterêts, our second battle of the Marne story began.

Our road southwest from Reims took us close to the edge of part of that ground where they had gnawed at the east side of their pocket. We could have seen Marfaux had there been more light on the way to Ville-en-Tardenois. But light was going now, visibly each few moments. Had the day been with us still, we should have seen clearly just the same sights as those of the morning hours, desolate fields, desolate houses, emptiness. As it was, the sharp edges of this perpetual spectacle began to dissolve in the quiet gloom. Cruel shapes grew gentle in

the vagueness, standing fragments softened, smaller fragments melted away; until discernment of our road and
what lay to its left and right, ended, and one merely felt
the presence of whatever objects we passed.

Reims was present, too, in this voiceless obscurity, casting over France its ceaseless influence. As Amiens stood
by the Somme so Reims stood by the Vesle, and these two
great guardians were stretching their suppliant towers
unseen in the night. "Do not weep for us, but continue
us."

Dormans came. We had already descended from the
higher land of Tardenois, and crossed the Marne at Bas-
Verneuil. Along the river we felt the trees passing, and
here and there passed little lights, with wide blank spaces
between them. The ground over which our cautious speed
was now increasing had been the uttermost goal of the
Hun, it was the outside limit of his onset from the Chemin
des Dames; here, as if he had struck some surface, he
rebounded, and his backward steps to the place whence he
had come, began. He counted, during the height of his
fierce advance, 209 divisions against those 192 that had
met him. France gave 103 of these, England 58, ourselves
17, Belgium 12, Italy spared 2 from her own desperate
struggle with Austria. While these were contending, even
in the days of gloom that so filled the weeks of this spring,
leaflets of ill news were floating down upon Germany from
the sky. They told those who picked them up that six
hundred thousand Americans, young, strong, fired with
zeal, were now landed in France and ready. They came
through the air with French aviators, who dealt them out
like packs of cards foretelling misfortune. These leaflets
sailed in little balloons devised in England; their messages
of truth, well chosen to strike chill, were written at Crewe
House by Sir Campbell Stuart. They fluttered down, and
the mailed fist was never able to seize them all before they
had done their work, undeceiving its dupes and weakening
the beats of their discouraged hearts. When our 4th of
July came, it was no longer six hundred thousand of us,

but more than a million, that were present in France, with
more arriving each day; and this, too, was wafted down
upon Germany from the little balloons.

Our speed increased as we went along the valley with
the sense of the great trees at our side and overhead. We
ran out of them into darkness that continued, but across
which some distant light would shine, then the nearer
darkness would again shroud us.

"That was Jaulgonne," said our captain once in the
silence, as a far light showed and sank behind.

Below Château-Thierry we crossed the river again, our
road improving as we dived forward into the endless gulf
of the night. No one came by, but lights single or by
twos and threes shone from time to time across succeeding
distances. After Meaux our pace quickened still more
and presently seemed to double itself along the empty
road. Sometimes upon a rise the upward slant of our head-
lamps would reveal tall tops of trees between whose
steady avenues we were rushing, and sometimes our flying
light would glare for a second upon a kilometre stone; but
when I thought of the towers, they seemed as near as ever.
It was as if the silence were filled with their quiet presence,
this silence that brooded over the night as it had dominated the day. After a while the lights of Paris began, and
at eleven we got out at the hotel.

XV

I WAS tired, but also I was wakeful. Deeper than before, deeper even than at Amiens, I seemed to see into and comprehend France. My thoughts turned also to the living, whose flesh and bones were crushed, who had known the wild raptures of the blood, the calm rapture of exaltation, and who now were knowing the empty stages, where rapture and exaltation are not. Upon sticks and crutches, if not still unhealed in bed, they were facing, not death, but life. I had seen them at home, and in England, and now here. "Do not weep for us, but continue us." The boy who was dead had wanted no tears for the dead, but he would have pitied these living. They had to continue upon their sticks and crutches, dragging themselves somehow across the desert stages where there is no exaltation. I trusted that in most of them that thing was alive which Thor cannot smash. Without it, it were far better that they were wholly dead. Those of them that had the habit, or the occasional mood, of prayer, pagan or Christian, or a blend of both, which is the most honest and most human kind, were doomed, like all of us, to pray sometimes to emptiness. Neither the deepest grief nor the bitterest remorse equals in its desolating chill the sensation of unanswered prayer. The vision came to me of these maimed survivors, these fragments of men, the halt and the blind, all over the world, a vast horde, crawling painfully about, like insects that have fallen upon the table from a burning lamp.

Does war make more men than it kills? I wished that I had thought of putting this question to the Tommies at Albert, or to the military policeman from Kansas. Some kind of answer I should certainly have received, though nothing like so mature an answer as would have come from a *poilu's* more subtle and intellectualized Latin intelligence. I went back the few steps from the hotel entrance to the Place du Havre; Kansas was not upon his island, nor anywhere else to be seen tonight. Returning, I sat down in the adjacent café, ordered a bock and a brioche, and opened my map upon the table.

Some tables away in the almost empty place sat a creature whom I was sorry to see, for I feared that he would see me and come over. He did not live in my hotel, but evidently somewhere in the neighborhood, and sometimes frequented its reading-room and hall. Taking me for a brother American he more than once had attempted to invade my privacy for longer stretches of time than the natural rights of man justified, or my view of my own rights would allow. I had hitherto managed not to swallow any large dose of him. He was no brother of mine. Kansas on the island was a brother, and many of our doughboys, and many more people still: but not this kind. It takes all sorts of people to make a world, and all sorts of people to make a United States; and I exceedingly regret that it does so. I felt in my bones that this American belonged to the numerous and noisy tribe of conscientious objectors to common-sense. Hundreds of these had come over to Europe to teach Europe how to suck eggs.

His face and clothes were exactly alike, if you understand what I mean. He was the sort of person who at home hands the plate on Sundays in the sort of church where the minister improvises prayers which last an hour, reads aloud passages from *The Literary Digest,* and misquotes Longfellow. The rising and departure of two Frenchmen exposed me to his full gaze, and I saw this fix itself upon me across the intervening table where their glasses stood. Oh, yes, he was coming!

"Well, now, who'd have thought a man like you would be sitting up here this late!" With this greeting, he seated himself opposite me, and smiled. He had a vaguely lustrous eye, and his teeth were too long, and slanted outward.

I pulled out my cigar-case and was stretching it over to him, but he lifted his wide, limp hand against it. I had a box of cigarettes, and these I offered him.

"Thank you, I never use tobacco."

I tapped my glass of beer.

"Have one," I suggested, and signalled to a waiter.

"I never use alcohol in any form, thank you," he said.

The waiter came.

"Bring this gentleman a cup of coffee. I hope you will keep me company in that?"

"Thank you, I have had all the refreshment I ever take before retiring."

"At least let me order you a toothpick!" I exclaimed.

"Sometimes I think you must be quite a joker," said my man. "Well, now, I think you're right to joke. I've seen sights in France—well, now, there's times when a joke helps some."

"Yes," I assented, wondering if I had misjudged him. "Yes, indeed. How long were you at the front?"

"I was not exactly at the front. But I have served. My viewpoint is that in all walks we can find some way to serve. And I have seen sights and sights."

"Were you too old for the front?"

"No. Not too old. Not too old in years, that is, you understand. But at Fort Oglethorpe, they found my heart was not what it should be for my age. I am twenty-nine years and seven months now. Unmarried. My uncle in the Surgeon General's office wrote them about my heart, because he knew more about it than those medical reserve doctors did. But I was determined to serve if I was strong enough. I was going to get over here somehow."

"Couldn't you find any chances for service at home?"

"Ah, but I wanted to be in the thick of it! I'm no stay-at-home."

"Oh, I see."

"And will you tell me what life is without service?" he demanded, slightly chanting the words.

"Lots of fun," I answered. "Especially when you're under thirty."

"Now you're joking again. So my uncle got me a position in an uplift mission."

"How very interesting! Which one? The tuberculosis caravan? or the pædiatric unit?"

"Peddy—I don't think I have heard that mentioned."

"A number of Americans are going about in camions from place to place, showing the French how to have and rear children."

He cast down his eyes immediately, and was silent.

"Pædiatric is the name for that unit," I explained. "It comes from the Greek. It is a perfectly nice word. Even a lady uplifter can use it without any risk."

"My viewpoint," he now resumed, "is that we should all avoid certain language. The unavoidable use of it by doctors does their tone no good. And between tone and action the distance is very short. Did you go out to any of our training camps?"

"Yes."

"Did you hear the language of the young men? But you would get no slant on that, because they would be careful before you."

"Won't you tell me some of the sights you have seen?" I asked.

"Well, now, you don't have to go far. This great French city right now is full of evil."

"Isn't your city in America?"

"I never got a slant on our cities, though I have sensed them, visiting. Father intends to buy a new home in Little Rock. Have you noticed the man out there?"

"Where?"

"There is a military policeman out there some nights. He makes no attempt, no attempt at all, to use his authority."

"Why, I thought he did."

"No attempt. He allows young soldiers to walk right by him, when anybody could see they intended to practise immorality. If a person like you spoke to him and got his reaction, some good might come of it."

"Well, I don't know about that. Do you mean that you spoke to him?"

"I did, sir. I felt it my duty, even if I was no longer officially connected with uplift."

"You spoke to him about stopping——"

"I certainly did."

"Jimminy Christmas! And what 'reaction' did you get?"

"I will not soil my tongue with repeating the language that he used. But a man with a viewpoint like his is a disgrace to our democratic army."

"You're not now officially connected with uplift, as you express it?"

"Well, not just now. But when I was, I used to come out between vaudeville acts and speak to our boys about social purity and kindred topics of a serious nature. It was against my principles to issue cigarettes to them."

"Do you mean those cigarettes that people in America had bought for them and that were sold to them instead?"

"That was a mistake," he replied.

"A mistake! Yes. Quite."

"The gift cigarettes were unpacked along with other cigarettes that we had bought to sell the soldiers at cost. The two lots got mixed up. That was all. And so when the soldiers opened packages that they had paid for, and found slips inside printed, telling they were the gifts of some society at home, why their reaction was based on a mistake. We tried to give them the right slant, but somehow they never got it. My uncle——"

"What more sights have you seen?"

"There is immorality and intoxication everywhere you——"

"Yes, I know, I know. But everybody isn't drunk. And you seem to me to have immorality rather prominently on your mind. Believe me there is not much true 'service' in making a military policeman angry. You have no idea how easily I can guess the names he called you. Having to bear these patiently isn't very strenuous service, is it? And, to be quite frank with you, I think service ought to cost a man something—his energy, his brains, effective exercise of skill, or good will, something like that—for many hours each day, and given freely for nothing. You needn't wait for your uncle to get you another job. Jobs lie thick ʹhere all around you."

Had my deliberate testing him succeeded or failed? Would he not, if he were a self-known hypocrite, have got up by now and gone away? During my probing words I had watched in vain for that special look, the glare of mingled injury and vindictiveness, which flashes across the face of the hypocrite found out. If he had that sensitive spot, my probe had not reached it yet.

"I would feel indebted to you," he said with unction, "if you would mention some job I could do here, without overstraining my heart, that is. I am a stranger here."

I bethought me for an instant. I could give him some addresses where good workers were welcome—but could he be any sort of a good worker? France was afflicted with too many like him, come over from America for the "uplift" as he and they called it, but which was no true uplift at all, was merely a mask, concealing to others— and to themselves at least partially—the subtle disguises of a central and impregnable egotism. Swarms of these psychologically diseased people were pervading poor, sad, scarred France with their intrusive "missions," and these brought really valuable missions of relief into disrepute.

"Charity begins at home," said I lightly, but watching him close. "Don't stay over here. There are many hundred wounded soldiers in the Walter Reed hospital, near Washington. You could be of help to some of them every day, by reading aloud to them."

He immediately spread out his hand against this suggestion. "I cannot bear the sight of human suffering," he said. "I find it too afflicting."

A psychologic doctor would have been quite satisfied

with those two statements. Added to what had gone before, they were enough to rip the veil away and disclose the true nature of this case. But it interested me to go fishing for some more "reactions."

"Well," I said, "the Armistice saved much additional human suffering. I suppose that we should rejoice that it came."

"I certainly rejoice," he stated.

"And yet, do you know," I continued, "sometimes I do not wholly rejoice. Sometimes I ask myself, may it not have been premature?"

He sat erect. "Premature? When it stopped the war?"

"Yes, if it stopped it too soon for the wholesome instruction of Germany."

At the word "Germany" I thought that I discerned some fleeting change in his face. But he said:

"Would you instruct anyone, even your enemies, by means of war?"

"Certainly, if there was no other way."

"Then you are quite against universal disarmament?"

"Universal? How do you know that everybody will come into that game or keep the rules of the game if they do come in? Don't forget the Scrap of Paper! Don't caress yourself with the thought it will be the last Scrap that the world ever sees!"

"I am sorry to hear you speak like this," he said. "I never allow myself to be cynical."

"Just as much as we insure against fire," I pursued, "we must insure against war. Never in making our national plans and preparations can we reckon without the possible chance of war."

"I can't bear to hear you say that," he said.

"Oh, there are compensations," I replied, very lightly and deliberately. "War makes more men than it kills."

He threw both his flabby hands above his head.

"You have no idea what a horror I have of war!" he intoned.

"I'm quite sure that you have!"

This slipped out before I could stop it; but he missed it. His vague, lustrous eyes were filled with his chronic preoccupation.

"But please don't imagine," I amplified, "that you own the copyright of horror of war. That is no monopoly of yours. It is shared by a good many millions of us who would like war to become impossible, and yet who would make war at any moment in the name of righteousness and to defend the liberty of the human soul."

"I have thought it out clear," he intoned. "I know where I stand. The most sacred thing in the whole world is human life. Therefore anything that takes human life is pure evil."

"You're a Christian, I presume," I said.

"It is certainly my effort to be one," he replied.

"Then what do you make out of the Crucifixion?" I asked.

I knew quite well how he must have dealt with that, or would now deal with it, if my sudden question had never till now presented itself to him. He would push it quickly out of his mind, as he pushed out every fact of history or nature or human nature that caused the clockwork of his toy idealism to slip a cog. But I was not prepared for the ingenuity with which his subconscious self would instantly protect itself.

"I cannot discuss with you the Founder of my Religion."

"No, you can't," I murmured, lost for a moment in admiration, which he took for defeat. I had pushed him pretty close. He was not a self-known hypocrite. But his under-self had felt the approach of my probe to the spot it was hiding, and its resentment had peeped through in a hard flash from his eye and a brush of color that had already faded out of his cheeks. In his eye was now a reproof at my irreverent introduction of the Crucifixion. Well, I would try for one "reaction" more.

I tapped upon my map, which lay spread upon the table.

"By the way," I said, "there is service that you can do. Of course you've seen all this?" And I swept my hand in a general way from Amiens and Picardy eastward and south across Soissons and Reims to the edge of the Argonne, which was as much of the devastated regions as this particular map included.

He leaned over and looked at the map, and then he shook his head.

"I have been able to travel very little," he said. "My duties have been confining."

"Then you have not seen anything of the devastated regions?"

"No."

"Go and see them. There is your chance for service."

"I have no permit," he said. "It requires influence."

"You forget your uncle. I'm seeing them, and I have no uncle. All I did was to explain to the proper people that I wanted to visit the devastated regions in order to see with my own eyes what the Germans had done to France, and then go home and report it to Americans."

"I have no wish to report it," he said coldly. "I do not consider that any true service."

"Why?"

"It has been too much reported already."

"You're mistaken. It cannot be too much reported."

"May I inquire your reason for such an opinion?"

"Because there is a pernicious spirit at home which masquerades as Christianity. It preaches the doctrine of forgiving and forgetting what the Germans have done to France and Belgium. Of course nothing could please or could profit the Germans quite so well as that the world in general and America in particular should forget what they did, and believe that they would never do it again."

By the changes in his face I could read that in this final attempt my success was going to be perfect. When I had spoken of a pernicious spirit as "masquerading as Christianity," the same hard gleam which I had detected once before again flashed in his eye. By the time, however, that I had finished speaking, he had schooled himself for the moment. It might have been a preacher that now addressed me in accents reproachful yet mild.

"Do you not think," he said, "that we should forgive our enemies?"

"I'm afraid that you'll have to put that question a little plainer before I can answer it," said I.

"Could anything be more plain than the words themselves? Are we not told in the Bible to love our enemies and do good to them that hate us?"

"We are. I don't, however, remember that we're anywhere told to forgive other people's enemies."

His control held. He was still the benevolent, Christian preacher of the Gospel of Peace.

"How does this strike you?" I asked him. "The United States standing up with its hands outspread in an attitude of blessing, and saying to Germany: 'I forgive you for carrying away French wives and daughters to slavery and prostitution; I forgive you for throwing poison gas into the hospital and streets of the French town of Mézières in the last few minutes before the Armistice was signed, and thus killing the defenceless French whose town you were leaving in haste.' Does that sort of forgiveness strike you as costing the forgiver very much?"

He took instant and adroit advantage of my phrase.

"Need forgiveness cost us anything?" he asked, raising one of his tell-tale hands. "Did it cost the father much to forgive his prodigal son in the parable? I admit that we should hate the sin, but let us not hate the sinner. Remember the prodigal son, and how freely he was forgiven!"

"Aren't you omitting a rather important part of that parable?" said I. "The prodigal son said, 'I will arise and go unto my father, and will say unto him, Father I have sinned against heaven and before thee, and am no more worthy to be called thy son.' Has Germany said anything like that?"

It may have been from his talks to soldiers about social

purity beween the acts of vaudeville entertainments, or
it may have been from other previous experiences, that
he had learned his various uses of adroitness. Wherever
he had been, he was certainly skilful; and his skill was,
of course, seconded at every turn by that under-self in
him who was hiding the spot he wished to remain unknown both to himself and to all the rest of the world.
My facts about French wives and poison gas at Mézières
he did not take up; he pushed them out of his mind
automatically, because they interfered with his psychological clockwork. That mechanism was constructed to ring
melodious bells and thus drown the noises of reality
whenever they threatened to disturb his artificial and perfectly sterile idealism.

"Both sides have been guilty of much that you and I
would condemn," he now said, intoning slightly again.

"If you mean that men in hot blood commit acts they
would be ashamed of when they were cool," said I, "that
is not what I am talking about. I am talking about a plan
of atrocity worked out by the German Staff in advance,
the proofs of which you can see for yourself if you visit
the devastated regions."

He smiled. "There has been so much exaggeration."

"Exaggeration? I don't know what you call Lord
Bryce's report. Or the French report of Monsieur
Bédier."

"But they were enemies of Germany," the uplifter reminded me.

"Have you read their reports?"

He paused. That was in order to look as if he had read
them, and was now being judicial about their contents.
I doubted his ever having heard Bédier's name before;
but he could hardly have escaped hearing something about
the investigation of German atrocities in Belgium conducted under the auspices of Lord Bryce. Our papers had
spoken of it, and the facts presented in the pamphlets
had been upon many lips. He would be well aware that

these facts, like the sights in the devastated regions, would
be disturbing to his psychological clockwork. Therefore,
to avoid the trouble of putting them out of his mind, he
would never let them come into it.

"Lord Bryce," he began in a weighty and dispassionate
manner, "is an eminent man. He is an honest man. We
are all convinced of his sincerity."

"Quite so," said I.

"But we must not forget that Lord Bryce may have
been deceived. He was not on the spot. He did not see
those alleged deeds committed with his own eyes. How
could he be sure that the witnesses were telling the truth?"

"Don't you think that with his long career in Parlia-
ment and in public life that he would have become fairly
expert in such matters, pretty careful to sift what was laid
before him?"

"My dear sir, mature judges have been deceived before.
Who of us is infallible?"

"But there was the Supplemental Report, containing
photographs of letters written, and diaries—all in the
handwriting of Germans, who recorded not only the
atrocities they saw others commit, but the atrocities they
committed themselves. They were photographs, remember, with the dates, and the names of the writers, their
rank, and the regiments to which they belonged."

He smiled again. "Can you and I be sure that these
photographs were not forgeries?"

It was growing late. No one was left in the café but
ourselves and the waiters. These were noisily lifting
chairs from the floor and piling them upside down upon
the empty tables, casting upon us the while looks of increasing inhospitality. I decided that I must bring him
to a boil. So long as he remained tepid—and he knew the
strategic value of a moderate temperature very shrewdly
—he could not be surprised into that final "reaction"
which would complete the *quod erat demonstrandum* of his
case. To surprise him circumspection was needed, and
therefore I began my approach from quite a safe distance.

"Of course I cannot prove to you that those photographs of letters in Lord Bryce's Supplemental Report were authentic documents. To do that I should have to show you the letters in the presence of those who had written them, and have the men state under oath that it was their own handwriting. But on the other hand, how can you prove to me that they were not genuine?"

"I admit freely that I cannot. Therefore I hold my opinion in reserve. That is what I so wish you would do about all these matters."

He did not know how nearly this remark brought *me* to a boil. But I continued to stalk him.

"Have you heard anything about Shantung?" I inquired. "Hints reach me that it is giving them trouble at the Peace Conference." I spoke softly.

"Oh, no," he replied. "I am not near enough to anybody there."

"I've never been to Japan," I said, "or to China either. China must be still a very strange place. Is it Canton or Shanghai that's the capital?"

"Why, Peking is the capital."

"You've seen it? How I envy you!" I spoke more softly still.

"No. I have had no opportunity to visit China."

"Then how do you know that Peking is the capital?" This I almost whispered. A sudden change had come into his look, but he was too late.

"You have never seen Peking with your own eyes," I pursued. "You cannot know that it is really the capital of China. You have taken the word of maps and geographies for it. How do you know that they are not forgeries? Should you not hold your opinion in reserve?"

He rose abruptly. "I will bid you good-night," he said. "I thought I was talking to a man who lived on a higher plane."

He was gone at once. More slowly, I folded my map and slid it back into its cover, and left the café to the piles of chairs and the impatient waiters. I had brought him to a boil, the lid he so tightly kept upon his under-self had come off, up from the bottom had bubbled the key-word that unlocked him. This case of diseased psychology was demonstrated.

France was filled with "uplifters" such as he, conscientious objectors to common-sense, all living upon the "higher plane." So, unluckily, is America.

XVI

EARLY the next morning after my talk with the up-lifter, I entered the Gare de l'Est. Above the streams of travellers on their way to the platforms of the Eastern railroad in Paris, beacons a white dial, a meeting-place for many. Swarms of our doughboys surrounded it; French passengers were lost in this crowd. To these American soldiers returning from their *permissions*, the sight of themselves here, and the sound of their own voices was nothing out of the way, but it was like a dream to me. I had sped past the dial so often in other days, that now to come upon this flood of the New World in khaki beneath it, literally submerging the Old World, made me stare.

The New World flooded my train, part of which was going to Metz, and part to Strasbourg. After some five hours it would divide at a junction which lay to the south-east of the St. Mihiel country, the next step of our pilgrimage. All the way we should run just within, or just along, the edge of battle-grounds as ancient as Cæsar and as recent as Foch; through Meaux and La Ferté-sous-Jouarre on the Marne, whence the Hun had been beaten back in September, 1914; through Château-Thierry; through Mézy, where on July 15th, 1918, the 38th Regiment of our 3rd Division with a platoon of the 30th had won its name, "The Rock of the Marne." All the more because we had passed some of these places yesterday, either in daylight or in dark, I was glad that they were to come by again, and I should have liked to get out and walk and linger over all that ground where our soldiers had stopped Ludendorff. Right down the time-table of our Strasbourg express, name after name sounded the overtones of historic association: Jaulgonne and Dormans

141

rang with American dash; Épernay bubbled with memories of golden wine; farther up the valley we should follow the Marne and be running to the south of Blanc Mont and Suippes, and the Main de Massiges, that Champagne country where Gouraud had splendidly halted Ludendorff. Then, with Chalons-sur-Marne behind us, our train would run on eastward below Ste. Menehould, below the Argonne, beyond the Marne, the Meuse, the Moselle, and so after dividing reach its two destinations over rails now once again wholly upon French soil. The last time that I had travelled on this Chemin de Fer de l'Est, my course had been from Strasbourg as far as Avricourt across land of the Kaiser's, descended to him from his grandfather, who had torn it from the map of France after the Bismarck victory in 1871. After forty-seven years Alsace and Lorraine were French once more, and America had helped to bring this about. I thought of the crowds beneath the clock and of the trains drawn up by the platforms during the years before we came in, the black years of Verdun, and the mutiny of 1917. Those trains had carried soldiers daily up the Marne valley, grave soldiers in blue, going to Ste. Menehould, the Argonne, Vaux, and Douaumont, many of them destined never to see the clock again.

Today it was our soldiers who crowded the train. They were returning to their regiments at various places, each fresh (or stale) from his "permission" in Paris, and the scene recalled to me in a way certain trains at home between New York and Boston, when our boys are going back to their various New England schools after the Christmas holidays. As I walked slowly beside the long train, its open windows hummed with the sound of voices jocund and youthful. No more than the school-boys converse about Cæsar and his Gallic war, did these doughboys make references to the historic interest of the journey before them. Bits of their talk reached me from the windows and it was all what you would naturally expect and some that you would naturally not repeat. Dearly should I have liked to join them and hear something of their Parisian adventures and impressions, their murmur sounded so buoyant, so charming to my elderly ears. Thus certainly did Cæsar's legionaries, and possibly even Attila's, gaily converse between slaughters, without any more suspicion that their deeds were destined heavily to bore the school-boys of today than these vivacious fellows from the Hudson and the Mississippi, whom the train of the Chemin de Fer de l'Est would presently be rushing over Cæsar's and Attila's ground, were aware that their deeds, too, would heavily bore the school-boys of the future. They in their turn had made history, and farther from home than ever Cæsar or Attila had been able to get. The train was not starting yet, and I continued to walk along it, looking at this new vision of America in the Old World. Some tales of ill behavior on the part of our men had reached me, to be sure, and of certain harsh and even cruel punishments, which a young soldier friend has since told me he believed on the whole timely, in spite of their widely published excess. I can quite believe it. Upon thousands of lusty youths, far from home, let loose from military discipline upon a great metropolis, a firm hand needed to be kept. But ill behavior was not the prevailing characteristic of our boys, and a picture of them has been drawn by a Frenchman, André Chevrillon, whose delightful pages, entitled "The Americans at Brest," give what I fancy represents the impressions which France will retain of us when incidental memories of roughness and discord have died away. In the first days of their homecoming our soldiers, just like those I had met in Paris streets, cherished some resentments, chiefly connected with high prices; but two years later, the officers and enlisted men whom I happened to tell that I was going back to take another look at France, never failed to exclaim, with light in their eyes, that they wished they were going too. And quite often they would add, that if I should visit such and such a place, would I look up a certain house where they had been billeted, or a certain corner where they had

been wounded, or some other thing, some hill or wood or
street or bank or stream that was now become a magnet
in their memories, drawing their spirits back to France,
the country of their great adventure. That is what Time
does for us all.

Not every window of this long train was filled with a
doughboy, nor was every car dedicated to them. At
certain windows French travellers stood and stared out
with that particular glare, which we all assume in
European trains, to discourage everybody else from entering our compartment to take a seat. But these glares did
not worry me. Our young captain whom we had begun
to see at 37, Rue de Bassano, and begun to know at
Belleau Wood, had us still in his charge and had taken
every care of us in the matter of tickets and reserved
seats in this early-starting and thickly-peopled train.
Our car was of German make, allotted to France after the
Armistice, and of better build, more solid and handsome
in every respect than French cars. After we had attained
full speed it was a cautious rate, never above thirty-five
miles an hour. Owing to the dilapidations of road-beds
during four years of fighting, all trains ran slower, those
between Paris and Strasbourg now taking from twelve
to thirteen hours instead of seven or eight. Over this line
three expresses now ran daily; in 1914 there had been
nine or ten. The great through expresses to Constan-
tinople, Carlsbad, and Berlin, for instance, had of course
all been abolished. About twenty express trains were now
running in the whole of France.

Special trains were arranged for our doughboys between their various important camps and the different
leave areas, but these could not wholly relieve the regular
trains of their burden. From certain of the best expresses
the enlisted man was excluded by order—and this most
naturally was a challenge to his young spirit; he got
aboard them whenever he could dodge our military police,
and exerted his entire guile to stay in them without being
discovered and turned out before the journey's end.

Soon after we had reached the Marne, I made a progress of exploration through the congested corridors of almost all the cars. I squeezed my way through knots of doughboys blocking the passage, leaning, smoking, loquacious, thinking little of other passengers, few of them intentionally rude, most of them merely young and rough and in high spirits. As I worked along back and forth through the long train, and realized that trains all over France, every day in the week, were running to and from the leave areas bursting with young America, I felt more indulgent than ever to the French impatience with us. I could have put the case better now to the discontented soldiers with whom I had reasoned in Paris streets and shops.

The wide-awake fellow from Danbury had said:

"Do you think if they had come over and saved New York and Bridgeport and New Haven for us, we'd be showing them the door like they're showing it to us?"

"Yes," I should certainly now have replied. "I think we should be showing them the door, and less civilly. Would you find it easy to say to them every time they swarmed into your train, trod on your instep, shoved their elbows into your ribs, and filled your face with tobacco smoke, 'Keep it up, dear saviour of my country. How can I ever forget that nine months ago you fought at Mézy?'"

Lovely in the quiet rain was this valley of many wars, seeming to grow greener as the drops continued to fall gently upon it. It was as if May each hour were turning higher the lights of spring, and spring were visibly feathering the trees along the Marne. We passed the tower of Meaux, the fields sloping up to woods, the steeper banks, the levels by the winding river. To our right at first, then after Trilport to our left, it curved constantly across our way, and sometimes we lost it in the sudden darkness of a tunnel to emerge upon it again in the sudden light. We soon passed into the zone of ruin. Not the least gruesome sight here were solitary houses, off on the hillsides, gutted within, with grey walls standing roofless, and black window-holes like eyes that watched you though they were blind: mile after mile of this among the ploughed and sown slants of cultivated soil, that chequered the sloping boundaries of the valley. The land here had been less wrecked than the buildings and was coming to life again, but they were not. And out there beyond sight across the river to the north, if you followed those little roads up the hills, you would come into the plain of Tardenois and be swallowed at once in the wide-stretching desolation of the Ourcq and the Aisne and the Vesle, and could go on to your right or your left or in front, and look at Reims, Soissons, Coucy-le-Château, St. Quentin, and so to Ypres, and never take one step that was not upon the grave of something.

At Épernay we made a considerable pause, and I got out, and on the platform beheld the manufacture of some international hate. A boy of about eighteen had rolled the customary two-story edifice of trays on wheels along beside the cars. Bread, oranges, champagne, with other food and drink, filled the trays, and the doughboys were stretching their arms out of the windows toward these refreshments. I didn't catch what prices the boy had asked for his wares, but I came in time to hear the loud results. Some of the soldiers had jumped down and surrounded him and his rolling booth, and stood with the buns and the bottles they had picked out, cursing him for a robber and a cheat. On him was evidently pouring their accumulated resentment for many over-charges. He stood dazed and sulky amid the storm of language, speaking not a word of English, but perfectly able to understand that he was being called obscene and filthy names for what was no fault of his. He hadn't made the prices, they had been set by the proprietor of the buffet in the station. And he was so much younger than the soldiers!

"Say," shouted one of them, "you ought to be glad for our buying your stuff."

And another from the window, pointing to some eatable:

"Say, Rain-in-the-face, how much is that?"

I couldn't help laughing at this and at several more of
their violent remarks; but I was ashamed of them, and
of myself, too, for not protesting. How often had this
boy been forced to receive similar insults, what sentiments
toward America was he going to retain and spread, how
many such scenes had been enacted throughout France?
And if this was exceptional and I had chanced upon a spot
of blackguards in khaki, would such spots stain all the
decenter rest of us in the French memory?

Of such spots I had heard elsewhere. Every day to some
soldiers quartered in the north, a lady of the neighborhood
sent good things from her kitchen garden, and, constant
in her appreciation of our coming over, had made these
soldiers welcome to the pleasant grounds of her estate.
This did not stop some of them from loud and unfavorable
opinions of the French, expressed continually in a trolley
car that ran through the district. There they sat talking
one day, and there sat the lady too; and an army surgeon,
who could bear it no longer, rebuked them and was told
to mind his business. But he reported the scandal to the
commanding officer, and there was no more of it. Which
was France going to remember, the army surgeon or the
"roughnecks"? It was not only enlisted men, it was
officers as well, whose words and conduct spotted American reputation. As when, for instance, a certain general
accompanied a film machine and a certain benevolent
organization to a certain hospital, and there ordered out
the convalescent men and staged a moving picture which
"featured" himself. Assuming his posture, he ordered
the patients to race and pick up little gifts flung to them
by the benevolent organization. When the photograph
was finished the little gifts were taken back from the con-
valescents, and the general with his benevolent apparatus
marched on to a new place and had more films made. Or
again, for instance, when a certain officer issued an order
that "The —th regiment will de-French and de-louse at
——, and embark on the —th." These examples—more

could be given—should suffice to remind any American, inclined to complain of French shortcomings, that the boot is not always on the same leg. That the conduct of our enlisted men was on the whole more creditable than that of their commissioned officers is something that I have heard too often from commissioned officers themselves not to believe. Some of the unfit were weeded out, but the Armistice came too soon for this process to be complete. Quite naturally, much more impregnable conceit was to be found among the middle-aged vegetable officers of our regular army than in those who had come from successful responsibility in civil life. While discussing our army with me, a French general said:

"When an American officer told me that I need not tell him anything, I knew that I had a bad soldier to deal with. When an American officer asked me to tell him what to do, I knew that he would prove a good soldier." He went on to explain with illustrations how admirable he had found the Americans, how quick to seize a point. "Make them understand a thing once," he said, "and you need feel no more anxiety. They will carry it out."

Among our doughboys the roughness at Épernay is the only case that I saw, and this makes me sure that the French are sincere and not merely polite when they express admiration of us, as they do today: our general tone must have been wonderfully decent. Two years later, when a lady who lived on a great estate in the eastern part of the country was speaking to me of the war as it was after we had come in, and of the Americans who had during some months in 1918 occupied part of her ancient house and part of her land, she had such cordial words to say that I exclaimed:

"Well, I hope that you are not telling this to me just because I am an American! I hope that our boys did conduct themselves pretty well on the whole?"

"But they were charming! We shall never forget them: so gay, so athletic, and some of them so good looking! And they always thanked us for the little that we could do for them." Then she smiled and shrugged her shoulders. "Some little Americans are running about in our village today; but that was quite likely the fault of our own lasses."

"You are very indulgent," I replied; "and from the chronicles of chivalry it would appear that wandering warriors have always been apt to leave their portraits behind them."

It was none the less new to think of: our doughboys home by the Hudson and the Mississippi, or sleeping in their graves by the Marne and the Meuse, and little Americans strewed about in Lorraine, and Dauphiné, and Anjou.

Nobody ever seemed to get out of this train; they seemed only to get in. They had an excellent opportunity to leave us at Châlons-sur-Marne, and one other at Vitry-le-François, but these they neglected and stuck to their seats closer than brothers, while the corridors remained congested with standing passengers. Everyone was apparently bound at least as far as we were, and when an emissary in uniform from the restaurant car pushed his way past the door of our compartment, announcing—

"Déjeuner deuxième! Deuxième service déjeuner!"— I felt my approbation of the French system increase. The steward's announcement may well be translated into the rubric that I once heard a black waiter upon the Michigan Central poetically chanting through my Pullman:

> "Second call
> In the breakfast hall!"

We rose and manœuvred towards the distant food, our minds at rest. At home, with the number of passengers upon our train, and but one restaurant car, attaining a meal would have proved a struggle to which we very likely might have preferred starvation. In France there is no standing for thirty or sixty miles at the door of the dining-car, or lurching about in its vestibule, till your turn comes. Before you get into your train, you stop at the steps, where the steward gives you a ticket for the service you prefer, unless you are late, when you may have to take what you can get. Sometimes there are three services, each lasting about an hour. Once you possess your ticket, your cares are over, you sit quiet until your "service" is called, and then you go and find a seat ready for you at a table which has been cleanly re-set. To all this our vigilant captain had attended. While we comfortably ate, drinking good white wine with it, the landscape flattened and widened, marshes passed, and spreads of water, in which many stunted willows stood in lines or clumps like children wading. Behind this untroubled scene of spring, lay always the country of ruins and graves, Massiges, St. Menehould, the Argonne.

East and west every day travelled our doughboys on this Chemin de Fer de l'Est, upon which I shall never travel again without affectionately thinking of them. Like the Chemin de Fer du Nord and no other of the great French railways, its main lines and branches crossed and pervaded the upheaved regions of the war, and upon both I have made many journeys to the land of silence. Over most of their miles of track nothing was running in May 1919, their rusty rails stretched through emptiness, or were torn up. Whilst I have been travelling in their cars, I have thought often of those trains that during the years of strife had taken soldiers of France and England, not to the land of silence, but to the land of bombs and gas and flames. My own safe journeys can never be forgotten, and pictures of various fellow-travellers remain vivid in my memory, especially those of the Chemin de Fer de l'Est, of which my impressions are more copious. Once along the Meuse, I was going to a small village to find, if I could, the grave of an American boy. I had the compartment to myself until at our second stop the door opened and in got a rosy French girl whose eyes sparkled upon a young Frenchman as

rosy. They sat opposite each other by their window, I sat
at mine. Unless it was the better to gaze at each other
I couldn't imagine then, and can't now, why they were
not sitting on the same seat, for really, such honeymoon-
ing I have never beheld by daylight, and I am sixty-one
years old. Not to be in the way, I looked out of my window with the utmost delicacy, and repeated verses from
the "Song of Solomon." But at a sharp slap I jumped
round.

"Isn't she wicked?" he asked me, gay spirits and
tenderness blending in his tones.

"Yes, indeed!" I exclaimed. His cheek was red from
her hand.

What was the use in looking out of the window?

They went on quite regardless of me, until the train
slowed for a station. Then he gave her such a kiss that
she protested.

"But the monsieur doesn't mind us," he assured her,
and both their glances appealed to me, hers saying, "You
see I can't stop him!" and his, "You understand!"

We halted and she got out. At the open door a little
baby was lifted up to her, evidently by its grandparents.
She took it from them, while he waved ardent good-byes
to her and the family group.

"Then you're not getting out with her?" I exclaimed
to him in surprise and sympathy.

He was not, he had to go to his work at another place.
He had been taking her for a little holiday. Soon I had
left the train, and was walking by a broken wall among
crosses, reading the names of the dead and of the battles
where they had fallen.

The Chemin de Fer de l'Est has furnished my memory
with many pictures. That harsh scene of our doughboys
and the French lad at Épernay has been softened by time
and reflection, and also by a sprightly performance, in
which I played a slight part. We had got into a Paris express at Bar-le-Duc, and according to my wont I began
after a time to wander along the corridors to see what I

could see. Disappointment was my first "reaction" (that uplifter has poisoned my vocabulary with his canting jargon), I found neither honeymooners nor doughboys, but only the average population of any French express train. As I was standing in the corridor of a second-class car, looking out of the window and thinking I would give up my search for local color and go back to my own car, the door of the lavatory opened and three doughboys came out. Why three at once in a lavatory? And why only three on the whole train? And why had I not seen them when I was exploring? I wanted to ask them how long they had been in there, but this seemed too leading a question for an entire stranger. They stopped beside me and stood watching the scenery with what struck me as an interest more lively than it justified: flat fields, marshes and stretches of water with willows, should hardly absorb three doughboys, unless they were all landscape painters. Nothing was said by any of us for a while, until at last one of them addressed me with a certain hesitation:

"Do you speak English?"

"Oh, yes."

"Could you tell us how soon we get to Châlons?"

"Well," I answered, "at a guess, I should say in about forty-five minutes."

Why did they all laugh?

This I did not inquire, but asked:

"Are you getting out at Châlons?" at which they laughed still more.

"Oh, no," one said. "We've got three days' permission for Paris, but we're not allowed to ride on this fast through train. Our police will pull us off at Châlons if they see us. They nearly caught us at the last stop."

"I'll not tell," said I. Then we were all merry together.

"Have you ever been in the States?" asked one.

"God bless your heart, I've been there for two hundred years!" Then we fraternized more than ever.

"The French military police are all right," they told me. "It's ours that make the trouble for us."

Presently I returned to my compartment, and there

found that I had given wrong information to those three confiding boys. We were due at Châlons at six, thirty minutes sooner than I had told them, and it was now five minutes to six. I hastened back to them with this news, at which they immediately rushed tumbling into the lavatory.

"If the police comes," said one, "tell him there's a lady in here." And they locked the door. The little indicator by the handle turned to "occupied." I should think it was!

I stood guard. We reached Châlons at six and left it at six-twenty-two. No police came, but one passenger tried the door three times, and I shall never forget his face. As the train began to move out of the station, I felt that I had done my duty, and returned to our compartment, and narrated the circumstances to my companions. Just as I was finishing, the three boys came by, looked in, and on seeing me they all laughed joyously.

"We made the riffle!" cried one.

On the whole I think that the Chemin de Fer de l'Est is my favorite railway in France.

XVII

F, in the silence of that wounded land which I had come to see, one visited a town not wholly dead and empty, those living there were making the best of it, were meeting life, with such a spirit and aspect that their effort was simply never visible. One had come to know so well the seal which the war had set upon all faces, that attention noted it no longer, but took it for granted, unaware, and looked at other things. At the time I was immersed in my journeys, the sorrow of it prevailed in my imagination; today, as I think back, it is the pride in human nature which can so splendidly meet distress as these French were doing that dwells chiefly in memory. Never was such horror dealt to any people, never have any people so indomitably faced it, not at the moment of stress alone, but in the forlorn prolongation of its after-math. Here at this little town of Bar-le-Duc, though noon was gone and we had watched ruins since early morning, the work of bombs still was visible. Far behind us on the Marne—a hundred miles, I suppose—we had passed the wrecks of way-stations, such as Dormans, and here also the station roof was shattered, walls had jagged holes in them, and in the platform itself was a descent to some hiding-place, where the railway people had gone during hours when the Huns were sailing overhead.

The town had suffered in no degree comparable to such places as Albert, through which the tides of obliteration had raged back and forth. Bar-le-Duc stood on the outer rim of a storm-centre and, saved from the worst, had not been put out of existence, but retained all its features whole—streets, houses, statues, churches, park; and its shops were open, with iron crosses and other still rather fresh relics for sale. After getting away from the ruins

154

at the station, you might not have seen anything to remind
you that war had paid this place a visit, but for those
painted words upon so many dwellings: "Shelter,"
"Cellar," "Vaulted Cellar." These, which I had first noticed at Noyon, and met continually since in many towns,
showed that war had flown here through the air. It was
the starting point of what came to be known as the Sacred
Road, over which rolled the endless chain of camions that
during so many months brought supplies to Verdun. This
road had been a creation of General Pétain's resourceful
mind; without it Verdun could not have stood, with it he
was able to make good his quiet, great word, "They shall
not pass." The main line of the Eastern railway is connected at Bar-le-Duc with Verdun by a branch, a feeble
affair with but a single track in 1914; and one cannot help
thinking that the French Government, had it been the
German Government, would have been careful to make it
solid and ready for war emergencies, long in advance of
the event.

In the streets and by the station, some of our officers
and men in khaki made visible the presence of America,
and the rule of the military police was, as we found one
afternoon, still rigorous. As we strolled along the Boule-
vard de la Rochelle, the time of day suggested tea to our
captain and beer to me, so we sat ourselves at a table on
the pavement in front of the Café de Commerce. We
could hardly have touched our chairs when out flew the
lady who commanded the café while her husband was in
the army. We must come inside, she declared; it was not
allowed for an officer in uniform to be seen drinking in
public.

"But, madame," protested our captain, almost piteously.
"Since it is only tea that I ask for!"

"No, no, no, monsieur le Capitaine, it won't do at all.
I cannot serve you here, not even tea. If it was only your
American police, they are so kind! I would not fear them,
but our French police, it is they that are the bad ones, ah
yes! You must not stay here. Enter, I pray you."

We entered, and retired meekly far back into the corner, where my friends had their tea and I my beer. At another table sat two healthy little boys, one in knickerbockers, each sedately having his glass of beer too.

Upon the wall above our table still hung the proclamation of the Armistice, its words tingling with joy and patriotism.

> Mairie de Bar-le-Duc
> Mes chers Concitoyens
> Le Jour de gloire est arrivé!
>
> . . . .
>
> Vive l'Alsace-Lorraine!
> Vive la France! Vive la République!
> Vivent à jamais nos Alliés!
> le Maire,
> J. Moulin.
>
> En Mairie à Bar-le-Duc, 11 November, 1918.

The eleventh of November, 1918! The brightness of that day, not yet six months ago, was even now beginning to darken. Some minds already saw that the work of the politicians was going to undo much of the soldiers' work, and that the "new heaven and new earth," announced to mankind by the Prime Minister of Great Britain, were of the same substance as the rest of his abundant phrases. Here in Bar-le-Duc an American officer perceived and spoke the truth about the allotting of Shantung, torn from China by Germany, to Japan.

"Japan," he said, "sat into the game and never spoke till she knew her time for a bluff had come. Then she told them that if they didn't pass the stolen goods on to her, she wouldn't join their League of Nations. They passed the goods all right, but that puts ridicule on the League of Nations."

"Our doughboys," said I, "seem as anxious to leave France as Mr. Wilson was to come to it." With military correctness he ignored this reference to his commander-in-chief. "The French are equally anxious to move back into their houses, which we are occupying; in Verdun a Frenchman is living in the tunnel of the citadel, waiting for Americans to get out of the only habitable room left in his bombed house."

"I've been urging some of our boys," said I, "not to be too hard on the French."

"It's the howlers who tell of French prices," he said. "In a town in Oklahoma where I was, prices were just as bad. Personally I have met more generosity here than at home. In this town there is a manufacturer whose sheds I have been using as a garage. He had to remove all his stuff to make room for me. I wanted to pay him, but he refused to accept a cent. He said, 'You came over and saved us. It's very little for me to do.' Keep up your talk to the complainers," he added. "It's astonishing how few understand that we must make allowances for other people's ways."

One of the "ways" of Bar-le-Duc is renowned, and no allowances have to be made for it. I allude to a sort of currant preserve; and when my second glass of beer was finished, I asked the lady of the café for some, but she had none. In response to my expression of genuine woe, she told me how to find my way to the factory where the delicacy was made.

It was not at all far away, I was soon ringing the bell. They had none.

"No, m'sieur. None since four months."

"Madame, mademoiselle!" I cried, "don't say that to me."

"Alas, monsieur, not one since four months."

"Madame, mademoiselle, I have come expressly six thousand kilometres. Pensez y, madame!"

"Ah, m'sieur, it is you Americans who have them all eaten. You are such sweet tooths."

"Oh, madame, now I shall go home six thousand kilometres, blushing for the greediness of my compatriots."

"Eh, m'sieur, it is not a mortal sin, the greediness! But

see, when we have sugar again, we shall be able to make
your currants."

"Ah!" I exclaimed. "It is the absence of sugar, not
the presence of Americans."

"It is the sugar, monsieur. But without doubt the
Americans quickly discover what is good."

Currants might be wanting in Bar-le-Duc, but the
French spirit was here, smiling, joking, going on with
existence undaunted. The commerce of the place was
killed, not the courage that would bring it again to life.

The town lies enclosed by hills quite near together, and
to the south it has climbed part way up their sides; so
that one-half the population looks down from among its
plentiful trees upon the roofs steeply mingling in the
bottom of the cup. It is only a little cupful of France,
but into it great tradition has been stirred. The statues
of two marshals, born here, rise in their separate squares,
and on the pedestal of one, Exelmans, stand the words
that Napoleon spoke to him: "One cannot be braver than
thou." I came upon this after crossing a bridge with a
little, ancient tower upon it. The bridge was small, the
river narrow, but a marshal of Napoleon had walked there,
and long before his day, the Dukes of Bar. The little river
ran between a vista of poplars, beneath arches of stone;
and though the houses along the quays by the poplars were
not fine dwellings, old French masons had proportioned
their lines, and French grace filled this formal avenue
made by the river upon which their windows faced. Yes;
Bar-le-Duc has more than currants to give its inhabitants.
Over the entrance to its shady little park is the admirable
text: "Plus penser que dire"—"More thought than
speech"; and a notice within the gate reminds one that,
"this park being common property, is placed under the
safeguard of the townsfolk." The back of the Hôtel de
Ville forms one corner of these lawns and walks, stone
steps lead down from it to them, and its walls rise above
them, not high, but proportioned by old French masons,
and stained with the seasoned hues of time. On each side

of the stone steps couches a lion with a conversational expression; one lion seems slightly to be pouting, as if he would say: "Lunch was not what I had a right to expect;" the other smiles sleepily, and he would certainly say: "Lunch came up to my ideas." The sky was blue as I sat on a bench near these decorous beasts, water trickled down the carvings of a fountain into a slumberous basin, flowers framed the borders of the lawns and daisies starred their sod. The tops of trees new-leaved rose like green islands in the sea of steep roofs, and loveliness hung quietly over the town. It is by no means a town of the first rank in beauty or interest, but its present is mellowed with the glow of messages from the past. Did our dough-boys, when they had eaten up the currants of Bar-le-Duc, find any of this nourishment of the mind and spirit, or had wise Kansas, on his island, been right when he said that unless you brought education with you to France, France would teach you nothing except riper modes of sensuality? I wondered if the stone arches over the river, its gracious avenue of poplars, the little old tower on the bridge, the marshal of Napoleon, the wise legend over the garden-gate, "Plus penser que dire," had not perhaps left a memory and a yearning here and there in the American mind; if perhaps some of our soldiers, after getting back to their own thriving, well-drained, well-lighted towns of the West, might not sometimes miss that inward illumina-tion which shone here as in every old town of France, and which even the most improved light-and-power plant cannot provide.

XVIII

THESE French and these sights of France that I was seeing, hour after hour, and day after day, would sometimes string to its highest tautness every nerve of attention, and sometimes slack and stupefy me into those trances wherein I seemed for awhile to notice nothing of the world external; the only thing that they never did was to stale my interest in this spectacle of gigantic ruin: not a mile of it, as it unfolded through those four hundred miles that I travelled right and left within it, ever grew dull through sameness. If this seems strange, if any one who has merely been told about the ravage, wonder how a panorama of changeless wreck, of houses, farms, churches, villages, and forests chewed up and spit out by the jaws of war, can fail to weary in the end, it is because the visible unrolling of all this nourished and enlarged, not knowledge alone, but also emotion. The variety was within, and never died. No battle was like another nor any individual story of man or woman: so that into one's streaming thoughts came constantly the words, "This, too, the Germans did," or "This, too, France suffered," and absorption grew under it as does the scholar's who pursues a chosen path, or as something new fills every moment the over-sheltered body that has gone for breath to the mountains or the ocean. Such a breath of pity and awe blew here, that into the stream of thought often came also the words, "Who, after seeing this, can ever be the same again?"

Our first few miles out of Bar-le-Duc are nearly a blank, scarce more than a general green and loveliness of spring present upon changing slopes, no clearer memory than this, because the nerves of attention had slacked and I was thinking of Nauheim, not of La Voie

160

Sacrée. I had strolled about the German resort in May and June, 1914, admiring the order, the system, the thoroughness, the thoughtful care of detail, the plan wrought out to success. During one of these walks a Zeppelin had sailed over us, and this apparition suggested that Germany would devote the same care to planning war as she did to planning peace.

"It is quite likely," said I to my companion, "that in their War Office at Berlin they have blue prints and specifications of every bridge, tunnel, signal-tower, and siding of the Pennsylvania Railroad."

In less than four weeks, Ferdinand the Archduke had been assassinated at Serajevo; in less than eight, more Americans than we were beginning to suspect the care which Germany devoted to planning war. One evening of that first winter, after the French at the Marne and the British at Ypres had blocked German plans, and 468 miles of fortified trench ran across France from the Channel to Switzerland, I was sitting at dinner next the president of the Pennsylvania Railroad, and I repeated to him my remark at Nauheim.

"Why that's not so far from the truth," he said. Then I learned a tale of German thoroughness, new and typical.

As far back as 1903, there was usually an engineering attaché at the German Embassy in Washington. To him or his emissaries the Pennsylvania Railroad was accustomed to furnish free transportation as well as information about mechanical appliances and improvements, including all the blue prints that they asked for. But Germany did not return the compliment. In March 1904, when the Pennsylvania's chief signal engineer came home from a sort of roving commission to visit and study certain European railway systems, he made in his report particular mention of the courteous treatment accorded his committee by all railroad officials with whom he came in contact in England and Scotland; but about Berlin he was entirely silent. This was because in Berlin he had found the door shut, and was told that the Kaiser had the

key. In consequence of this experience, the president
in 1905 officially declined a request to furnish free transportation to an engineer then arriving from Germany.
Later, in the days when frightfulness was spreading
flames and human lamentations wider and ever wider
through defenceless villages and miles of horror, the
railroad whose blue prints Berlin had secured was led to
do what it could to make safe the yards and system of its
tracks on Long Island, in case—— But frightfulness in
uniform did not step ashore over here; it merely sent
vessels to the bottom along our coast just after our
Secretary of War had come back from Europe and told
us that the war was 3,000 miles away. In August 1914,
the British fleet became our wall of safety, and behind
this we dwelt unscathed. I was brought back from these
memories by our captain, who showed me two "pill boxes"
bordering the road, little squat turrets, solid, with peep
slits for guns, and fantastically painted. Nothing but a
bomb falling straight upon their roofs could smash them,
and their roofs were colored according to the laws of
optical illusion to escape the eye of the aviator. Some of
these contrivances suggested large fat toad-stools, others
the machines on dinner tables for grinding pepper. From
their insides, men could train guns as from a compass
upon all points and be almost safe. After we had left
this lonely couple behind us, the scars of war thickened
rapidly, trenches, barbed wire, roofless walls; and the
silence was here, waiting for us, even though some of the
trenches were already being filled, some of the barbed wire
already rolled up from the liberated fields.

Do you know the extent of these fields of France which
frightfulness in uniform laid low according to its careful
plan? To read the cold figures is one thing, to feel what
they mean is quite another: the dead decimals and integers
do contain, but they also entomb, the story; they need
translating into life. Of farmland, seed and harvest land,
1,757,000 hectares were devastated, and if to this be
added the land that was in pasture and forest, the total is

3,800,000 hectares. A hectare is 2.471 acres—nearly two
acres and a half; and so, in terms of acres, the devastation
covers 9 million 389 thousand 800 acres; and as 640 acres
make one square mile, 14 thousand and 670 square miles
of France were devastated. This exceeds the area of
certain of our smaller states, but it would not cover quite
half of Maine, not quite a third of Pennsylvania; and
when you come to some of our Western States, in their
vastness, it would be well-nigh swallowed up—Texas
alone is some forty thousand square miles larger than the
whole of France. But what if we had been devastated,
not in this same actual amount, but in the same proportion to our total, as France was? To lose one leg is a 25
per cent. loss for a dog, a 50 per cent. loss for a man: the
whole area of France is 204 thousand and 92 square
miles, and its devastated region is between one-thirteenth
and one-fourteenth of the whole. The area of the United
States is three million square miles, we are more than
fourteen times as large as France, and if one-fourteenth
of our soil had been devastated, it would cover more than
two hundred thousand square miles—the whole area of
Maine, New Hampshire, Vermont, Massachusetts, Rhode
Island, Connecticut, New York, New Jersey, Pennsylvania, Delaware, Maryland, and some of Ohio. I select
the northern and eastern part of our country for my
comparison, not only because it is geographically the
same portion of France which has suffered, but also because it is economically parallel, the great coal, steel,
wool, and other centres of industry being preponderantly
situated in the north and east of France, as they are in
New England and the Middle States.

I have been at pains to understate the matter in my
own multiplications and divisions, by disregarding certain decimals which would have somewhat increased my
final figures, although not enough to go beyond Ohio.
Unless these calculations err, a man could start in a car
at Vanceboro, Maine, and go through Bangor, Portland,
Worcester, Springfield, Albany, Utica, Syracuse, Roches-

ter and Buffalo to Pittsburgh, and not reach the western
limit of devastation. He could wind to the north and the
south of this route, and pass Manchester, Lawrence,
Lowell, Fall River, Bridgeport, Trenton, Bethlehem,
Reading, and Scranton, finding all these towns totally
or partially destroyed, their great manufacturing plants
not only silent, but deliberately paralyzed by the removal
of their machinery and the flooding of their mines. Not
alone these larger places whose names I have set down,
and others of the same kind that I have left unmentioned,
but also every isolated dwelling and farm and village
between them would be wrecked, just as Lille, Lens, St.
Quentin, Chauny, St. Gobain, Coucy-le-Château, Soissons, Reims, and Verdun, and the homes and hamlets
between were wrecked. Four thousand and twenty-two
villages and towns were destroyed in France, and of these,
every one east of the front in 1917 was scientifically
blown up, in obedience to the principle laid down by
the rule of the German Staff before the war began—
that the enemy be *spiritually* and *commercially* crushed.
The attempt at spiritual crushing is visible, for instance,
in the cathedral of St. Quentin, where ninety holes were
systematically cut in its supporting pillars to receive
dynamite. It was never placed there. The pillars stand,
supporting still a noble church which is only half in
ruins. In their 1918 retreat, the Huns had not expected
the Allies to reach St. Quentin quite so quickly, and
hence (as at Laon), they were surprised like burglars
at work drilling a safe, and had to flee.

The attempt at commercial crushing is visible, for instance, at Lens. Before the war, these mines produced
annually four million tons of coal, eight hundred thousand of coke, thirty thousand of tar; their employees
lived in eight thousand houses. When the war was done
and the French came back, of these eight thousand
houses, sixty that could be repaired were left. When the
Huns came to Lens in 1914, they stopped the pumps in
the mines and measured the rising water each day. It did

not rise fast enough to please them, so they broke the
jackets of cast iron which encased the shafts, and through
the holes blasted in them, the water from the wet surrounding stratum of soil poured in to speed the general
drowning. Fifty millions of cubic metres of water flooded
the mines. The machinery was smashed, or removed to
Germany. Lens was reduced to a sort of ash heap. The
Huns when they came, set fire at once to the plant where
the naphtha and tar were made, because the sight of the
flames made fireworks for their diversion. They watched
them at a safe distance, laughing. Ten years after the
Armistice, the mines of Lens may be again whole and
completely at work—in 1928—perhaps. Lens is merely
one of the industrial centres which was destroyed in order
to crush France commercially. Of homes, where men and
women and children lived, three hundred and four thousand were totally obliterated, and two hundrd and ninety
thousand practically—by cannon, or by fire, or by mines.
This we may call a mixture of spiritual and commercial
crushing. This devastated area, though it was but a fourteenth part of the whole of France, paid nevertheless
nearly one-fifth (18.5%) of the whole taxes, even as
New England and the Middle States, because of their
denser population and more concentrated area of manufacture, pay more of the taxes than such areas as Texas,
New Mexico, Arizona, Utah, Nevada, and California and
much of the South.

Besides poison gas and like inventions for the killing
of men, German ingenuity created devices for the killing
of things—the incendiary fire engine, for example, which
rolled methodically through village streets, setting fire
to houses instead of putting them out; or the pastilles of
the chemist Dr. Otswald, conveniently portable, and so
skilfully compounded that one, if lighted and left in a
hall or dining-room, would suffice to reduce the dwelling
to cinders. They had, too, a machine for tearing up railroads as you went. This was hitched behind the tender
of a locomotive, and as the engine puffed along, it rooted

up the sleepers and rails behind it. Of the main lines in France, 1,500 miles were destroyed, and 1,490 miles of local and branch lines—2,990 miles in all. The total mileage of railways in France is 31,992—more than one-tenth was wrecked. If one-tenth of our railway mileage were wrecked, it would be 25,682: that very nearly equals the whole of the Boston and Maine, the New York and New Haven, the New York Central, and the Pennsylvania systems; it comes to more than double the whole Southern Pacific.

Upon our journey in the wind and the rain from Amiens, through the battle lands of the Somme, the road to Arras beyond Mailly-Maillet, near Beaumont Hamel hill, had perished in a world of featureless mud and ghost-like splinters of trees. That was but one case. Throughout this devastated fourteenth part of France, country and town alike were locked away from the living world by the obliteration of the thoroughfares. The traveller threaded his way through broken landscape and broken village, easily blocked, often obliged to turn back, if he was not well guided. So we had found it beyond Amiens, so next near Soissons and Reims, so now, where flowed the waters of the Meuse and the Moselle. The Sacred Way, the great highroad over which supplies had gone to Verdun during its fearful siege, was still one of the few open channels. From this we had turned off, not many miles out of Bar-le-Duc, and as we penetrated deeper into the destroyed country amid the thickening vestiges of violence, the wonder returned as to how this region was now supplied, how did food or anything at all reach those who lived here? The answer was simple—the silence was the answer. Almost no one did live here now. Like the lady who had come back from Nevers to look for her house at Noyon, and the brave wife with the gash in her forehead at the estaminet, most of those whose homes these ruins once had been had taken refuge in other parts of France, the old, the women, the children; and very few of them had as yet returned. Their return was beginning; they, too, like all France, were determined to come back and to go on, and the signs of their determination were the small patches of ground, cleared already of barbed wire and shells, lying like scattered aprons amid the rough bristling wreck of the land. Thirty-two thousand, nine hundred and fifty-eight miles of French roads had been destroyed, and six hundred and forty-eight miles of canals. Four million and a half people had lived in the devastated fourteenth of France— one-tenth of the whole population. Their live-stock had been taken, thirteen hundred thousand head; twenty thousand, five hundred and thirty-nine of their manufactories had been levelled to the ground, or gutted of their machinery, and of themselves, two million and seven hundred and thirty-two thousand had been driven out of their homes; while the remainder, nearly two million, had during four years been forced to pay war levies, and to work half starved beneath the hand of the invader, which often held the lash; or else they had known exile and prison.

Is it wonderful that devastated France was silent? It seemed, as one went onward and onward through the barbed wire and the trenches and the empty walls, as if nothing would ever be able to break this silence. Our American artillery, during four hours of the brief battle of St. Mihiel, had fired more than one million shells. The rusting fragments of those shells were now to be gathered up by the peasant whose pastures or fields they littered. If one million shells were scattered in four hours at one place, what was the number that, during four years, had torn the ground in all places? The question cannot be answered, but to ask it is enough. And the barbed wire?—those skeins of fierce strings that stretched tight across such uncounted acres, making thick webs, enmeshing hills and valleys. The amount of this has been computed—there were three hundred and ten

million square metres of it (a metre is more than a yard).
Of trenches to be filled up, there were two hundred and
seventy-seven million cubic metres.

We passed the town of St. Mihiel without stopping,
and left those assembled ruins behind us to come to others
and again others, both assembled and solitary. If we
looked up a hill, its side was pocketed with shelter holes,
if we looked down at a plain it was drilled with dug-outs,
ditched with trenches, blurred with barbed wire—worried
out of all semblance to serene nature; and if we went
through a wood, its trees were naked shreds. Germans,
French, and Americans had fought hereabouts. The
flames and rage of conflict had been less blinding, perhaps, than in the days of the Somme in 1916, but quietness had departed hence in September 1914. Two Crown
Princes of the Huns, William and Rupprecht, had set
on Verdun during the first battle of the Marne. Their
success might have made that battle a failure. They
failed. Soon they began again, and by the end of the
month, St. Mihiel was German territory. It made the
bottom of a pocket not unlike the one which Ludendorff
dug to the Marne. The Germans stayed in it until we
drove them out exactly four years later; but they were
seldom left in perfect peace, either along the north or
the south edge of their pocket. We were going now along
its south edge, following the road to Pont-à-Mousson,
following it too quickly; for here were the Bois Brûlé,
and Apremont, Flirey, Limey, presently each in turn
to brush our very sides, each brooding with tales and
memories, each deserving to be stopped at and listened
to with reverence for the dead and the surviving, while
not far away, to our left, were the Mont Sec and Seicheprey. We could not stop, we could not listen to any wayside tales, though it seemed as if the earth and the torn
trees themselves were waiting to tell them. At Brûlé
Wood, right on the south seam of the pocket, fifty yards
and no more separated the German trenches and the
French lines, and so it was for months: scarce ever a day

without flames, explosions, death—a man must not speak,
must not smoke, could not sleep—and eight days of such
a life were generally the limit that human nerves could
stand: each spent battalion had to go away and rest, and
be replaced by a fresh one. Once, in April 1915, after
three days of fierce fighting for a trench, it was taken
and new men sent to keep it. Upon these the Germans
suddenly fell and threw them into fright and flight. The
trench was going to be lost. This was seen by an officer
who had helped to capture it. He was resting with his
men, but he called upon them to go back, and back
they went with him. They took the trench again from the
Germans; but it cost time and struggle and so many
lives that the exhausted living faltered among the corpses.
In this moment of suspense the officer saw defeat approaching and—let his name be told once more—Adjutant
Jacques Pericard looked around in desperation at his
wounded and fallen men, and cried:

"Debout, les morts!"

And they rose and went on. So was one trench retaken
at Bois Brulé.

How many tales of death and life and the soul of man
should we know, could the ground or trees in those fourteen thousand, six hundred and seventy square miles of
devastated France whisper them? And what traveller
who has once felt that great silence which we entered
first at Compiègne will ever wholly forget it?

From Brulé Wood we came at once to the nothing
which had once been Apremont—no house left in it, holes
and heaps where the church had stood; and a few steps
off, a symbol of Germany, solid and substantial, a shelter
of concrete. This thick thing wore an ornament on its
wall, a German gun, well carved. Symbols of Germany
were everywhere, always thick built, dominating; thick
statues, thick monuments, thick tombstones, heavily
lettered. Just here by crumbled Apremont was a whole
Hun village quarried deep in the hillside, full of elaborate
comfort and relics of efficiency; the slopes terraced,

plants on the sills, carved woodwork, stolen tapestry; little, nice things, all stolen from the neighboring piles of rubbish which had been French homes once. This was just here by the road. Just such another was there across the valley on the opposite seam of the pocket—Les Éparges. In that snug burrow of the Huns was a system of electric lights, an officers' club, an elevator, a narrow-gauge railway;—and more little, nice things, stolen from crumbled Frèsnes and crumbled St. Rémy, Hannonville, Vigneulles, all lying shapeless in the plain below, symbols of Germany too;—but over in Germany, no such symbols; not a shell hole, not a trench, not a scar; not a church tower fallen, not a single stone of a single home displaced; every picture safe on the wall, every chair safe in the room, every silver spoon safe in the drawer. In France were four thousand destroyed villages, twenty thousand destroyed factories, five hundred thousand homes in dust. Of little, nice things, pictures, silver, home tokens and treasures, personal property, in short, the Germans had destroyed or stolen twenty-one billion francs' worth; beside the barbed wire and the trenches, there were forty-two million cubic metres of rubbish to be got rid of by a country that had one million, three hundred and eighty-five thousand men killed outright in action—workers who never would rebuild any more than many of the two million and a half of wounded. About three and a half per cent. of the whole French population were killed. Had a proportionate loss been ours, our dead would have numbered every man of the 2,084,000 who got to France, and more than 1,000,000 more at home. Thus France had her maimed country to rebuild with her maimed hands.

In 1916, true to the system and the thoughtful care of detail of Germany, some German composed a manual of 482 pages for the benefit of the German Army. It was issued under the auspices of the Quartermaster Department. It tabulated the destructions accomplished so far, and the further destructions contemplated. It was based on that part of the Hun doctrine which forms the supplement to atrocity to non-combatants in order to win quickly—commercial destruction of the enemy in order to make gold from blood and iron. French industry was to be put out of business, because, for instance, "French railroads, in consequence of the destruction of car shops, will have to equip themselves in Germany"; by the destruction of looms, because, "resuming operation will be very difficult, and an enormous market for German products will be thus created." The sugar industry "must disappear from the world market for two or three years"; and it is pointed out that "mines are paralyzed for years by the dismantling of the machinery and the flooding of the pits."

Armed with this book, and with the other tools needful, the German soldiers paid their visits to the various mines and factories in this fourteenth of French territory, and left behind them, destroyed with Germany's thoughtful care of detail, 55% of the total national coal-producing capacity, 94% of the wool manufacturing, 90 of the linen, 90 of the mineral, 83 of the smelters, 70 of the sugar mills, 60 of the cotton mills, 45 of the electric power—I will not continue the list; is this not enough to suggest why the devastation of this particular fourteenth part of France should deprive the country of almost one-fifth of its taxes? Many of the destroyed industries which I have named will show more clearly to the reader the economic parallel between this region and our New England and Middle States. In 1870 Germany overran France, and in 1871 she demanded an indemnity after her victory. Not an inch of Germany had been hurt then, any more than now. It was France that was hurt, France that was beaten, and France that paid. The Germans occupied her soil and her cities until every last cent was paid. They withdrew by instalments, according as they received instalments of the indemnity. This time, though France is hurt and France is victorious, she sees reparations that were promised her by treaty incessantly cut down, postponed, excused. Too many people both in talk and in books use indemnity and reparation as meaning the same thing. They are quite different; uninjured Germany

made France pay an indemnity in 1871, devastated
France demands reparation from Germany.

Our wheels beyond Apremont rolled eastward upon and
across the front line of battle. We had no time to look at
any ruins, but time was not needed to see that they were
close at hand, sometimes near enough almost to be
touched, sometimes up a hill or down a hill; Bouconville
village like a mouth with but few teeth; and next, a sullen
glimpse of barbed wire and distance stretching to sombre
hills; and after this, the shattered tower of Beaumont
Church, sticking up against the sky with ruins encumber-
ing its feet. Xivray, where the French right made contact
with our 1st Division's left on the night of September
11, 1918, was scarce two miles off, and Seicheprey was
nearer still. We should have liked to stand in Seicheprey,
upon the ground won in the spring of 1918 from the
Germans by our 26th Division, known as the Yankee.
That was our first little independent fight, the beginning
of the Yankee Division's renown. We were sorry not to
visit the spot. Beyond it not very far was the Mont Sec,
a sullen hump rising out of the plain. There, too, we
should have liked to climb—into its elaborate tunnels,
upon its fortified top, whence the Germans during four
years had watched the plain. In the shape of a smoke
screen, the curtain fell upon their long, safe watch. We
should have liked to stare down at the land where, behind
the smoke screen, our 1st Division advanced twelve miles
from Xivray north into the heart of the pocket, and met
near Vigneulles the Yankee Division coming south from
Les Éparges; so that the Germans were stitched into
their pocket before they could get out of it as they
were planning to do; and the pocket became ours, and
we put them into it—16,000 prisoners, and 443 guns,
with other useful chattels, and very little loss to ourselves.
It was all quickly done—over in 48 hours—and then we
pushed our line west of the Moselle farther than had been
laid down. Our divisions fought harder and longer soon
after this in the Argonne; but their action at St. Mihiel
accomplished what Foch asked of them, performed it

smoothly and speedily; and what was done here, was the
doing of an American army, commanded by an American
general, its individuality attained and asserted, not
without some friction and delay. Four French and fifteen
American divisions constituted the force assembled here,
and from Beaumont east to the Moselle at Pont-à-Mousson, our road ran where many American feet must have
trod:—feet of the Rainbow Division, of Wood's Own, of
the Second, of the Red Diamond, of the Alamo—all along
this way through Flirey (a total wreck) and Limey,
another, and between ceaseless holes and graves and fragments of many things. A railway bridge was one of the
larger fragments somewhere near Flirey, topped and
slanting helpless; no trains ran here, or for a great distance to our west. To our east we came upon one at Pont-
à-Mousson, steaming and crowded with passengers from
Paris. It was on its way along the Moselle down to Metz.
Its open rails were like the open road we had come, a
single working channel of communication, lonely among
countless channels that were stopped. Of tunnels and
bridges the Germans had destroyed 3,603.

In Pont-à-Mousson, bruised by shells, is a square,
the Place Duroc, beautiful and French, with its arcade
in cracks but not in ruins—though by the ninth month of
the war Pont-à-Mousson had been bombarded one hundred
and ten times. Here indeed I longed to pause amid the
surviving charm before plunging into more desolation,
but time forbade it. This was the east limit of our drive.
We turned, re-crossed the Moselle, and bore toward Thiaucourt. We were all the while within the battle-ground of
our first American army's first exploit. We passed between pale, broken trees, and concrete caves, and many
crosses where the dead lay; and everywhere here, since
1914, blood had flowed, German and French, long before
our divisions came. Sometimes we got out to walk the
ground and listen to our young captain, who had fought
here. The places had names—the Widow's Wood, called
so by the Germans, and another the Priest's Wood, named
by the French; and within its dead and tragic trees was a

spring where both sides came by turns for water, no man
shooting while his enemy drank. Sometimes we returned
into sight of the sullen, distant hump of the Mont Sec,
rising over open miles of loneliness, sometimes woods shut
us in, and now and then we passed more shattered
houses; but whatever it was, earth or building, it had
always the look of a witness who has seen something
which has blinded it to all other sights, so that, no matter
what else may pass before it, it will for ever see only
this. Our divisions had swept across here, the 82nd, the
90th, the 5th, the 89th, the 2nd, as they pushed the
Germans out of the pocket. This work done, they were
fresh still and ready, without any rest, for more;
but their high spirits had left no echo behind, and the
ground over which their fierce gay steps had gone bore
no trace of their gaiety. The Somme had been more terrible to the eye, and so had Berry-au-Bac; greater sadness
I had not yet seen than in this region about Thiaucourt,
and in the Woëvre plain beyond that ruined town.

Thiaucourt, St. Bénoit, Woël, Joncourt, St. Hilaire,
Frèsnes-en-Woëvre, Étain—these are the names which
plot our course from Pont-à-Mousson west and north
towards our night's lodging. All along the way, we
were skirting at no great distance the boundary of the
St. Mihiel advance, where the line, for the time being,
had been stabilized. At Frèsnes we were upon this line;
when we reached Étain we had passed beyond it to the
north, and I understood more about the "operations in
the Woëvre district." There was much water because
there had been much rain. It lay to one side or the other,
in irregular ponds reflecting the afternoon sky, or in
round pools which were shell holes, or in oozing trenches,
with barbed wire posts sticking and leaning out of the
ooze. Water and plain stretched away to right and left;
far to the left Les Éparges was dimly visible, sullen like
the Mont Sec, a ridge which had become a gulf of mud;
where half a hill slid down, where planks were laid five
times and sank, where men wounded and not wounded
went down and could not be saved. As the light grew grey

and more grey, its veil softened the sharp edge of the ruins. The tower of the church at Étain was the last ruin that we saw clearly. Étain had been bombarded for thirteen hours one day in August 1914, and again on the day following. Many people were burned in its flames or buried in its ruins. The last message sent by a girl who stayed at her telephone post informing Verdun every fifteen minutes how the destruction progressed, was: "A bomb has just fallen in the office."

As we had watched them soften and dissolve in the twilight of preceding journeys, again this afternoon the forms of all ragged objects in the wide wet plain of Woëvre melted into the enveiling grey of dusk. Whether these towns had been wrecked by French or American or German shells, all were the victims of German invasion. Latest, as always, to remain distinct were the dead trees. Their skeletons stuck out of the level dimness like crooked fingers scratching the horizon. These woods had been lacerated by shells; others all the way from the war zone across France to the Pyrenees had been levelled by the axe to keep the war going. To meet our heavy needs, more were chopped down when our soldiers came. Until the war, the thrift of France had kept her growing forests ahead of her use of their timber. Had she wasted them, as we wasted ours during the 19th Century, an American forester has said that the Allies might have lost the war. Some will recover in from ten to twenty years, it will take others thirty years, and France meanwhile must rebuild as best she can. Just to our west and left, lay the forest out of which the Germans had come down upon Verdun in February 1910. Beyond it, a little south of Spincourt, we turned west from the main road, reached a village corner, passed through the sound of American voices, and soon after came to a stop. Here was our night's lodging. It was long since we had left what the French call La Voie Sacrée, but our course had been never once away from ground where privation and grief and courage lived, and many thousands had died. Every road that we had travelled was a sacred way.

XIX

IT was like a scene in a play: once again reality suggested this image. In the early stages of our journey, when devastation was a sight novel to our American eyes, the rearing splinters of homes, the walls and windows without insides, had seemed like the unreal aspect of what meets one behind the curtain. That was over long ago. It never looked to us like stageland now, we knew it well as war land, real, mangled, dumb, its hollows thick with unheard sorrow and the crowded, unseen dead. From this deeply familiar actuality through which we had been moving but a few minutes ago, we walked up some steps and entered upon the serene welcome of candles lighting a hall and pleasant stairs. An American captain, whose voice came from the South, greeted us at the hall-door, and behind him shone the candles. They were tall, like those in a church, and so arranged as to make almost beautiful the almost plain interior of this house. They were few in number, and stood at various levels, one or two here in the hall below, one or two upon the newels of the banisters which framed the right-angled ascent of the stairs in two short flights to a gallery above, and one or two along the gallery, upon which several doors opened. They gave light enough to see, yet left the agreeable mystery of limits and corners not quite visible, of hospitable nooks beyond, which might extend to many secluded wings and passages. Had this Southern captain, perhaps, learned his art of candlelight in some plantation house, into whose old, ample rooms not electricity, or gas, or even oil, had intruded? I never asked him; but if ever he sees this page, he will know how much more I thought than I said about our nights beneath this roof, where he was master for a while.

176

"If only we might stay here for a week!" I thought. The candles and the quiet were so good after shell holes, and barbed wire, and ruins, and dead trees.

The seeing eye, the shaping hand, and a military sense of order had filled this bare house with objects collected from war and arranged with skill. Merely to study the contents of its rooms and what hung on its walls would have taught one as much as many lectures. To look at them while the captain or his lieutenant talked about them was better than any lecture. Whoever made the collection was able to draw upon a rich territory, and had not wasted his chance. This farm lay in the Woëvre plain, and battles had been fierce on every side but its north. The Meuse was not far off one way, the Moselle another, Verdun was some twelve miles southwest of it; distilling itself from various marshes in the Woëvre where blood must have flowed, the little river Loison slid through its domain. The village near by, where we heard American voices, had been occupied by the Germans since 1914, never disturbed until the end. They had left their mark—various marks —and from their bill-posters forbidding this and that and the other, a humorous selection had been made, and these now helped to decorate the walls and edify the guests. How many of these guests were edified by the veritable museum of war which surrounded them, is something I have often wondered. Taken over by our army soon after November 11, 1918 (I surmise), this French farmhouse became the resting-place for travellers privileged as guests of the American army to visit this part of the devastated region which was allotted to our care. For their benefit the wonderful museum and relief maps had been arranged, and for their welcome the tall candles burned in this hall. They certainly gave it the look of a scene set equally well for mystery, or crime, or comedy.

Any one who has had to drink water made sanitary by chlorine will not forget its flavor. This water is the only circumstance which I would have had different at our meal; and, knowing the South, I am sure that our

host, had the regulations permitted him, would have de-
canted for our refreshment nothing of the sort. What we
ate I cannot remember, but only that it was good enough
to turn conversation upon the cook. She had four service
stripes, the captain said. Three, but soon to get a fourth,
his lieutenant corrected; and for a moment I, in my
ignorance, imagined wildly that she had been in the
trenches and gone over the top. But she had merely boiled,
roasted, stewed, and otherwise concocted their meals during a period equivalent to the stripes—and I am inclined
to think that they were afraid of her. These commissioned
officers with decorations for bravery smiled about their
cook; but to me it looked remarkably like the smile of
men in the proximity of a powerful personality. Candor
bids me confess that the few words which I exchanged with
her may have helped this opinion. I went out to see her,
to make her compliments on an omelet. Upon my standing
at the threshold of her kitchen, she turned and contemplated me. She was wide, she was thick, she was round,
she had a shining forest of black hair, a thick throat, an
eye of domination, and a moustache. I imagined that
my opinion of her omelet would warm the influence that
proceeded from her. It did not. Her reply was civil—but
I didn't stay. If they weren't afraid of her, an army commission must toughen you. Any civilian would have given
it up as I did.

The captain and the lieutenant talked of the war in
general, and of incidents in particular; a very pleasant
meal. And if they did not stand in awe of their cook,
I know that they were afraid of the lady of the house.
She was not here now, of course; but since their occupation of her premises, she had paid her house visits enough
to make a formidable impression upon the captain.

"She's crazy," he told me.

"From the war?" I asked, prepared to hear something
painful.

"I think her state of mind antedates that, but it may
have been emphasized by it. They tell me that at the

dinners she used to give, she put all the old people close together at one end of this table and all the young away far off at the other, so that the young ones shouldn't hear her jokes."

"I suppose," said I, "that as they grew older she moved them up."

"Well, from what they say about her jokes," returned the captain, "I'm not sure that I am old enough to be moved up for quite a while yet."

"I wish that I could have met her," I sighed; "she would not have respected my youth."

"Last time she came in here," said the captain, "she saw one of her old family portraits on the wall. Heaved a log right through it. She didn't like it because German officers had been looking at it four years."

Like many men from the South, this captain maintained a certain gravity of bearing rarely practised by Northerners, who often plunge into a jocosity somewhat premature. His stiffness had been augmented by almost daily experience with the American congressmen whom he had to make welcome. To find that we were not politicians was a visible relief to him; on this first evening he steadily unbent. He told us that the British, New Zealanders, and Americans had exchanged whisky at the front.

"A better exchange than personalities," said I.

Some men of our Bloody Hand Division had given rise to merriment unintentionally at times when laughter was scarce. This division was not wholly organized at the time of its landing in April 1918, and it was broken up and brigaded with the French. Six hundred were killed, two thousand wounded. The survivors seemed to be enjoying France. They had met with a social success beyond any which they knew at home.

"Those darkies are having the time of their lives now," said the captain; "they have known less agreeable days. One of their regiments was with the 4th French Army at Wesserling. Some soldiers built a fire with the purpose of boiling a kettle. They set four unexploded shells upright, laid the fuel between them, set the kettle on top of them, and lighting the fire, sat down to watch the kettle boil. One of them was sent for by his commanding officer, and was away for a few minutes. Upon returning to the spot, he found no kettle, no fire, no comrades, and a large hole in the October mud. Immediately he rushed back and cried out to the officer:

" 'Cap'n, dat coffee he done blow up!'

"Yes," he continued, "when they get home, they'll never need to stop talking. A couple of them got more fighting than they approved of over on the west edge of the Argonne, and they were running away. They reached one of the long straight roads bordered with poplars and marked with the distance, and along this they ran on and on. At length one said:

" 'Say, dis hyeh is de longest graveyahd I ever saw.'

"And his better-informed mate corrected him:

" 'Them's not gravestones, them's kilo*mm*etees.' "

The captain gave us, by his use of one happy word, an indelible picture of the survivors of the Bloody Hand Division, elated by social success in France.

"When the darkies mount guard," said he, "they don't walk; they syncopate."

A wood fire burned in the room where we sat after supper until an early bed-time. An upright piano was there and open, with a look of having also merited service stripes. I asked, did it belong to the house? It did, and had been there during the four years of German occupation.

"Then," said I, "when they had to get out and you came in, did you find the piano——?" I did not complete my sentence.

They nodded. "We had to scrub it out."

I told them the remark of a major in charge of the interned Germans at Fort Oglethorpe, in whose company I had visited the internment camp at that place during the preceding fall. We had spent more than an hour in going over its various parts; where they ate, where they slept, where they took the air, where their possessions were stored. They were made much more comfortable than our own people who were being trained to fight them overseas. At the end of our inspection, I asked the major:

"Have you made any generalization about these Germans? They are of every station from ragged bomb-throwers to New York merchants and Prussian Junkers. There is even the leader of a famous symphony orchestra here. Have you been able to observe any one trait which they have in common?"

"Yes," replied the major. "One and all, their personal habits are filthy beyond my willingness to describe."

This caused our captain no surprise: he had seen the piano. I told him that it had fallen to my lot to read certain confiscated and impounded letters, written by the conductor of the famous symphony orchestra. These had led the court to give him his choice of submitting to internment without more ado—or of being prosecuted under the White Slave Act. They contained passages which would stain any decent lips.

As my years have increased, bed-time has grown less unwelcome than once it used to be—but I could have listened all night to this captain and his lieutenant. Perhaps it is as well for the reader that I can remember distinctly but one of the curiosities of warfare which they showed us; otherwise I might have been tempted to describe every object in that museum. You have sometimes, no doubt, walked behind the counters of chemists' shops into the precincts where they keep their jars and bottles and retorts. If so, you may have derived an impression of cylinders and cones and tubes of various unearthly shapes, standing on shelves or the floor. That is in a way what the museum looked like, only the unearthly shapes were not of glass, but metal. Shells and bombs of many varieties had been gathered here, and some of the engines that projected them—such as could be got conveniently inside a house: so that you saw the instruments which had blasted the salient of St. Mihiel and the plain of Woëvre into that welter of dead fields, dead houses, and dead men, through which our journey upon this day had been. There they stood. Some were German, some French, some American. These glistened, those were dark. Some tapered to sharp points. Others were round. One specimen was not larger than a baseball. One was thicker than a big man and as high as my shoulder. Smaller shells stood on exhibit like flower vases when you are looking for wedding presents. I touched them here and there, while the lieutenant explained their natures and uses, how far they could fly, how big a hole they could dig, how many bodies at once they could behead and disembowel. Their assemblage exhaled a silence—these bombs that could deafen—but a silence perfectly different from that which hung over devastated France. The lieutenant put one little brass bulb into my hand, and asked, could I guess what it was? How could I? He took it, seemed to press and turn it, and perhaps touched some mechanism at its top, and it split apart in halves with saw teeth. Its insides were not simple enough for me to be able to describe them clearly. It was a mechanical carrier pigeon; German, I think. In its brass guts a message could nestle and fly from a gun safe to its destination; and I believe that it had some sort of fuse of special construction which popped or spat or flickered or otherwise indicated its identity after it had alighted at the proper address. Bombs, belts, guns, grenades—altogether an interesting, sinister company, with gas-masks among it like faces left behind, staring glassily.

Less sombre were the maps in another room, artillery fire contour maps, and relief maps of terrain. Upon the ridges and hollows of these you could look as from an aeroplane upon the Woëvre or the Argonne, and follow where our divisions had climbed down, or climbed through. There was the Meuse running, and the Moselle, and the little Aire trickling along the bristly rises of the Argonne, and Varennes and Cheppy and Grand Pré and Mouzon and Sedan, that we were to see, with Thiaucourt and the

Bois Brulé and all the rest which we had seen. Thus, with
the point of a pencil touching here the Mont Sec and there
Les Éparges or Vigneulles, one could clearly follow the
pivoting of our 1st and 26th Divisions on those two September days when they stitched the Germans into the
St. Mihiel pocket.

Not by going over the actual hills and valleys of any
battle, nor yet from study of their miniature on a map,
can one completely grasp the detail and the total of what
happened. Both are needed—first the real country and
after it the map. Thus it results that I could very nearly
explain St. Mihiel and the Meuse-Argonne, because I
went over their ground and followed later a pencil point
over those relief maps in the house where we slept well:
whereas about Belleau Wood, over which we only walked,
I am quite vague, although it was a much simpler action.
The reader need not dread any attempt of mine to explain
to him either St. Mihiel or the Meuse-Argonne. Let him
study, with its subjoined maps, the report of General
Pershing.

While, by means of relief maps and tales of darkies and
coffee-pots, we were enlarging our knowledge and equip-
ping our intelligence, the doughboys were dancing. I
doubt if they went to bed as early as we did. The captain
had sent them all off to the neighboring village of Billy-
sous-Mangiennes. I don't know how many of these Billys
there are in France, or in which of them our doughboys
put their American arms about French waists to the ac-
companiment of music, and after the music had ceased.
The captain told us that wherever they went they got up
a dance.

XX

SPLENDID day. The first one in France."

I find that the hour at which I wrote this in my diary up in my bedroom was six-thirty the next morning. Eave-martins were flying in and out of the big windows, a chirping of neighboring birds filled the air, and upon looking out I saw many in the trees and farmyards at their May morning's work. There was a glitter from the sun that made the young leaves glisten, and a glimpse of wet meadows beyond the enclosure, sparkling with little pools. It was strange to see in the midst of this, just by the house, a wrecked aeroplane; this glared out of the serenity of everything else. I do not think that it had fallen here, but that they had brought it as an out-door part of the collection.

Voices in the house were audible through the seams in the bare plank floors, or through many large windows, all of them open; and as I strolled about in a free exploration of the second floor, a voice beneath came up to me, and I stood still.

"Bon jour." The words were quite correct, but their pronunciation had been born very far away from France indeed, although French experience was audible in it; I did not need to see him through the floor to know that he was a doughboy.

"Bon jour," some one answered him. I did not need to see her either. That was the cook. Her voice went with her eye and the Olympic amplitude of her bosom: not harsh, by no means soprano, and with many lazy overtones of command. He seemed to be walking about.

"Comment te trouves-tu ce matin?" she inquired.

"O tray bien, mairsee."

What was comical was his perfectly correct speech and his khaki French.

"As-tu bien dansé avec la demoiselle?" the cook's deep voice went on musically.

"O je ne say pah."

"T'es amusé, hein?"

"O wee, wee."

One deep melodious chuckle now came up through the floor. That was the cook. It now struck me that she was addressing him in the idiom of the second person singular; also that in his tone there was something—I couldn't be sure whether it was sheepish, or a lack of ease, or merely impatience, and if he were entirely conscious of it himself.

"Quand on est jeune, faut bien s'amuser." (When one is young one must have a good time.) As he did not reply to this, she pursued: "La sagesse attendra, hein? Faut pas gaspiller tes vingt ans." (Time enough to settle down later, eh? Mustn't waste your youth on that.)

His reply was to begin whistling a tune as he moved about the room. She seemed to be stationary, probably by her fire; for I now heard some rattle of pans or lids before her next remark:

"Et la demoiselle? Elle t'a trouvé gentil?"

"Ah, comment es-ker-je say slah?" he now broke out.

Was there to be no more of this dialogue? Alas, there was not! His spurt of damaged temper and equally damaged grammar proved to be his parting remark, and I heard his steps go out of the kitchen. Like all international conversations, there was so much more in it than the mere words! But I doubt if that particular cook and that particular doughboy ever held talks together for very long at a time, and I think it likely that most of their conferences terminated abruptly, on his side at any rate. She could not have ruffled Kansas so easily, and Kansas (if he possessed fluency in French) would have been able to return her fire—but then he was out of the common. There is no play of the intellect which the general American mind comprehends less, and resents more, than veiled irony. We are just civilized enough to feel it vaguely, and not enough to deal with it lightly. It needed but little

imagination to see in my mind's eye that cook and doughboy, she old and massive over her breakfast pots and
pans, he young and defenceless beneath the lazy indul-
gence of her phrases. No conversation that I had heard
in France, nothing that was told me, threw so much light
upon how the peasants—especially the women—must have
come in time to regard these vigorous children so fresh
from the Western world.

I went back to my room, where presently he came,
bringing some hot water and my boots. The boots, after
yesterday in the mud, had needed a good deal of his
attention. He was a shock-headed boy, very blond, from
Arkansas. There were two of them who looked after us,
the other being from Louisiana. This latter told me, with
a sort of disdain, that he understood what they said in
French pretty well. I did not need to ask this question
of the boy from Arkansas; what I had heard through
the floor sufficed to show him already apt in the language
beyond many a college graduate. His appearance suggested that his fluency had been attained through the
tutoring of various romantic experiences. His body was
slim, he was light in his walk, and almost certainly he
knew how to dance in a manner that would please. I was
tempted to ask him how he liked the cook, but I abstained.
His way of replying to questions discouraged asking them.

He went out, leaving my boots and hot water; and while
I shaved, I heard in memory the cook's ironic intonations
and comprehended everything that her tawny voice had
said without words. She was much more than herself; she
was her race, her continuous history, ancient France,
where Cæsar had been, and Roland, and Diana of Poitiers;
France, whose basking shores the Latin and Greek Mediterranean caressed. In her syllables and between them,
laughed quietly the long-memoried Mediterranean which
had known the Argonauts, and Salamis, and the keels of
Cleopatra, and had heard old Triton blow his wreathéd
horn. The spirit of the peasant cook contained all that,
while the boy contained not much except the Declaration
of Independence. She had addressed him with the intimate

"thou," instead of "you," because her age confronted his youth like some antique sybil gazing from a grove at a faun, smiling at his physical charm, and bored with his emptiness. At her birth she was older than he would be at his death. What the ancient Mediterranean, speaking through her person, said to him was really this:

"You are engaging and attractive because you are young. I like you, but I like you at a distance. You have explored and peopled a continent, but you have not yet explored and peopled Time. Intellect and Art know nothing of you; you have not approached near enough to them to be visible. We can see your skyscrapers, your Olympus not yet. Your material science creates in you the illusion that there is a short cut to education, to reflection, to maturity. There are no short cuts to anything except perdition. You think that to build many churches is to have much religion. You hold meetings, even your women hold meetings, I am told, where resolutions are passed and laws are made, and by these paper toys you imagine that you have caused reality. Such things do not cause reality, they merely express it.

"Never suppose that I am not dazzled by the flame of promise which burns in you with such energy. See to it that it be not put out by the poison which our fatigued old world pours into your still clean and lusty veins. I hope, and sometimes believe, that a great past will be yours in time to come, because I have seen and can never forget what you have done for me, and the reason that made you do it. You are fierce in battle; I love that. You are good to children; that, too, I love. Grateful I am, but am no mistress for the lover who has but one thing to say, no companion for one whose future is his chief tradition.

"Go home to your new world, handsome and vigorous young barbarian! You still imagine that there are answers to everything, that you have found most of them, and are going to find all. Remain in your intellectually virgin world until your mental and moral adventures shall have brought you into that place which lies beyond discourage-

ment, and when in your ripeness you can smile at all
things, even at yourself, without being paralyzed. Remain
there until you have learned that there is no answer to
any of the great questions for ever asked by man; that
the game is not worth the candle, but that we play it to
be worth a candle ourselves—and that to be able to make
interesting love, one must be complicated.

"I see and praise your restless intelligence, upon which
Time has not yet chiselled a single line of grace. I enjoy
your gaiety, which proceeds from a soul beneath whose
surface Adversity has not yet begun to dig the first approach to depth. But alas, I cannot long be sympathetic
in the company of one who, no matter how capable, is
still psychologically illiterate and spiritually infantile:
such is the price which you pay for your youth, and be
assured that youth is worth this price, and more. Be less
sure that the quick and great success which you have had,
is a blessing. Ease may tarnish the beginning of our
days; it polishes their end.

"You are still merely a work of nature. A civilized man
is a work of nature too, but he is also a highly wrought
work of art. Come back in a thousand years and let me
see you, and then, O strong and handsome boy, perhaps
you will be ready for me."

Thus, in the voice of the cook, spoke the old Mediterranean, the mellow, subtle, cynical, sensual sibyl. The
cook herself heard none of these words, because they didn't
sound in her brain, but echoed in her unconscious blood,
and she knew little more about them than any telephone
knows.

What if young blond Arkansas had been able to hear
them, instead of only vaguely and angrily to feel them?
Instead of ineffectively flying out at her with his "Ah,
que sais-je," what adequate reply would he have found?

By the time that I had read the inner meaning of their
colloquy, my shaving and toilet were finished, and I went
down to breakfast.

XXI

WINDING in many curves upon the map which I carried at our journey's end as I had carried it since the beginning, the crosses plot our road through the Meuse-Argonne country. Each cross is set against the name of some town or village, where another broken church tower rose like a bony, up-stretched arm; or walls of broken homes stood waist-high and knee-high amid gaping cellars; or where the town had been struck out wholly, dashed into utter invisibility, and you could not have known it from the ground, save for the sign-post bearing its name and sticking in its dust. Like this were Hautcourt and Malancourt —just names on a board—and Fleury by the forlorn wayside between Vaux and Douaumont. Others there were; but of these slain towns, of whose very bones not one remained, I shall name no more. He who did not see, and never now can see, France flayed and raw as she lay before healing had set in, may try to conjure into his fancy the look of it: stretch after stretch of riddled earth, horizon after horizon ragged with stark trees, emptiness strewn with distortion, walls, towers standing like limbs whose bodies have been hacked away, and short sign-posts like headstones over the graves of places dead and buried. He who did not see this may try to imagine it—and will fail; he who has seen it may try to forget it—and will fail: somewhere in him that sight and that silence will live as long as he lives himself.

Of this particular piece of the war country General Pershing writes:

"The Meuse-Argonne front had been practically stabilized in September 1914, and, except for minor fluctuations during the German attacks on Verdun in 1916 and the

French counter offensive in August 1917, remained unchanged until the American advance in 1918. The net
result of the four years' struggle on this ground was a
German defensive system of unusual depth and strength
and a wide zone of uttter devastation, itself a serious
obstacle to offensive operations."

Yes; a wide zone of utter devastation. Wrecks, half
or whole, are the towns in it, almost all; nearly every
name on the map of that three-cornered country is a label
of obliteration. Go northwest down the Meuse from
Verdun to Sedan, come south from Sedan, skirting the
Argonne to Clermont, turn east back to Verdun, and you
will have enclosed a region wherein many places had in
them shelter for not a living soul in 1919, and two years
later, when next I saw them, it was still the same with
many. Grain was green and swaying under the wind
where holes and shells had been, much of the earth was
breathing again; but from the dust of Fleury, Hautcourt,
Malancourt, and many another, nothing had as yet arisen.

A wide zone of utter devastation: with more to its east
through the Woëvre to the Moselle, and more to its west
across Champagne, and then more.

It is a large looking country of many distances. Across
it the eye often sees far. At all its edges and also within
it, hills rise. Numerous ridges roughen and streak it,
valleys furrow it, patches of woodland darken its open
stretches; yet its spaciousness of line is the chief aspect
that sweeps over the memory, with mounded blurs a long
way off. In it, as in the Somme region, our Western bad
lands were suggested once or twice by the huge, bald, discolored slants of excoriation. Nevertheless it resembled but
little any other of the battle lands that I had seen. Many
wars had made it their arena, but this was true of the other
regions also, and with them it had in common that look
of a place where something has happened, of a witness
to deeds that will never be absent from the eyes again.
But as I watched it from many changing points beneath
the sunshine of these final days, I knew, without being

told, that its serene amplitude in other days of sunshine had been of a sober rather than a gay serenity. There are faces which show the mark of much agreeable society, of many acquaintances, of talk and laughter; while others reveal that meditation has been their chief adventure. The Meuse-Argonne country has communed a great deal with itself. To the understanding imagination it seems to say: "Fourteen hundred years ago I saw Attila. He, too, like these later ones, left me for dead. These are worse than Attila, because they knew better."

Fourteen hundred years after Attila, the Meuse-Argonne saw his successors. They came, turning into deeds the words of their high priest, "the sight of suffering does one good; the infliction of suffering does one more good," and those other words of their high priest, "when one country conquers another nothing should be left to it but eyes to weep." The best of them came here, well taught and faithful followers of their Bismarck. Over them was their General von Mudra, with their Crown Prince over him—but prudently tied to the apron-strings of Marshal von Haeseler. These tutors were to place upon the royal young brow the laurels of their conquests, which would then furnish the theme of happy telegrams from his father to his mother—those despatches that used to run, "Willy and God have done nobly today." Thus the Fatherland could hail and love the youth. He must have also caused many German eyes to weep, for he was perfectly generous in throwing away other people's lives. Many thousand German bones lie in the territory of his failures: at St. Hubert and around Four-de-Paris, which he tried to take, from October to January of that first year; at Fontaine-aux-Charmes and Bolante Wood, where he was next active; and at Les Islettes in June, which he missed in his effort to seize the railway from Ste. Menehould to Verdun. He scattered German bones prodigally at all these places, and at many others—no need to recite his failure at Verdun in 1916: sitting at Montfaucon safely encased, he watched operations through thirty feet of periscope.

This pipe reached him where he hid underground and directed the bone-scattering right and left of the Meuse, all the way to Vaux and Douaumont and Dead Man's Hill and the other places of which we all heard so much during those six months of French agony and glory.

Even though long lulls intervened in the bone-scattering from 1914 to 1918, the Meuse-Argonne had little respite for communing with itself. The tough ridge of the forest was eaten beneath with galleries and mines, its beech and oak thickets on top were gashed with paths, strung with wires, sawed short by shells; while out of the woods to its east the open country, from the little Aire at its base to the larger Meuse over the hills, was bled white and left no eyes to weep with. I have seen them—the empty hollow on the hill where Vauquois stood, and Charny, Samogneux, Consenvoye, Dun-sur-Meuse, Chattancourt, Avocourt, Varennes, Cunel, Romagne, Buzancy—villages crushed, lying among crushed woods and pastures crushed, —a wide zone of utter devastation indeed.

Hither on September 25th, 1918, came our divisions to fight their hardest fight of all—made harder and delayed by a bad choking of their supplies along the few difficult roads: a task allotted to them because it was so difficult, the tough hog-back of the Argonne so mired and enmeshed with defences, and they the only men not tired by four years of strain and struggle. Where they had bled and died and won so splendidly not yet six months ago, we followed their course as they had gone pushing north and east. We went over much of the very ground of their exploits, in sight of more, and never far from any of it. The mud was still in many places strewn with the broken machines of war. In it these lay flat, or tilted, or stuck half sunk, rusting slowly as the wet weather leaked among their stiff joints. We saw where their victorious line had been when the Armistice stopped their onward rush for Germany, and they had flung down their baffled guns, and cried tears of disappointed rage, all the more bitter over the knowledge that the Germans had been permitted to get up from their supplicating knees, and march home with their arms and banners like an undefeated army. There is a legend that the great Foch himself shed tears on that day of fateful blunder. We skirted the territory of their quick advance during the first days of the battle. Then in the dismembered woods through which all sorts of fragments lay strewn, and the wires sagged tangled among the broken branches, we stepped where the mud allowed us in order to see more sacred ground. It was where, in the long slow time of hunger, horror, thirst, and impregnable determination, American grit had been tried out to the full and proved more than equal to the test.

We had gone up the hill from Varennes and turned in among the thickets; and as we passed safe through all this extinct, monstrous turmoil of war that lay everywhere over the land like a contorted fossil, once again—it might well have been for the hundredth time——I asked myself, "What was this like when it was alive?" We must not forget! We can forget injuries to ourselves but not a wound half-mortal to mankind, not, at any rate, until the offender show by sustained deeds that his spirit is changed. Long ago, in 1915, I had said that a full comprehension of this war would burst any human brain; I thought it again now, and that from the thousand chronicles of personal experience which will be written, the future will distil, not the total reality, never that, but the final impression: and that will rise and loom above the general level of history, a terrible spectral shape.

To stop us in the Argonne the Germans brought more and more of their best divisions, piled them in our way— and could not stop us. They piled them here because this ground was now their foot-hold for the whole: knock it from under them, and they must fall their full length, from the sea all the way south. We knocked it from under them. To keep us from their railroad thoroughfare between Metz and Mézières, along which, as one might say, their life-blood was pumped to the whole body, they threw

against us fifteen reserve divisions, while two of our own
had to be taken from us and sent to help in Flanders:
nevertheless we could not be kept from the railway. When
the wooded ridge of Barricourt was gripped and held by
our divisions—Wood's Own and Alamo—on November
the first, Foch, on hearing the news, exclaimed, "the war
is over!"—for that ridge commanded the Meuse and more
than threatened the life-blood thoroughfare beyond the
Meuse.

Not ignorantly, nor yet with an open guide-book merely,
but with at least some seasoned knowledge should one go
over this ground: Barricourt, Buzancy, Beaumont, Létanne, Mouzon, Raucourt, and beyond to the line where the
Armistice halted us. All of it is territory where our soldiers—colonels, captains, lieutenants, sergeants, privates
—by deeds of single daring won honors that are recorded,
and deserved many more that never will be known. As
day followed day their dash increased. They had pierced
almost at once beyond the line planned for the war to stop
at and wait until 1919 should see its finish. They changed
the date of that finish to 1918. Six divisions of them were
ready to go eastward through Briey into Germany, on
November 14th, with twenty French divisions under General Mangin. Four were already starting their march on
November 11th. General Foch had at his disposal two
hundred and five divisions in all, the Germans but one
hundred and eighty-seven, of which the seventeen in
reserve could not have reached the Lorraine front in time
to stop us, because we had cut their railway. The Germans
were already evacuating Metz and Thionville, knowing
themselves impotent to stop us. Their whole army was
helpless from Holland to the Saar, incapable to move its
vast demoralized mass. Catastrophe was imminent, inevitable; retreat was impossible. Even after the Armistice,
the German command left all of its material on the spot,
gave it up, and crossed Dutch Limbourg. Organized to
crush down a robust opposition on the Lorraine front, the
Allied offensive would have there met with but feeble opposition at the first line of defence, and would have gone

on almost without loss. At a blow the whole German front from Switzerland to Holland would have crumpled together. It would have been done within ten days. So the Germans in terror fell on their knees, the Armistice was signed three days before the Lorraine attack was to begin, the German army escaped disaster, marched home with its arms and banners—and our doughboys who had come three thousand miles to do a clean final job, dashed their arms down and cried bitter tears.

And who were our soldiers that fought this Argonne fight? What sort of men were they who took Montfaucon Hill by noon of the second day, making eleven kilometres through the entangling defences by that evening, and, by the next, so alarming the enemy that he threw six new divisions into first line? Such was the start these Americans made in the Argonne, delivering a direct frontal attack through barbed wire, machine guns, cross fire, bad country, deep mud, thick fog: seven days of this forward striding, and then that long, slow, second chapter which filled nearly the whole month of October—from the fourth day until the last. The final chapter like the first was short—eleven days—with a return to the stride forward, the enemy's last defences smashed, the stride quickening to a pursuit. We may think, then, of the Meuse-Argonne battle as thus divided: a swift beginning, a swift end, with a middle twenty-seven days long—days of holding on, of crawling on, of torment and great loss, a test of every quality and resource which combine to make successful aggressive warfare: and when the test was over, the survivors ready for more, getting out of their Argonne woods, getting up on their Barricourt heights, knocking the enemy off the heights of Dun-sur-Meuse, driving him back faster and faster out of the home into which he had broken, and when halted in full stride, weeping with rage at being thwarted in catching him in his own home, for which he was making in such haste.

Who was this doughboy that did this? Who were they that helped him?

The front he held was seventy-five miles wide. More

than a million of him held it. Behind him from where he fought, all the way across France to the shore where he had landed, all his machinery was working to feed and arm him and care for his wounds. It was not perfect—how could it be? But daily it was growing towards perfection. Though still so new at the vast, terrible game—three years (and in most cases nearly four years) newer than his allies—once fairly in the game, he caught up with them with a speed that astonished them, and which they remember with the warmest admiration.

To General Mangin I said on a later day, purposely: "And I hope you found that our soldiers did fairly well?"

The tone in which he answered was like a rebuke. "Fairly well!" he exclaimed, "but very well! very, very well."

He spoke without reserve and all the more cordially, perhaps, because during the talk which had preceded this question of mine he had found me not unaware that we owed to our Allies quite as much as they owed to us; that the moral tonic of our coming *in* had been weakened by our delay in coming *over;* that twelve long months after we had come in, only 300,000 of us had got over; that nothing but the terrifying imminence of disaster, in March 1918, had started the getting us over in adequate numbers, and with proper speed; that, but for the help of British transports, more than half of us could not have got over even then; that nothing but the superb sticking to it of British and French armies during 1917–18, and General Nivelle's attack in 1917, without waiting for our coming, had held the Germans off, and thus given us the time in which to get ready; and that during this time our private citizens by the thousand, Americans on whose shoulders rested great private responsibilities, had dropped their work regardless of their politics, and dedicated their unrewarded ability to propping up the most incompetent and most ungrateful administration which we have thus far staggered along under. The French had helped us out with nearly three thousand airplanes—we had nothing of this kind ready. As to guns, even by Armistice day we had on our front no 75's, 155 mm. howitzers, or 155 G. P. F. guns—the French equipped us from their our plants with this artillery for thirty divisions. During the Meuse-Argonne battle our remount resources fell so short that Marshal Foch turned over to us 13,000 animals from the French armies. Our men had been dragging the guns through the mud themselves, leaving behind their rolling kitchens in order to do it, and eating roots. One division had been obliged to do so much walking in other regions that it named itself the Sight-Seeing Division.

A word about our deficiencies, the lightest acknowledgment that we did not win the war alone, that General Gouraud, for example, with the 4th French Army was fighting west of the Argonne while General Liggett with our first army was fighting in it and east of it, and that together we broke the evil spell and at the finish were, so to speak, flying to victory—any syllable of such recognition brought instantly its generous response from any Frenchman just as well as from General Mangin. What they liked, what opened their hearts, was a word, or even a sign, which expressed appreciation of their courage and suffering during the three years before we brought any courage or suffering into it; receiving such word or sign, they would say readily enough that we had saved them in 1918. What they did not like, what shut their hearts, was to hear us boast. It is difficult to pay compliments to a man who has already begun to pay them to himself.

But who were these American doughboys for whom General Mangin had such handsome compliments?

Four French and twenty-one American divisions fought the Meuse-Argonne fight, and of our divisions five were regulars. All the rest came from civil life, like the embattled farmer who in 1775 at Concord and Lexington fired the shot heard round the world. Every trade, profession, walk in life from all over the country united to make that roar which spoke to the enemy of American courage in the Meuse-Argonne.

And who were the enemy? Germany's best troops, prepared from the cradle for this day, their minds put in uniform at the kindergarten. So fierce became the American onset that when a German division had once got into it, it had to stay in, it could not be relieved. Twenty divisions were taken from the French and one from the British front to pile in the way of the Americans. Forty-seven days of this, forty-seven days of the worst battle Americans have known from Lexington and Concord to the Armistice, and it was over. Not as at the second battle of the Marne, or at St. Mihiel, where we attacked on two sides of a pocket and squeezed the enemy out of it, but in a remorseless frontal attack, did our divisions fight through the Meuse-Argonne, managing entirely by ourselves for the first time the whole mechanism and apparatus of it—communications, dumps, telegraph lines, and water service. We lost some 117,000 in killed and wounded, captured 26,000 prisoners, 847 cannon, 3,000 machine guns, and large quantities of material. Except by the five divisions of regulars, it was not done, it could not be done, with the technical experience of regulars. Life was wasted:—seeing the waste at times the French exclaimed, "they're crazy": and perhaps General Pershing's words about it belong here:

"The less experienced divisions, while aggressive, were lacking in the ready skill of habit. They were capable of powerful blows, but their blows were apt to be awkward—teamwork was not often well understood. Flexible and resourceful divisions cannot be created by a few manœuvres or by a few months' association of their elements. On the other hand, without the keen intelligence, the endurance, the willingness, and enthusiasm displayed in the training area, as well as on the battle field, the successful results we obtained so quickly would have been utterly impossible."

Let this page therefore chronicle the names of those

sixteen divisions who by a few manœuvres and a few months' association in the training area were able with our five divisions of regulars to obtain so quickly those successful results.

That splendid 26th Division, the Yankee, came early to France, fought early, and fought late; the 28th was the Keystone, and saw war from the second Marne to Varennes and Apremont in the Argonne Forest; the Blue and Gray, or 29th, captured Haumont; the Terribles, or 32nd, knew the Vesle and met the 4th Prussian Guards, and was twice in the Meuse-Argonne—especially at Cierges and Romagne, and its name does not disclose that it came from Wisconsin and Michigan, but only that the Frenchmen who gave it this name thought that it knew how to fight; the Prairie came from Illinois, it was the 33rd, and fought with the British in July, and along the Meuse in October; the 35th, or Santa Fé, did not come from the ancient city, but from Missouri and Kansas, where the trail to the ancient city began, and after being in the Vosges it came to the fight, especially at Vauquois and Cheppy; the Buckeye, or 37th, naturally came from Ohio, and most particularly took one side of Montfaucon Hill while the 79th took the other; it was a devastating piece of courage; the true cause of the 42nd being called the Rainbow Division was not, as has been repeated, any incident in the sky, but because men from twenty-six states and the District of Columbia were in it, and of its record it has reason to be proud; it knew the July fighting in the chalk-white country east of Reims, and the Aisne-Marne, and St. Mihiel, and came in for the flying finish of the Meuse-Argonne; I do not know whether the 78th got its name from the New Jersey men in it or not; men from New York and Delaware were there too, and it was called the Lightning Division; it came into the fight by Grand Pré, where it relieved the heroic 77th after the bitter struggle through the Argonne Wood, and had a bitter struggle itself to take the Bois des Loges; the Liberty or 79th Division came

from Pennsylvania, Maryland, and the District of Columbia, and after its share at Montfaucon and its extra rush
to Nantillois, went east of the Meuse and was headed
for Lorraine; the Blue Ridge began the Argonne early
at Béthincourt, fought through the whole of it, finishing
after the capture of Beaumont and Yoncq; the Wildcat
fought east of the Meuse, and took Chatillon and other
towns; and the reader will expect to hear that it came
from North and South Carolina and Florida, but it also
came from Porto Rico: the All-American, or 82nd Division, came from thirty-seven states, though it was the
National Guard of Georgia, Alabama, and Tennessee; it
fought through October, taking Marcq, Chehery, and
other places; the 89th, at whose capture of Barricourt
heights Foch exclaimed "the war is over," was called
Wood's Own, and I think that Leonard Wood must have
liked that name as much as did the men; they came from
Kansas, Missouri, Colorado, Nebraska, North Dakota,
New Mexico, and Arizona; they began to fight in the St.
Mihiel, went into the Meuse-Argonne, capturing other
places beyond Barricourt, and found themselves beyond
the Meuse on November 11th. They derive pleasure also
from remembering that they were the football champions
of our entire army. The 90th, the Alamo, from Texas
and Oklahoma, came into the fight in October, and stayed
till the end, capturing ten places and advancing eighteen
miles against resistance. The 77th, the Metropolitan
Division, had a somewhat special chance to suffer and to
triumph. They happened to be placed in the thick of the
Argonne Wood, on the worst side of that bristling hog-
back, their period on the front line during the difficult
advance which constitutes the second chapter of the
battle being longer than that of any other division. They
fought from the first day until October 15th, and again
from October 31st to November 11th, and their losses
were severe. One incident of their fight has become
widely known; we read of it in the newspapers each day
while it was happening, we have read of it since. Three

whole years after it occurred, we were all reminded of it again by an event of piercing sadness. Through the romantic phrase of a newspaper correspondent, a misrepresentation was unintentionally spread, and though the error has been corrected and Major Whittlesey set right, an established mistake needs to be set right more than once. His battalion was not a "Lost Battalion," as it was called in the despatches.

After the 77th Division had been advancing six days, through the bristles and across the slits in the hog-back, a wickedly hot fire stopped it, notwithstanding which it was ordered to go on. Near a place called Binarville, fairly west through the wood from Varennes, trickle some marshy tributaries of the Aisne, down the west side of the hog-back. These make swamps and come to junctions, over whose wet ground rise high, steep, wooded rocks in walls. Companies from the 307th and 308th Infantry with some of the 306th Machine Gun Battalion, formed the battalion which Major Whittlesey was ordered to take into one of these junctions and hold the position. He carried out the order, working through the meshes of wet growth, losing near a hundred men, raked by fire, and taking prisoners nevertheless. Here he was to have been supported on the west by some of Gouraud's 4th French Army, and on the east by the 307th Infantry. These flanking supports failed to make the planned parallel advance each side of him. Being thus the only one to succeed in carrying out his orders, he found himself cut off, surrounded, with food for one day, and set about making the best he could of it. He got one message back to headquarters by a carrier pigeon; the man he sent for food never returned. His general had ordered Whittlesey to stay, and now did his best to get reinforcements to him. For three days the battalion listened to German voices, returned German fire, and grew more hungry, more thirsty, and fewer in numbers—from more than six hundred to two hundred and fifty—but they kept off the Germans, who asked them now and then

why they did not surrender. On the fourth day, with still
no food, with scanty water, and groaning wounded, and
lessening ammunition, they still held on, refusing the
German invitations to surrender. The last of these
invitations was not shouted from the enemy line, it was
a note brought by messenger—a captured American
soldier. Part of this note read:

"The suffering of your wounded men can be heard
over here in the German lines, and we are appealing to
your humane sentiments to stop. A white flag shown by
one of your men will tell us that you agree with these
conditions. Please treat Private——as an honorable man.
He is quite a soldier. We envy you."

That was a handsome message, and Whittlesey made no
comment as he read it; it is said that he smiled. After
showing the note to officers standing near him, he put it
in his pocket. It was the men who shouted their defiance
pungently and unprintably to the enemy when the news
of the note and its contents got about. They preferred
death to surrender, and death it would have been that
evening for them all, but they were saved by the arrival
of the 307th.

There is the story: Whittlesey had orders to take and
hold at any cost a certain position. He did it, and
through his dogged courage our line was pushed forward
and stabilized.

Whittlesey is dead. Three years after those Argonne
days, he jumped from a steamship to his death at sea.
We must suppose that his nerves had received a bruise
incurable. This war with the horrors of its new science
seems to have destroyed the mental or physical health
of many who came bravely through it unhurt, so far as
appearances went at the time. Its work on mind and
body resembles the burn of radium on occasions, invisible
at first, a deep sore later, hard to heal, and sometimes
fatal.

Bruised nerves, the radium burns of the war, can be
seen today in many hospitals and asylums. A lady where

I live wished to arrange a little music for the entertainment of some patients, and asked that these sick soldiers be allowed to assemble in a large hall where the concert could be given.

"They cannot be allowed to go there," said the superintendent. "They are seven hundred and fifty men permanently raving mad."

On many acres in the Meuse-Argonne countless great deeds were done that never will be known. The hero that lives in most men and may sleep in them through a whole life of week-days, waked in this fiery month of battle and made of it a sacred day, frightful, consecrated, divine through sacrifice. The nameless unrewarded dead, the seven hundred and fifty madmen, are less sad to think of than certain of those who lived and came out whole, in whom the hero has fallen so fast asleep again that his very existence seems doubtful now.

Scarce three miles through the wood from the swamps and tangles of the Beset Battalion, is quite another sight. Prince Rupprecht of Bavaria lived in the trees above Varennes most comfortably. To see his thoughtfully constructed quarters was ample compensation for not seeing the elaborate conveniences below ground that the Germans had made for themselves at Les Éparges. I have been twice to Rupprecht's look-out. It must have housed more enjoyments and relaxations for his royal senses than Montfaucon supplied to the Crown Prince. I cannot blame a prince for taking such good care of his pleasures so much as I blame those unthinking American soldiers who, as soon as they got out of war-stricken France into unscathed, whole-skinned Germany, began to prefer Germans, merely because they found it more comfortable on the uninvaded Rhine than on the shattered and bleeding margins of the Marne and the Meuse. It is a pity that these doughboys were capable of so little reflection—thought more like children of eight than men of twenty-five. Elaborate thought was apparent everywhere in the quarters of the Bavarian prince. One descended concrete

steps so solid and shapely that they were like what you
see in some large handsome garden conducting from some
terrace or arbor to some lake with lilies and goldfish;
there, one's eye followed a substantial balustrade, again
like something in a park; down the first flight, in the
rooms, were wainscotted walls, excellently finished; apartment led to apartment, one imagined where the electric
lights had shone on games of cards, and where music and
song had made the nights agreeable—all in the middle
of this muddy, wild, disordered wood! Brick heaters
were there to keep Rupprecht warm; one room had a
bay-window like a city house; there was ornamentation;
there was a theatre; in a trench to the left of Rupprecht's
exit was beautiful concrete work; a fine stone chimney
stuck up into the wild, disordered woods from a heavy,
sunken concrete roof—probably a division headquarters;
the place was a veritable city; the dugouts went down
sixty feet and connected right and left. We did not go
into a quarter of it.—And then on the walls of Rupprecht's parlor, "Dubuque, Ia." scrawled in a clear hand.
Also, "Oscar McLeven," and "Robert B. Franklin," and
"Little McCarthy."

"During that battle?" I inquired, astonished that they
should have had time to write their names—or anything—then.

"No," said our escort. "Done since by visitors." He
had "jumped off" at Cheppy, just north of Varennes,
and knew that our men had been otherwise occupied.

Such was the scene inside these concrete caves; traces
—almost echoes—of comfort, pleasure, luxury; and outside, at their very doors, the wild, disordered wood,
littered with leavings of war. Not yet were the little
wooden cleats along the wet paths disarranged, nor yet
the fragments among the sodden leaves disturbed, and
through the branches everywhere hung the telephone
wires. We picked up, on another day, two or three pages
from a book, muddy but legible still, libidinous and
intimate, written to stir youth and to goad age. To many

an American boy it would have been like the first dose of frontier whisky to a Cheyenne or a Sioux, only more potent in its appeal and more ravaging in its possible influence. Had the volume belonged to Prince Rupprecht's library? Had it dropped from the kit of some soldier of the 77th? Or had Little McCarthy brought it? Well, we were not likely ever to know.

Not on the walls alone had the Little McCarthys begun to leave their defacing mark; names and initials were already carved upon the trees. This was not the only place where such records were to be seen; they covered the walls thick over at Montfaucon. Names were scribbled by the hundred in that house on the height where the Crown Prince through thirty feet of periscope had safely watched other people fight and die. These names were not going to secure much immortality, however, for the people who had written them; already this snug abode of the Crown Prince was going the way of all flesh and plaster and mortar and everything else. Its gaunt shape reared up on the hillside, and it was ceasing to be a house and beginning to be remains; in a little while it would be like all the rest of this village. We entered the gaps that had been its front door; explored its rotting premises, walked up its as yet safe stairs; looked out of its window-holes over the wide, mournful country towards Verdun; watched the swallows flying in and out of these holes; stared at the disintegrating walls; stared most at that observatory which had been built through the centre of the house for the Crown Prince. That was a structure indeed! It ran up through the building which served as a concealment of its identity, as camouflage. It was reinforced with steel and sand bags and concrete. We admired this symbol of the solid, thorough German character—and of the precautionary valor of the House of Hohenzollern. We mounted to the roof and stood there to look better across the wide view, the woods and fields over which the 37th and 79th Divisions had made that devastating frontal attack by which they took Montfau-

con. It had been said that you could not take it. It stood
up there about midway between the Meuse and the Argonne, strengthened and protected by three years of
German military science—but they took it. Perhaps it
was wasteful tactics, certainly it was splendid courage.

Still better could we see the ground over which they
had come from a point on the hill, which rises higher
than the lookout of the Crown Prince. There was much
in that graveyard to lead one to stand still: another torn
acre of tombs, another church that never would be a
church again. It made a high point in the silence—one
of the places where this enormous stillness came flowing
in from every quarter of the horizon, flowing and flooding over ridge and wood and field, coming to the base
of the hill, rolling up its steep sides, and meeting and
settling on top in a great wave upon which human voices
and the sound of birds made not the slightest mark. I
remember that all the time we were there a cuckoo was
singing ceaselessly. He was as filled with spring as was
the sunshine, and the green of the new leaves; but he
made no difference, nothing made any difference, in this
sea of silence that stretched around us, west to the towers
of invisible Reims rising above it, and still west to
Amiens; and east also beyond where eye could look.

I had copied no names in the house of the Crown
Prince, but in this graveyard among the heaved-up slabs
and ripped interiors where open coffins lay, I wrote: J^n
F^{ois} Drouet, Docteur Medecin, 1795–1849; H^{yte} Hector
Guillenot d'Alby, 2me régiment de cuirassiers, 1814–
1855; Anne Brouchet, Epouse Drouet et d'Alby, 1820–
1880. These names were on the tablet of a tomb broken
open, and they belonged to the corpses which had been
scattered into sight. The tomb was one of several fine
monuments and had been wired for the telephone and
made an observation point, but this was no excuse for
the wanton desecration of the dead.

From here we could see the entire upland of the heights
of the Meuse, as well as the ridge of the Argonne Forest.

and no place was better for relating the parts of this
large country to the whole. We adjusted to each other
the points where we had been, and some of those still to
come. There to the south we could make out Hill 304,
where our 80th and 4th Divisions had begun their part
of the Meuse-Argonne battle near Béthincourt and Dan-
nevoux, pivoting on Verdun and swinging northward.
We knew Hill 304, for there we had been already in the
course of our circuitous wandering. We had gone in and
out of the folds of the landscape, and far and wide,
seeing various signs of the war scattered broadcast
through the region. Once, between Étain and Damloup,
we had passed a Baldwin locomotive, alive and steaming,
recalling home, and symbolizing reconstruction. Tank
traps had been placed along that road. These consisted
of very strong stone posts set in the ground something
like gate-posts, and between them would be strung heavy
chains. We had passed squads and squads of German
prisoners, dull in their dingy green. These were at work
upon the roads, and they worked as little as they could.
Alike in the knobbed and gnomish countenances of the
old and the pleasant ruddy faces of the young, I seemed
to descry the same look of puzzlement. Were they heavily
wondering all the while how and why they had come to
be here, or had they worked beyond this to the later stage
of wondering how soon they would be able to revenge
themselves? We passed Russians too—strangely different
from any one else. Our escorts could not tell us what
they were doing or what their status was; and I doubt
if they knew this themselves. They had saved France as
much in the beginning as we had saved her in the end;
they had fought bravely, had been vilely betrayed at
home, and slaughtered pitifully by the thousand, and
now their country—the one that they had known—was
weltering in disaster, no longer herself. I gather that
they had been treated very stupidly by the French
Government, and that their souls must have been poisoned
by a sense of ingratitude. Over all this unearthly mix-

ture of Baldwin locomotive, cheerful doughboys, saddened peasants, German prisoners, Russian exiles at work or at idleness, amid mounds and holes and obliterated roads and villages, shone a bright sunlight upon the trees. In their branches the mistletoe bunched like crows' nests; while above them in the blue soared many larks like floating dots of song. Their music fell upon the forlorn fields in scattered drops of sound which might have been made by silver hammers tapping upon a crystal vault. German words were painted large and black upon many a village corner, sometimes naming a street, sometimes an office or headquarters; and from these still habitable edifices we would pass almost in a breath to zones where all had been blasted flat, and it was rare to see any fragment that still resembled a house. Along much of these winding journeys, camouflage of various patterns remained, whole or in rags; and this also touched with unearthliness a scene where shell holes lay like giant soup plates, scummed with motionless bubbles and awful liquid.

And yet the fury which had reduced the world to this, produced—otherwise man would have perished as much from horror of the brain as from wounds of the flesh— songs, and jokes by the thousand, and philosophy, and in many cases deep, ultimate, serene belief in God. A piece of *poilu* philosophy from the trenches has been translated into English and applied to our doughboys; but by an American brain no such train of logic would have been formulated, although, once it was formulated, American brains might readily have assented to it:

With the *poilu* everything might be worse.
Of two things one is certain—
Either you're mobilized or you're not mobilized;
If you're not mobilized, there's no need to worry,
But if you're mobilized, one of two things is certain—
Either you're at the front or behind the lines.
If you're behind the lines, there's no need to worry,

But if you're at the front, one of two things is certain—
Either you're in a safe place or you're exposed to danger.
If you're exposed to danger, one of two things is certain—
Either you're wounded or you're not wounded.
But if you're wounded, one of two things is certain—
Either you're wounded slightly or you're wounded seriously.
If you're wounded seriously, one of two things is certain—
Either you recover or you die.
If you recover, there's no need to worry.
If you die you can't worry, so what's the use?

The gaiety of this, which flashes through it like a blade of well-tempered steel, strangely ratifies a word of foresighted discernment spoken by Bismarck in 1874. That was three years after he had defeated France and taken Alsace-Lorraine from her. He was passing with a friend through some German city—it may have been Stuttgart—and in the evening went to hear *La Fille de Madame Angot*, whose words and music were then quite new. It came from Paris. At first Bismarck was much diverted, and laughed and enjoyed himself. Gradually he ceased to laugh, became graver and graver, until he was so dark and silent that his friend in surprise asked him if he did not like it.

"Not at all," he said. "For here is an enemy singing and dancing, and an enemy who can sing and dance like that is not conquered."

In those days and long after them, as late as 1914, indeed, the rest of the world—and even France herself—would have heard in the sportive measures of *Madame Angot* nothing but an irresponsible, if agreeable, levity; but canny old Bismarck heard that philosophy of the *poilu*. One remembers it was in the following year, 1875, that, if he had been allowed by certain other powers, he would have invaded France again in order to "bleed her white" so that she should stay so. Very obviously the gaiety of *Madame Angot* contributed its light straw to his perfectly wise and perfectly savage intention.

Along the valley of the little Aire we followed very

intelligibly the advance made during the first eleven days
of October by our 1st Division. While Whittlesey was
across in the wood west of the river, perhaps six miles
off, they were working along east of it, capturing Baulny,
Exermont, Fléville; and there was but little along this
ridge to hinder our view of the whole of this. Down below ran the river pleasantly, its valley green with marshes
and busy with birds and looking like something at home
—very different from the sights on the ridge. To tell a
reader about mud is hardly worth while, therefore I will
say no more of it than that later, beyond Grand Pré,
and between Buzancy and Raucourt, we grew venture-
some in our exploration, and for a while I wondered if
I were not going to be sorry that I had come. But we
got out of it at last, and I must certainly tell you about
the bells of Autrecourt, another of the villages taken
by our 1st Division, in their fight during early November.

On the River Meuse, upon that reach of it which saw
us come after the Huns in the final days, are Mouzon,
Létanne, Angecourt, Autrecourt, with Beaumont and
Yoncq not far off; all names full of memory to our
divisions who pushed to the river or beyond it during
the flight to victory just before the Armistice. Mouzon
has a most beautiful little church, but its bells are gone.
So are the bells gone from all of the churches there-
abouts, save only the church at Autrecourt. This has
one, the others followed where went their neighbors of
Mouzon and all the other places. Their bells were removed by the Germans for the sake of their metal. One
evening, just about the time that the order went forth
to take away all the French church bells that they might
be melted down in Germany for the better destruction of
the French, some Hun officers were enjoying themselves
in Autrecourt. They were supping freely and easily. So
were the few other Germans who were there. The village,
like all of the Meuse-Argonne region, had been in German possession since 1914, and the officers had made

themselves much at home. That night during the supper, fire broke out in the German military stores. As this mishap was not at all one which concerned the French, they became the pleased spectators of it. Can you see those French peasants and villagers, with their hands in their pockets, watching the fire get the better of the German stores? When it was quite too late to do anything in the way of prevention, somebody came out from supper and saw.

"Mein Gott!" he very naturally exclaimed.

But this did no good, nor did any of the various other expressions which followed from him and his brother officers, as they came piling out.

"Why did you not tell us of this?" they demanded of the villagers. "Why did you allow it to get beyond control? You should immediately have sounded the tocsin."

But to this the villagers had no answer except to smile agreeably while they shrugged their shoulders.

So it all burned to ashes and more had to be sent from Germany.

"Very well," said the officers, "for your pig-dog disrespect for the property of the All Highest, you shall receive punishment. During three months, beginning tomorrow, every day two citizens shall ring the tocsin for fifteen minutes."

This sentence was forthwith put into effect, and while it was in mid-execution came the people to carry out the order from Germany and remove all church bells. But if you have no bell you can sound no tocsin. Therefore from the church at Autrecourt only two bells were taken in order that two citizens should be able to carry out the punishment by ringing the third bell for fifteen minutes every day till the three months had expired.

Today, therefore, while all neighboring church towers are empty of their chimes, you can hear one bell at Autrecourt calling the peasants and villagers to their prayers.

It was at Mouzon, next door to Autrecourt, a mile or

so up the Meuse, that the village apothecary told me this, after he had accompanied me in a vain search for the grave of an American boy, and we were inside the exquisite church. Throughout all of this woe-begone country it was merriment bubbling from the eternal masculine heart that helped that tough heart to beat on sanely till the tempest was over; and when we wander among the crosses where lie the dead men whose hearts were stilled during the storm, we shall not imagine it rightly if we imagine it as going on without laughter. There is no laughter for us among the crosses; but of them that were in it, few who survive, I think, could have come through and remained at all themselves, had they not been capable of mirth. Therefore when I think of the men who fought and suffered so well—French, British, Americans—I know that most of them joked well too—know that nearly every day they must have exchanged words such as these between two American doughboys talking about a third, and overheard by an officer:

"He's got just about no sense at all."

"No. If his brains were gunpowder and went off they wouldn't blow his nose."

The "buck privates" whom we saw in the streets of Sedan looked as if almost any of them could talk like that in almost any circumstances. Sedan they had not entered at the end of their rush during those early November days of 1918; this particular act had been most fittingly done by the French; it was right to heal, so far as ever it could be healed, the wound and the outrage dealt there by Bismarck to France in 1870. Do you remember the outrage? There it was that the Emperor Louis Napoleon surrendered, and a great disaster fell upon the French army and nation; and while that surrender was taking place, Prussian trumpets blew the strains of the Marseillaise into the ears of their vanquished foes. Oh, my friend, when you hear talk about the "irritating" attitude of France since the war, put yourself, whose country has never suffered anything like this, in a Frenchman's place; and remember the indemnities which Germany purposed to exact from France, England, and ourselves, if she had won!

Just across the bridge over the Meuse as one came from the south into Sedan, was the house where Louis Napoleon had been on that day in 1870. Not far away on the other side of the street was an old lady in a booth selling picture post-cards of the place, and of her I bought at once a picture of that Napoleon house.

"I shouldn't have wanted to own this before," said I.

"Oh, no, monsieur," she answered, "but now it makes one joy, does it not?"

Our doughboys seemed to swarm in the town, in the middle of the street, on the sidewalks, and in the house and tree-grown yard of the Café de la Soquenette. This pleasant establishment did a brisk business, and as we ourselves sat there pausing before our plunge back into the zone of utter devastation, the voices of the doughboys came to us from tables adjacent.

"Well," said one, "I'm told that the boats on the Rhine have square port-holes to fit the heads of Germans."

We left them and Sedan behind us. We had come into the town by the road above which they had been stopped by the Armistice, in their forward rush. This road, the Meuse, and the railway, are all close together at this particular point, to which three of our divisions came— the 1st on November 7th, the 42nd on the 7th and 8th, the 77th on the 10th and 11th. To mark this farthest fling of their victorious tide, a memorial stone stands today above the road. This I passed in those later days when the ticket agent was so civil to me upon finding I was an American. I hope that I shall drive along that road some day again. I find myself wishing to linger in words upon it now, instead of getting away from Sedan. It is because of our doughboys. This is my last chance

to talk about them when they were at their best, and I
am loath to leave it. Discipline and a great cause lifted
thousands high above their daily selves for once at least,
and for this they should feel gratitude instead of demanding pay. The flash of Cantigny revealed their mettle; at
Belleau Wood and the bridge-head at Château-Thierry it
flashed again; in the second battle of the Marne the
flash widened to a steady blaze of established certainty;
St. Mihiel was a feat well and quickly done: but the
Meuse-Argonne, though less imprinted on the popular
mind, rises above them all. It was truly a long and tough
battle, and virtually all their own. It was difficult in
every way; through bad weather, through bad country,
inexpertly fed and supplied at times, on account of the
mud and the strangulation of the few highways of supply—and against more and more of Germany's best men
fortified behind Germany's best defences: forty-seven
days of it; nothing like it in the whole history of the
nation. If there is such a thing as being too proud to
fight, the American doughboy was sorely lacking in it.

You must not look at human nature with a microscope
alone; distortion is the consequence. Even the calendared
saints were sometimes sinners, and the doughboy was no
saint. Moreover, in his mobilized ranks abroad were enlisted professional criminals, who escaped from discipline
and degraded his name by their foul deeds in Paris until
a heavy hand closed upon them—while in his demobilized
ranks at home are guard-house lawyers, politicians, pension sharks, who also degrade his name and drive many
of the best of him to resign from the organization which
held at its beginning a hope too ideal to come true in a
world like this. None of these things has anything to do
with the doughboy and his battles in France. He came,
often most unwillingly, from a nation that hates war, and
once in it he so conducted himself in that quarrel that his
adversary was ware of him. Then he lived his great
moment when discipline and the cause made him more

of a man than he had ever been before. He showed himself a terrible fighter—those other terrible fighters, the
Australians, found him "a bit rough." He proved a
soldier dogged, aggressive, enterprising, and humorous—
nobody better than he at the game. He also showed
himself a lover of children, an adept in athletic sport, a
too lavish spender, and keenly appreciative of hospitality: not in every case, of course: avoid the microscope.
A good name lingers behind him. I wish that all of him
were still as worthy today. And so my chances to dwell
upon him, my American brother, end. My last close
sight of him was in Sedan, gay beneath the trees of the
Café de la Soquenette, conversing about Rhine steamers
that fitted their port-holes to the square heads of the
Germans.

We left Sedan by another way and went along by
another river, la Chiers, which comes into the Meuse just
above Sedan, and goes through Carignan, Montmédy, and
Longuyon, as we also did. All that road was also along
or near the Metz-Mézières artery, whose strangling by us
throttled Germany's last breath and threw her on her
knees, praying to be spared. There was no way of not
granting that petition; but prayers granted to Germany
do not improve her soul. Greater tragedy than the premature Armistice and the belated Treaty cannot be met
in history. We saw the chimneys of the Briey basin,
whence Germany got much mineral help for the war,
until we cut it off from her—and then in one of those
strange moments that was like some evil magic, growing
trees and living houses ended, and we re-entered the
awful Thing and the awful Silence.

"For mark! No sooner was I fairly found
    Pledged to the plain, after a pace or two,
Than, pausing to throw backward a last view
    To the safe road, 'twas gone! grey plain all round:
Nothing but plain to the horizon's bound.
    I might go on; nought else remained to do.

"As for the grass, it grew as scant as hair
   In leprosy—thin dry blades pricked the mud
Which underneath looked kneaded up with blood.
   And more than that—a furlong on—why there!
What bad use was that engine for, that wheel,
   Or brake, not wheel—that harrow fit to reel
Men's bodies out like silk?"

Had he who wrote that passed in vision seventy years
beforehand over this ground of the Woëvre and the
Meuse-Argonne?

XXII

VERDUN

SOMEWHERE far back along our way, near its beginning, I had remembered that line of mystery in *Lear:* "The worst is not so long as we can say 'This is the worst.'" The words came back to me as we for the first time neared Verdun; and Verdun has caused my speech to die away at every sight of it that I have had since. On its heights and in its hollows I have walked with friends, none of us speaking a word. Nothing that I or any man can say, or any picture, will make you know what Verdun is. Music might steep the spirit in the same mood. It is best such a thing should have to be seen, should cost effort; could its whole reality be carried about in books and spread on laps, even it would be cheapened. As it is, you must go there to know it all, you must climb about among its barbed and wasted mounds, and stand high up a long while, and look slowly down over the torn sea of shell holes to the bottom and across the wide plain there, pock-marked and patterned by the blasts of war. Whiffs of the rotting dead are no longer blown to your nostrils as you go about; on that first day they were. Written in my notes on the spot, at the moment, is this:

"Douaumont. Pools, humps, stones, corrugated fragments, dead distance, dead nearby, stumps, steel rail, rusted bits, whiffs from the dead, human bones (a German grave, his shoes, his bones, a cross of twigs unnamed), a pool with thirty dead in it, and larks in the sky."

Sitting at Douaumont and staring, it seemed as if all the miles of sacred ways we had travelled led here; as if we had been coming here ever since Compiègne, through Amiens, Reims, everywhere, the whole journey being in-

evitably to bring us to this. In my thought I could see
Reims and Amiens back on the road—truer to say, they
came and stood in my thoughts suddenly. They were this,
and this but a piece of them, just like the French boy
who wrote the letters, just like the whole of magnificent,
tragic France.

As you come in one way from Étain, the white dead
fingers of the trees begin their stiff gesture along the
ridges. They beckon motionlessly, spreading their ranks
over the undulating dearth. Stark and thin, with crazed
knuckle joints, they show that something wrong has happened to them, that they did not die naturally, but were
murdered. They stretch around Tavannes and on to
Vaux, in groves, or by twos and threes, or sometimes just
one flayed bone, sticking up from meshes of barbed wire
and bumps of slaughtered earth. This ground, Vaux and
Douaumont, just these two fortresses, only a part of
Verdun's large circle of strongholds, was where during
four months 10,000 shells of 8 inches and larger fell
every day. Multiply it—one hundred and twenty times
ten thousand. How is it that any trees at all still stand
to show that they were murdered? What wonder that all
the men still alive by the ninth day of it were weeping?

"They shall not pass." That was Pétain's promise
about the Huns.

Before they knew that they never could pass, the earth
had become like this, and it was November—they had
begun to try to pass in February. Over at Les Éparges
not very far to our southeast, 70,000 French had been
killed; of these dead, there were 8,000 not in shreds, the
other 62,000 were mere nameless drops of blood and bits
of flesh. That seems bad—but what was the cost of life
here to prevent the Germans passing? To save Verdun,
four hundred thousand French were killed, and of these
were found eighty thousand that still were human bodies.
Of these bodies about one-half could be identified. On
the forlorn hill beside the road, and opposite the path
that leads to Douaumont, is a wooden building, a sort

of chapel for the fragments of the featureless, dismembered dead. A good man, the Padre Noel, lives here in the wilderness, to be near these bones and give them sacred shelter as fast as they are found. They are being carefully searched for and almost every day more are collected. Some came from quite near, in a pinched little gully, the Ravin de la Dame. Five hundred were killed in this place and buried; but later fighting wiped all these graves away. In Padre Noel's chapel stood fifty-two coffins full of nameless bones on the last day I was there. More are there now. All will never be found in that wild continent of obliteration; but in time, instead of the wooden chapel, houses more permanent for those bones will stand there; churches where all the bereaved of every faith may come and say their prayers —a church for Catholics and one for Protestants, one for Jews and one for Mohammedans; the families of every race that died fighting for Verdun will have a sacred roof beneath which they can kneel and feel at home and think of their dead. Or, if they live too far away, or are too poor to come, they can know that Padre Noel is there watching over the coffins, and that when his watch is over, another will follow him. Of the four hundred thousand French killed at Verdun, eighty thousand were fairly whole, forty thousand recognizable: our American total of deaths (to September 1, 1919) was 81,141, of which 35,556 were killed in action—or about the same number that were recognizable after Verdun.

I wanted to climb down to the bottom of Vaux. It was a good long descent; but with the earth in natural state, half an hour would have been more than enough. With the earth as it was, I got a little way below the flat top of the fortress and went no farther. I was among barbed wire, I had crossed some sagging strands of it, more of it was ahead; all the way down, fence after fence of it encircled the slope, each but a few yards apart. This was to climb over, with a ground to walk on that was ditched deep with trenches and so tossed and gutted that, had I made the attempt, I should have been letting my body down into holes and pulling it up at every dozen steps. It would have taken all that morning, even if none of the wire proved impassable. So I stopped where I was and looked at the great view. I had seen it before in the days when no moving or living thing could be descried. Today the slow smoke of a train, creeping out from the deep folds of the hills on its way to the open spaces of reconstruction, marked the solitude. Its sound did not come up to me as I watched it wind out of sight. It ran on a road-bed between shell holes, dug-outs and the blur of barbed wire, and once it stopped at a demolished station. Beyond this, the hills opened upon the plain stretching to the forest of Spincourt. It was from this wood that the Germans descended upon Verdun. The distance was wan, effaced, of hues lighter or darker, according as the land was open or wooded. Thus the distance; near at hand, the broken upheaval, the bristling wire, the waste of splinters, slanted weeds, and stones. A grave was here. No others. It had the hill to itself. It was close against one of the barbed wire fences. I made my way to it and copied the inscription on the wooden cross:

Léon Fautier
30 Avril 1916
119ᵉ Regᵗ d'infantrie

That day had been the 38th of the siege of Verdun. How many shells by then had fallen on Vaux? And why was Léon Fautier not sleeping in some cemetery with comrades for company? Had he fallen here, and had his people wished that he stay here? The cross was set in rubble and supported by stones and the rusting shells of the 75 gun. Not a wreath, not a leaf, lay on this naked grave.

Such is Vaux. Such it was in May 1919, and two years later it was unchanged. Exactly like it is its neighbor

Douaumont. In both you may descend and be shown
their dark interiors: a great disappearing gun with its
levers and machinery; the hospital; the surgery; the
chapel; where the commander slept; where the soldiers
lived; their well of water; the place where the Germans
came in; the gallery of a frightful battle—the walls look
stone-deaf from it; and other galleries and labyrinths
which you do not explore, but merely peer into; all by
the light of a lamp held up for you by a grave *poilu*.
He points to where the tunnels lead to the tunnelled
citadel in Verdun itself, ten miles away. You can visit
likewise this enormous underground place and its galleries; its chapel; its dining-room; where soldiers and
civilians lived in shelter during the siege of the city in
which every house was struck but one. It is all strange
and solemn; not to be missed; but you will learn more in
the outside air. Books have been written about Verdun,
many books already, a shelf of them, well-nigh a literature. They are good, too, some of them, well worth
reading—the last days of the Fort de Vaux, for instance.
But you will learn more in the outside air. Walk in the
city, walk in the plains, go up the hills and look down.
Find some chauffeur who fought through it all the four
years, and is here still, and will tell you about it, if he
feels that you care. Talk to Padre Noel among his coffins.
I walked away from him across the road and wandered
along the path that leads to Douaumont. Presently this
changes to planks and later accompanies the light rails
of the little war railroad. It goes among and over
trenches. Some of them are kept as they were, but most
are melting in the wet and crumbling in the dry. In the
bottom of one of these shelters I passed near two women
in black. They were so still that they might have been
something come from another world. They held a paper
and looked down at it. I went on to where the path and
railroad end below the abrupt, gashed summit. This was
two years after I had written in my diary upon my first
sight of Douaumont. In the later diary come these words:

"Walked to Douaumont. Rusted débris—lumps—larks—pools—silence." I climbed to the top. There was the unchanged sight, the descents of barbed wire, the unfolding hills, the stretching distance, wan, effaced. I explored for a while, and came down the steep banks to the plank path again, and so back among the trenches. Still the two women were down in that shelter, motionless, black, their paper in hand. I guessed right what brought them. Every day, I learned, came women like this with papers by which they are guided to the spot where their living became their dead. There they stay, remembering.

Thus, walking about in the air, and stopping, it sinks into you: the murdered trees, the forts, the scarred hills rising out of silence into silence, and motionless women in black, pilgrims to the foot of earth on which their sons and husbands fell.

After such a sight, more sights followed, as the road from Padre Noel and his house of coffins sinks to levels below; it passes the Trench of Bayonets, the ravine where the buried dead were torn out of their graves by later violence; it winds through a tormented region, gashed, discolored, quarried with shelter holes like rows of ovens, scribbled with trenches, blotched with craters—the Côte du Poivre; then it comes out beyond these ravaged steeps and slants to the level ravage along the Meuse, the tumbled village of Bras, the impassable streets of Verdun itself.

One road threaded through the town; into the others, as at Reims, the houses had fallen, barricading passage. By climbing over their heaps one could make one's way on foot from one end of a street to the other, but in no other manner. When next I saw these stones two years later, they were not yet built back again into houses; that will take a long time; they had been cleared away from the streets and stood upon their land, symmetrically piled in level cubes, each stone numbered to mark its identity. The jostled disorder of races at Verdun in the early day was as mingled as the stones which blocked the thoroughfare. We had our lunch in a Y canteen that had been a house of which enough remained for this purpose. Its street front was fairly whole, its back gaped upon a court into which the rest of this house and parts of its neighbors had been hurled. Timbers lay there, and the twisted iron of a balcony, and a plaster Virgin, and over these things hung a pair of drawers recently washed. Eating together in the room were Russians, French, Americans, negroes, and behind the counter serving them stood American women in blue caps. Here and there in doorways stood German prisoners. Near me was a negro soldier from Virginia who told me that his name was Lee; behind him sat a boy from Oklahoma who said that he was glad he had come because "he had it to do," but now that it was done he would like to get home.

Upon the townsfolk and the peasant mind, what mark was left by this huddled medley of races suddenly pitched everywhere into the quiet midst of France? A very slight mark upon their minds it must be, after four years of fighting for their lives. To those who came through that, no sight can ever be strange again, no matter what is destined to enter Verdun by its ancient gate, beneath which have already passed so many centuries of sights. It will leave but a faint impression upon the French mind. The mark upon the French race might be deeper, did heredity cope evenly with environment—but it does not. Those half-French offspring of unforgiven, over-tempted mothers, begotten by Mongolians, Slavs, Teutons, Africans, English, Americans, may—some of them at least—have tragic childhoods; to the nation they will make but little difference, and most of them will come to count as wholly French.

Verdun as it had fallen and still lay, was without shape; Verdun with its stones piled in the blank spaces where its houses had stood once, was like a mouth with many teeth gone. But no gaps were in the sane, determined spirit; not a voice, unless after some intimacy of acquaintance, told you of loss, or of hardship, but only

of going on, of determination to come back to full life
and vigor, no matter how long the struggle might be.
By the Meuse, where it runs through the town sluggishly,
is a little public square, the place Chevert, named to
honor a soldier of Verdun. With top-boots and sword,
his spirited statue rises in the middle of the square;
underneath is his name and rank: Chevert, Lieutenant
General, 1695–1769. Upon another face of the pedestal
are words recording that the fact that he never became
a marshal is a loss, not to him, but to those who choose
him for their model—and then, upon still another face,
an account of him so proud that I wish the words into
which I must translate it could equal the fire which thrills
through the original:

Without Ancestors,

Without fortune, without influence,

Orphan from childhood,

He entered the Service

aged eleven years.

He rose in spite of envy

by force of merit,

And each upward step

was the reward

of a noble act.

"Well," I have thought more than once, as I have
come to that French soldier's statue in my walks about
the streets of his native city, "he was like France in these
present years—without fortune, without influence, rising
in spite of envy, each upward step the reward of a noble
act."

It is to Verdun, indeed, that all the sacred ways conduct. Even after travel along the others, by the Lvs, by

the Somme, by the Marne, and east to the Vosges by Thann and Massevaux, something more which these have not spoken, is heard in that silence there, and one comes from it with knowledge of France still deeper than even Reims and Amiens could impart.

Go, after seeing Vaux and Douaumont and all other spots which are included in the word Verdun, to the Mort Homme. Do not be content to look at that hill from your car at Cumières; leave the car and walk to the top of Dead Man's Hill, and stand there beside its monument. Give to this an afternoon, so that the light of the ending day may shine upon that sight and mingle with your thoughts. From there each way they came upon Verdun is plain; first on the east side of the Meuse to Vaux and Douaumont—which you can see far across the gulf of silence; then, because the fire from the west side forts raked them—Fort de la Chaume, Fort du Chana, Fort des Sartelles, Fort de Choiseul, Fort de bois Bourrus, Fort de Marre, Fort du Vacherauville—they changed their plan of siege and came on the Mort Homme side of the Meuse. They fell by thousands day after day, but still came, rising as it were out of the earth. The French did not learn for some time that it was really a tunnel through which they made their way under the hills from the northern slope towards Forges. Hill 304 was part of this battle-ground. In a circle stand the heights from which the French poured their fire. Sometimes this huge cup of country was a roar of flames to its rim, and it wears today the charred look of ordeal. It puts you once more in mind of the four hundred thousand French who died here, of whom forty thousand could be recognized. Those men had to fight so hard lest the Huns pass that there could be no stopping, they were given no breathing spell, until 70 per cent of any command was wounded or killed; then the surviving remnant could pause and wait a while until its strength was filled by new men, and sleep and change had made it fit to go in again.

Over Dead Man's Hill the sky itself seems to grow

more solemn. From its summit the earth sinks away,
north, east, and west, in furrow after furrow of fragments. The receding lumps merge and stretch to the feet
of distant hills, or to the horizon. The eye looks across
the wide valley to Vaux, or toward Montfaucon, over a
world that might be a planet after death; a planet that
did not burn out and chill gradually, but was violently
killed through some last encounter between the forces
that created it. One thinks, Will man's engines, greater
than he already, break wholly from his control and in
the end be able to tear the world to dust, so that as dust
it floats on through space—or will man sometime be so
taught by what war has done that he will cease to wage
it and will not have to die before he find peace?

Nothing that you see from Dead Man's Hill gives an
answer. You go on looking at the sky, at the quiet, pitiful miles; and here, still more than at Montfaucon, the
tidal wave of silence rolls in and covers the place deep.
It is gigantic, but yet so wistful, so yearning, so potent,
that you come to feel it is a sort of being made of a
million beings, and has a message, and might speak if
rightly commanded.

It went with me away from the hill, north to Brieulles
and across the Meuse there. As we came back along that
east side of the river through Sivry, and Consenvoye
where the German line had been, and then Brabant where
had been the French line, and the ground and the ruin
never changed, it seemed to enter me. Rain began to fall
and light was leaving the day. Every village was a heap
of stones, many houses blown out of all shape. In some
houses that were half left, a single light burned, and you
saw a peasant, man or woman, after the day's work upon
the shell holes, entering home for the night. Along this
road, I think in Consenvoye, one half-ruin had passed
by upon which remained the solitary German word:
Spielhaus.

PART SECOND

TWO YEARS AFTER

In the long run even a gloomy
truth is better company than a
cheerful falsehood.

AUGUSTINE BIRRELL, *Res Judicatæ*.

—

XXIII

OLD ACQUAINTANCE

SOON after seeing Verdun I came home, where, with far too many Americans, the war was out of sight and out of mind. Moreover, great numbers of my fellow-countrymen were still of the stale, misdirected opinion that we owed our ally, England, nothing but a grudge. Whether we like it or not, England is quite the best thing since Rome, better than Rome, and not only the real cradle of American liberty but its constant friend, although she once tried to upset the child and has since then rocked it rather violently at times. History, which has been concealed from American youth by the grudgers, shows unanswerably that England has never allowed other nations to be rough with her offspring, invariably saying "hands off" to all comers who meditated assault—to Germany last and most emphatically in 1898. A century of suppressed facts shows the distortion instilled into the American mind by school histories and politicians who want Irish votes. These facts I gathered and printed, and it took a long while to make a short book. Then I set to work upon my second debt of honor, this time to

227

France who, next to England, is the greatest thing since
Rome, and our next best friend. The truth is that since
the surrender of Cornwallis in 1781, France on the whole
has been less good than England to us, and has given us
more occasions for a grudge, if grudge were possible; but
it is not; no American can forget what France did for us
in the darkest day of our childhood, and the high example
of generosity which she set in the first treaty of alliance
that she made with us: she was to receive no compensation
for her help. This was unprecedented in history, and our
following the precedent in 1918 squares no account in
decent minds, because between friends there can be no
question of such accounts.

More than a dozen of the preceding chapters had been
written; it was late in 1920; I had not been back to see
the devastated regions, but many whom I knew had been
there. Had they all told me the same story, there would
have been nothing to do but believe them and go on writing
this book; but the stories would have bewildered any one;
France was doing very well, France was doing very badly,
she was rich, she was poor, she was working nobly to get
on her feet, she was perfectly idle and waiting for Germany's reparation money, she was militaristic and making
all the trouble there was, she was not militaristic and she
wanted only to be left alone. What was there to do but
go over again and see for myself? I went accordingly
for two months—and stayed eight, because to see everything and hear everything and after that to know my own
mind clearly, was quite beyond my powers, unless I took
my time over it. I did not see everything, but certainly I
saw France, and I heard everything else from very close.

My pilgrimage in chaos tangible had ended at Verdun,
and now began a journey in chaos intangible, chaos politic,
moral, financial, paper nations, paper money, crumbling
friendships, gathering hatreds, misery and menace so appalling that the tragedy of the peace grew blacker to me
than the tragedy of the war and for a while I could not see
the wood for the trees. Merely to read the morning paper

was to renew each day yesterday's restlessness, as in the war times; but this new restlessness was as much subtler than the old had been as poison gas is more subtle than bullets. Good news came during the war sometimes, it never came now; in a word, civilization, after its four years' sleepless battle for life, had entered upon no healing period of rest, but had merely passed from one state of insomnia into another. What was happening to Wrangel? Was Austrian starvation being relieved? Were the English miners to strike? Was the plebiscite in Upper Silesia to be dominated by Prussia? Was the Irish question nearer solution? Were they going to cut down Germany's reparation any further? Would she pay her next instalment? It was for answers to such questions as these that one opened the morning paper, instead of to see what was happening on the West Front. There was no west or any other front, no Hindenburg Line between warring forces, the new evil was invisible and crossed all fronts like a pestilence. Paper money is the morphine of economic insomnia, as vain and dangerous a drug, and many governments in Europe were giving themselves weekly injections of it. Through the continuous convulsions in exchange, a traveller with American money could live in Vienna or Warsaw or Buda Pesth luxuriously for about ten dollars a week, while on the other hand an Austrian who had buried in his garden a fortune equal to a thousand dollars in 1914, would find it equal to less than two dollars if he should dig it up. While these earthquakes rocked the buying and selling of Europe, England's unemployment dole had merely helped to beget industrial paralysis and a breed of bribed idlers. These marched through London streets in small, mean processions flanked by policemen, their flags and their faces all one piece of ignoble discontent. Everyone in England seemed to be hard at work except the laboring classes, whose aim, apparently, was to make a second Russia of Great Britain. I know of a gardener who gave his employer notice, and on being asked if he was dissatisfied replied, no, but that he could get higher wages for walking in the procession of the unemployed.

Such was the background of my new pilgrimage, every day being crowded with experiences and conversations so vivid and engrossing, that only at certain times when I was alone did the menace which threatened us all—and is nearer now—darken my enjoyment.

I went over every foot of the devastated regions that I had seen two years before, and all the rest that I had not then seen—from Ypres to Alsace and everything between; the Somme four times, the Aisne four times, Champagne once, the Meuse-Argonne twice, St. Mihiel once, the Vosges once. I began these journeys early in February and finished them early in August, able so to watch the land in different seasons. I went as the guest and companion of French and English officers, with friends, and alone; meeting everywhere official and unofficial courtesy all the more friendly when it was discovered that I had come on my own errand, the representative of nobody and nothing except my own desire to ascertain the truth and tell it. I spent one deeply interesting week at Geneva, meeting under auspices that I can never forget the members of the Secretariat of the League of Nations. I heard of their work from themselves. I saw where they did it, I talked with several of them at length. I felt as if I listened to statesmen, not to politicians. I came away to grow steadily more sorry than ever that the reservations made by our Senate should have been rejected by Mr. Wilson. In the opinion of Lord Grey they were proper, and M. André Tardieu, one of the ablest minds in France, has written in his book that they were no grave modifications of the general document. I wish that Mr. Wilson had not kept us out of the League of Nations; we could do no better thing than to join it intelligently; various small countries have brought their difficulties to it with success, and its action seems steadily to be enlarging in scope and gaining in authority. Any device so new cannot win immediate acceptance, and none so complicated should have

been set going all at once. I am even of opinion that it
would be well if France could persuade herself to admit
Germany into the League if ever the improbable happen
and Germany give to her and to the world more solid
proofs than she has so far of "moral disarmament." I did
not travel in Germany, but I met, sometimes daily, English
and Americans and French who had just come from there,
and whose reports did not seem to me wholly reassuring.
Fortunately, the convictions which I have been able to
extract from my second pilgrimage in chaos are few and
clear:

Is France militaristic? No.

Is France idle? No.

Is France well off? No.

Are those Americans right who wish to keep up American isolation? No.

There they are, my four convictions; but before dealing
with them, I must say that nothing I found over there
so concerned me as the falling apart of England and
France and the falling together of England and Germany.
It seemed to me that England was forgetting "Der Tag"
rather soon, her battles in Flanders and Picardy rather
soon, and rather soon the twenty thousand manufactories
and five hundred thousand houses that in France had
been laid in partial or total ruin. Some of the reasons
were natural but none of them wise, as it seemed to me,
unless there were complete "moral disarmament" in Germany; and I remembered Benjamin Franklin at the
signing of the Declaration of Independence, when some
signer had remarked, "We must all hang together,"
and Franklin rejoined, "Otherwise we shall all hang
separately." It seemed to me that the English were forgetting prematurely that in 1914 Germany's plan had been
to hang several nations separately, and that only their
hanging together had stopped her.

Beneath the commercial reasons for this estrangement,
lurked two which may be termed psychological. There was
some jealousy. Each had been necessary to the other's

salvation, each would have liked it better if it had wholly saved the other—although, could this have happened, the other (whichever it was) would have been still less pleased. Second, the principle of old acquaintance was asserting itself quite obviously in a sort of inverted manner; one heard of unnatural friends and foes. Centuries of enmity lay between England and France, and but four years of a common cause. Once the common cause was removed, old acquaintance would not be forgot, and this acquaintance was hostile, while a long past of friendship lay between England and Germany. All this was very natural —and very undesirable. It was made worse by a misapplication of one of England's most magnanimous characteristics, shaking hands with your enemy and forgetting all about your quarrel, once you have soundly thrashed him. This does very well, provided two things are true: your enemy must give you an honest hand, and he must be your enemy alone; you can't gracefully shake hands with somebody else's enemy. It does not seem to me that Germany has given an honest hand to anybody (unless this has happened very lately indeed) and I know of no compelling reason to believe that she has ceased to be the enemy of France. Why should she? Why should she renounce—and especially in the circumstances of the Armistice and what has followed it—a plan of world dominion for which she has skilfully and subtly been made ready for so long a time? Prussia began to train the grandfathers of the Germans who fought this war. Every toy, every song, every book, every teaching from their nurseries to their manhood has instilled three generations with love of the Fatherland, contempt for other nations, faith for the sacred mission of Kultur, and conquest of the earth to spread its blessings—and for other benefits of a more material kind. Just because she failed in 1918, is all this to drop off Germany's back like a change of linen? Were I a German and had the deep and sincere belief and love of the Fatherland that is so fine a passion with them, it would not drop off me; it would be part of my soul.

"Oh, you're pro-French!" said an English friend to me.

Well, it must have happened to everyone to agree some-times with one friend rather than with another, and in this case I am bound to say that I think France has the right of it. Some of her spokesmen have put her, by their impatience, seemingly in the wrong; but in all faith and justice she is having what Americans call a "raw deal."

Besides the causes of disagreement already named, is one for which it is more difficult to find any solution. Without two things no nation can live; these are food and safety. To buy food England must sell goods and she needs Germany as a market. But France has to be safe; she has seen Germany overrun her twice in fifty years and these were not the first times, and Germany has a population of sixty-five million to France's thirty-eight. Moreover, France has to be rebuilt and this will keep Germany poor if she pays. But if Germany is poor, how is England to buy bread, since so much of her money comes from what she sells to Germany? If Germany is rich she can invade France again. Having just been half-killed, France does not wish to be wholly slain.

Here is a clash between two national instincts of self-preservation, and both are perfectly just; England must live, France must live; and this pressing fact causes each to have an inlook which is larger than their outlook.

To an Englishman one can say:

"Are you quite sure that Germany will never come after you again? Don't you remember how sure you were that she wasn't coming in 1914? Are 'Der Tag' and 'Gott strafe England' wholly turned to milk and honey? And aren't you forgetting France's experience? When you talk of her greedy indemnity, aren't you confusing indemnity with reparation?"

To a Frenchman one can say:

"Do you want England to go under? Don't you think she might be useful again some day on the Somme? And are you quite consistent when you insist—as at times you do—that Germany must be kept poor but that she must also pay you about eight hundred million dollars in gold a year?"

But to an American one must say:

"If you continue to consider that none of this has anything to do with you, you are the biggest fool of the lot."

They are all pushing each other off the plank. But need old acquaintances fall out so? Must either England or France go under? The thought is unbearable. Is there no way of taking turns at the plank, and making land together somehow? The question is really much wider and far worse than this: more than two nations are struggling in the water with not enough plank, the whole of western civilization is barely keeping its head above the surface; and I have slowly and very reluctantly been forced to the conviction that we Americans must throw this civilization a life-preserver; not because it is virtuous or humane to do so—although I think it would be that— but because I believe that, if we do not, we shall in the end be dragged under ourselves. Our ship of state is no longer a solitary craft sailing her own voyage to her own port, she is one of a fleet, and the ports are all the same: science has enabled such increasing millions to survive who used to perish; electricity has so enmeshed the world in its net, that we and our various welfares are all crowded and woven together in one vast common interest; we cannot get out of the net if we would, it is ultimately sink or swim, live or die together. Difference of race, of speech, of government, of religion, of anything you please, cannot outweigh the huge identity of bread. We can raise enough for ourselves no doubt for a while, but does any one who has grown beyond having a brain of one dimension, and can see commerce steadily and see it whole, imagine that we should do well if all the rest of the nations were to die of starvation? How about Utah Copper, Baldwin Locomotive Works, Amoskeag Mills, how about Lowell, Lawrence, Manchester, Fall River, Bridgeport, Pittsburgh, Birmingham? Could all the industries of our country sell each other enough to keep paying dividends

or the interest on their bonds? Were these to fail, all
fortunes in the country would be wiped out, there would
be no money to pay labor for the work of its hands, no
money to pay taxes to run the government, none for anything, and everything would stop; we should arrive where
Russia is. All Europe is in sight of such a state, and if
it overtakes Europe, our turn will inevitably and im-
placably be next. Ruin will stride over the sea and tear
tariffs and senators to scraps of paper. Since ours is the
only ship at present afloat, we shall have to throw some
sort of life-preserver to Europe. Our contribution to the
war should be, and will be, supplemented. Much money
that we lent England she spent upon our own munition
plants when they worked for her; only through this ex-
penditure were they sufficiently equipped to work for us
when we came into the war; without it, they could not
have supplied us. If we count as our supplemental contribution every dollar that we lent England which she
spent, so to speak, at the front, or which she loaned her
allies to spend there, we shall do no more than right.
We shall do less than right if we fail to do this.—But
when a man has wrecked his own life, it does not become
him very well to patronize those who are helping him to
repair it. Europe, through jealousies, meanness, greed,
and incompetence, has brought herself to grief. Less pat-
ronizing on the part of Europeans towards Americans
would oil the machinery quite a little.

France's irritation with the world in general and with
her recent ally, England, in particular, is just as natural
and just as little wise, as the feeling in England is about
her. France is not idle, not militaristic, nor well to do;
she knows that she is by no means out of the woods, and
she feels that she is forgotten.

Her enfevered state affected the pulse of almost every
sustained conversation that I held with her people. I
recall how it disturbed the serene and mellow loveliness
of a Sunday afternoon in Beaune, when spring was coming slowly up that way and the winter twigs seemed

visibly to be growing warm. I was defending England,
when my companion broke out:

"It is easy for them. They are as uninvaded as Germany herself."

"Think of their dead on your soil," I responded.

"We do think of them. Do they often think of ours?
They do not see our graves, while we see both ours and
theirs."

"They are not having an easy time. Their unemployed——"

"We have our own unemployed, as well as our own
dead."

"Yes, but yours—why, compared to theirs, your unemployed are a handful. Theirs run to the million, and yours
not even to the hundred thousand."

"I wonder if you think us French a little—Chinese?"

"Since you have said it—may I agree? Perhaps you
will not think it quite such bad manners when I add that
we Americans are also somewhat Chinese, and that I
fancy every nation has always been so, either moderately
or excessively; but I find only two great nations worse
than the French, Germany—and the Chinese!"

She laughed.

"I think that England is the least Chinese of us all,"
I ventured to add.

Her laughing stopped. "One sees well that after all
you are pro-English."

"My dear lady, in London they called me pro-French,
and two years ago our soldiers eyed me askance because
I insisted in speaking well of you to them. They were inclined to suspect that I was pro-everything except proAmerican. Sometimes I feel that the north pole must
be the only agreeable place left in the world because
nobody lives there. Now, at the risk of your displeasure,
I repeat, that to every unemployed Frenchman England
has about four hundred, and that compared to their need
to sell their wares, yours is almost negligible."

After a short silence, "Do you think," she asked, "that

if it was their Birmingham, their Leeds, their Sheffield,
their Canterbury Cathedral, that were in ruins, and their
wives and daughters who had been deported and debauched, they would enjoy hearing us ask them to excuse
Germany's debt?"

I could only meet it by saying, "Do you ever think
that what you French lost more than a hundred years ago
and have adjusted yourselves to, England lost all in a
moment in this war?—At Mons in 1914, at the Somme in
1916—the whole flower of her race, madame, her youth,
her promise, the fit lovers for her fittest maidens, the fine-
tempered steel of her future strength in peace or war, all
in a moment, madame, burned off the face of her world
like a beautiful forest."

Perhaps it made her think of some of her own dead,
for she flung up her hands.

"Ah," she exclaimed, "the horror of it all!"

"Horror indeed!"

More than once, that chill returned which had shot
through me as I went along the street in Amiens in April
1919, and I asked myself again the same question that I
had put then—were the signs of life around me true
stirrings of convalescence, or the last mechanical gestures
of a man who does not know that he has been killed?

I recall another talk, in Paris this time, and with an
American. He had prophesied the war in a book entitled
"Problems of Power," which Roosevelt advised all Americans to read, if they wished to understand Europe. Most
Americans have no such desire. His sagacity and knowledge are better appreciated in Europe than in this country; and as he continued to unfold and discuss one depth
after another of the world's desperate plight, it seemed
almost as if the lights grew dim.

"What you're saying, if it's true," I remarked, for my
pilgrimage was still at its beginning and my eyes not
yet half open, "is that you and I, sitting here at this
table, are living in the presence of a tragedy that beats
Æschylus and Sophocles and Hamlet and Lear and

Othello and every worst thing in history that we can think of, all rolled into one."

"I think so."

"You might almost imagine," I continued, "that malignant gods had sat above the world, up in some hell, and deliberately thwarted by black magic every human effort to save us from this, and deliberately helped every blunder and ignorance and vanity that would plunge us deeper into it."

"Yes, it tempts one to that superstition."

"And here sit you and I, enjoying a good dinner!"

"Would it noticeably help matters if we abstained?" he inquired; "the milk is spilled."

XXIV

OVER THE SPILLED MILK

THE reader will recognize almost every fact in this chapter, of which not a word would need to be written, were our memories more retentive and coherent. History sweeps through each day in a pouring spring flood, and on its surface events come whirling by like the leaves of a torn book. We see each leaf, it rushes on, the next follows; none are put together in our brains, and so the import of what is a continuous story and a significant warning sweeps by us in uncomprehended fragments.

In March 1918, Germany showed what she thought of the fourteen points set forth by Mr. Wilson as a basis of peace. She launched an attack upon the 5th British Army which came within a hair's breadth of taking Amiens, of cutting apart the British and French, and of winning the war; she continued to launch attacks until she saw that the jig was up. We knew what her peace terms were to be, did she win. These were not at all like the fourteen points; those were a repudiation of the spoils system between victor and vanquished in war; by Germany's terms her whole war bill was to be paid and whole countries were to be annexed.

Not quite five months later, Ludendorff perceived that Germany had failed and must ask for an armistice. His opinion gradually prevailed in his country. One does not see what right Germany in her hour of failure had to peace terms which she had not accepted in the hour of success. It is as if the owner of a race horse had rejected an offer of twenty thousand dollars for the animal, and then after it went lame, stipulated for the same price. Germany was encouraged to do this by the letters which

239

Mr. Wilson wrote to Max of Baden without consulting the Allies, who at that time were driving the German Army out of France from the Channel to the Vosges. One can see that American prestige, our help that saved the day, led to the fourteen points being accepted "in principle" by the Allies as a basis of peace; at such a moment, whatever the Allies might think, they could not ignore the apparent spokesman and actual symbol of the United States.

Through October 1918 the speed of our success heightened until it became what General Mangin has called it, a flight to victory; and during these days Foch was turning over in his mind the terms of the Armistice. In meditating what terms should be exacted, he said one day:

"They have fought bravely. They shall keep their arms."

It was the word of a gallant soldier, it was a chivalrous gesture to heart-sick thousands who had bled in the German cause, and whose fault the Prussian crime certainly was not. Grant at Appomattox did the same to Lee, and his act and Lee's equally generous response to it have set both men on a high pinnacle in history; but Prussia does not resemble Robert E. Lee.

General Bliss, our member of the Supreme War Council, was of a mind different from Foch. On the 28th of October he offered an addition to the terms of the Armistice, of which the following is a translation of one paragraph:

"First, the Associated Powers exact complete disarmament and demobilization of the enemy on land and sea, leaving only a home force deemed sufficient by the Associated Powers for the maintenance of order within the enemy's country. This of itself means the evacuation of all invaded territory and its evacuation without arms, not by soldiers armed or partially armed."

On the ground that it would be difficult to carry out, Foch had already rejected a similar proposal made to him by M. Clemenceau, and probably for this reason the suggestion of General Bliss was not sent to him.

Ignorant of these important links in the chain, I had constantly inquired, first in England and then in France:

"Why was the German army allowed to go home with its arms and banners?"

"Oh, one didn't want to humiliate them too much!"

This was the answer of a distinguished British general.

"But do they seem to have appreciated such magnanimity?"

He admitted that they had not.

When I asked the same question in Paris, a member of the government replied:

"Foch never dreamed that the Armistice would not be soon followed by a peace treaty, signed in Berlin with the Allied armies standing at attention, and the German people looking on."

I must have asked six or seven Frenchmen about it, and perhaps what one elderly and seasoned diplomat answered sums it up:

"Foch spoke like a soldier." And then, after a pause, he added with a gentle smile: "but it is a pity."

A clue to what Foch had begun to think by March 1919, with four months gone since the Armistice and no treaty in sight, has been dexterously pulled out of the tangle by Mr. Fullerton, the author of "Problems of Power." Speaking at a public dinner, the marshal had said: "An armistice is the equivalent of a capitulation." When his speech appeared in print, he had made one change: "An armistice is merely a capitulation." Mr. Fullerton adds that although Foch did accept the Armistice, it was in the faith that statecraft was not extinct. The reader will find translated in Appendix B, the strange, sad interview given by Foch on November 8th, 1920.

We have the word of Colonel House (*Public Ledger*, Philadelphia, July 12th, 1920) that a plan for peace at once had followed straight upon the Armistice; a pre-

liminary treaty to be signed by Christmas, covering
broadly the army, the navy, reparation, and frontiers;
and that this would have been the natural step to take
while all the Allied armies were confronting Germany,
full of fight and elated with victory.

Then why was this step not taken? Terror filled the
German generals during these October-November weeks:
one of them cried out frankly to his colleagues that their
army was demoralized, incapable any longer to stave the
Allies off, and that if a halt were not called they would
be soon in Cologne. These generals were too elderly, too
unstrung, so they themselves declared, to meet Foch, and
so Erzberger was sent in their stead. Later, as we know,
he ceased to be Prussian enough for the Junkers, and
they assassinated him.

But, if it was the natural step, why no treaty by
Christmas?

During the October week when Foch was pondering
the Armistice, I was staying at Sagamore Hill; and,
"Can you explain," I asked Mr. Roosevelt one day,
"Mr. Wilson's writing notes to Germany over the heads
of the Allies when Germany is in full retreat?"

"Don't you see?" he said. "This war may last until
spring, or it may finish any day; and Mr. Wilson intends to go over and sit at the peace table and be the
first president of the League of Nations. He is writing
these notes to prepare for that."

It was not then known so generally as it is now that
the idea of being world mediator had been present in
Mr. Wilson's mind since 1916. Mr. Roosevelt probably
guessed it from the readiness to offer Europe the benefits
of his mediation which Mr. Wilson had already displayed.

Whatever we may forget, all of us remember Armistice Day. Our cities danced in their streets, scraps of
paper fluttered down like golden snow in the sun from
twenty stories of windows to the pavement, bands and
leaping processions came round corners, a belt of steam

whistles blew among the suburbs that encircled our industrial centres. In Paris our doughboys rushed along in camions, whirling girls from the sidewalk up into their arms. London became a wilderness of joy, relief made us ready for the new heaven and new earth which Mr. Lloyd George later promised us; we were with him when he said in December that Germany must pay to the last cent for the wrong she had done, and again when he said that the Kaiser must be tried at Westminster.

Just before all this rejoicing, we had held an election. Mr. Wilson had requested us to vote only for Democrats, as he needed Democrats to support his policies. It was remembered that upon the day he gave his war message to Congress, the leader of the Republicans had tendered him that party's cordial and total help in carrying on the war, and it was also remembered that numerous Democrats in both the House and Senate had voted against measures of defence and preparation offered by Republicans. Mr. Wilson's request did not have a happy effect upon the country, and was disregarded at the elections; but this failed to reach the general mind of England and France.

No treaty was signed by Christmas, but Mr. Wilson sailed for Europe, as Mr. Roosevelt had predicted. A group of senators, by no means negligible in number, somewhat formally sounded a note of warning that they would not accept certain provisions if these appeared in any draft of a League of Nations. The rumor will not quite die that this and other later and important news was prevented from crossing the ocean both east and west. I know that the result of our November election, and the warning of the senators, and the fact that Mr. Wilson did not represent the unanimous opinion of our country, came to public attention in Paris through a series of articles by M. Chéradame in *La Democratie Nouvelle*. How much impression these made I cannot say. But it is plain that no matter what was known in

England and France, they could hardly ask the President of the United States for his credentials; as the editor of *Punch* put it to me in London:

"We had to behave."

So did we. How were Americans to repudiate their own President, and even had they wished to do so, by what means could it have been done? Such a thing as an American President twice in two months sailing three thousand miles away from his desk, and staying away four months the second time, was something new; but the cause was new. Americans looked on with various opinions, and hoped for the best.

Early in 1919, Mr. Wilson returned from his first absence, and during his brief stay here he spoke about the League of Nations in glowing general terms, but without making clear its concrete significance for us, or answering the specific doubts of the dissenting senators, except by somewhat sweeping denunciation and one threat. He would weave the Peace and the League, he said, so completely together that they could not be severed. This was his parting word, he sailed the next day; and I think it may be safely assumed that what he counted on was not so much European ignorance about the November election or the American Constitution as that the Senate, when he should press against its head a treaty signed by England, France, and Italy, would not dare to break the\heart of the world (as he phrased it later) by refusing to go along with him. His miscalculation involved us all in European displeasure for a while; even two years later I met the lingering resentment.

"Does your country always change its opinions so easily?"

"I am not quite sure that I follow you."

"Your President demanded a League of Nations. We bowed to his pleasure—and failed to please you."

"Do your public men always represent the whole of your public opinion? Allow me to felicitate you."

"We express our dissent."

"We expressed ours in the election before Mr. Wilson went to you."

"Ah yes, your elections! But you have so many and they are so far away. We do not understand them."

"Quite evidently you misunderstood that one. But there was something less recent. By our Constitution treaties are to be made by the President with the advice and consent of the Senate. Our Constitution has been in print a hundred years."

"We know so little about your institutions."

"That is equally evident. But I have never heard that ignorance of the law constitutes any defence in either civil or criminal cases."

Of such conversations I held a number, sometimes less sharply edged, but once or twice more so, when I found myself adding:

"You have always shown such a sincere interest in our dollars, and lately so much in our military aid in case of further unprovoked assault from Germany, that I wonder if it would not be well for you to turn your attention to some aspect of us less directly useful to you?"

I had to shade my replies according to the shade of civility meted to me on each occasion, and I was always glad when the talk ended amicably, and never sorry when it did not. It was every American's duty to set his country straight, after the miscalculation of Mr. Wilson.

No man's landing on a foreign shore was ever like Mr. Wilson's first coming to Europe. That had been awaited like an almost miraculous event. The people, the simple rustic people, broken in heart and fortune, thirsty for some ideal, longing for some touch that should lift them from despair, stretched out their hands to him. They had read his words and they passionately believed that he was bringing to them a gospel of balm which should heal their world. His picture hung on the walls of expectant thousands. Even their more sophisticated leaders, with whom he had said that he was going to

match his mind, supposed that a matured plan lay behind
the vision which he had belatedly borrowed from the
League to Enforce Peace, and that it was not all mere
lofty words. His first landing was in December. When,
after half a year, he started home the second time, his
picture was gone from the walls, and Europe's moment
of idealism had passed into cynical laughter. The recoil
was also like nothing that history had ever seen. Mr.
Wilson had matched his mind with his colleagues'—and
the wave upon which he had ridden first to Europe's
shores had ebbed as far below the level of justice to him
as it had previously surged above it. He had come to the
conference with a noble idea—the only man who so came,
and he came asking for nothing—the only man again.
What had happened?

Because of his letters to Max of Baden, Germany, who
had no moral right to his fourteen points, trusted that
these would yet save her skin; upon these same points
each country based various hopes of peace and prosperity.
All were disenchanted soon or late.

One point of the fourteen, the freedom of the seas,
had gone early in the game—for game it turned out to
be, every one for himself, and Mr. Wilson no match for
any of them. To keep his League of Nations afloat he
flung overboard all his other points: Shantung went to
Japan; open covenants were not openly arrived at—they
cannot be, they can only be adopted openly—but when
one day it leaked out that Mr. Wilson was dealing openly
with one set of Russian delegates, while he was privately
dealing with their antagonists, a large piece of popular
faith in him cracked off. Self-determination was enforced
where it was not wanted, denied where it should have
been in all fairness applicable; Italy, Hungary, Austria
were alike aggrieved, the confidence of friends and foes
was equally destroyed. Germany found that through a
trick at the eleventh hour, and in spite of the unanimous
opposition of the American experts, Mr. Wilson had consented that her reparations include pensions for injured

French soldiers as well as damages to French civilians. For this and the taking of her colonies Germany fell away from him. An early and deepening chill had cooled French enthusiasm; day after day he put off his visit to the devastated regions. The French had expected him to go at once, and see with his own eyes what they had suffered.

"Is he going this morning?"

"Didn't he go today?"

"Isn't he going tomorrow?"

These questions were asked all over France each day after his arrival; and his explanation that he feared such a sight might prejudice him too much against Germany did not help to keep him warm in the popular affections, any more than did his gaiety at lunch in Soissons on the one day when he did finally visit the ruins. This disappointment to the French heart changed to a more active sentiment when it turned out in later days that his promise of future military aid was, without senatorial endorsement, void. It was after this that his name one night was painted out by unknown hands on the signs along the avenue that bears it.

In various books and in many discussions, the weight of blame for the treaty's shortcomings has been laid upon this or that particular pair of shoulders among "The Big Four";—they were more often the Big Three, if Signor Orlando took as little part in the other discussions as he did in those concerning Upper Silesia, which are given in Appendix A. This way of fixing the responsibility is not borne out by such facts as one can learn; good and bad were alike the collaboration of all, because all in the end accepted or rejected the wishes of any one; Mr. Wilson happens to have suffered from a heavier popular reaction because higher popular hopes were set upon him—and, to my thinking, his own contribution remains the finest in idea. Unluckily, to gain its adoption he assented to many less admirable provisions.

The British Prime Minister's lack of plan seems due

to the financial and labor powers behind him at home;
his zigzag moods too much resembled the gestures of
something jerked by strings with no mind of its own,
and they brought upon him that caustic comment of M.
Clemenceau, that Mr. Lloyd George thought only in
terms of parliamentary majorities. Like many democratic leaders he was unsteadied by the eternal jar between
domestic and foreign policy. Very late indeed in the
deliberations of the Big Three, he returned one morning
from one of his swift visits to London, and proceeded to
insist upon the uprooting and reversal of so much which
had been settled, that silence fell around him. Mr. Wilson was described to me as leaning his deacon's head
against the back of his chair and gazing immovably at
the ceiling, while Mr. Lloyd George harangued with increasing energy. When after some fifteen minutes he
came to a stop, Mr. Wilson uttered four words:

"You make me sick."

If the Upper Silesia conversations are a fair sample
of the rest, it is evident that M. Clemenceau was far
clearer sighted and much better acquainted with Europe
than either of his colleagues, and he seems to me to have
risen nearest to the level of statesmanship; but he had
too much inlook, too little outlook, saw France as a horse
in blinders sees the road ahead of him and nothing each
side of it; on that road was Germany to be got out of
the way, no matter what else happened. He did not dis-
cern that right and left loomed a menace to everybody,
more imminent than the German danger to France. None
of them seemed sufficiently to have perceived and guarded
against this; they were blind to the economical prospect,
they saw the political only, they failed to recognize that
henceforth commercial and financial team-work between
all nations could alone repair the destruction already
wrought, and make safe the bread and the money of the
world; that whatever image and superscription a coin
may bear, whether it be Cæsar's or the American eagle's,
humanity has in the end a purse in common. This is

clearer to many today than it was then, but warnings
were not wanting—for instance, that of Garvin, editor
of the London *Observer*, in his book on what ought to be
the economic foundations of the peace. In a word, Foch
the soldier did a clean job in the fall, and in the following
spring the politicians—did not. Mortals could not have
dealt successfully with a task so monstrous; the blunder
was not to have set themselves a simpler one.

And Germany? What of her during the fatal and
precious months between the Armistice and the com-
pletion of the treaty?

On November 11th, 1918, Foch had beaten her to her
knees; she was in deadly fear, abject, unnerved; she
thought the Allies would be in Cologne within a few
days, and she threw up her hands and cried "Kamerad!"

Not such was her attitude on that May 7th, 1919, when
she received the treaties from the hands of her conquerors.
She had regained something more than confidence. Very
naturally she had kept her ears and eyes open while the
Allies delayed and discussed. She had seen no peace
signed in Berlin by Christmas; what she did see was her
army returning with its arms and its banners; what she
heard was, that it was undefeated. She erected arches,
she strewed flowers, she played triumphant music for
this undefeated army. She got up from her knees and
listened, and looked all the harder. She saw the sailings
back and forth of Mr. Wilson, she saw Signor Orlando
rush away from the conference to Rome in a rage over
Fiume; a hundred signs during those weeks showed her
that her recent enemies who had stood together and so
defeated her were now falling apart; and her despair
changed to hope. Who can say how much of the increasing gossip and cynicism in Paris, as the conference
wrangled on through those weeks, did not reach her
attentive ears? She must have heard that they were
"making the world safe for Hypocrisy"; that when
Orlando went to Rome, the French had struck Italy's
name from the list of contracting parties in a docu-

mentary preamble to the treaty, and had to be persuaded
by their colleagues to re-insert it quickly in ink, lest
Orlando return and discover the meditated slight, and
deplorable discords ensue. It was told at dinners in Paris
that one of the army of experts gathered there had been
reproached by an actress for rewarding her too slightly
for the pleasure of her company.

"My nature is not thought stingy," he replied. "Only
this morning I gave a whole province to some people I
have never seen."

If, in April 1919, I could hear comments like this upon
the lightness with which the old nations of Europe were
being sliced and repasted into new ones, is it not likely
that the acute ears of Germany heard much more than
did my innocent American ones?

When her emissaries came to Versailles to receive the
treaty, she had been up from her knees for a long while.
This was plainly to be seen by their deportment on that
Wednesday, May 7th, 1919. On the day preceding, at
the brief, stiff ceremony when these delegates presented
their credentials to M. Cambon, the fewest possible words
had been spoken, and nothing was to be observed except
the gait of the approaching Germans and the color of
their complexions. The satisfactory inference drawn
from these signs was dispersed next day in the dining-
room of the Trianon Palace at Versailles. The great
ceremony was held there, all the council present, splendid
sunshine pouring in upon the room, blossoms on the
fruit trees outside in the garden. The Allied delegates
sat waiting amid a silent swirl of historic association,
especially the memory of that 18th of January, 1871,
when Bismarck the conqueror sat here and dictated German terms to the French. The door opened, a voice
announced the German delegates, the council rose. The
Germans walked to their chairs and sat down forthwith;
then, noticing that the company was standing, they stood
for a moment and reseated themselves. M. Clemenceau,
presiding, said a few words, Brockdorff-Rantzau was

handed the text of the treaty; he set it on the table, laid
his gloves on it, put his spectacles on, and read in German a lengthy and unexpected address. While the inter-
preters translated each passage twice, into English and
into French——

"Come nearer!" snapped M. Clemenceau, "I can't
hear you."

The address went on, and the sad-eyed Foch sat there
with his colleagues, present against his will, because he
thought his absence would show the enemy that he dis-
agreed about the terms of the treaty. He dissented deeply
from its insecurities, and had said so, and had been
ignored. He looked at the German's manner, noticed the
tone of his voice, and heard from him that the German
people had gone to war in self-defence, that there should
be a committee of neutrals to examine who was guilty;
this and more he with the Allied council heard said by the
seated Brockdorff-Rantzau during the better part of an
hour, and then the ceremony ended.

"It is galling," said Mr. Lloyd George to M. André
Tardieu as they came away, "to be the winner and have
to listen to such words as those."

They would not have had to listen, there would have
been no such words if, instead of dialogues, delays, and
discords for six months, the German army had gone
home without its flags and arms, and the German nation
had seen a treaty signed before Christmas at Berlin, with
the Allied armies present. The object lesson, the fruit of
victory, the chance of peace, all was missed by the
politicians in the spring after the soldiers had done a
clean job in the fall.

"Our alliance," wrote Pertinax in the *Echo de Paris*
next morning, "has not based its provisions as prudence
should have dictated, on the assumption of the worst, on
the possibility of a Germany that may regain its strength
and its unity."

A German in Switzerland, Carl Rosemeier, published
on that same morning a plainer piece of prophecy:

"They will cheat you yet, those Junkers! Having won
half the world by bloody murder, they are going to win
the other half with tears in their eyes, crying for mercy."

A verification of this began immediately; all Germany
at once set up an outcry over the treaty, and this served
its end during the days between May 7th and that June
day when the treaty was signed. Apparently, as is to be
seen in the conversations about Upper Silesia which
occurred in this period, the outcry alarmed Mr. Lloyd
George more than it did M. Clemenceau or Mr. Wilson.
They do not seem to have been afraid that the Germans
would refuse to sign the treaty; he seems to have been so
nervous and restless about this that he proposed soften-
ings and conciliations with which his colleagues seldom
agreed, and which brought one day that remark from
Mr. Wilson as he leaned his head back in his chair. Mr.
Lloyd George carried some of his points—it can never
be known whether or not they were necessary—and the
treaty was signed.

"The Germans will not observe the most equitable
stipulations," remarked M. Clemenceau on that day,
"unless they feel that force stands behind justice."

That was in June 1919, and in May 1921, a German
said to a friend of mine:

"As an American this will not interest you; but Germany does not intend to pay France, and France is not
clever enough to make her. Were the situation reversed,
we should be clever enough to make France pay."

Equally plain talk came from General Ludendorff later
in the summer of 1920. In addressing the students at
Koenigsberg, he referred to Upper Silesia, and said:

"I have no doubt that our country's destiny will sooner
or later be decided by a battle for the eastern region. . . .
The greater our country's need, the closer shall we rally
round the Prussian flag."

No blame or shame attaches to him for that; it is the
word of a man true to his country and his faith; the
blame falls on those who shut their eyes to all this.

And so, seven months after the clean job of Foch, the peace was signed, giving us Mr. Lloyd George's new heaven and new earth, and the labors of the "Big Three" were ended. Upon M. Clemenceau fell unjust wrath; the jar between French foreign and domestic policy shook him from public into private life. He deserved better from his people. Mr. Wilson came home bearing the treaty like a magic talisman, flawless, to be accepted just so. Apparently he knew about nothing it contained except his League of Nations, was unaware that he had helped to establish a spoils system in the teeth of his fourteen points. He had made promises alone which two were needed to make, and wrath fell upon him at home and abroad. Mr. Lloyd George came off best at home, hardly as well elsewhere. Together, the three had invaded commercial thoroughfares as Germany invaded Belgium; had shuffled and re-dealt frontiers as if they were a pack of cards; and many of their arrangements seem as if they had supposed that they could change human nature with a drop of ink. The new heaven and new earth in which we are living is their work.

XXV

WHEN Germany threw up her hands and cried "Kamerad!" she was spared having that done to her which she had done to others; not one blade of her grass was trodden down, not one invading footstep crossed her boundaries, not one hair of her head was singed; but her conquerors were agreed that she must make good the havoc she had wrought. Then these conquerors failed to strike while the iron was hot. They doubled the error of a premature armistice by a belated peace, and by so doing handed over their victory to Germany; and Foch, who had delivered the goods, saw these not only squandered but never paid for. To the tragedy of the war is added this sardonic mockery of the peace: defeated Germany, who was spared invasion, is now not only to be pardoned her sentence of reparation, her conquerors must also stretch out united hands and help to lift her from the economic collapse which she brought upon herself by her assault upon them. Our civilization must heal Germany or perish itself by the contagion of economic pestilence. To some men of finance there seems no other way out.

Does any literature of any age contain a drama parallel to this?—wherein the half-killed victim of an enslaving tyrant in order to save his own life must nurse the sick tyrant back to health, knowing all the while that once the tyrant is firm on his legs he will try the same trick again? Let us talk and reason moderately and try to keep our heads if we can.

The opinion of these financiers would weigh more with me did I not recall their prophecies at the outset of the war and during its course. They proved that the war would be short, because no nation could go on paying for it; it was Kitchener, a soldier, who said that it would last three years. The view of the financiers looked at the time unanswerable on paper—I confess that I cannot answer their present view—on paper; I can only reflect that human effort contains surprises which upset the wisest calculations, and that perhaps there is more life in us and in Mother Earth than appears. Nevertheless, that is no warrant for a blind optimism such as Americans love to indulge in; the early spoken warning of Mr. Keynes has come nearer the truth than the new heaven and new earth promised us by Mr. Lloyd George, and the United States can no more turn its back on the illness of Europe than one Siamese twin can ignore his brother's jaundice. We shall have to do something, and the sooner the better, but not over-hastily. Just how extinct is Germany, just how much is she shamming dead? It will be very well indeed to keep in mind the warning of the German Carl Rosemeier, published the morning after the treaty was delivered to his fellow-countrymen:

"They will cheat you yet, those Junkers."

Once a Wall Street financier, imprisoned for his misdeeds, was pardoned by President Taft upon a doctor's word that his health was failing. Upon being set free, his health returned immediately. It is well known that women often have sent flowers and refreshments to a condemned murderer, but bestowed not a crumb or a thought upon the family of the victim. Should not the quality of mercy be more strained than this? Too many people today go about talking of the hardships of Germany, and quite pass over the hardships of France. Many of these persons wonder if the fault was Germany's, or are sure that even if she may have been guilty, she is sorry for it now. If they are asked the reason for their opinion, they fade into vague generalizations. Even a simple question to the point has been known to embarrass a financier; one banker who had recently returned from Germany and was asserting that she had no money wherewith to pay her reparation, was asked why she did not get some of the millions which her profiteers were investing all over the world. He replied:

"Oh, that is another story," and proceeded to enlarge upon how hard Germany was at work.

We do not need to be told that. War has not made Germany idle or inefficient. The superb manner in which she ran her administrative machinery, the perfect physical training of her body politic and economic, put all other nations to shame, and made our own municipal and State and Federal Governments look like flabby amateurs beside a professional athlete. We could do nothing better than imitate her methods in political housekeeping, and the nearer we came to them the better off in health, and safety, and order, and pocket we should be; but what we particularly need to do in these days is to find out how inanimate Germany really is, to watch the straws that show which way the wind blows, to judge her by what she has done and is doing: "by their fruits ye shall know them"—that is the eternal test.

The German people are most certainly at work, and I doubt if in any of the Allied countries a list of dividends like the following could be paralleled:

	First year after the war per cent.	Second year after the war per cent.
Bremen Linoleum Company	10	30
Unger and Hoffman	15	15
German Rail Transport	15	40
German Wool Manufacturing	10	30
Saxon Cartonnage	17½	20
Ottenser Iron Works	10	15
Leipsig Cotton	21	25
Poppe and Wirth	20	30

These figures were published in the Norwegian *Courier* of March 8th, 1921.

For the third year since the war the dividends were as

large and larger, and I could give a longer list of them, but the above seem enough for my point.

Where does the money go? Industrial leaders in Germany are known to have on deposit, at home and abroad, securities worth one billion dollars. Germany taxes her people $13.88 per head, in France it is $45.22. Bread in Germany costs three and a half cents a kilogram, in France eight and a quarter. A ten-ton railway car can be transported a thousand kilometres in Germany for sixty dollars, it costs nearly one hundred and eighty in France. The German foreign debt is less than one billion, that of France more than ten billion.

It seems to me that straws like these show which way the wind blows; and here are two others of a different sort:

A friend of mine, lately in Germany, looked out of his window at the Hotel Bellevue in Dresden. The Opera House stood opposite and some heavy scenery was being brought in a dray and unloaded. Some five or six men lifted ponderous columns and steps of temples out of the dray and into the Opera House in some five or six minutes. These men did not make a needless movement of arm or leg, it was all a precise piece of team-work with them, and their job, performed by our undrilled American methods, would have taken at least half an hour.

My second straw is an instance of mental and moral drill. This same friend was in Berlin, and was being shown a particular quarter where the mob of the brief revolution had swept through. A space of lawn lay in their course, and my friend pointed to the rich and flourishing grass.

"No revolution ever trod on that," he said; "that shows years of care."

"They went round it, naturally," said his German companion, and pointed to the sign "verboten."

Drill did its magic work when our soldiers came to occupy Coblenz and its neighborhood. They were not well received during the first hours of their arrival; they met with sullen manners and scowling looks, which is hardly to be wondered at. Had I been a German at Coblenz, I

should not have felt like greeting the American army with
a smile and a hand outstretched. The next morning, all
was different at Coblenz; it was welcome, and geniality,
and What-can-I-do-for-you? The doughboy did not reflect
deeply over this agreeable but unnaturally sudden change,
he merely began to like the Germans better than he had
liked the French. It was his officers who used their reason
and discerned that some wise observer had sent word to
Germany's control office of the rudeness shown the new
arrivals, and that the office had at once given out the needful direction, changing German manners overnight.

Many accounts of Germany's actual political state reach
us, some quite plainly meant for uncritical and credulous
readers, but others as plainly honest and well observed.
One derives from these latter the impression that the
present German Government wishes to fulfill its obligations to France and the world—is, in a word, reasonable
and well disposed; but that it is weak, that the true power
lurks behind and is in the hands of a few very able captains of industry, who are playing chess with the Reichstag and all other pieces on the board—pawns, knights,
bishops, castles, and even kings—for their own benefit.
What is their own benefit? That question is answered
satisfactorily by no one; we are left uncertain what these
strong and resourceful men, who seem to be the real rulers
of Germany, intend. Are they at the bottom of the unrest
which has been playing like sheet lightning over the question of Upper Silesia? Were they of General Ludendorff's
mind when he told the college students of Koenigsberg
that a battle would some day settle that question, and
Prussia's army would be victorious there through the same
drill and discipline and trust in its leaders which had
won at Tannenberg? I don't know; but when I meet those
who are inclined to release the prisoner because his doctor
says that he is dying, or who are sending flowers and refreshments to the outlaw across the Rhine, I think it well
to remind them of that billion dollars invested in foreign
securities, of those dividends paid by German corporations

since the war, and of the difference between the German and the French tax rate.

"They will cheat you yet, those Junkers."

I do not say that they will, I do not know that they will not; I know only that straws show which way the wind blows.

Returning travellers bring word of the shifting tides in Germany's party politics—which currents are flowing strong and which seem to be weakening; and these reports do not always match. All are interesting and none seem important, because they tell of what goes on near the surface and not of the invisible ground swell, at which one can only guess. There is something to be gathered by the number of seats which this or that party has lost or gained in the Reichstag; socialism would seem on the whole to be on the wane, with a tide setting toward the return to traditional institutions, by no means forgotten, tenaciously remembered, increasingly regretted. In the deep woods are huts upon whose walls the royal portraits still hang, they are being put back upon walls from which they were removed three years ago; it is against the law, but the law does not seem to mind. One may be fairly sure that when a dreamy, poetic, and long-memoried people, with a strong accumulation of legend in their subconsciousness, have gone to war, and drunk their beer, and begotten their sons, for centuries under the rule of dukes and princes and kings, serving their families, wearing their colors, singing their songs, dancing at their pageants, dying in their battles, and faring all the while as well as their neighbors, that the taste for their old leaders will die hard in them, and they will not immediately drop it all and turn into a self-governing race because they have been prescribed a tablespoonful of democracy three times a day after meals. But even if we do wake up some morning far or near to see a throne in Germany once more, and some dynastic family from Prussia, or Bavaria, or elsewhere seated upon it, not even this seems to me the important point for us: it is not what form of govern-

ment this strong-souled and persistent people may keep
or change to, it is what of their ambitions will survive
beneath any garb, what they are going to do, what will be
done through them, what young Germans who are now
five, ten, or fifteen years old are being taught—since they
are the Germany of tomorrow.

Well, some of this is known. Old Germans are saying,
and young ones are believing, that in 1914 the Fatherland
was obliged to fight a war of self-defence, particularly
against Russia; Russia had been making ready to attack
it for months. One does not know how an old German
would meet such a comment as this:

"But you know that on the night of July 31st, 1914,
when Austria was showing signs of drawing back from the
gulf to whose edge you had pushed her, and had entered
into amicable conversation with Russia, you cut it short in
haste and declared war upon Russia yourselves."

I cannot say how this would be met, but in the Fatherland it does not have to be; the unfledged nestling German
asks no questions, he opens wide his mind and what he
is to know is dropped into it by the Prussian parent bird,
and consequently, when he flies from the nest, it is with
a string from Berlin tied securely to his brain. Did the
war break that string? Hardly. The great skill in the
devising and instilling of lies for an end, by which Germany was duped and directed into the war, is not at all
defunct. It does not invent imaginary bombs at Nurem-
berg any more, or publish Roosevelt's congratulation to
the Kaiser on his victorious entry into Paris, or stamp
the compressed fuel-bricks for locomotives with "Gott
strafe England"; but it circulates almanacs with saint-
like images of the Hohenzollern family and their military
glories, and pious texts beneath them; and it makes toys
for children, boxes of little French houses and churches,
and little guns with which to knock them down on the nursery floor. Could anything be more natural, more excellent
for the young of a nation that had a great predatory pur-

pose to implant in its people? And what people has ever proved by temperament more politically docile than the Germans, less instinctively revolutionary, better adapted to receiving impressions like wax, and retaining them like adamant? Their subtle educators never miss a trick. On the morrow of Mr. Hughes' proposal for disarmament, out came the German papers, like the well-drilled chorus that they are, with exclamations about "Yankee hypocrisy." There again they present us with a straw for our guidance: the word "disarmament" is to be associated with the word "hypocrisy," and thus dropped into the docile German mind. It matters not whose the mailed fist be at present; whether imperial or industrial, it is there; a soft glove has been drawn over it, that is all—and sometimes there are little holes in the glove through which the metal gleams.

As no people is more politically docile than the Germans, so also none has ever run more true to form. Merely as a revelation of the changeless persistence of their character, it is deeply interesting to read that, in the first century after Christ, a Roman general named Velleius Paterculus wrote of them that they were "cunning in ferocity, born to lie"—to read this and to remember that in 1914 at Fontenoy, they displayed flags of truce, and when the French accepted this signal in good faith and walked up to receive the surrender, the Germans killed them; to remember that in 1918 near Cambrai, they left behind them as they retreated that live kitten nailed above the concealed mine which killed the British soldiers who hurried to release it from its torture.

Equally interesting is it to find Tacitus writing in the fourth book of his history:

"There will always be similar motives to excite the Germans to invade the Gauls. It is lust, greed, the desire to change place, to quit their marshes and solitudes, to seize upon a fertile soil and its inhabitants——"

And after this to read in a number of that illustrated

family paper the *Gartenlaube,* published in 1874, an article with pictures of the Marne valley, by a German who had walked through it, and who concludes:

"Your heart bleeds in your breast to think that this splendid region does not belong to Germany."

And finally to read the remarks of two Prussian generals, von Clausewitz and von Schellendorff:

"Let us not forget the task of civilization which providence by its decrees lays upon us. As Prussia was by destiny the kernel of Germany, so Germany regenerated shall be the kernel of the future empire of the West.

"That none may go in ignorance, we proclaim that henceforth our continental nation has a right not to the North Sea only, but also to the Mediterranean and Atlantic. Consequently we shall absorb, one after another, all provinces which border on Prussia; we shall annex successively Denmark, Holland, Belgium . . . then Trieste and Venice, and finally the northern part of France from the Somme to the Loire."

General von Schellendorff, in commenting upon this prospectus, said:

"The style of old Clausewitz is very soft. He was a poet who put rose-water in his inkstand. Now it is with blood that matters of war should be written, and the next war will be atrocious; between Germany and France nothing but a duel to the death is adequate. To be or not to be, that is the question which can be settled only by the ruin of one of these antagonists.

". . . We shall annex . . . the north of France from the Somme to the Loire. This program, which we announce without fear, is no fool's work; this empire which we intend to found will not be a Utopia: we have in hand even now the means of realizing it."

In nineteen hundred years, the marshes and solitudes across the Rhine have become miracles of fertility and comfort; but "the greed, the desire to change place, to seize upon a fertile soil and its inhabitants," which Tacitus recorded, we too have beheld; and in thinking it over, once again the acute judgment of Heine is borne out.

"The German is stupid," he says; "educate him and he becomes malignant."

Prussia's intensive education of the race of Luther and Beethoven has made it the race which bombarded the cathedral of Reims and nailed the live kitten to the door.

Midway in the long chain of testimony comes Dante, with his word about the *Tedeschi lurchi*. This poet of Latin race and refinement had seen plenty of Germans in Italy, and his word *lurchi*, though it is not quite easy to find any single English adjective which expresses it perfectly, is exactly translated by the use to which the piano was put by the German officers billeted at the farm where we slept; by what I heard about the daily personal habits of the interned prisoners at Fort Oglethorpe; by what I read in the letters of the orchestra leader; and by what the Germans did in public to Belgium women—all is a translation of Dante's word *lurchi*. It does not mean those excesses of hot blood common to all warfare, but the quality which showed itself in the German caricatures, and which impelled German officers, after living months in a French house, to defile it when they left. It is perhaps Tacitus rather than Dante who is recalled by Bismarck's speech concerning the indemnity that he was imposing in 1871:

"If France does not meet her obligations, we will do as caterpillars do that invade a tree. We will eat her leaf by leaf."

It was Frederick the Great who said that he first did what he chose, and afterwards could always find pedants to justify it. Did he inherit this from the days of Dante? At any rate he transmitted the custom; and we still remember that manifesto of the ninety-three professors in 1914, who told us under their ninety-three signatures the truth about the Fatherland.

"It is not true," they declared, "that Germany provoked this war."

"It is not true that we criminally violated the neutrality of Belgium." Their own Chancellor had admitted the contrary.

One understands why Schopenhauer wrote in his *memorabilia:*

"In anticipation of my death I make this confession, that I despise the German nation on account of its unlimited stupidity, and I blush at belonging to it."

The ninety-three did not stop there; they, and others to what number I know not, were busy through four years, justifying the acts of their Kaiser until he ran off to Holland—it may be that they have also justified that; but they produced a mass of pamphlets and addresses proving heavily to the entire satisfaction of their readers the righteousness of any number of things. I do not know what they may have had to say about such incidents as this, of which there were a great many:

From the diary of Private Hassemer, 8th corps, September 3, 1914, at Sommepy:

"Horrible carnage, the village burned and razed to the ground, the French driven into the houses in flames, civilians and all burned together."

I have read in the writings of German generals, that work like this is done in order to discourage further resistance on the part of the enemy, and so to make the war short: one of the objections to such policy seems to be that it did not achieve its purpose. Would it have provided Schopenhauer with another reason for blushing? We can imagine his cheeks growing hot over a solemn pamphlet which proved that the Meuse country was Germany's by historic right, since *Verdun* had long been known in Germany as *Wirten,* showing that the town must have had a German origin. The trouble about this argument is, that there are twelve other Verduns in France, six of which are in the south, quite beyond the inroads of all Hun invasion from Attila down.

Strasbourg was full of printed arguments like this, little books, little lectures, that fell into the hands of the Allies after the Armistice. They form a library, and they draw a map of the German mind, a portrait of the German spirit, carefully, by its own hand, not an enemy's. I can

not choke this chapter with one-half or one-tenth of these
touches which go to make the portrait; three or four
must suffice:

What us the World War bring must, is the excellent
title of a work published in 1914, and I will not disarrange
its sequence of syllables. It seems addressed to mothers,
but to mix its genders:

"Enough of the twaddle about morality! . . . now is
the moment thou noble . . . woman, Germania . . . to
suppress manfully such moments of pity . . . nations at
war find themselves in a pure state of nature . . . all
feeling of generosity is to be silenced . . . even if a
state of panic amongst women and children is to arise!"

Professor Fleischner, of Berlin, published in 1915 at
Frankfort his opuscle entitled, *Of the War against German Kultur.*

"The greatness of Germany," says the professor, "has
not been wrought by her merchants, diplomats, scientific
men, or artists. . . . Only the mailed fist can establish
it. . . . Hit and destroy. . . . O German spirit . . . with
the strength and simplicity of the bear and the child."

Professor Lasson tells his fellow Germans that—

"To observe a treaty is not a question of right but of
interest. . . . Force can create what we call right . . .
the weaker becomes the prey of the stronger . . . and
this . . . can be called moral as well as rational."

Professor Kohler writes in his "Holy War" that—

"Might overrules right. Americans . . . never understood the philosophy of Law. . . . We may smile . . .
that the vulgarity of our critics . . . shows where barbarism and ignorance are to be found in this War"—this
war, with whose causes and objects Mr. Wilson told us
in 1916 that the United States was not concerned.

But on the whole I like this next selection best, as a
portrait of the German mind. It is Dr. H. U. Schmidt,
of the University of Göttingen, who speaks about the destruction of the cathedral of Reims in an address of March
22nd, 1915, one of a series entitled *German talks in heavy*

time. His thesis is, that the French deserve to lose Reims, because it was built when they were more worthy of it than they are now. The doctor says (and I will not disarrange his style) :

"More and more vanishes of course the German element also out of the north and east of France; ever less will henceforth the possibility for the French be to understand what great and genuine in the German, yea in the Germanic nature, is. Ever stronger must through this the chasm between France and Germany, but also between modern France and her own pasthood be. The world story is often symbolic, and the sacrifice of the cathedral of Reims—since about that is it being dealt—can as the symbol of the estrangement of the French people from their own pasthood, how it itself even wider yet with necessity be drawn must, taken be."

I sometimes wonder if the best portrait of the German mind—its shape, not its content—is not perhaps the syntax to which it has given birth.

We see it from the religious angle in an interview which the renowned chemist, Professor Otswald, accorded to "Dagen" of Stockholm.

"Question. What do you think of the more and more decided part which the different churches are playing in the countries that have thus far suffered invasion ?"

"Answer. That is a consequence impossible to avoid. The present situation necessarily invokes atavistic instincts in many regions. I will say, nevertheless, that God the Father is reserved with us for the personal use of the Emperor. Once He was mentioned in a report of the General Chief of Staff, but, note this well, He has not reappeared since."

In his talks with Eckemann, Goethe says:

"I have often felt a profound grief in thinking of this German nation, which is estimable in each of its individuals, and collectively so wretched. The comparison of the German people with other peoples arouses painful sentiments which I have sought to escape from by every possible means."

This was said in days when Prussian education of Germany was in its infancy; after it was full grown, and the mailed fist had flung Germany against civilization, Germany's Prussianized voice spoke true to form, true to the word of the Roman general, the word of Tacitus, the word of all ages, in this outburst:

"Let us give up our wretched attempts to excuse Germany, let us cease from casting unfounded accusations upon the enemy. It is not against our will that we have thrown ourselves into this gigantic adventure. It was not forced upon us by surprise. We willed it, it was our duty to will it. We do not stand before the tribunal of Europe, we recognize no such court.

"Our might will create a new law in Europe. It is Germany who strikes. When she has conquered new realms for her genius, then the priests of all gods will praise the holy war. . . .

"Germany does not make this war to punish the guilty or to liberate oppressed peoples and rest afterwards upon the consciousness of her disinterested magnanimity. She makes it in the changeless conviction that her exploits give her the right to more space. . . .

"Spain, Holland, France, and England have seized and colonized large territories, the most fertile on earth. Germany's hour has sounded. . . .

"Come, is Germany strong? Yes. What stuff are you telling us, professors in spectacles and theologians in slippers? That right exists? Do those lofty notions amount to anything? . . . Force; a fist; that's all! . . .

"Get used to the idea that in German land live barbarians and warriors. . . .

"When Tangier and Toulon and Antwerp and Calais belong to the Barbaric Power, then we will condescend to talk to you sometimes."

This was Maximilian Harden in the *Zukunft*.

After the thorough education which Prussia had been giving Germany for several generations, this changeless conviction is perfectly natural; but what is perfectly extraordinary is to hear people excusing her on the ground that she was merely doing at last what other nations had done at first. The other nations could not have done it and would not have dared to do it, if the weaker peoples whom they conquered had been strong enough to stand them off. By like reasoning, the apologists who offer these extenuating circumstances in Germany's case, would invite Mr. Smith to forgive a burglar who had been caught breaking into his house, because previous burglars had successfully stolen the silver spoons of Mr. Jones.

Is the "changeless conviction" changed?

When the iron was hot, and the fierce shock of the war was stinging public attention awake, the words of Harden were vividly familiar, often quoted together with many others like them that are faded utterly out of the general memory, now that the iron is cold. When reminded of them today, the apologists not infrequently reply:

"Ah yes; but we have a new Germany since the war. She has seen a great light. She is industrious and peace loving. If any of the old Junker spirit survives, it is a negligible influence, and on the wane."

But is the conviction changed?

Some signs of this were apparent, to be sure; some editorials, some public utterances, showed a new spirit. *Vorwaerts,* the Berlin paper, declared that "the German Republic must repair the crimes of Imperial Germany ... and that is why it should silence the admirers of the old régime who now would lift up their voices in reference to this question."

Such opinions did not strike me as plentiful, they seemed confined to the small handful of bold and liberal papers. The *Deutsche Tageszeitung* was more representative.

"The hate between Frenchmen and Germans is ineradicable," it said. "Europe will know no repose until the eternal peace disturber is annihilated politically and militarily; and this moment is perhaps less distant than may be thought."

To any eyes on the watch for them, gleams like this of

the mailed fist shone through not infrequent holes in the soft glove. While the laments over Germany's poverty and her utter inability to pay the reparation flowed copiously, in a daily stream, from the pens of editors and the lips of politicians, now and then something like this, from the *Welt am Montag*, would appear:

"Everybody knows that millions in paper money have been hidden away to escape from taxation. It must also be recognized that agriculture is rolling in wealth. . . ." And the journal is so incautious as to publish specific details of prosperity:

As against a five per cent. dividend the year preceding, the Rheingan sugar refinery had this year declared forty-eight per cent.

The Sugar Trade Union of Hamburg had risen from sixteen and a half to forty-eight per cent.

The Düsseldorf Blast Furnace Company in 1920 made a profit of twenty-two million marks on a capital of three million six hundred thousand.

The Sandloch Lead Works, capital one and a half million, made a profit of seven million marks.

The Concordia Chemical Factory paid eight per cent. one year, seventy-five per cent. the next.

The North German Iron Trucks rose from eight to sixty per cent.

Observing travellers in Germany noticed a curious difference in appearance between those parts of the Fatherland under military occupation and in the beaten routes of foreign travel, and those parts where foreign travel was infrequent. In occupied Rhineland, stoves were in the restaurants and hotels, trains were cold and bad, streets were unlighted; France was envied the coal she took from Germany and did not need, while here it was needed so sorely. But if one penetrated into districts more intimately German, where nothing had been arranged for effect on foreign visitors, bread cards, though required by printed rules, were never asked for; there were no temporary stoves, the central heating systems were going, the hotels and trains were so hot that windows had to be open; in short, lignite was taking the place of coal very satisfactorily, there was plenty of it, and there was an effort to hide this fact from the Allies. Travellers who happened to visit Turkish baths, circuses, cinema shows, merry-go-rounds, outside the zone of foreign visitors, were not at all deceived as to the camouflaged dearth of coal. They noticed, too, even while they were hearing the cries of distress and the assertions that German industry and prosperity were paralyzed, that forests of fresh scaffolding bristled in large towns where corporations and banks were in the act of erecting palatial quarters wherein to house their expanding needs; they observed that a vast new underground railway system was being pushed forward in Berlin; it seemed odd to them that if funds were so scarce, two millions should have been voted to the State Fair at Leipzig in 1920, and twenty millions to the same enterprise in 1921. This grant was made at a time not remote from the London Conference, where Dr. von Simons assured Mr. Lloyd George that Germany could not possibly pay in reparation more than two billion and a half pounds in forty-two years, instead of the eleven billion and a third demanded by the Allies. At that moment, the tax per head in Germany was three pounds, while in England it was twenty-two.

Mr. Lloyd George broke off his conversation with Dr. von Simons, and said later to his English and French colleagues:

"If we had let him talk for ten minutes more, we should have been owing Germany several billion."

In those days when Dr. von Simons was explaining to Mr. Lloyd George that Germany had nothing wherewith to pay her reparations, the news that her factories were doing a disastrous business reached America, and Americans at once made large offers to buy these ruined German plants. Not an offer was accepted, not a factory was for sale!

When an American in search of them visited the great

Krupp establishment at Essen, he did not find it shut up. What he found was a place where workmen worked for one-seventh the pay of English labor, and did not strike; where they worked full hours, and so far from being anarchistic were they that they touched their hats to their employers and went to it with the same drill of mind and body which had unloaded the scenery from the dray in Dresden, and kept the revolution off the grass in Berlin; a place that was turning out three hundred locomotives a year, three thousand cars a year, trucks in proportion, cinema apparatus, sewing machines, everything in short that can be made of steel; and a place which had employed thirty-five thousand men before the war, and was now employing forty-five thousand.

If this American traveller had continued to go about the Fatherland in quest of factories for sale, he would have found:

1. Jena, turning out cheaper and better optical glass than any competitors; from furnace to show room a gigantic organization busy over every stage of construction from the making of the glass to the mounting of it in microscopes, cameras, field glasses, cinema projectors, theodolites, ultramicroscopes, nautical and astronomic instruments; and ten thousand serious workmen employed upon this. For these men in times of recreation, libraries, reading rooms, parks were constructed.

2. Leipzig, printing newspapers, periodicals, illustrated colored plates, Latin and Greek books, catalogues, trade papers of fifty pages, and sensational novels—all cheap. Pulp is plentiful because Germany used Polish forests during the war, and saved her own for peace.

3. Dresden, making pianos, organs, steam organs, instruments to suit all national preferences, little grands for bridal housekeeping, tall uprights for Spain, Italy, South America; and wires for these, as well as for violins, mandolins, and guitars. Beside this industry of Dresden are the porcelain works at Meissen, where workmen proud of their hereditary descent from those selected for the

works by King August II in 1710 were making fake antiques for New York dealers, telegraph insulators, handpainted sets of egg-shell china, crucibles for scientific use, electric lampshades, statuettes, vases and plates imitating the wares of Copenhagen, Sèvres, and Limoges. Living is cheap in Meissen, and the workmen's houses clean and pretty.

4. Pforzheim, carving bone for combs, pendants, necklaces, beads; handbags, umbrella handles; little cats and pigs in bronze or celluloid or imitation crystal for the watch chain; every sort of cheap jewelry; souvenir brooches with Venice, Seville, and the Passion Play at Oberammergau done in color on their glazed convexity; souvenir spoons showing the ruined cathedral of Reims; and, to advertise a certain make of automobile, neat pencils lettered in six different languages and distributed free throughout the world; knicknacks inscribed with publicity matters in Turkish, Japanese and Russian characters. Wages at Pforzheim had gone up.

5. Frankfort and Mannheim fabricating cheap dry goods, employing as many hands as before the war.

6. Berlin and its suburbs equally busy; east Berlin over enamel ware, pianos, optical goods, furniture, textiles, domestic chattels generally, including jewelry, confectionery, carved frames and cases, perfume, fans; north Berlin over heavier work, electric and railway supplies. In the science of perfume several experiments were being successfully made—in dry scent, for example, a powdered perfume which dissolves when sprinkled upon a warm hand; synthetic essences, smelling like strawberries, pineapples, mushrooms, that never saw a strawberry or pineapple or mushroom; soap in quantity, in spite of the loudly alleged shortage of fat. At another suburb, Charlottenburg, drugs and medicines. These had been made near Cologne until the Armistice, and they were then hurriedly removed out of reach of the Allies' observation, lest these chemical secrets should become known outside of Germany. The undivulged processes are now producing

medicines in far greater volume than before the war. They are in demand all over the world and their retail price is three and four hundred times the cost of production. To escape export duties a brisk traffic in smuggling goes on at various frontiers. I skip Chemnitz and its dry goods, and Plauen with its lace and dyeing and bleaching, and other places.

None of these establishments was for sale; it was the same everywhere; the American quest would have been fruitless in purchases, but very profitable in experience.

In their offer to buy German manufactories, our business men had meant business, had been perfectly serious; they believed the "hard luck" stories so ingeniously circulated. Their failure to find any acceptances of their offers revealed to them that what they had unwittingly done was to "call a bluff."

It may be said that among all the industries in which she excels, propaganda is at the head of Germany's list; the organization of private industry stands second, but still so high as to overtop anything of the sort in those countries which are her competitors. This organization is being perfected every day; Germany's set-back has vitalized her energy, while the Allies' has been slackened by their sterile victory. She has carried Trusts into higher terms, under the title Community of Interests Association, whereunder all productive factors, from the raw material at the bottom to the finished article at the top, are gathered and co-related under a single management. This is known as the "vertical line" system. For instance, if a company made telephones, it would acquire control of all the areas from which all the raw materials needed for a complete telephone are drawn—mines, forests—and also the corporations which manufacture wire, or electrical apparatus, or fixtures such as hotels and offices use, switchboards, everything necessary to a system in complete working order. Or again if coal is at the bottom and hardware of every description at the top of a vertical line of production, one huge hand of the Community of Interests Asso-

ciation grasps both ends and everything between, and
conducts the whole work harmoniously, with the least
possible waste and the greatest possible gain. Meanwhile,
the workmen of Germany who carry on the physical part
of this vast activity retain their habit of drill, have no use
for strikes, and are satisfied with their state. Small concerns outside the association of giants have come to grief,
and these cases have been adroitly used to convey the idea
of a general collapse.

"They will cheat you yet, those Junkers."

With such organized energy, it is not wonderful that
industrial dividends went from eight to sixty per cent.
and that a billion of profit is already invested in foreign
securities. Germany, with masterly self-control, made herself ready to sell to the world, and now the world has
begun to buy from her. Before the war she saved ten
billion marks a year; were she to save eight billion now,
it would more than meet the requirements of her reparation. It is to be noticed that one of the leading financiers
of New York—not affiliated with German concerns—has
stated that the payments, spread over forty-two years, if
capitalized at $8\frac{1}{2}\%$, will form a sum of about thirteen
billion dollars, which Germany can pay easily. Under the
Treaty of Frankfort, when she was victorious in 1871, she
laid down and acted upon the principle that the nation
provoking the war ought to pay the costs of the war. She
has not been dealt with according to her own rule; the
Allies deliberately have not asked Germany to pay one
single mark for the cost that they incurred in defending
themselves: therein lies the profound difference, both
practical and moral, between the *indemnity* exacted by
Germany in 1871 from France who had provoked the war
and was beaten, and the *reparation* demanded by the Allies
from Germany for the injuries that she inflicted upon the
land, the houses, and the manufactories of France. Most
financial writers that I have read constantly speak of the
indemnity demanded from Germany: this is false to fact,
and it misleads many readers who have not gone into the
matter.

It seems to me also that these financiers are themselves confused by the horrible condition of state finance in Germany, while they overlook the vigorous health of private finance, the large dividends, the invested billion of profit. No doubt the government has paid the deficits of railroads whose transportation was artificially cheap, the losses on exports sold needlessly below cost; has rioted in paper money, kept a huge army of salaried Junkers in office, and is consequently without funds to pay its current expenses. What has that to do with the reparation? How is it that new banks and buildings are going up, and twenty million marks are voted to the Leipzig Fair? If private Germans are making millions, whose fault is it that the public purse is empty—if it is empty? A man who kept two bank accounts, one overdrawn and a thousand dollars in the other, would not be allowed to plead bankruptcy.

The financier who was pardoned by Mr. Taft on account of his ill health, ate soap for days to make himself an emaciated and pitiable object. When he was let out he changed his diet and soon resumed his old appearance and previous habits. It looks more than likely that the German Government has been eating soap. I suggest that the financiers inquire a little further into the case before they ask France and the rest of us to commute the Fatherland's sentence of reparation. I think that they ought to remember more often than they do, how sure they were that the war would be a short one; and that before asking the world to help in lifting weak Germany on her legs, they should make us all sure not only that she cannot get on them by herself, but also that when she is up she will not promptly knock us all down.

What is the mailed fist doing beneath its glove, meanwhile?

Articles 160 and 178 in the Treaty of Versailles are definite:

"The number of effectives in the army of those states which constitute Germany must not exceed 100,000 men, and shall be exclusively for the purpose of maintaining order and for policing the frontiers.

"All measures of mobilization are forbidden."

Article 176 forbids military academies. Berlin had one, Munich another. Over these the glove was drawn. In each of the division staffs, staff courses of lectures were created, to which the entrance examinations were like those of the military academy. The documents of the army were collected at Berlin in a war library. To sort and classify these and to aid in research and historic study, officers were summoned from time to time. It was not mentioned that those officers permanently in custody of the library gave courses of lectures and conducted exercises. The officers who formerly taught at the military academy no longer wear uniforms, but frock coats instead and are under civil jurisdiction; in these circumstances they continue to teach what they taught before —for the instruction of their "Sipo," their Sichereitspolizei—their police. These police forces are most remarkable. Each man has a gas-mask, although Article 171 forbids the further manufacture of poisonous gas.

Up to October 1919, the demobilization bureau retained lists of reservists, but as these men were slowly dispersed the rolls of their names were distributed among the local recruiting bureaus, which are conveniently called pension bureaus. By their means mobilization could be rapidly effected. In 1920 the old army, apparently dispersed in accordance with the treaty, was replaced by the "Reichswehr," to which the regulars of the old army can be despatched by means of the rolls of their names at the local "pension" offices. In his Koenigsberg speech, Ludendorff in August 1921 lauded the excellence of the old army, which he declared the Reichswehr must imitate.

"Think," he said, "what won us Tannenberg: the will of the chiefs, faith in them, discipline and courage in the face of death. . . . The greater our country's need the closer will we rally round the black, white, and red Prussian flag."

This Reichswehr numbered 300,000 men in August 1919, 320,000 in November, and 370,000 in February 1921. If to these be added two corps organized in Lithuania and Lattonia, and the regulars retained under the treaty, the total mounts above 420,000 in February 1920. On February 18th, 1920, Mr. Lloyd George granted an "extension" to the time limit for German demobilization set by the treaty. This caused much Teutonic joy.

The treaty was signed June 28th, 1919; by July Germany had created a State Police force in addition to the force existing before the war. That was divided into two classes, Ordnungspolizei—Order Police—and Kriminalpolizei—Criminal Police—each a body for maintaining law and order in cities, in other words, a municipal force, armed with revolvers only.

This new Sichereitspolizei—Safety Police—was for the repression of mobs. Its organization was military, with companies, battalions, regiments, brigades, divisions; its equipment was the same as that of the Reichswehr, even to cannons, minenwerfer, and liaison material. Its uniform was green, the old police wore blue.

By October 1919, this "Sipo" was already a little army, its Berlin contingent commanded by a brigadier general, its complement three corps of 3,000 men, with two parks of artillery, 1 squadron, 1 liaison detachment. One-third of this force was in service, one in readiness, one in repose. In the spring of 1920, exercises between it and the Reichswehr redoubled. In June the Allies at Boulogne made a sign of expostulation; they shook their finger at it, and said it must stop. Three months later it was somewhat larger than in June. The Fatherland professed herself deeply alarmed by her state of internal unrest; still, her desire was only to please the Allies. Therefore, being composed of 18 sovereign states and 13 of these having a "Sipo," 10 resolved to disband it and one joined them later. Sipo disappeared, but immediately appeared a new force, named the Schützpolizei. The entire Sipo passed into this, dropping in its metamorphosis some inferior material and replacing this with younger and better stuff.

During April 1919, an agitation in Munich made the establishing of the Einwohnerwehr most easy and convenient. The citizens had been frightened and this new force gave them peace of mind. This body had been started by a law passed on the 12th of the preceding December; the events at Munich gave it fresh impetus. Its ramifications spread through the Fatherland, it was provided with arms. To the world outside it was presented as a defence against internal disorders; the trouble appeared on investigation to be, that Germany had so little disorder and so much defence, and that such an amount of arms which by the treaty should have been delivered to the Allies is not plausibly represented as essential to this defence. Constant meetings of the young, who formed the Einwohnerwehr, kept their hands and eyes skilful at target shooting and other military accomplishments. Under the pressure of remonstrance, this vigorous training society, like Sipo, dispersed as mercury when pressed beneath the finger; and, when the finger was removed, came together again. A new set of labels was invented for it, very long names like Schützorganization and Selbschützorganization; but underneath them, there it was. Bavaria was very slow in performing the dispersal.

Behind all this disguised militarism, work some societies who are loyal to the old German traditions, and to whom democracy is distasteful. The animus of these societies may or may not be the cause of that setting of the tide away from the communistic parties and towards the traditional dynastic form of government; certainly there is a close correspondence between the facts. It is, however, probable that quite independent of any secret organization, the wish to return to the old ways lies deep in the breast of many a German who is not a member of any of them. The Orgesch is the principal secret society of this sort in Bavaria, in the Tyrol

next door it is the Orka; there is reason to suppose that
in this part of Europe, as in several others, the frontiers
which were shuffled and redealt so lightly at the Peace
Conference will not remain in their present arrangement:
it was too often a derangement—a violence to ancient
association, a dislocation of beneficent channels of trade,
and a hurried and ignorant tying up of the dog and the
cat in the same bag. Bavaria may loom a very important
nucleus of a new Central Europe empire, when the
various organizations that I have mentioned will play
their thoroughly rehearsed parts. At certain schools
today, two months' military instruction has been slipped
into the curriculum.

All the while that these activities have been going on
beneath the nose of the Entente, news has been constantly
coming of secret stores of arms. Throughout my eight
months in Europe, one read almost every week of these
being discovered. It would be in East Prussia, where the
key to some door was "lost" when the Entente inspector
came his rounds. The door was forced and thousands of
rifles were hidden there; or it would be in Berlin that
a treasure house of military telephone and telegraph
apparatus was unearthed. In many directions these
"caches" of every kind of implement and munition of
war, great and small, were being found; while on the
other hand, some gigantic objects, like the Big Bertha
guns, have never been found at all. The explosions at
chemical and dye works, far more frequent in the Fatherland than ever before, lead one to wonder what the
Germans can be making: one recalls those gas-masks of
the polizei. Now and then, too, comes another gleam of
the mailed fist through some incautious hole in the glove;
on February 11th, 1921, the *Volkzeitung* said:

"That nation will be victorious which shall have discovered the most virulent germ to spread in the country
of its enemy and the surest vaccine to render itself
immune. Fifty agents would be enough to infect as
large a country as Germany."

Months later, General Ludendorff, running true to form in his new book, "Politics and the Conduct of War," says:

"Conflict for the individual as for the State is a permanent natural phenomenon, and is founded in the divine ordinance of the world . . . we must have done once for all with the talk of such things as eternal peace, disarmament, and reconciliation of mankind . . . war will continue to be the last and only decisive instrument of policy. . . .

"There must again be a Kaiser . . . the birth of Prussianism must again be blown into the administration framework. . . . Political leaders . . . are to be trained in school and university in the doctrines of Clausewitz."

Quite near the time when this book appeared, during the last months of 1921, six hundred howitzers of large calibre were found walled up in the Rockstroh near Dresden. The Entente investigators were discouraged in their search by many artifices and objections, but they went on.

Dr. Wirth was sure that these arms had been made before the war, and were concealed to be broken up as old material. Is this innocence on the part of the Chancellor? But what if it is? The guns were made after the Armistice. Breechblocks and other parts of 342 howitzers were next discovered, five rifling machines were hidden under the floor, seven times the number of howitzers allowed by the treaty were discovered in this one factory, with official invoices directing the guns to be kept here and not forwarded, as usual, to the arsenal at Spandau. At Spandau were found two rooms packed from floor to ceiling with papers concerning the strength of the German army at the time of the Armistice; these, when asked for at that time and ever since, were reported as "lost." The Entente investigators, who would appear to be among the most humorous characters alive, left them under a guard of the Spandau military authorities overnight, and returned to get them the next morning. They were all lost again.

In Upper Silesia, since October, the French have

reported numerous discoveries of concealed arms—seven since January 1st, 1922, six hundred shells for heavy guns found in a barn; in a coach house the equipment for a company of infantry; others in the park of a country house, in a music hall, and in a deaf and dumb asylum. At the end of January the Germans made an armed attack upon French who were searching for concealed arms, wounding twenty and killing two. This was about six months after General Ludendorff's assurance to the students of Koenigsberg that the fate of Upper Silesia would be decided soon or late by a battle.

Where is the moral disarmament, where the changed intention? What converted and pacific Germany is to be found in all this? And what matters it whether Chancellor Wirth and his government are the deluded or the conniving cats' paws of Kultur? Since the Armistice, as before it, Germany has run true to form, and by her fruits any one can know her. The mind's eye sees the big dividends secretly shuffled into foreign investments, the big guns secretly manufactured, the thousands of young students secretly drilled—and the renowned chemist, Dr. Otswald, closeted over test tubes, retorts, and microscopes with his scientific brethren, trying for new explosives no larger than an egg, but able to flatten Paris, London, and New York to dust; and trying for a new germ, bred from all the deadliest contagions that will mingle, and capable of rotting any community to deliquescence in twenty-four hours.

Such a people may not be precisely lovable, but they are in truth a great race; their industry puts us all to shame, and one bows to their impregnable steadfastness to themselves. One can hardly over-praise the power of their team-work, or over-damn the wabbling incoherence of some of their adversaries, into whose feeble political hands Foch the soldier delivered them in November 1918.

Is there in the whole course of history a spectacle more stupefying?

XXVI

TO divert attention from herself, Germany has been pointing the finger of accusation at France.

"Behold the trouble maker!" she says to her own people and to the Allies; "see what a big army she is keeping up."

It is an old trick. Policemen are familiar with it when there is disorder in the street, and they have been known to arrest the wrong man. Of course the German people are taken in by it. Under the forty years of drill to which their minds have been subjected by Prussia, they accept all official statements automatically; they have believed and will go on believing anything that Berlin tells them. At the age when the children learn the Lord's Prayer, they have been taught the following words:

"Germany is my fatherland, a country surrounded by enemies."

Upon a soil so carefully tilled, the seed of any lie will grow. This Prussian perversion continues unimpeded, and the preparation of no germ or explosive could be more dangerous, since it is the man behind the gun that counts. Therefore it is wholly natural and inevitable that sixty-five or seventy millions of Germans should believe Prussia when she accused France of militarism. But why should anybody else? Why should English and Americans look in the direction that Germany is pointing, and express themselves as shocked at the large army of France at a time when all really good persons are talking about disarmament? It is remarkably like the policeman arresting the wrong man in the street, and it is also a piece of the whole stupefying spectacle.

At the Peace Conference, France asked for a Rhine

282

frontier by way of protection against further invasions
from Germany. This she was prevented from getting
by England and the United States; but these friends of
hers offered her something in exchange for what she
gave up; they would bind themselves to come to her
help in case Germany should ever assault her again
without provocation. Renouncing her Rhine frontier, she
accepted this offer. Then her friends went home. Mr.
Lloyd George had been careful to make England's
promise depend upon America's; so that when it turned
out that Mr. Wilson had promised more than he could
perform, it all fell down. France had given up her
Rhine frontier and got—nothing; she was left by England and America to take care of herself.

Against sixty-five million Germans, France counts
thirty-eight. Her people saw German hordes come in to
pillage and burn before the land was named France, or
the invaders were called Germans. From the year 102
before Christ, when the Cimbri and Teutones got almost
to Marseilles and were stopped by the Roman general,
Marius, down to Ludendorff's last lunge at the Marne
in 1918, the land of France has been incessantly trodden
down by the barbarians. Sometimes they got no farther
than the Oise, or Verdun; sometimes they swept to the
Somme, or overran Franche-Conté and threatened Italy
from the stronghold of Besançon; sometimes they
swarmed into the Rhone Basin and destroyed Lyons.
There were centuries when they broke in several times,
and again a long period would pass without a visit; but
it has been computed that there has been an average
of one invasion of France by Germans every fifty years
for fifteen centuries—and the fathers of those who fought
in 1914 fought in 1870. Had it not been for European
intervention, Bismarck would have tried it again in 1875,
because he was not satisfied with his job five years
earlier.

Is it not conceivable that England, had she suffered
from a habit of German invasion so chronic as this,

might have been more acutely attentive to the warnings
which Lord Roberts gave her through those seven years
before 1914? Had she renounced a Rhine frontier and
got nothing for it, would she not be likely to want an
army? To call France militaristic in such circumstances
looks somewhat like putting the cart before the horse.
France seems to me more like a man who goes about his
premises armed with a revolver and a big stick, because
he has lately been twice sandbagged, and the police have
all gone away.

I have never noticed that England, or America, or
any nation enjoyed misrepresentation and abuse; yet they
are calling France militaristic and accusing her of impatience because she resents it. How satisfactory to
Germany, their enemy, this attitude towards their friend
France must be! How perfectly this carries out Germany's plan that the Allies should fall apart!

Yes; France is being accused of impatience, and I
am afraid that it is true; the marvel is that she has
not been much more so. Her newspapers are intemperate
at times—are they the only ones? At Washington her
delegates made a righteous case seem wrong for a while,
and were surpassed in urbanity by the delegates of
Great Britain. But put yourself in her place, review the
story of her recent experience:

One-fourteenth of her territory devastated; four million men lost in killed, maimed, and wounded; a frontier
renounced in exchange for a broken promise; the German damages awarded her by the court whittled down
under British pressure while the German fleet is safe in
the British pocket; her demand at Washington to increase
her own greatly reduced sea power, skilfully distorted
by the press. Her naval plan was held up to the world
as an enormity, when in fact, after the cobwebs of misrepresentation had been brushed away, what she asked
was very close indeed to what Mr. Hughes proposed.

By the reporters she was made to appear as intending
to have completed ten new dreadnoughts of 35,000 tons

each by the end of ten years; as a matter of fact, they were to come at the end of twenty years; at the end of ten she would have just two. This was the first distortion by the press.

France had built no new ships for seven years; she had turned over to England, for war purposes, what vessels she possessed. Some had been lost, and her plan when truly stated came to nothing more than replacing superannuated tonnage at the rate of one new ship in two years. According to this plan, she would have at the end of the "ten-year holiday," counting six old ships and two new ones, 200,000 tons instead of 175,000—only 25,-000 more than the ratio first proposed!

Her tonnage in existing capital ships is 283,923; Great Britain's is 1,031,000; ours is 628,390. France has a colonial population 20 million greater than at home; a colonial area of 13 million square kilometres to our 9 million; she has a coast from Belgium to the Bay of Biscay, with Ostend, Calais, Havre, Cherbourg, Brest, St. Nazaire, Bordeaux, among the harbors which she must defend, and Marseilles on the Mediterranean, with her two African ports, making a triangle. Since the beginning of the war she has built 5 submarines; since the Armistice, the United States has built 44 and is building 38 more, while Great Britain has built 41. To put it in another way, our total tonnage in submarines existing and to be built is 82,105; Great Britain's is 82,464; France has 42,949, and is building none, while we propose to build 38, having officially declared that the submarine is a defensive weapon, which is precisely what France has contended.

France was obliged to stand in a false light dexterously thrown upon her during the Washington Conference, to hear the outcries of editors based upon distorted news, and in the midst of this din a congressman introducing a bill demanding immediate payment of money owed to us by any European nation that had announced its intention of increasing its navy. Patience is always desir-

able, but in such circumstances is impatience wholly unnatural ?

So much for the charge that France is militaristic.
Why it is made by Germany is perfectly plain; why
it is made by England is not so plain, because the safety
of France from Germany is just as important to England
now as it was in 1914; but as the general British mind
could not take in what Germany was getting ready to do
during the seven years before 1914, it is equally unable
now to imagine that Germany will do anything more.
The war is over, the German sea power eliminated,
and England set upon resuming her interrupted trade.
The French army seems to be a disadvantage to this,
and consequently the British mind does not see why
France should be needing something that is unnecessary
to England.

"Why does she not disband her army as I have done?
We beat Germany." That is virtually the thought in the
British mind, because it lacks imagination, and without
this you cannot put yourself in the other man's place;
you always put him in yours.

Mr. H. G. Wells says of his own countrymen:

"Most Englishmen, even those who belong to what
we call the educated classes, still do not think systematically at all; you can not understand England until you
master that fact; their ideas are in slovenly detached
little heaps, they think in ready-made phrases, they are
honestly capable therefore of the most grotesque in-
consistencies."

Why Americans should call France militaristic, and
why a congressman should offer such a resolution as that
demanding immediate payment of money owed to us by
any European power intending to increase its navy, is
because many congressmen, as well as many of those
who elect them, are in the habit of thinking that they
know all about everything when they know nothing of
anything.

XXVII

AS I travelled back and forth through the land of France, after two years, I watched the winter go, the spring come and go, and a part of the summer. What I saw and heard of France in her great emergency of peace through those months would fill a book—and must be condensed into a chapter. The mere aspect of things was often so contradictory as entirely to explain the discrepancies between the various reports of her state which travellers had brought home; all depended upon where they had gone and how long they had stayed. At the bottom there was no contradiction, everything that I had been told was true, except that France was idle and that she was prosperous; she was neither the one nor the other. Perhaps the only unchanged things that I found were her sane and gallant spirit, and her deep, unspoken sadness.

"See, monsieur," said Madeleine, my chambermaid, after she and her husband and I had come to know each other well, "Nicholas and I, we are working and saving to have some day a home where I can take care of him, though he doesn't know that. You did not see him before the four years of prison with the Germans. He is changed, monsieur, changed inside, and it is for me who have not been in prison to take care of him."

I saw many brave women and broken men like that, who said no words to me such as Madeleine's, because we had not gone far enough into friendship, but whose state a glance or a whisper would reveal; at Bléran-court, where American ability and devotion are lifting to health the crippled communes of the Aisne; at Arras, St. Quentin, Soissons, Albert, Bapaume, Reims, Verdun, Thiaucourt, Pont-à-Mousson and along

the roads between—where did I not meet with this?
Many of the men lacked an arm, or a leg, or breathed
with lungs that had been gassed; there they were, in
the fields, in the estaminets, going on as well as they
could, each with a woman working hard all day, and
taking care of her man, because, monsieur, he is not
the same as he used to be!

I saw those orchards which the Germans had cut
down, still kneeling as if in supplication, and some
of their trees like true French trees were trying to
go on when April came; a rag of bark and wood still
tied them to their roots, and through this still flowed
the sap, breaking into white blossoms that leaned and
bowed close to the ground.

At Péronne, the German placard, "nicht ärgern nur
wundern," was gone; Péronne had manufactured sugar,
and while she waited for the rebuilding of her destroyed
machinery to resume her ancient industry, she was by
no means idle. She was sowing wheat in her reclaimed
fields, and barley, and was raising hay. In centuries
past she had been a storm-centre of history, and had
counted many beautiful old buildings which I had
seen shattered and demolished upon my last visit. She
was but a tomb of beauty now. She recalled the mining
camps of the eighties in our West. Scarce any movement had been in her wasted streets in 1919; they were
wasted still, raw, without order, something like a face
that needs shaving, but life was bustling in them. The
stumps of the dead trees, with glaring new board shacks
scattered like litters of boxes among them, might have
been Montana forests cut down to make way for civilization. Here was a cinema in a tent; there was a phar-
macy in a shack; there in another was a shop with a
proud name like Grand Magazin de Paris, with boots and
buttons and spoons and shovels and nearly everything
else for sale; long new wooden barracks like bowling
alleys housed the homeless people of Péronne; this
once symmetric and historic town was now as ugly and

shapeless as any six months old place I had ever seen
in our Rocky Mountains; and to look at it and reflect
that this identity of aspect came from destruction in
one case and advance in the other, was strange and sad.

The woman who kept an estaminet here where I went
to drink coffee and get warm, was as lively and com-
petent as my friend Madeleine.

"Until '16 I stayed here in Péronne, monsieur, and
then I had to go to Amiens. At Amiens they complain
too much. We have suffered more here, do you not
think?"

"I certainly do."

"As you see, this café is made of wood—double planks
with paper. And the bedroom is very cold, constructed
by my husband. When the Boches were here they made
men and women and young girls work beneath the stick.
There are Boches and Boches; but you know, the best of
them don't come high."

The startling resemblance of these French towns that
were being built again to those camps in our West was
a common sight which met me all through the devastated regions. In their ruins they had been noble and
pitiful, and now this dignity was gone, and the stage
through which they were passing wore a degraded and
sordid appearance, where the beauty which had been
blasted away was replaced by unsightliness. Yet even
this disorderly make-shift and improvisation of existence had been touched with grace already by the French
hand. Amid the raw square shacks and the rusted sheets
of corrugated iron that arched the beds and kitchens of
these encamped townsfolk, flowers, blue and white and
pink, would be growing along some sill in a box, or
in the earth of some tended corner, and new-washed
curtains veiled the little windows with the caress of
neatness.

At Cuisy-en-Almont, I passed a new house two stories
high, and very pretty, which a man and his two daughters
had built entirely with their own hands. In certain of

the larger towns, such as Soissons, those residents who
had been well-to-do and had some money still, were not
waiting for help from the government to rebuild their
houses; and wherever this was the case, the new residences stood out very plainly among the general ruins.
They were apt to have red roofs, or to be of brick, and
were often ugly in shape; and before long it became
easy to judge from a distant sight of any village how
far its restoration had progressed, so very marked and
so very small in amount was the new construction amid
the old destruction. Help from the government came,
but it had to come slowly, and by instalments. If a
destroyed house had been worth 25,000 francs in 1914,
to rebuild it in 1919 would cost three or four times as
much, according to the fluctuations in the price of material. Its owner would be given its value, in 1914, as
damages for his loss, and supplementary sums to cover
the excess price of replacing it. But to establish his
claim to any of these subsidies, he must return to the
place where he had lived and stay there, or within a radius
of 50 kilometres. Many were living in any fragment of a
house that they could find, and many in holes, asking
merely for somewhere to come back to for rest after
each day's work. Many villages from which the war had
swept all life were still lifeless and in dust, still totally
dead, and some of these would never be alive again;
others were a quarter alive, or half; while some towns,
less destroyed and with more resources of food and
shelter, were harboring not only their own population,
but refugees also; Arras, for example, had numbered
25,000 people before the war, and now had 50,000. But
Arras, like other towns where I ate or slept, showed
the shock of shells not only out-of-doors, where the
cathedral and Hôtel de Ville had been purposely destroyed, and many streets were walled by hollow ruins,
but indoors, too, where big holes were in the ceiling of
one's bedroom and big cracks in the mirrors of the
restaurant. I walked about in Lens, where the water

was gushing copiously out of the vent as they pumped it from the flooded mines, and where 1,000 houses had been built of the 12,000 that were needed, and 6,000 men were now working. These mines were spending a million francs a day, in a year it was expected to be many times that sum, and they were making a loan of 20 milliards to cover their coming expenses. At Ronssoy, north of St. Quentin, there was a graveyard where the Germans had emptied the bones from all coffins of lead, of which metal they stood in need.

The aspect of the French country varied as greatly as that of the towns, but it had recovered in far greater proportion. The first labor had been spent upon the more fertile and valuable areas, and there were other wide stretches where nothing as yet had been done at all. Miles of shell holes and barbed wire that I had seen in 1919 were now smoothed and plowed, waiting for the spring; as the season advanced and I passed them several times again, I saw these acres rise into life and become a waving sea of crops. Nothing among or near them would have led a traveller to suspect that they had been a wilderness, two years ago, except the large coils of barbed wire, which had been removed from them, and often lay piled along the roads. These roads ran through other miles where the wire and the shells and the holes still spread across the desolate surface, over which no change had come save a growth of rank weeds and grass, robbing this land of its tragic appearance without redeeming it from its bareness. So it was by Beaumont Hamel, on that road beyond Mailly-Maillet towards Arras. Not even the road had been there in April 1919, and now it was the only thing there. It was worse beyond Bethune and Neuve Chapelle; indeed, in that direction, there was still almost perfect desolation all the way through Armentières and Messines to Ypres and the Menin road and the ridge of Paschendael. Towns and lands alike still lay in wreck and obliteration unredeemed, not a fragment seemed to have been touched among the

mounds and the holes and the wire; along the main road
I saw a thighbone sticking out of a pool. This part of
the battle-ground was one of the few that remained
where it was still difficult to find one's way; we were
turned back twice, and once had to make a long détour
in order to gain a road that was open. This happened to
me in only one other place, between the Aisne and the
Chemin des Dames; through all my other journeys, although one came at times to roads that were still impassable, there were other roads open near at hand; progress
had virtually ceased to be the picking out from many
ways the only one not closed, and had become the avoiding among many ways the only one not open. France
had re-established her channels of communication in a
very large measure, both her thoroughfares and her railroads. These latter on their main lines were nearly
normal in the service of their trains, and the speed,
though still not as fast as it had been before the war, had
decidedly increased. It was only a certain small number
of branch lines that were still unopened.

While the various voices were busy reporting that
France was not trying to pick herself up, but was lying
on the ground, supinely waiting until Germany should
pay her reparations, this is what I found she had accomplished by January 1st, 1921:

Of the 277 million cubic metres of trenches to refill,
219 million had been done; of the 310 million square
metres of barbed wire to uproot and remove, 249 million
had been done; of the 3 million 8 hundred thousand
devastated hectares to be brought back to safety and
fertility, 3 million four hundred and fifteen thousand
had been purged of live shells and projectiles, and 3
million 126 thousand had been made level and normal.
Or, to put it in another way—

Of shells removed 89%
Of land levelled 82.2%
Of barbed wire removed 80.1%

Of trenches filled 79%
Of wreckage cleared away........................60%

in 18 months, with a male population reduced by 4 million, and a debt increased tenfold. And again—

Of 1,757,000 hectares destroyed, 1,669,000 were levelled, 1,405,000 were cultivated, 1,000,000 were sown.

The French harvest in 1919 had been 24% of the harvest before the war; in 1920 it was 50%.

By January 1, 1921—

334,000 hectares were sown in hay.
304,000   "   "   "   " wheat.
57,000   "   "   "   " beets.
39,000   "   "   "   " rye.
37,000   "   "   "   " barley.
150,000   "   "   "   " other crops.

Of main line railroads restored....................96.6%
" local railroads...............................28%
" canals and navigable streams..................93%
" engineering works 70%
" roads 64.7%

Three thousand six hundred and three tunnels and bridges had been destroyed, one thousand four hundred and ninety-eight remained to be repaired.

That is a part of what idle France had been doing in 18 months—from the spring of 1919, when she was able to begin work, until January 1st, 1921; and here is more of it:

In November 1918, twenty thousand five hundred of her manufactories were paralyzed, either knocked down and without machinery, or left standing without machinery. After 18 months, 18% of these were going concerns, 26% in partial activity; but 56% were still stationary. The German work of destruction and robbery could not be repaired very rapidly, and so, while German

factories were whirling full speed at night as well as in
the day, earning those 30 and 40 per cent. dividends,
more than half the industry of France was still a total
wreck.

But it was in making new houses for her homeless
millions that France was most behind. She had so
little money to spend at all, that she devoted most of
it to what would immediately increase her income with
the least outlay; therefore her first care had to be for
her fields and her channels of communication. Meanwhile, those homeless French lived near their place of
work in any shelter that could be found or improvised.
In their anxiety to return to their homes and reclaim
their land they came back from their exile in a stream
with which no reconstruction of the demolished farms
and villages could keep pace; especially in a country that
had lost one-fifth of its revenue, and had been spending
9 billion francs a year in self-defence. This outstripping
of the sheltering capacity in the devastated regions by
the returning peasants caused a very heavy shortage
of every kind of habitation, adequate and inadequate.
Five hundred and ninety thousand dwellings had been
wholly or partially destroyed—293,000 were wiped out,
the remainder left in various stages of ruin. By January 1921, 40,000 of these were rebuilt, 280,000 made
partly habitable, and to this housing capacity 40,000
barracks, 60,000 shacks, and 29,000 shelters of other
substances had been added; this had to accommodate
one million seven hundred thousand people. The total
insufficiency of housing in ratio to the housed was 24%;
of repaired or provisional houses in ratio to the population in 1914, 33.1%; the insufficiency of normal houses,
96%. Since January 1921, the energy of France in restoring herself has never flagged; today more than six-
sevenths of her schools are reopened, nearly half of her
destroyed homes are permanently or temporarily repaired, more than three-quarters of her productive soil
has been reclaimed. This she has accomplished in spite

of having been compelled to buy from abroad much
wheat, sugar, coal, and other necessaries which she had
produced at home before the Germans destroyed her machinery and sources of production. To rebuild the destroyed areas, the bridges, roads, railways, telegraphs,
to set industries, commerce, farmers on their feet, France
up to the year 1922 had devoted fifty-six billion francs
since the Armistice.

Yet Germans have intimated and others have echoed
the intimation, that France has been lying idle, waiting
for Germany to pay the reparations! It is singular that
Germany should expect such a tale to be believed, because
the idea that any nation which had to go on living should
voluntarily expire makes a very feeble appeal to human
reason; more singular still is it that any one should have
actually believed it. It is somewhat as if a man who had
been crushed by his neighbor's automobile should wait
to be paid the damages before he went to a hospital.
Germany has given the world another suggestion about
France, certainly more plausible on its face. France
refused Germany's offer to send workmen and rebuild
her ruins for her; had she accepted this offer, says Germany, France would by now be rebuilt. Without taking
into consideration the problem of feeding a large army
of strangers when food was scarce and expensive, and
also the feelings of the French at having to see again
and to live side by side with those who had wrecked
their homes, killed their brothers, and debauched their
sisters, there is something else; with that offer which
Germany made went stipulations about the comfort and
food and general well-being of her workmen, while they
should be in France, which it would have been perfectly
impossible to meet, and the Germans knew it. They did
not intend that France should accept their offer, any
more than they had intended on July 23d, 1914, that
Serbia should accept Austria's ultimatum. Acceptance
of the scheme would have flung Germany into the same
flurry of indignation at the "duplicity" of France that

they improvised when Serbia took them aback by accept-
ing the ultimatum. The offer was what we call a "frame.
up," something to be used for effect, quite like the
incident of Casablanca in 1907. That was a "cause of
war" with France which Germany had been carefully
engineering. Germans with a past, who had enlisted in
France's Foreign Legion, like many others with a past,
were induced by German secret agents to desert, and were
to be represented to the world as being worthy subjects
of the Kaiser, whom the French Army had kidnapped
and enslaved. The trick was played prematurely, before
the Kaiser felt ready to fight; and he backed down in the
face of the energetic position then taken by M. Clemenceau, who was President of the Council.

"Born to lie," wrote the Roman general in the first
century, and this pattern running through the German
character shows no sign of fading out, after two thousand years. Its color has glowed brightly whenever,
after some conference at which Germany has asseverated
to the Allies that it is out of her power to pay her reparation, they have taken, or have even threatened to take,
steps to enforce payment under the sanctions of the
Treaty of Versailles, and the cash has been forthcoming
at once.

"You have answered all sorts of questions," I said
to a member of the French Government, "and now I
am going to ask you one more—and even then it may be
that I shall not have finished!"

He bowed. "You know I am always at your service."

"It is this: how about your taxes?"

"That is our weak point," he answered with immediate
frankness. "We have not been able to collect our tax
from the profiteers as successfully as England or yourselves. But Germany has this same weak point, as well
as a number of others. Don't forget that!"

"I don't!"

"And that she is the culprit while we are her victims."

"No American who has seen your devastated regions will forget that."

"Also, it is not that we are conniving with our great industrials, that they may escape the tax and hide their profits in foreign investments. That is the second deep moral difference between Germany and ourselves in this matter of taxes. First, she is the guilty debtor, we the injured creditor; second, she deliberately winks at the diversion of large sums of money into these foreign investments, which by the treaty should go to us for reparation. She violates the Treaty of Versailles every day. With us it is inefficiency. We are violating no treaty, and it is only we who suffer from our own—well, call it timidity, if you like. The French people hate direct taxation, and ministers fear to push them too far. Our leaders, like yours, I fancy, find their position difficult when it comes to a clash between domestic and foreign policies."

"England has the same embarrassment," I said.

"But not Germany," he answered. "Whatever it looks like on the surface, they stand together at bottom, because they are just as much against the world in peace as they were in the war, and this keeps them unified. Yes, I admit that we fall short of you in the matter of taxes. Only half a million Frenchmen paid a direct income tax in 1920, when about four million ought to have paid. But who does that hurt except ourselves? And in spite of it, we have not remained at a standstill."

"I am very well aware of that!" I exclaimed.

"Yes; but do you know that our exports have increased some 16 per cent. over last year, while our imports have decreased 45 per cent.? That will come to an export balance of nearly a billion francs against an import balance of almost 28 billion last year. And by our bookkeeping we have continued so far to keep our heads above bankruptcy. Our public debt amounts to—in dollars—$1212 per capita against England's

$875 and yours of $240. But of this debt of ours—about
forty-eight billion and a half dollars—only 8.4 per cent.
is external debt. And—have no fear!—France will meet
her obligations. It is not in her tradition to repudiate.
Only—may we not have time to build ourselves up before paying? Who is the real debtor—France, or the
one who forced us to spend these billions to save our
liberty? And one word more, monsieur——"

He paused a moment, as if to be able to continue his
calm manner and speech:

"Do you think if Germany were just across the river
from certain bankers and politicians, that they would be
quite so ready to invite us all to deny ourselves for her
sake?"

"Don't let them make you give up your army!" said I,
"whatever else you may have to deny yourselves."

"Oh, we shall keep our army! Mr. Lloyd George is
not our Prime Minister, you know."

"He almost seems so, at times," I ventured to murmur.

He let this go. "They tell us, monsieur, that we are
asking from Germany more than the true price of our
damage. That is very easy for financiers to say, but not
so easy to prove when exchange is in such rapid and
constant fluctuation that what we have correctly cal-
culated on Monday will have become false on Tuesday.
Let Germany pay us until our regions that she devastated
are rebuilt, and then we will excuse her whatever excess
we asked."

"Nobody has ever suggested that," I said.

"Is it not perfectly simple and practical?"

"Perfectly. But they say that Germany can never pay
the true cost of rebuilding."

"And in reply to that I say, monsieur, that when
France, short of men, short of money, and with her
industries paralyzed as you have seen, has been able
in two years to rebuild herself in the manner that you
have also seen, that Germany, who has not a wheel cracked
in her vast industrial machine, can pay perfectly well,

and in a shorter time than they have allowed her. No,
monsieur! This is how it is: Either Mr. Lloyd George
and his friends know better, or they do not; either they
understand Germany, or they do not. It comes to the
same thing in result—that they are the best friends that
Germany has, and are aiding her in her plan which
France clearly perceives. That plan is to delay her payments and so compel us, who cannot go on living without a roof over our heads, to pay for the new roof
ourselves—and with the generous help that you and
other friends are sending us. Germany intends the Allies
to heal their own wounds—and to deal them some new
ones, perhaps, before the old ones are cured. Meanwhile,
her democratic workmen are very respectful to those
above them. When they declined to launch for Monsieur
Stinnes his new ship the *von Tirpitz* because of its name,
he dismissed 3,000 of them. Since that they have launched
the *Hindenburg* and the *Ludendorff* for him with the
most correct and obliging politeness."

I slept two nights among the ruins in the department
of the Aisne, whence the violence of war had scarcely
been absent at all during the four years. In that
region, out of 841 communes, 814 had been demolished;
of 590,000 people, 290,000 had fled; of 736,000 hectares,
730,000 had been plowed up by projectiles; of 10,000
kilometres of road 6,000 were still impassable, and to
rebuild them one million seven hundred thousand tons
of stone would be required. Of 489 kilometres of main
line railroads, 489—the whole—had been destroyed, and
of the 648 kilometres of branch lines, 609 had been
destroyed. The little town of Coucy-le-Château—and
nowhere in France was there a gem of more exquisite
beauty—stood on its hill as silent and dead as Hercu-
laneum, destroyed by no volcano, but by the eruption of
wanton, baffled German hate.

At Anizy-le-Château on the Sunday that I spent in
this region, the croix-de-guerre was given to 21 of the

devastated communes by Marshal Fayolle. The people
came from their own ruins through the dead forests to
the ruins of Anizy, and assembled round a platform in
the sunlight to listen to the speeches. These were eloquent
and moving, made by prominent men who spoke to the
bereaved and hard-working people of their beloved
France. Bright flags covered the little broken place,
hanging quietly in the warm and motionless air. Beyond
these and across the tiny stream, the Ailette, rose the
forest of Pinon, grim and leafless, never to be green
again, every tree a mere dead spike above the marshy
green of the new grass by the river. Twenty thousand
dead had been in the forest of Pinon in September 1918.
The great silence was living here still; but as those
Frenchmen spoke of France and I listened to the solemn
and passionate devotion of their words, and looked at
the forest beyond, it was easy to imagine unheard music
floating from the depths; the songs of the mothers bidding their dead sons to sleep and dream proud dreams
because they lay in the bosom of their country that they
had saved; the songs of young mothers over their cradles,
bidding their new-born to sleep and dream proud dreams
because they would in their turn live for France and,
if she asked them, die for her. The heart of the ceremony was the conferring of the war cross to each one
who stood forth to represent his commune. Its name
would be called from the roll, and at this the representative approached Marshal Fayolle. Then the roll of
the commune's dead would be called, name after name;
and after each came the answer:
"Jules Touzet."
"Mort pour la France."
"Léon Jourdois."
"Mort pour la France."
"André Renard."
"Mort pour la France."
Always the same reply, "dead for France," commune
after commune, until all the twenty-one had been dec-

orated with the cross through their representative by
Marshal Fayolle. Not only did it not seem long, but
time ceased to be, the sacredness of it was a moment of
eternity; and through it sounded the unheard music
from the forest of Pinon, and it seemed as if the whole
company were sitting in the cathedral of Reims, invisible, a wreck no longer, made whole and rising glorious
beyond the grave.

The people of the communes had wished so much to
make the marshal and all their guests feel that they were
welcome, that they had spent themselves to provide, not
a meal, but a feast. They had done far more than was
needed, they had determined that none of their poverty
which could be hidden should be seen today; and their
endless bill-of-fare, printed with such zest, contained
both a smile and a heart-break.

It had been the plan of the ministering spirit who
presides over the American Relief of this department to
reduce and simplify, for the sake of expense, each
detail of help that should cease to be needed. It had
been hoped that after two years the surgical help might
cease. Nothing else could; not the little shacks for
school children; not the little new brick libraries
scattered through the wasted region; not the automobile
service, or the assembly rooms where the people came
at night to see moving pictures, or the dispensary, or the
dentist, nothing that meant help to work, or to instruct,
or to amuse, or to keep well; but war wounds had either
got well or had been placed in the care of more central
organizations. Nevertheless, surgical equipment had to
be continued by the American Relief in the Aisne, because of the bombs that were being removed from the
fields, the unexploded hand grenades. A special force was
being employed all through the devastated regions to find
and take away these live shells. In the department of the
Aisne, 648 men had been doing this work in 1920, of
whom 100 had been killed and 38 wounded. The French
shells were more dangerous than the German on account

of their mechanism; they had a spring which caused the fuse to ignite. In time and under exposure, this spring became rusty, so that sometimes the lightest touch, or even a jar caused by the earth pressing against it where a man had set his foot, would snap it, and the man might lose a leg, or be blown to atoms. Consequently the surgical equipment had to be retained.

In the windows and on the counters of the bookshops all over France were the signs of a great change. Innumerable pamphlets and periodicals were now published to teach and encourage out-of-door competitive sports. One of these was called, "How to become a good player of Football Association," another, "Football Rugby," another, "Feminine Basket Ball." These were but a few that I noticed. Not one of these publications had I ever seen before, and until the war the French had paid but scant attention to the games of England and America. Competitive sport had not been a habit or a tradition with them, and to this fact one weakness in the national character may be ascribed—the absence of the instinct of team-work, of co-operation, straight through the entire social and economic structure of the country.

Two officers, a Frenchman and an American, were talking together as they watched a line of our doughboys standing in a heavy rain growing wetter and wetter, each soldier patiently waiting his turn to have his supper handed to him. This astonished the Frenchman. "Are your men willing to keep in line like that?" he asked the American.

"Yes. Why not?"

"French soldiers would not endure that deluge of rain. They would all crowd each other to get first."

What they saw of the British and of ourselves during the war, of the games we played, of our generally athletic habit, has evidently made a deep impression upon the French. They constantly spoke to me of the size of our men, and of their broad shoulders. It has not stopped there, they have done more than talk about it;

broad shoulders and the instinct of team-work and fair
play have seemed to them something worth acquiring,
and they have set about doing this systematically. Football has been made compulsory in the French army.
When the government is able to pay Soissons the money
which rebuilding will cost, it will also return to the
American Relief in the department of the Aisne their
outlay in developing the play grounds at Soissons and
at Reims. The 67th regiment was stationed there at the
time of my visit, and its team played a game of basket
ball with a team from Couy—a neighboring village of
which not one stone is left upon another. The score
stood 9 to 9 close to the finish, when the soldiers in the
Couy team made a desperate rally—and won.

"What made you play so hard just then?" an American asked them.

"Because, if we won, each of us was to get a permission of forty-eight hours."

The ministering spirit of the American Relief found
at first a grave obstacle in the absence of all sense of
co-operation, or wish for it, among the peasants. They
had always done their own work, they had no desire
to do their neighbor's. But France was too short-handed
now for such individualism; if the fields were to be reclaimed, if the crops were to be sown, the farmers must
come to each other's help, and this they were learning
to do. They were also adjusting themselves to waiting
their turn to use the farm machinery which was being
supplied to the department by the American Relief.

If competitive sport and the habit of co-operation out-
last the emergency of the peace, and persist when normal
conditions are wholly resumed, something so new will
have taken root in France, that a marked and salutary
modification may be looked for in the national character.
Quite as odd and novel as the sight of the books on sport
for sale in the shops was the spectacle of little boys of
eight and ten years old, kicking footballs in the various
French towns where I stayed; more interesting still was

a game played near Paris between an all England and
an all French team, in which the French outplayed their
adversaries during the second half, and at which fifty
thousand spectators looked on. It was a sight as new as
aeroplanes were once; it may in time become as familiar.
If the war so far has done anything but harm to the
world, it is in the awakening of the French to the value
and the practice of outdoor competitive sport.

Another new sight in France was a large official
placard in the railway stations and in other public places,
exhorting young husbands to beget many children, and
specifying the graded sums that would be paid by way
of support and reward to parents with families of three,
four, five, and more. Not infrequently I saw couples
who were evidently quite fresh from the marriage service
reading these notices. Once at Meaux, I spoke to such a
pair.

"In Germany," I said to them, "I understand that
this sort of encouragement is not needed."

"It appears so, monsieur," said the bridegroom.

"Well, young man," I returned, "I am sure you know
the words of the Marseillaise: 'Allons, enfants de la
patrie.' "

"C'est juste, monsieur!" cried the bridegroom with a
gleaming laugh. The bride had walked a few steps away
so that she might seem to be out of hearing.

But to Nicolas, who brought my hot water morning
and evening in Paris, and to Paul, who took me so often
and through so many miles of the devastated regions
in his car, I said more. Nicolas had been telling me
how he came to be taken prisoner in the early days of the
war.

"I was of the 8th corps, monsieur."

"That was away off in the East, wasn't it?"

"Yes, monsieur, in the Vosges. We were led by persons
who made some blunder every day. We were marched
round and round without any point. Once we rambled

about in various directions for fifteen days. We had
been at Gerard Mer and at other places in the Vosges,
and finally one morning in a fog we were on a plain near
Ste. Die, and the battle of Lunéville began. We were
left without any guide, with the Germans on eminences
all round us, and our whole battalion was captured.
Others, who were better led and were not helpless,
escaped."

"What did they do with you in Germany?"

"They put us to work. I was at Ingoldstadt, and also
at Bayreuth. I did work in the railroads, and of course
we never got any news that we believed, but we learned
how it was going by the difference in the manner of the
Boches. In 1915 the German soldiers who passed us on
their way to the front used to shake their fists at us.
They would have massacred us if they had been permitted
to do so, but we were too useful. Thus we knew things
were going well with them. Then there were times in
'16 and '17 when those going to the front did not shake
their fists at us. Their heads hung down. By that we
could tell that things were not going so well for them."

"Were there no German workmen with you?"

"But yes, monsieur, naturally. Ah, those workmen
in Germany, they are slaves! See! whenever the ingénieur was coming near us—every time and each time
he came, no matter how often—they bowed low to him,
just as low as the first time. In France, after you have
once touched your hat and said good-morning, you don't
keep on doing it. *C'est une platitude.* But they would
say to us, 'Hush! The foreman is coming'; and they'd
start bowing. As if we cared for the foreman! They
work through fear. Ah, they are slaves. Voilà. And
that is why they are doing so well now in their business,
because those workmen work through fear. And after
the Armistice they saw their soldiers come back heads
high, with their arms and banners, wearing flowers. So
they strewed the streets with flowers and hailed their

heroic army and believed that the war had finished *en queue de poisson*. They will come again, monsieur, one knows that. And they outnumber us."

"Whose fault is that, Nicolas?"

"It is not our fault that they are barbarians and have a child every year."

"Well, Nicolas! Then you will call me a barbarian because I have six children! Listen! You have heard of Mr. Roosevelt?"

"Oh, yes, monsieur. Every one has heard of him. He was here and made a fine speech at the Sorbonne."

"Mr. Roosevelt told us Americans that we were committing race suicide. He said that the richer we became the fewer children we had, while the foreigners in our slums were having many, and that it would be merely a question of time when the old American stock would die out and our Republic fall to pieces in the hands of races that did not have the tradition or the power of self-government in their blood. Now I think at this rate you French will commit race suicide. You wish us to come back and help you fight the Germans if they invade you again. But if I say to American mothers that we ought to do this, that we ought to save France, they will reply, why should we bear sons to be killed in France? Let French mothers bear more sons! After all, Nicolas, in Brittany your peasants do have large families."

"They are Catholics, monsieur."

"Well, on too many of the crosses in your cemeteries, I read the names of men who are described as the only son of the family."

"It is because the parents wish to have the little share of land which they have owned for generations descend as a whole to that son. They love it and they wish to keep it whole, and not have to divide it among several as they are compelled to do by the Code Napoléon."

"I don't think our American mothers will be impressed by that argument, Nicolas."

He now became philosophic. "Yes, monsieur, it is

true. The Frenchman is an egoist. He does not wish to be burdened with the support of a family so large that he has no time to enjoy himself. In Germany life is easier, and their ways do not induce them to limit their families. And when a family grows to eight—or perhaps it is ten—children, the Kaiser has always stood godfather to that last child. So you see, with their feeling about the Kaiser, they have had a strong incentive. We, with our love of our land, have that reason for making only one son to inherit all of it."

"Now that the Kaiser is gone, Nicolas, perhaps those families of ten will stop."

"That is not very probable, monsieur. You see, when one has got the habit—" and Nicolas shrugged, "Ah, oui," he concluded. His generalizations almost always ended with "ah, oui."

Paul, my chauffeur, also had his philosophy, like most Frenchmen of every class, and, like most Frenchmen, he had the art of expressing it. We had come into Amiens one afternoon, and I got out on the steps at the west front of the cathedral.

"Paul," said I, "I wonder if I could guess your age?"

"If monsieur will try," he smiled.

"I think that you must be about thirty-two."

"That is my age, monsieur," he said, with a tone of surprise.

"So you were expecting me to get it wrong?"

"I thought that you would say that I was older." He stopped, and into his face came that look which I had begun to know in April 1919—the look of having been changed by sights and by knowledge that would never be forgotten, and that were always present. Then he said quietly and simply:

"The war has made old people out of many young people."

"Yes, Paul. And I suppose the only way to look at that, is to think that any man like you, who were in your twenties when that whirlwind caught you up from

ordinary life, would be no true man at all if he were not
many years older in the spirit when the whirlwind set
him down."

"Yes, monsieur."

"Are you married ?"

"No, monsieur. Oh, no. Not that."

"Well, but you're thirty-two. It is quite time."

"Perhaps. I have never turned my mind in that direction. It may be that I shall come to it."

"Don't wait too long !"

"Hé, monsieur, le mariage est si bizarre !" And Paul,
like Nicolas, punctuated his generalization with a shrug.

The remarkable and unanswerable adjective which he
applied to marriage stuck in my mind, and on a sub-
sequent day, I said to him:

"Paul, if the idea of a wife does not appeal to you,
here is something that will. I see the old people that
the war has made out of young people. I see them everywhere, and it is very sad. But I am sure that the years
of rebuilding which lie before you all will not be as dreary
as they look. Don't think about them as a whole, don't
imagine their united weight as pressing down upon every
day. It will be dispersed, only a little of it will be in each
day, and it will always be growing less."

"That is true," said Paul.

"And to see France reviving, to be part of it, to cause
some of it yourself, will carry you through each day,
and you will find, beside plenty of hard work, plenty of
laughter awaiting you. Perhaps even plenty of children !"

"Children will not be a laughing matter !" said Paul.*

It was easy to talk to him, and to any one before whom
a possible future stretched, a span of years wherein to
rebuild and refill an emptied life;—but there were others.
There was a custodian in the museum at Dijon. He grew

*Note. One year later, in 1922, I returned to Amiens, hav-
ing telegraphed for Paul to take me through the Somme
region. Another chauffeur met me. Paul was being married
that day at Nantes.

to know me as we walked among the pictures and while
he told me about the dukes of Burgundy, whose tombs
are there; and one day he talked about himself. He was
sixty-seven, he had seen the Germans come in 1870, he
had seen France recover from the war only to be thrown
prostrate again in his old age.

"There are people," he said, "who can make new
friends when they have lost old ones. But if one loses
one's only son, one has nothing left. Life is a burden.
One *is* not sure that one wishes it any more."

What could I say to him?

Again there were others, many others all over France,
who had gone a step beyond him, and had become sure
that they did not wish life any more: Clerks, small
officials, employees faithful and of many years' service,
whose fixed salary was no longer enough. It had sufficed
them, they had felt safe, they had built their lives upon
it, a roof, a family, books, perhaps a garden. Suddenly
the bills for food, for all necessities, trebled, and they
found themselves past their middle years—and unable
to pay. The salary grew no larger, they faced implacable
debt and want at fifty. They had no spring with which
to start afresh. They drew down their window shades
—and freed themselves from the burden of life. Perhaps
some might have persisted but for the four years' draft
upon their fortitude. To meet the war they had drawn
upon their courage every day; there was no balance
left for further stress.

It is hard for us, whose lives and property no invading
enemy has ever disturbed, to think of what living near
that war was like. Abbeville was a large place near
enough to it to be bombarded every night at times. The
shells came in the dark hours. The citizens attended to
their daily affairs in town, but they dared not sleep there.
Every evening a special train took them away, out into
the country, and there in the fields, or in any shelter that
they could find, they slept; and each morning the train
took them back to their business. The aunt and uncle of

a young lady who told me this came into Abbeville by
the train one day, and found the house that they had
locked up the night before was no longer to be seen;
it had been dashed to atoms.

What inhabitants of Philadelphia or St. Louis, or anywhere here, can imagine what it was to live through
weeks and years of such experience? Had they done so,
they would hardly be asking if France intends to "insist" upon the whole of her "indemnity" from Germany—
that "indemnity" which has already been cut down by
about one-third of the sum set by the Treaty of Versailles. And those Americans who talk about the line
between us and Canada, unguarded for a century, and
ask why France wishes an army, would they like to
change places with France, and have an unguarded line
between them and a race that has invaded them every
50 years for 15 centuries?

At Massevaux in Alsace, I found the curé's door, and
wrote "de la part de M. Clemenceau" on my card, and
sent it in. The curé came, and I said:

"Clemenceau sent me here. He told me to come and
see two of his friends in Massevaux and Thann, and say
that he had bidden me to do so, and they would talk
freely."

"Come in," said the curé. And he took me first up-
stairs to his room. There the windows looked out upon
his church.

After explaining what had brought me to France, I
continued:

"Is that the church where you took Clemenceau and the
generals that day of 1918, when Massevaux had ceased
to be Germany and was France again after 46 years?"

"But certainly," said the curé.

"You went with him and the generals and their soldiers in there, and after standing silent for a while, you
all sang the Marseillaise together?"

"But certainly."

"What deep and great happiness, mon père, to be

able to sing that song aloud again and not to have to say French prayers in silence any more!"

Then we spoke of Alsace, France, and the future.

"Have you talked with many Alsatians?" he asked.

"I wish that I could. I am afraid to begin politics with them—and I think they are with me. Who can be sure who any stranger is? Germany haunts their minds, I feel that, and it haunts their manners also. What do you think of this? When I changed trains at Cernay to come here, there was a woman getting into the car. I drew back and motioned her to go first—and she said, 'After you, monsieur,' and waited till I had preceded her. That is a little thing, mon père, but does it not reveal much?"

He nodded. "If they became willing to tell you what they have in their hearts, you would find that they all expect the Germans to come back in ten years."

"In October 1918," I said, "when Mr. Wilson was writing those notes to Max of Baden, I published a little piece in our papers in which I said that if we trusted Berlin when it cried 'Kamerad,' our children would pay for it with their blood."

"People in Mulhouse spoke to me of such a piece," said the curé. "They said it was by an American.—Alsatians believe that Germany will never pay the reparations, but that they would have forced France to pay most of it by now, had the situation been reversed."

"You are not the first person who has said that to me," I responded. "The present situation seems to me to be chiefly the fault of Mr. Wilson and Mr. Lloyd George. We are more fortunate than England. England still has Mr. Lloyd George. I was indiscreet enough to say to M. Clemenceau that it seemed to me Mr. Lloyd George, if he continued on the way he is going, would end by achieving what Napoleon Bonaparte failed to achieve—the destruction of the British Empire."

The curé looked at me. "And what did M. Clemenceau say to that?"

"Naturally he was discreet. But he talked much of India."

"Have you ever heard any one say that Mr. Wilson sent a message through Lloyd George that if the Allies did not accept an armistice, he would withdraw the American troops?"

"I have heard that several times, but never at first-hand. I hope it is not true."

"Listen," said the curé, "in September 1918, Foch was here, in Massevaux, and so was General Castelnau. I said to Foch, 'How is it going?' 'I hold them,' he answered, 'they are done.' 'Then why go on?' I asked him. 'Because we must enter Germany and finish there. Otherwise they will say that we did not win, and there will be no finish.' So said Castelnau also. And then, why did they not finish in Germany? The greatest victory in history was turned into an abortion."

"It is very grievous for me to think," said I, "that we are responsible for that."

"Oh, we all understand now that it was not you. Mr. Wilson was without your mandate."

"We could not tell you so," said I.

"Nor could we French tell him so. By his own arbitrary act he placed us all in this false position."

"Then you think that Foch——"

"Foch—what was he to do but to be loyal? He sank his own—judgment, he stood by what was forced upon him, and said to the world that an armistice gave us all that we wanted without the sacrifice of more lives. But do you think that he, who told me in September that it must finish in Germany or remain unfinished, had changed his mind? Have you ever heard that one afternoon when Clemenceau and Wilson and Lloyd George were sitting in council together, Foch came in to speak to Clemenceau, and Wilson said, 'Who is that military man? I will not have military men in here.' And Clemenceau, to save the situation quickly, rose and said, 'It is five o'clock. Let us go to tea.' Have you heard that?"

"Never. Couldn't that have been invented?"

"Oh, yes, it could have been invented; but no invention sticks which is not characteristic. We know that Mr. Wilson had no power to promise us your help in case of another invasion. But the next war, should it come, would be over before you could reach us. People will never march to any war again, they will fly through the air."

We must have been talking for an hour, when I rose.

"Let me show you our church, where we sang the Marseillaise," said the curé.

He accompanied me out and across the street into the church. There he pointed up to a broken window.

"A bomb did that," he said. "It also killed the only man who had moved into Massevaux for safety. He was an old man. Here is where we stood and sang the Marseillaise."

I stood there with him for a while; and after he had shown me the rest of the church, and the very fine organ, I took my leave. His farewell words were:

"I have known the Germans for forty-five years. They are a curious race; like no other. And they have won the peace."

On such another afternoon as this I made my way to Thann. The light of May was shining upon the Vosges, hill and valley were filled with it, the fruit blossoms glowed in it. Thann was neighbor to Massevaux, separated by one of the wooded ridges of the Vosges; and along the valley where it lay, the mills of a large and long-founded industry extended. The house of the present master of this industry stood on a hill overlooking his manufactories and the village where his operatives lived. Once again the name of Clemenceau opened doors to me, and the master took me into his study; once again the understanding of America was clear and cordial. The responsibility of the evil Armistice and of all that followed was fixed where it belonged, not upon

us or our Senate, and the good that we had done was
also fixed where it belonged, not upon the man who had
"kept us out of the war," but upon the heart and mind
of the nation that had ended by seeing the true meaning
of the war in spite of him. This French gentleman had
seen many of our officers, and these had told him the
truth about our country.

In one of the front windows of the room where we
talked, a bullet had drilled a splintered hole through
the pane; another had dug a cavity in the wall while
the daughter of the house had sat at the desk where
her father was sitting now. These were the only injuries
the house had suffered. Both the master's sons had been
killed. After speaking of the North and the South he
asked me about our Middle West.

"They were slower," he said, "to realize the war, were
they not?"

"For this reason," I answered. "They were misled
by our President who told us in 1916 that we were not
concerned with the causes or the objects of the European
conflict—and they are a community deeply absorbed in
its own development. They are not inclined to look
out of the window. But when they finally did look out
and saw what was happening, the manner in which
they rose and set to work was truly magnificent. They
can do anything, once they are aroused."

"Is your industrial crisis over?" he asked; and for
a while we discussed that and our labor difficulties.

I discovered that he was a man who certainly looked
out of his window and saw long distances. In speaking
about some of the French methods of business, he said:
"We are Chinese." Presently he turned the talk to Alsace
and its special problems. I had spoken about the *double
personality* which I felt in the people of Strasbourg.

"I am travelling second and third class in the trains
here," I said, "because it is in those cars rather than in
the first class that I seem to see the Alsatian more distinctly. I notice that the people glide from French into

the local dialect here, and back again into French, almost in the same sentence. And I notice also that their appearance is rather German than French."

"That is quite true. Their bodies have the heavy character of the German physique—but not their minds. Have you observed their manner of speaking?"

"I am not quite sure what you mean."

"There is a lightness, a turn of drollery and of wit in what they say which is not at all like the heaviness of their flesh. Their spirit is French. They have not dared to be French outwardly since 1871. In November 1918, some soldiers of our army who had entered and were marching by a field where stood an old peasant woman, saw her suddenly burst into tears; and she cried out to them that it was nothing but happiness at being able to speak French aloud again."

"Have you any idea how much German sympathy is lurking among the people?" I asked.

"Broadly speaking, I think it is among the lower classes that the German spirit hangs on, but it is by no means universal there. In spite of all that they could do during 46 years, they did not manage to make us love them. It was a rule of fear. You have heard of the Saverne incident?"

"Where the Prussian officer cut the face of a lame cobbler with his sword because he was not wearing a sufficiently German expression? Oh, yes. And the Crown Prince sent him a message of congratulation."

"But do you know about poularde?"

"Poularde? No."

"In the café at Saverne which the Prussian officers frequented, there was a bill-of-fare on the table one day, upon which, among the German words, was the French one, poularde. A young Prussian lieutenant was so enraged by the appearance of this that he drew his sword and cut the bill-of-fare in two where the word occurred. His name was von Forstner. It was in the Restaurant à la Carpe d'or, opposite the Place du Château, where this happened.

If you have time, pay Saverne and that restaurant a visit.
The lady who saw the whole poularde affair still keeps it."

"That whole brutal outrage of Saverne," said I, "was
a sort of rehearsal of what they did next year in the war
—a specimen of what they would have done to the world,
had they won."

"Yes, they did their best to Prussianize us and divide
us against each other, by encouraging disunity in both
religion and education. They had separate schools for
Catholics, Protestants, and Jews—but always with the
Kaiser as the centre of worship. I have heard a pastor
say in a pulpit 'you must not consider the Kaiser as God's
deputy, but as Jesus Christ himself.'" He added that
it was German policy with the young to educate "le conscience contre l'intérêt."

"How long do you think it will take," I asked, "for
Alsace to become completely French?"

"A generation should accomplish it. All the children
are eager to learn French, and certain troubles which we
are having now will be adjusted. There is a difficulty
about the church. The clericals naturally resist a change
to the present system in France which would deprive them
of the direct control of their office and estate. This would
never have come about in France if M. Combe and the
Pope had either of them been capable of compromise."

As he talked on about Alsace, and France, and America,
I listened and replied, feeling all the while a sympathy
for him that I dared not express. His mills in the valley
of Thann had been going for a hundred years, owned and
conducted by his family from the beginning. He told me
that he had never had any trouble with his operatives.

"I have a system of pensions, and I have always remembered that these men are human. There came a time when
they demanded syndicalization. I made no objection to
this. 'You have the right to it,' I said to them. 'But I
have a right also. I will deal with you directly, and not
with any outsider; and I will treat non-syndicalized men
exactly on the same footing, neither better nor worse.' I

thought that I knew what would happen, but I did not expect it so soon. In six months all of my workmen had left the syndicate."

I wanted to stay on and listen to this French gentleman. His father had been president of the Senate during the Dreyfus case, and was one of the first to believe that Dreyfus was innocent—a stand which cost him many friends, and his office. He in his turn was now a senator.

"And so M. Clemenceau sent you to me," he said. "I have known him since I was knee-high. What a man!"

"He made me think," I answered, "of Mr. Roosevelt when he was our President. Whenever I paid him a visit, I always felt as if I had been talking to Vesuvius in active eruption."

Yes, I wanted to stay; but I had been here an hour, and so I rose.

"But at least you will let me get you some refreshment?" he said; and when I declined, "Then I will go with you to the station."

It was about half a mile; and as we walked down towards the valley, very beautiful church bells sounded from below, their tone floating up through the quiet air among the woods and ridges. It was May 1st, and as we drew nearer the village, we heard a strain of thin false brass music. Presently we turned a corner, and a very small company of "reds" marched by, blowing trumpets to the glory of disorder. A few ragged children followed them. The master pointed to them, smiling.

"Not a large proportion for a great industrial community," he said.

Once more I looked at him, a senator, a captain of industry, the establisher of pensions, friend to his men, and owner of a mass of buildings which stretched far down the valley; and with both his sons killed in the war. I could not help speaking:

"Is there none of your blood to follow and take this from your hands?"

"Not any longer," he replied quietly, "I am the last."

I went to Saverne and the lady of the Golden Carp enacted the whole scene of the poularde for me as I sat drinking coffee at the table in the back of the room where it had happened. But the youth, or the beauty, or some attribute of Lieutenant von Forstner, had softened her heart toward him.

"He was only 19," she said. "It was the fault of his colonel." And she told me, among other things, that all the children of Saverne were eager to learn French, and that the girls were quicker at it than the boys. Were I Alsatian, I, too, should wish to learn French;—here is some Alsatian:

"De reizigers gelieven niet op het privaat te gaan zoolang de trein in eene statie stilstaat."

As I talked with General Humbert in Strasbourg, a budget of papers lay upon his desk.

"This," he said, laying his hand upon the heap, "is my latest secret information from Germany. They are not disarming. They are merely changing the name of the Polizei which they agreed at Spa to disband into a Polizei with a new name." Then he gave me the details. "And they are practising gunnery twice instead of once a week." And he thumped the papers lightly.

"I am being indiscreet every day," I said, "and now I will add one more to my indiscretions. Some of your recent allies are calling you impatient. What strikes me is the extraordinary patience of France under repeated provocations."

As I was going, he suddenly spoke of America, of our army, of our soldiers and officers, with such a warmth and enthusiasm that I will not repeat it; and all I could reply was:

"My lack of French prevents my expressing to you, as I should like to do, how deeply your words touch me."

Anywhere that you went, anyone that you saw, it was the same; if you were silent on the subject of our contribution to the war, they would introduce it sooner or later, and always with generous and cordial words; but American boasting had not pleased them any better than it pleased those Americans who did not boast.

From Guy Ropartz, the distinguished French composer, and director of the conservatory of music at Strasbourg, I heard most interesting facts about music there under the German rule. His Hun predecessor had done his best to extinguish French music in the town—none had ever been taught, and none had ever been played at the concerts. Ropartz found the young people of Strasbourg entirely unaware that any French music existed; they had never heard of Saint-Saëns, or César Franck, or Debussy, or Berlioz, or apparently of anybody except Germans. But he found something even more interesting than this. The Hun predecessor—whose name was Kitzner, I think—had introduced many improvements into the symphonies of Beethoven; he had not only made cuts in them, he had put in his own orchestration and made changes in the notation. Ropartz was obliged to spend much time in restoring Beethoven's own instrumentation in the scores of the symphonies.

"I always admired greatly the calm conducting of Hans Richter," he told me. "It was not only deeply understanding, but it was also always reverent. His aim was never anything but to learn the composer's intention and then to carry it out. But after the time of Nikisch and Weingartner, it became the fashion of German conductors to use the symphonies of the masters merely as vehicles for themselves."

"I have heard Nikisch do that to Mozart in Boston," I told him.

During the war Ropartz had three sons at the front. He was then teaching at the conservatory of Nancy, and as that town was not safe, he sent his wife and daughter away to Brittany, and meanwhile kept the students at Nancy busy over the musical exercises.

"When the whistle blew to announce an air raid," he said, "we used to go down into a cellar and continue our exercises there until the bombs stopped falling and the safety signal blew. Then we would come back above ground again and go on with the work. The young people were perfectly calm. One day I was getting ready to go to Brittany for a short visit to my wife and daughter. I was writing and signing some papers at my desk before leaving, when the thought came to me, what a needless thing it would be to be bombed at such a time! So I took my papers to the cellar. While I was down there I heard a noise of an unusual quality, not like the sound of a Boche bomb, and I wondered if it might be a gas or a flame bomb. When I went back, my office had gone. A French bomb had fallen upon it. Now it would have been tiresome to be killed by that."

Earlier in the spring, before blossom time, while the peasants were plowing their fields, I spent a day in the St. Mihiel country. Much of it was still desolate with the shell holes and the barbed wire, but here and there were stretches that had been reclaimed. The earth was brown, and one could look deep into the violet grey of the woods. Where the fields rose to a ridge, the horses and the plowing peasants showed against the sky, and along the furrows went the sowers with their bags, flinging their arms with a forward gesture as they scattered the seed. Sometimes I got out and talked to those who were near the road. Often, as we talked, the sound of explosions came heavily from various distances through the quiet air, and the clotted pillars of their smoke would rise and hang for a long while. Those were the live grenades left in the soil by the battles and now having their stings drawn. The farmers were sowing oats to be plowed in later, and there was a growth of a bad weed named *chien dent* to be up-rooted. One peasant explained that no one dared to plow the soil deep.

"Because," he said, "ce n'est pas une noce to hit an obus. Those artificers who are being paid 35 francs a day to explode these shells are very unsystematic. They ought to do it progressively, like plowing, but they run here and there. If I am not blown up, after my oats next year, I shall plant potatoes. It will take me three or four years to get my ground clear of weeds. Yesterday I plowed up two obus, but I am still here, as you see."

On the way back, near Verdun, a puncture gave me a chance for a longer conversation with a farmer and his wife. One of their buildings was a complete ruin, with rusty shells lying around and inside of it, and wire ran tangled through the grass. They were living as best they could in a sort of hovel near by, where the woman was digging.

"How do you do, madame?" I said. "You certainly were not here during the war."

"No, monsieur, we were refugees."

"And where?"

"In Touraine first, and after that at Montpellier."

"And now you are back at work. Does it go well?"

"It is very hard to dig. The ground is full of stones and tin cans and saletés de toutes espèces."

"Well, madame, I hope you will have a good harvest."

"Oh, yes, monsieur, everything is going well."

At this point her man with a plow and two mules came up, having finished work for the day. It was a very light and a very poor plow, and I asked him about it.

"Yes, look at it," he said, with a sort of gruff joviality. "Everything is very dear now. Before the war that cost 125 francs. Now 700. And a good mule 5,000 francs now. Before the war 800.—So you are American?"

"Yes."

"We ought to have got some of those big animals that you left behind. They would have done our plowing well. But other people . . ." he completed his sentence by making a most eloquent and comical curving sweep with his hand behind his back, and this made his meaning quite plain.

"Alors vous êtes Américain?" he repeated jovially, "Have you returned to make some more war?"

"Ah, no!"

He stood straight and stiff, and his face changed to gravity. "Well," he said, with deliberation, "without you, this would be Germany today." And he pointed down to the earth.

"We are very glad if we were of any help," I said.

"This would be Germany if you had not come," he reiterated with emphasis.

"They should have invaded Germany," said I.

"Yes."

The chauffeur overheard this.

"That is true," he said. "Nothing more true. We wished to go on, but we were not allowed. Foch wept."

"Yes, I have heard that from many. General Pershing wanted to go on too."

That is the France which I saw for five months in 1921 and which some said (and are saying still), is idle, prosperous, and militaristic. Though some of those that have represented her have at times manifested impatience at the treatment she has received, and the perversions of her true position which have appeared in certain newspapers and fallen from the lips of certain public men, the plain truth is that as a nation she has been as patient with England about Germany as England has been patient with America about Ireland; and that is saying a great deal.

XXVIII

ALL through History are incidents which to their own generation have seemed important, and which have dwindled as the years left them behind, while the significance of others has steadily enlarged with time. To this latter class belong the Norman Conquest, the invention of printing, and the voyage of Columbus. When we, who have lived so close to the war that we cannot measure it, are long gone, and it has fallen into the motionless landscape of the past, what will it seem like then? Today we can hardly believe that it will ever cease to be known as the Great War; and yet, that is a question to be answered then, and not now; convulsions more gigantic may dwarf the terrible years of 1914 to 1918. But as time goes on, America's act in 1917 will not look smaller. It will grow in two ways, in relation to ourselves and in relation to our neighbors. We had risen to greatness before, certainly once, paying with our blood; but to keep the Union and free the slave was an act according to our faith, was carrying out into action what our religion declared and compelled; whereas in joining the Great War, in leaving our new world and crossing the sea to the old, we ran counter to an article of our faith so deep that it was second only to our belief in liberty defined and assured by law. Both—our liberty and our isolation—have been woven so close in our minds and emotions they can be called American instincts. And yet we broke from the second. It was like tearing apart one's brain. To go upon our own way, to mind our own affairs, to keep apart from others' quarrels, to stand aloof from the meshes of foreign jealousies, this course had been set for us, had been preached to us from the beginning, and it had been practised throughout a century of success. Every decade of

our national life had ratified and vindicated the wisdom
of our isolation; and yet we wrenched ourselves loose from
the embedded anchor. That small handful of Europeans
who have studied more about Americans than merely their
money, know this and understand that to take such a step
cost us a sort of mental revolution; they know that our
delay was inevitable, beyond our control, that a mental
revolution in a hundred million people is not accomplished
in a moment; especially under the powerful and confusing
influences that were at work in our midst, befogging us
night and day. Some of us, who saw where our duty lay
sooner than the mass, have been inclined to apologize to
Europe for our lateness. No apologies are due, except
from those Europeans who still, in cold blood and after
the event, have sneered because we did not do at once
what none of them have ever done at all in their whole
history.

One conspicuous demagogue has termed the European
conflict a rich man's war and a poor man's fight. Those
Europeans who have given us their intelligent attention
know that we fought for an ideal, that it was precisely
our *rich,* and not our poor, young men who threw themselves first into the war as a class, who enlisted in the
Allied armies, who formed the Lafayette Escadrille, who
offered themselves to the cause of Liberty before their
country had taken the step, who did not wait for the draft,
who shouldered arms *before the hour of obligation,* and
whose names now shine on the tablets of our schools and
colleges. It was our *sons of privilege* that showed themselves, as a class, worthy of their privilege, whose young
eyes discerned in 1914 what the whole country came to
see at last. Three words, spoken by one of these sons of
privilege as he lay dying, enshrine the whole truth, the
reason that he and his kind went at once, never waiting
for any call but the call from within. He came from one
of our great preparatory schools, he was a Harvard student, he enlisted in Canada, he met his death in Europe.

In the hospital where he was taken, the nurse asked him how it happened that he was in the war when his country was neutral. He answered:

"Our fight too."

The sentence is a parable. No orator, no statesman, no poet, could better say why America broke from that second article of her belief and poured her treasure and her life across three thousand miles of sea, and stood ready to go on spending herself to the last dollar and the last drop of blood. Nothing in that manifestation of our soul and strength more astonished the Europeans than how, once we were aroused and aware, we accepted conscription and required no law to enforce our self-denial. Did the Allies need sugar or flour? We went without them— it was the *kitchen,* not the dining room that rebelled; once again it was the privileged classes that saw their duty and did it. If oil grew scarce, it was only necessary to tell us, and thousands gave up the chief pleasure of their week and left their automobiles in the garage on Sundays.

No, it is not likely that our part in the war will dwindle as it grows distant in time; and the essence of the internal conflict that it costs us will be seen more clearly than it is today. Although we departed from our creed of isolation, that very departure was a passionate adherence to the first article of our faith—to liberty, defined and assured by law. The struggle was between those two principles, and the fundamental one prevailed; for in the last analysis, isolation is not a fundamental, but a temporary principle, and it is no longer a question of our renouncing it—it has renounced us. No matter how much some of us may wish it, Americans can no longer enjoy a brain of one dimension. It is not going to be a question of choice, natural laws have settled it for us. You may push facts out of the door, they will come in at the window. A natural law does not speak, it asserts itself in silence, and if you ignore it long enough, it will grind you to powder. Here we reach the second aspect of our part in the war, its relation not to ourselves but to others. Of those four years, we fought but half a year; it is not the size of our participation, but its consequences, that are now the point.

When the emergency of the war began in August 1914, we looked at it as one of those foreign complications with which Washington told us to have nothing to do. By August 1918, nearly two million Americans had gone to fight in France. We had been drawn into the emergency. Why? Look at the map, think of electricity and of steam, and you will have the answer. Is it very likely that Washington in April 1917 would still have advised us to avoid that foreign complication?

Next, the war was over, and in a way, won. We thought at the time that it was won much more completely than the ensuing years have disclosed; and with a deep sigh of joy and content our country came home—home physically and mentally. It turned its thoughts again to itself, and there was indeed plenty to think about. But the emergency of the war has been followed by the emergency of the peace. That is going on now; and once again some of us are quoting Washington. We can no more keep out of the present foreign complication than we were able to hold aloof from its predecessor. Just as much as that was, this is "our fight too"—not for reasons of sentiment, but for reasons of self-preservation. Why? Look at the map, think of electricity and steam, and again you will have the answer. War and peace are merely different processes of self-preservation, different means by which nations control and protect their existence, manage their affairs, survive. We like to hope that peace will some day be the only method by which nations live; but whether this comes to pass or not, if the fundamental state of the world is changed, and a great war draws everybody into its emergency, the emergencies of peace are bound to do exactly the same thing.

It would be good news if we did not have to think about Europe as a concern of our own, if foreign complications could be pushed out of our reckoning, if we could return to our brain of one dimension. But that comfortable day is done, and the truth is, that the word "foreign" has ceased to have any economic or political meaning; in that sense, there is little that is foreign in the world any more. We are all neighbors in the same street, and neighbors henceforth it is our destiny to be.

I do not wonder that great portions of our people sincerely believe what I wish that I could believe—that our going over to Europe was an accident, an exception, a parenthesis in our isolation, a closed incident; and that now we can resume our development and attend to our own housekeeping, and never think of Europe, or any other part of the world again, except when it pleases us to do so as a market for our wares, a playground for our holidays, or an object of our voluntary compassion and assistance, like Belgium. I wish they were right, I wish it were true. When I think of our pioneers, our backwoodsmen, our cowboys, I have a home-sick longing to be back in their simple day, and I desire to turn my face away from the welter that Europe is in—the deceits, the jealousies, the greed of conquest, the flare of discord, the collapse of prosperity. We are no more responsible for that state of things than we were for the war; why saddle ourselves with the burdens of others when we have enough of our own to carry already? Let Europe be satisfied with the help we gave her in 1918, and settle her present troubles for herself. That is what many Americans are saying and feeling, and it would make a strong argument, if isolation were a matter of choice in these days as it was in the days when George Washington wrote that Farewell Address which is being so freely quoted and misquoted just now on the subject of entangling alliances.

It is to be noticed how remarkably little we quote or follow a certain other piece of advice which Washington gave us in that same Farewell Address—that we should avoid occasions of expense by cultivating peace, "but remembering also that *timely disbursements to prepare for danger frequently prevent much greater disbursements to repel it."* Not once in our history have we followed that wise counsel; on the contrary, Congress has steadily opposed and obstructed preparedness for war; and every war which we have fought has caught us with our clothes off. The hasty toilet that we were compelled to make on the last occasion, in 1917, could not have been made at all if the British fleet had not stood between us and the enemy like a wall, behind which we were able to cover our nakedness before it was too late. Some day it may be too late. As it is, we are suffering from a heavy burden of taxes, due to the hurry in which we had to get ready at the eleventh hour, and which might have been averted, had Congress and Mr. Wilson heeded the advice of George Washington, instead of heaping every champion of preparedness, such as Augustus Gardner, or Leonard Wood, with falsehood, sneers, and abuse. Against stupidity the gods themselves contend in vain; and our politicians are quick to remember George Washington when they can use him for something that they like because it is easy and will cost them no votes, but they find it convenient to forget him when his advice is disagreeable to them. Consequently in these present days they are placing in front of the gloomy truth that America can no longer play a lone hand but must do team-work with Europe, the cheerful falsehood that Washington forbade team-work.

What did Washington really say about Europe and its relation to us in his Farewell Address?

"Europe has a set of primary interests which to us have none, or a very remote relation. Hence she must be engaged in frequent controversies, the causes of which are essentially foreign to our concerns. Hence, therefore, it must be unwise in us to implicate ourselves, by artificial ties, in the ordinary vicissitudes of her politics, or the ordinary combinations and collisions of her friendships or enmities.

"Our detached and distant situation invites and enables us to pursue a different course. If we remain one people, under an efficient government, the period is not far off when we may defy material injury from external arro-

gance; when we may take such an attitude as will cause
the neutrality we may at any time resolve upon to be
scrupulously respected. . . .

"Why forego the advantages of so peculiar a situation?
Why quit our own to stand upon foreign ground? Why,
by interweaving our destiny with that of any part of
Europe, entangle our peace and prosperity in the toils
of European ambition, rivalship, interest, humor, or
caprice?

" 'Tis our true policy to steer clear of permanent alliances with any portion of the foreign world . . . we
may safely trust to temporary alliances for extraordinary
emergencies. . . .

"There can be no greater error than to expect or calcu-
late upon real favors from nation to nation."

That is every word which the Farewell Address contains on the subject of alliances; and this document, dated
19th September, 1796, is being offered to us as a guide in
1922, with its language about foreign alliances generally
misquoted. Why not ask us to wear knee breeches and a
wig because Washington wore them? In the first place,
he expressly admitted temporary alliances for extraordinary emergencies, and in the second place his whole
thought is naturally based on the world as it was in 1796.
They pay a very poor compliment to the marvellously
observant and far-sighted sagacity of the Father of his
Country, when they apply his remarks to 1922, and assume that he would repeat them unchanged. In his time,
it took nearly two months to send a message to Europe
and receive an answer; today it can be done in a few
hours. Would Washington call Europe remote now?
Would he speak of our "detached and distant situation"
after seeing an aeroplane, and a submarine, and the
Baldwin Locomotive Works, or any other works which
sell our wares all over the world?

When he was notified of his unanimous election as
President in April 1789, Washington set out from Mt.
Vernon on the 16th and reached New York on the 23rd.
Had some neighbors in Virginia at that time asked him how

long one should allow for a comfortable journey to New York, the answer would have been seven days; and as Washington was careful about details, he would have told the neighbor where he would find the best lodging for the night at the end of each day's journey. Since then London has been reached in seven days by many steamers. To suppose that he would give us today the same advice about Europe that he gave in 1796, is precisely as sensible as to suppose that he would tell a friend that it would take a week to go from Mt. Vernon to New York, instead of recommending the express trains that do it now in five hours.

Washington's outlook was not narrowed by a brain of one dimension; he thought internationally, his policy was not shackled by obsolete conditions. Scarcely more than ten years after our Revolution, he declined to fall in with the wishes of France, who had been our friend, and made a treaty with England, who had been our enemy. For this he was violently abused by the brains of one dimension of that day, until the good results that followed from his wise policy put them to silence. If the changes in conditions after ten years could cause such a change in Washington's mind, it is hardly worth while to try to fit to the present day a piece of advice given 126 years ago based upon conditions that are no longer the same.

When we began our national life, the total population of the thirteen original states was less than that of the city of New York today; we exported nothing, the few articles that we made, such as glass, were of local use; our thin population was scattered in unrelated spots from New Hampshire to Georgia, with miles of uninhabited wilderness lying between them; travel on land was by horse, on water it was by sail. Similarly at that time, the whole world was inhabited in spots, no wires or rails tied nations together, the tides of trade and intercourse were few, and like thin streams, compared to the thick volume that pours back and forth between all countries now. Today, distance and time are virtually obliterated by electricity, Europe and America are no longer spots with space be-

tween them; they are confluent, with thousands of veins
and arteries of commerce and credit flowing through them,
making them like parts of one body. If one nation falls
a victim to any grave and prolonged economic disease,
the rest will suffer in time just as inevitably as blood
poisoning in a man's finger will infect his whole system
if it is not checked. Like neighbors in the same street,
the nations of Europe and America depend for their welfare more and more upon the same set of supplies, supplies of meat, grain, coal, hardware, and credit, especially
credit; in this essential above all they cannot get on without team-work. If Europe goes bankrupt, disaster will flow
through the arteries of trade and attack us too. The
American who shuts his eyes to this because it is a fact
which jars his ideal of isolation, is like a man who puts
off making his will because it is unpleasant to be reminded
that he is not going to live for ever.

As America was compelled to take notice of the war,
and submit to team-work in order to prevent a catastrophe that in the end would have reached her as well as
England and France, she will have to continue her team-
work henceforth. She can never break away again. Catastrophes are not over, and it is as unlikely that they will
ever cease in the future as that they ever ceased in the
past. The great difference between the future and the past
is, that nations used to be able to have catastrophes by
themselves, without one toppling brick pushing down the
whole row. Consequently, we must join hands with Europe
to fight all disasters that threaten.

And we shall play the part of creditor gracefully if
Europe plays the debtor's part gracefully: it isn't pretty
for him who stretches out his hand to be asking favours
with a sneer.

The signs are good. I can remember that long after I
was grown up it was a rare thing to hear foreign news
discussed by Americans of any class. It is now the subject of daily conversation, not only in marble halls but
in street cars. In the Back Bay station in Boston, there is
a boot-black who comments on France and Germany and

Mr. Lloyd George while he polishes my shoes; when I was an under-graduate I could have walked the length of Beacon Street with its most leading citizen and never touched once upon foreign affairs. That is because in those days, affairs could still be foreign, while now the word foreign is growing obsolete. As Columbus discovered us we are now obliged to discover Europe.

In his day, the world was said to be flat. When he proved that it was round a number of persons were highly scandalized. Today a number of Americans are highly scandalized to hear that our isolation is done for. But I do not think that the brain of one dimension is going to prevail now in the peace, any more than it did during the war. It came dreadfully near it, but it failed. We played team-work in time. We must not be too late now, and we shall not be. In some form, worked out by our men of affairs collaborating with our government, we shall bear a hand again to England and France. Nothing must happen to either of them. Whatever roughnesses there may be, they are the salt of the earth. The danger that hung black over them when we came in 1917 has been replaced by another danger, they barely keep their heads above water. If they sink they are certain to drag us down with them. For our own preservation we must throw them a life-preserver.

And not only for that reason! In those moments when France and England are at their best, they see a best in us that is not merely material. We have money, yes; but they know and we know (when all are at their best) that beyond and above money there is that imponderable thing which outweighs all gold. It is hard to name; the word ideal has been over-used; but it is what made us free the slave, set Cuba free, and come to help them in 1917. It is the thing that built Westminster Abbey, and the cathedral of Amiens, and made Washington come to New York to be President, when what his heart craved was to rest at Mt. Vernon beneath his own vine and fig tree.

XXIX

CAN THESE BONES LIVE?

IT is not alone in Flanders fields that poppies blow between the crosses. From Paschendael and the Lys, over the Somme and Aisne, across the Argonne and past Romagne and the Meuse and Moselle to Massevaux, the dead lie everywhere; the young dead of many languages, whose spirits at the end spoke a tongue universal. What they wrote to their mothers in a legion of letters that have gone to homes all over the world would have been understood by every mother bereaved of a son. Whether these last messages went to Warwickshire, or Inverness, or Dauphiné, or Ontario, or to the lands of the far Pacific, they could almost be exchanged by those who received them, so much do they all say the same thing. Their writers, while still in this life, had passed beyond these voices to a life where what was terror and horror to us who read of it, was to them a state of serene and even happy dedication to the will of God. As one passes their graves, and again more graves, and then still more, out in the open stretches, along the sheltering edges of groves, on the slopes of hills, among plowed fields or growing harvests, or near some lovely ancient spire, the silence of France is filled with the memory of them, and to each of those quiet hearts one applies the words that are graven on the stone of a certain boy who lies in a field of Tardenois:

He has outsoared the darkness of our night.

Thirty-three hundred British cemeteries are in France; we have four.

Much thought, much art, much care, went to the shaping of these cities of the British dead. They are very beautiful, and simple reverence lives among their paths and growing flowers, and consolation almost visible seems to be waiting for every soul who comes there in need. Each body that lies in them rests in the company of comrades, near the very spot where all offered together their last and highest sacrifice to the same great cause, and upon the soil that all helped together to save. To visit these assembled dead, come the living all through the year, each to seek some special grave. They take away a rich and twofold solace; they have seen how fittingly the ashes dear to them are tended, and they have felt the great unison of sacredness which comes from all these soldiers' graves, and is shed upon each one. They tell others what they have seen, and of the peace which the sight has brought them; and so to mothers in Canada, Australia, New Zealand, and every British land across the world is wafted soon or late the knowledge that it is well with their boys.

Along the roads from Ypres to Massevaux, to right and left all the way, the signs come by: British Cemetery, French Cemetery, Canadian, Australian, and sometimes American Cemetery; we still have four. From our chief one at Romagne, where once lay all our dead of the Meuse-Argonne, not quite one-half were taken from where they rested together, and were dispersed to rest alone, far away over the sea, in company that had not shared their errand or their sacrifice. Over the happy remnant at Romagne, France will bow her head on sacred days when she remembers and honors her own sons, through all the years to come. If Britain, whose killed were eight hundred thousand, counts thirty-three hundred cemeteries, how many must France possess, whose dead were not far from twice as many? But America still has four; and France will not forget them on her sacred days.

To see those British cemeteries that are finished, gives one the wish that one had the right to lie there too. The quiet and beautiful holiness that their paths and flowers and similar headstones make is like nothing I have ever seen. The headstones are all alike, proportioned with excellent skill, expressing dignity and simplicity; no upstart column or spike of vanity mars the solemn and sweet concord of the whole. One is moved to linger, one is led to read one name after another. Beautiful is the inscription without a name:

IN HONOR OF A
BRITISH SOLDIER
NAME UNKNOWN.
2nd July, 1916

KNOWN UNTO GOD.

The lettering and the graceful proportions of the cross reveal the same thought and art which are to be seen in every detail throughout.

These thirty-three hundred cemeteries are laid out, furnished, and maintained by subordinate camps which depend upon the general headquarters at St. Omer. The local camps are established in each of the regions into which the whole territory of the British dead is divided. From these are issued the headstone and the plants and other supplies, in accordance with the directions from St. Omer. At the camp in Bethune, for instance, is a nursery for plants; and in 1920 one-quarter of a million of these were distributed from here for the graveyards in that special region. At St. Omer are the various departments which plan and superintend severally the laying out of each ground, its grading and shaping in relation to its environment, its planting with trees and shrubs, its decoration with flowers, and its paths and arrangement of headstones, and the war stone and war cross.

Some cemeteries are larger; the one named TYNCOT on Paschendael Ridge contains 15,000 dead, while others are like country churchyards in size. For the 2,000 Chinese I saw some of the headstones at Bethune, lettered with their alphabet and carved with symbols strange to a Western eye; but with the date and a text in English. These dead have to be buried with their feet towards water, in accordance with their oriental faith. Among the English graves at Heilly were those of some German prisoners, tended with the same care and respect; and an altar which had been raised above these bore this tragic and moving sentence:

O freund wenn du nach Deutschland Kommst
  erzähle dass uns liegen sahst
  den Gesetzen unseres Landes getreu.

Suddenly overcome, I said aloud: "Peace to their souls! It was none of their doing."

At Louvencourt, English, French, and Flemish words were on the signs of a finished cemetery, where the war cross and war stone were in place, and around and beneath them, enclosed by the completed stone wall, generals, gunners, surgeons, lieutenants, trumpeters, drivers, able seamen—all ranks were lying beside each other, in the same majestic level of death. The emblems of their regiments were carved above them on each headstone, turf was green upon the walks. English daisies grew in it, and flowers grew round the graves. It was Sunday, and the bells of Louvencourt were ringing as I walked about and read the names.

How came there to be able seamen in so many of these cemeteries; privates of the Royal Naval Division, which

was the 63d? Because they had come from Gallipoli.
Battalions named after ships and admirals were organized
for Gallipoli and employed there for beach duty, the
landing of supplies and men. Afterwards they were
proud to be turned into a fighting division; and so these
able seamen retained their description but became soldiers and met their deaths on dry land.

The graves in the little plot at Warloy-Baillou were
beneath old apple trees, and once I was there when the
blossoms were at the full, and petals from them fell
quietly now and then upon the dead. Some of the trees
were failing, and there had been a thought of planting
cypress or yew or other churchyard tree in their stead;
but this has been changed, and apple trees will always
grow here and spread their branches and blossoms over
these graves.

Scarce a mile away from this cluster of the dead was
the cemetery of Forceville, also small, and also complete.
I returned to it very often, because it is not far from
Amiens, and in no other that I visited did reverence and
consolation seem more present. If the dead know and
care where they lie, those that are here must be content;
and the living who have come to see this place in anguish
and agitation, because it held the dust they mourned,
have gone away with spirits calmed. This I was told
on the spot. Mothers have arrived there in winter time,
distraught, out of themselves, asking wild privileges; they
must see their dead, the earth must be opened, they
must know how it is with him; perhaps he is cold; she
would like to make a fire for him. Wilder prayers than
this were made. After a little while, with that war cross,
and that war stone, in that holiness that hangs over
those clustered dead, generals, trumpeters, surgeons, able
seamen, she has found her self-control, she has not raved
any more, she has felt the strange peace of loss, and has
said that now when at home again and thinking of it,
she would not worry any more.

> He is dead and gone, lady,
>   He is dead and gone;
> At his head a grass green turf,
>   At his heels a stone.

Against this graveyard is an old French one with high
trees in it. As you approach from the road you pass
along the hedge by the French graves, and there among
these is a single new one, a British soldier. A splintered
tree stump, a foot high and soon to be hidden with
growing leaves, juts up close by. He had seen the shell
coming and stepped behind the tree, and along with it he
was dashed to fragments. What could be found was
buried here. A few steps more, and you come to the
stone gate where the British are. You pass under its arch,
through the solemn swinging door of iron bars that
show the peace within, and there the turf, the flowers,
the headstones, the decent order, possess you at once.
The war cross rises high, but not too far above your
head; first its pedestal, and then its slender shaft of
stone, symmetric, perfect, eloquent without words, nothing on it but a long slender sword in bronze. It holds
the eye, it compels to silence. It presides at one end of a
turf walk that runs through the middle of the ground
to the war stone at the other end. This is like an altar,
and behind it, as long as itself, a great stone bench, both
again compelling to silence. They seem to stand for
that greater thing of which Christianity is but the latest
part. The war stone and the cross mingle their influences,
which seem to flow from them, and bathe the headstones
benignly. Beyond the war stone, over the wall, a field
stretches away into quietness; beyond the war cross, over
the opposite wall, stretches another field but a little way
to the trees at the village edge, and through these rise the
quiet rustic roofs, and an old steeple. To one side lies
the French cemetery, and a field to the other; so is the
whole place set and framed in tranquillity. As one stands
and looks at this handful of British dead in France,

thought goes beyond them and their headstones, the gunners and trumpeters, to Thermopylæ, to Salamis, to Waterloo, to Gettysburg, to Verdun. All are of the same company. France is the home of those at Forceville who died in the battle of the Somme, at Paschendael of those who fell in Flanders fields, at Romagne of those who fell in the Meuse-Argonne; and France will care for them all perpetually, as for her own, whether Calgary, Melbourne, or Omaha was their birthplace, and no matter what their name or speech or faith; she is the true home of them all, and to her dust does their dust belong.

This is what our brains of one dimension could not see: that if all the rest of the dead were to lie in France, it would be exile for ours to be brought away from that great companionship. Ours alone have been brought from the sacred circle of all nations, and are now dispersed over a wide continent that did not witness their sacrifice or share their conflict. They lie apart from each other, instead of in a place consecrated especially to them, and they will be inevitably forgotten when those who mourn them now are followed to the tomb themselves and in their turn forgotten. Could those exiled bones of our soldiers speak through the ground to those who visit them now, there are few indeed who would not say:

"Mother, did no one tell you that I said I wanted to stay with the boys?"

Sad women all over the rest of the world know that remembrance and honor will continue to salute their assembled dead, when not a flower or a thought is any longer given to the dispersed exiles here.

Theodore Roosevelt let his son Quentin lie in the land which for ever consecrates his sacrifice. Happy are all those American parents who felt the true fitness of this as he did! Their grief and loss were not exploited by the well-planned campaign of that enterprising organization which styled itself *The Order of The Purple Cross*. They received no parcels of miscellaneous shreds from trenches where dismembered bodies had once been laid unrecog-

nizable, only to be subsequently grubbed up and boxed at
Government expense, $1000 per. . . .

More than two million lie in France between Flanders
fields and Massevaux. When they died, nations were lifted
as high above their week-day mood of getting and spending as they have fallen below it since. Sometimes, very
often today, as one reads the morning news, one has to
remember those cemeteries and the towers of Reims and
Amiens rising above that devastated land, in order not to
fall into despair. From what goes on, there is a tempta-
tion to believe that mankind spent its last drop of nobility
in the war, and has nothing left but its baseness. This is
not true now any more than it has ever been. Amiens and
Reims have stood through many tides. Other temples that
are crushed only made way for them, as their places will
be taken by still others. What passes is the Inn; what remains is the soul which builds the Inn and dwells there, but
for a time only. Those two million bodies in France prove
the existence of that soul. Just now it seems stifled and
extinct, as it has often seemed before, when other bodies
in other battlefields had proved its existence.

"Come from the four winds, O breath, and breathe
upon these slain, that they may live."

We must not expect to live above our week-day level
for any long time together; but may that level rise,
as the growth of pity shows it has risen. If it is to sink,
if the dead have died for no gain at all to the world, the
world were best unpeopled. Stray hints and projects of a
next war are given, a conflict waged with forces of destruction let loose by men who never see each other; new germs
of pestilence set going, which leave no living to bury
the dead, new gases made from the minerals and acids
of the earth, that with a puff blow out the breath of a
city.

To believe that wars will ever wholly cease while man
is here is difficult; but if that is to be war, if nothing but
more means for destruction have been learned, if that
alone is what science and human minds are making ready

for, then may the annihilation be complete! Let not only London and Paris and Berlin and New York, and all near and far, but Asia and Africa and every inhabitant of the globe, old and young be extinguished, and so be rendered incapable of further abuses of science. Then only the wild animals will inhabit the earth:—the wild animals, who, although they fight to kill, at least fight with tooth and claw, whose wars are at least redeemed by innocence of poison gas and politics; who do not pollute the streams, who do not burn and fell the forests, or despoil the caves of the planet of their coal and gold; who leave Niagara to flow in its natural majesty, who disfigure no mountain, and blacken no valley; who are innocent of chemicals and poison—the wild animals, whose character is honester than men's because they have no souls to corrupt and degrade, and who come into the world and go from it, leaving it unmaimed.

That would be best, if the Spirit of Knowledge prove for ever hostile to the Spirit of Life. Each time it has won and religion has gone wholly down, the civilization where such triumph occurred has perished. Better a world without man, if that is to be the end. We cannot know; but we can be calm, and wait until the bruised nerves which the years from 1914 to 1918 gave us all have recovered. There have always been an Amiens and a Reims to symbolize the Spirit of Life; never yet has there been a race wise enough to keep the hostile Spirit of Knowledge in its place. That is the recurring problem of problems; it dwarfs all others; and for a while at any rate it looked as if the agony of the war had brought us a step nearer to its solution.

APPENDIX A

The Supreme Council Differ About Upper Silesia

The restitution of Upper Silesia to Poland had been implied in Mr. Wilson's fourteen points, January 1918, and again in the statement issued by the Allies on June 3d, 1918. After January 1919, it was definitely to be given back to Poland; and so it stood in the treaty as delivered to the delegates of Germany on May 7th—but it did not stand so when the treaty was signed, June 28th. During the interval, Mr. Lloyd George re-opened the subject. He urged that Upper Silesia should decide by a popular vote whether to remain German or rejoin Poland. Messrs. Clemenceau and Wilson objected to this change of plan on the ground that German methods would prevent the election from being a fair one. The opinions and to some extent the characters of the three men are disclosed in the dialogues which follow, and which are directly translated from the French stenographic reports. These were put into my hands by an eminent Frenchman who was part of it all, and from whom I had leave to do with them what I saw fit. They were published in *The Saturday Evening Post* of December 3d, 1921, with some explanatory comments which also follow. They are among the few stenographic records of the Supreme Council's conversations still in existence. Most of these were destroyed by order.

The question was first brought up by Mr. Lloyd George on the 2nd of June, 1919. At this meeting he asked that the left bank of the Rhine be not occupied, and that the reparation clauses of the treaty be revised to provide for a lump sum to be paid down at once, reducing the German debt. Then he turned to Upper Silesia, and the material parts of the conversations follow, translated from the French record:

LLOYD GEORGE: My colleagues all say that the eastern frontier of Germany is inadmissible unless it is changed, and if Germany refuses to sign [the treaty] they all think that steps of coercion will not seem justifiable to the country [England]. Moreover they agree with our experts in thinking that as Upper Silesia has not been a part of Poland for six or seven centuries a plebiscite is indispensable. If the plebiscite is favorable to Poland it will be impossible for the Germans to talk of retaliation. That is what would have happened in 1871 if a plebiscite favorable to Germany had been held in Alsace-Lorraine. Besides, I am convinced that the plebiscite will be favorable to Poland.

CLEMENCEAU: First, as to Poland, amends are to be made for a historic crime, but also there is a barrier between Germany and Russia to be created. Read the interviews of Erzberger, who wishes Poland to be made as weak as possible, because it separates Germany from Russia. Mr. Erzberger adds that Germany, once she is in touch with Russia, can attack France in far better circumstances than in 1914. Is that what you want? Germany in control of Russia? That means that our dead are slain for nothing. That's all I have to remark on this point for the moment.

(June 3rd. Afternoon.)

WILSON: A plebiscite in Upper Silesia seems difficult to me; it would be necessary first to expel the German officials.

LLOYD GEORGE: Do you mean the petty officials?

WILSON: No. I'm thinking of those in charge of the administration.

CLEMENCEAU: Don't forget that in Germany it's the central power that appoints the mayors.

LLOYD GEORGE: I agree that the chief German authorities ought to go out of the country before any voting.

WILSON: Yes, but it's more than that. Fifteen or twenty big capitalists are the bosses in Upper Silesia.

CLEMENCEAU: Quite true. Notably Henckel von Donnersmarck.

WILSON: Unless the Germans are absent, a free and honest plebiscite, according to my expert advisers, can't be looked for in a country so long dominated and under constant fear of reprisals.

LLOYD GEORGE: Yet in 1907, in spite of this fear, the Poles won the elections. My experts foresee a plebiscite favorable to Poland. They believe that such a plebiscite will preclude later reprisals by the Germans.

WILSON: There's no trend of German opinion favorable to Upper Silesia; it's a capitalistic affair.

LLOYD GEORGE: Yet the majority of the German Government is socialist, and it is that which is protesting.

WILSON: Yes, for the benefit of the capitalists.

LLOYD GEORGE: I don't agree with you. It is national spirit. Upper Silesia has been separated from Poland for seven hundred years. I ask nothing unreasonable in asking that the inhabitants be allowed to vote. [Let the reader notice the word "inhabitants," used by Mr. Lloyd George. Later on, much turns upon this word.]

WILSON: But I repeat that a free vote will be impossible.

LLOYD GEORGE: Very well, we'll occupy the territory during the vote.

WILSON: Then they'll say that we brought military pressure to bear.

CLEMENCEAU: One way or another the Germans will always be protesting.

LLOYD GEORGE: None the less the vote will have been cast. Furthermore, how are the Germans going to intimidate a resisting industrial community? We've gone through that in Wales, and got the better of the big owners.

WILSON: You're comparing dissimilar things.

LLOYD GEORGE: But I tell you that the elections have gone for the Poles in the localities which concern us.

WILSON: Those were local elections and not a plebiscite to determine nationality.

CLEMENCEAU: We haven't promised any plebiscite in this region.

LLOYD GEORGE: It's Mr. Wilson who has proclaimed on every occasion the right of self-determination. We're providing plebiscites for the Saar, Fiume, Klagenfurt, so why deny one to Upper Silesia?

WILSON: I go back on none of my principles, but I didn't want the Poles to come under German pressure.

LLOYD GEORGE: You're employing the argument you opposed when Mr. Orlando was using it about Dalmatia.

WILSON: That is simply absurd. What I'm after is an honestly free vote. Now I am advised that the Germans are getting ready for military action in Upper Silesia.

LLOYD GEORGE: All the more reason for a plebiscite.

WILSON: Well, then, what are you offering us?

LLOYD GEORGE: The same procedure as in East Prussia.

WILSON: And if the Germans decline to obey the decision of the League of Nations?

CLEMENCEAU: You're going to ask them to promise; they'll promise, and they'll not keep it. Is that what you want?

LLOYD GEORGE: I don't exclude military occupation of the plebiscite zone as a hypothesis.

WILSON: I tell you that Germany will say that pressure was used.

LLOYD GEORGE: One division would suffice.

WILSON: Suffice for them to accuse us of pressure.

LLOYD GEORGE: I want peace. I know from a reliable source that the question of Upper Silesia is the most important one to the Germans. I prefer sending one division into Silesia rather than armies to Berlin.

CLEMENCEAU: Who says you'll have the choice?

LLOYD GEORGE: I don't want to repeat the madness of Napoleon in Russia, and be in Berlin as he was in Moscow.

CLEMENCEAU: It's a bit late to say all that.

WILSON: The point is to find out if our decision is equitable. Let them show a mistake as to race, and I am ready to correct it; but the threat that Germany will refuse to sign is of small interest to me. If the Germans have something valid to say as to Upper Silesia I'm willing to go into the question.

LLOYD GEORGE: It's not at all too late. The treaty of May 7th is not an ultimatum. We must hear the Germans. My colleagues in the government think so too. The Germans ask nothing unreasonable in asking that the inhabitants be consulted [Notice again the word ''inhabitants'' used by Mr. Lloyd George]; as to the freedom of the vote, that is our business: if Germany rejects a plebiscite favorable to Poland the British army will march enthusiastically to Berlin. That's what I require. I must have the English people with me in case of trouble.

WILSON: It seems to me we are further apart than we were at the start. My point is that a ''no'' from Germany isn't reason enough for changing our decisions. I am ready to change them in every case where we can be proved in the wrong.

LLOYD GEORGE: There are other considerations. Why refuse secondary changes if they facilitate the signing? It's my conviction that the plebiscite will both give Upper Silesia to Poland and facilitate the signature.

WILSON: Your intentions are excellent, but if we send troops we shall be accused of exercising pressure. I should prefer taking other guaranties to insure the freedom of the vote, and not sending any troops.

CLEMENCEAU: I have listened attentively to both of you, and here's my objection: you want to avoid difficulties, you're going to create worse ones. A plebiscite is ideal, but not in Germany, where liberty has never existed. To decide on a plebiscite and wash your hands of it would be very nice, but it would be a crime against the Poles. Occupation of the plebiscite zone remains, in which case Germany will say that pressure has been used—and do you know what will happen? In six months, in a year, right in the midst of peace you'll have all the bothers of war, and then the situation will probably be more difficult than it is today. You say, Monsieur Lloyd George, that you don't wish to go to Berlin; no more do I. If we have caused millions of soldiers to be killed it was to save our existence. You say that you want to learn the choice of Upper Silesia; I reply that under German rule Upper Silesia can't make a free choice, and that with interallied occupation the Germans will claim that the plebiscite was queered. You wish to quiet racial passions; you're going to inflame them. There are times when the simplest and wisest thing is to say no. We believe that we have made a fair treaty. Let's stick to it. A plebiscite and an occupation mean quarrels for tomorrow, battles perhaps; in a word, the very opposite of what you desire.

LLOYD GEORGE: But if you're afraid of German resistance it will come about much more if there is no plebiscite, and we must recognize that from the standpoint of right Germany will be in a better position than ourselves.

WILSON: We have said on our basis of the peace that all the indisputably Polish provinces must come back to Poland.

LLOYD GEORGE: But the Germans say that this is precisely not the case in Silesia.

CLEMENCEAU: What? You know perfectly well that German statistics themselves show a large majority of Upper Silesia to be Polish.

LLOYD GEORGE: But the legal aspect is not the only one; there's a sentiment, and I want to know that.

WILSON: The racial question is not doubtful. As to the rest I am willing to amplify what we have decided, but we are not obliged to do so by the basis of the peace.

LLOYD GEORGE: On the racial basis one would have to say that Alsace is German.

CLEMENCEAU: The case of Alsace-Lorraine, as you know well, is not analogous to any other.

WILSON: What I maintain is that our decision is not contrary to the fourteen points.

LLOYD GEORGE: Who of us had thought of Upper Silesia before the report of our experts had brought it to our attention?

CLEMENCEAU: You are absolutely wrong. All the Poles from the start have claimed Upper Silesia.

WILSON: Monsieur Clemenceau is right. When I received Dmovski and Paderewski in Washington I questioned them a long while, map in hand. Their claims were excessive, but we all agreed upon the formula "to give Poland all regions inhabited by Poles."

LLOYD GEORGE: I tell you again that we can never have thought of giving to Poland a province which has not been Polish for eight hundred years.

CLEMENCEAU: And I tell you again that the claim as to Upper Silesia has always been formulated by Poland and recognized as just by us.

WILSON: We must finish. We might consent to a plebiscite under the control of an interallied commission. We would declare the plebiscite to be void if the commission reported to us that pressure had been exercised.

LLOYD GEORGE: I fancy that Germany would accept an American occupation.

CLEMENCEAU: Well, I promise you that no matter who the occupiers may be, Germany will protest just the same.

WILSON: Germany doesn't love the United States any better than she loves the other allies. What is your decision? Do you want a plebiscite and do you wish an interallied commission to define how it shall be held?

LLOYD GEORGE: The German troops must evacuate Upper Silesia.

WILSON: Quite so, and the interallied commission must even be able to summon allied troops.

CLEMENCEAU: But what force do you think necessary?

LLOYD GEORGE: One division.

CLEMENCEAU: I'm not convinced.

LLOYD GEORGE: If the Germans refuse to sign I must be able to prove to my cabinet and to the people that the fault is not ours.

Then they decided that the experts draw up a scheme; and on the morning of June 5th they had in Mr. Paderewski, whom Mr. Wilson addressed as follows:

WILSON: They tell us that the most serious question is Upper Silesia. Our experts have prepared a note, which has been communicated to us. But before deciding we want your opinion. The material change will be the provision for a plebiscite. The population is Polish by a large majority, as we know, but some think that a plebiscite, held of course after the departure of the German troops, will give more strength to our decisions.

PADEREWSKI: The actual text of the treaty is justice itself. In Silesia there are two districts where Poland has an undoubted majority, and one where the majority is German. The part to the west, which is agricultural, is under the influence of the Catholic clergy, very dangerous from our point of view; it influences the opinion of the peasants. To the east the population is more thoughtful and freer, but if only the east becomes Polish, the whole industrial region will be close to the frontier.

LLOYD GEORGE: Which zone is the more densely populated?

PADEREWSKI: The east. In the mining region there are 900,000 Poles, 400,000 Germans. In the farming region there are 600,000 inhabitants; it is an indisputably Polish country.

WILSON: The Germans themselves recognize that the population is Polish.

PADEREWSKI: Yet, nevertheless, they claim Upper Silesia.

LLOYD GEORGE: If we were to speak of Silesia as a whole, and not merely of Upper Silesia, in its entirety it is mainly German.

PADEREWSKI: Yes, many people were speaking Polish at Breslau when I was there. [He means by this that in a German city much Polish was spoken just as much Yiddish is spoken in New York, and that these are not the facts which decide to what country a city belongs.]

CLEMENCEAU: But as to what concerns Upper Silesia, do you agree to a plebiscite after the evacuation of the territory by German troops? That's what we want to know from you.

PADEREWSKI: Such a change in the treaty would oblige me to resign, for the people to whom the text of June 7th [a mistake for May 7th] promised Upper Silesia would lose their confidence.

LLOYD GEORGE: We promised nothing at all, we wrote the scheme of a treaty, we didn't give it the form of an ultimatum. We reserved our liberty to examine the reply of the Germans, and consequently we have the right to make concessions if they are reasonable. What? Yesterday Poland was divided in three pieces, your fellow-countrymen were fighting separately against each other, and all were fighting together against the independence of their own country. Today you are sure of a resurrected Poland which will have 20,000,000 inhabitants; you're demanding in addition, for example, a population in Galicia which is not Polish. You're demanding all this from us; you, whose liberty has been won by the death of 1,500,000 Frenchmen, 800,000 Englishmen, and 500,000 Italians. It's our blood that has paid for your independence. If you kick against our decisions we shall have been mistaken in you.

PADEREWSKI: I confined myself to stating that I could not remain in office.

LLOYD GEORGE: We have given liberty to Poland, Bohemia, Jugo-Slavia; and those are the countries that kick against the plebiscite. They are much more imperialistic than the great nations themselves.

PADEREWSKI: I cannot admit what you say; you are merely reproducing newspaper talk.

LLOYD GEORGE: I say that you want to annex people against their will.

PADEREWSKI: Not in the slightest degree. We defend our countrymen when they are attacked.

CLEMENCEAU: I want to come back to the question of the

plebiscite. If it is held after some postponement and until that time American troops occupy the country, do you think the vote will be free and favorable to Poland?

PADEREWSKI: Yes, undoubtedly in the eastern part. As for the western part, the threefold influence of the freehold-ers, the officials, and the clericals will make the outcome un-certain. Furthermore the object of the Germans is to provoke a disturbance in order to have to repress it. They have 350,-000 men on the Polish frontier.

The conversation about Poland was resumed on the morn-ing of June 9th.

LLOYD GEORGE: The experts who have been at work over the plebiscite do not agree as to the interval between the signing of the treaty and the plebiscite. Now this interval bears upon the system to be established. We alone are able to solve this question. Do not forget that three of the experts are hostile in principle to the plebiscite.

WILSON: It will be enough to ask them to explain the two systems.

LLOYD GEORGE: That's it. Moreover, some proposals are not acceptable, such as the expulsion of the entire clergy. The commission who will be on the ground must be exempt from its decisions.

CLEMENCEAU: I recognize that it may be difficult to expel the entire clergy, and yet you cannot overlook the pro-Ger-man influence that it will exert.

LLOYD GEORGE: As in Ireland; and in spite of that we do not expel the Irish clergy. The plebiscite will deprive the Germans of all pretext for fighting. With concessions as to the reparations in addition, the Germans will sign.

On the afternoon of June 11th they returned to the ques-tion.

CLEMENCEAU: Do you wish to hear the commission on Polish affairs?

LLOYD GEORGE: That commission is very biased regarding Poland; I don't want to debate with it.

CLEMENCEAU: We'll debate only with each other, but we must first hear the commission, question it and listen to it. I desire to repeat once again that I am against a plebiscite in Upper Silesia. Since you all agree to the principle I'll be with you in a spirit of conciliation, but I can't forget that wherever the population has elected Polish deputies the plebiscite is useless. [He means that Polish deputies to the Reichstag count for nothing.]

WILSON: We can examine its limitations. I should add that my colleague, Mr. White, has also brought me reports of the pro-German influence of the Polish clericals.

LLOYD GEORGE: I'll bet those reports come from Polish sources. Look what the Poles are saying about the Jews. They claim to be giving them the best treatment in the world, and we all know it's not true. A plebiscite is a just thing. Without a plebiscite our consciences would not be at ease if British troops had to be sent to get themselves killed in Upper Silesia. A plebiscite put off for several months or an interallied occupation will give us free elections.

WILSON: You're very biased yourself. My information comes from Americans on the spot. You appear to have forgotten what the Germans can do in the way of propaganda and pressure. I know what they did in America. What will they not do in Silesia, where they are politically and economically sovereign? When it comes to the Germans I am against them and for Poland.

CLEMENCEAU: That's truth.

LLOYD GEORGE: I tell you again that if we have to fight about the east frontier of Germany our soldiers won't fight if Germany can prove that the plebiscite was rejected in spite of Great Britain's opinion.

WILSON: We've been making no sacrifice of our own interests; don't let us consent to them at the expense of a little country. [Mr. Wilson meant by this that after a lively discussion and upon the unbreakable opposition of Mr. Clemenceau the clauses relating to the occupation of the left bank of the Rhine and the reparations had been retained without change.]

LLOYD GEORGE: You know perfectly well that my sole object was not to give Poland territory that was not Polish. Were we to do that we could not fight to assure such territory to it.

WILSON: I'm sorry for the excitement into which I've thrown you. It's also quite certain that you've never changed your opinion about this.

LLOYD GEORGE: I want to avoid conflict. The Germans in Upper Silesia consider the Poles an inferior population, for whom they entertain contempt; and to put Germans under Polish rule would be to provoke trouble.

CLEMENCEAU: You'll have trouble, never doubt it, of all sorts, now or later, with or without a plebiscite.

LLOYD GEORGE: I hold an utterly opposite opinion.

CLEMENCEAU: The future will settle it, but I beg you not to forget what I'm saying today.

WILSON: The first thing to do, according to the experts, is to cause the withdrawal of German troops. Will British soldiers fight to make the plebiscite respected?

LLOYD GEORGE: Yes, because it's a just principle; and what I'd like to know is, if the French army would fight for Upper Silesia to become Polish without a plebiscite?

CLEMENCEAU: I reply yes, because the question is not as you put it; here's the one question: to know if the Germans will sign or not sign the treaty.

WILSON: The American soldiers will always fight against the Germans.

LLOYD GEORGE: I'm not speaking for your soldiers; I'm speaking for mine. You know how Lord Northcliffe is attacking me in his newspapers, and yet he is for the plebiscite in Upper Silesia.

[The experts are brought in—Mr. Jules Cambon, General Le Rond, Mr. Morley, and Mr. Lord.]

WILSON: In what do the experts agree and in what do they disagree?

LE ROND: We agree upon the territorial question, the coal question, and the financial clauses. We disagree upon the question of the plebiscite in Upper Silesia. President Wilson two days ago ordered us in the name of the Four to present two schemes—one for a plebiscite shortly, the other for a postponed plebiscite. In Upper Silesia the Poles are not their own masters. The big freeholders are lords of the soil; they are really feudal with more power than those of the thirteenth century, because they own not only the ground but what is beneath, and the manufactories and the capital.

CLEMENCEAU: Chiefly the bishop of Breslau, who is one of those big freeholders.

LE ROND: I'll speak presently of him. The big freeholders hold the country in a net, notably the clergy. The bishop of Breslau is particularly powerful. Since the armistice the Polish priests have been sent elsewhere. The Germans suppress the Polish newspapers and it's being said that if Silesia becomes Polish the money in the savings banks will disappear. According to the general opinion of the experts, serious precautions should be taken. The majority of the experts consider that a pretty long postponement is required; between one and two years.

LLOYD GEORGE: I accept.

LE ROND: Out of eight electoral districts in Upper Silesia, five were represented in the Reichstag by Poles.

CLEMENCEAU: Did these Poles claim they were independent?

LE ROND: They couldn't under the German system.

WILSON: There was a strong Polish party in Upper Silesia?

LE ROND: Yes.

LLOYD GEORGE: I fancy it's useless to bring up the question of an immediate plebiscite.

LE ROND: I'll speak of the preparation for a plebiscite. If it doesn't take place until after a fairly long wait you must give wider powers to your commission.

LLOYD GEORGE: The question is settled for me.

LE ROND: Who will settle the date—the Powers or the League of Nations?

LLOYD GEORGE: I'll accept either method.

WILSON: Can you inform us as to the Polish part of Upper Silesia?

LORD: There are two parties, one socialist, one not, but both are working for union with Poland.

LLOYD GEORGE: But is it not the same thing as in Ireland or in Wales—attachment to the nationality, but never until recently, even in Ireland, a serious idea of separation?

LORD: Separation was not in the program, probably because it wasn't supposed possible in the condition of Europe.

LE ROND: Since the war the movement in favor of union with Poland has been very active in the whole of Upper Silesia.

LLOYD GEORGE: I don't contest that, but what I don't know is the strength of Polish sentiment.

[The experts retire.]

WILSON: I consider that we must decide for a plebiscite

a year off at least, two years off at the latest. Mr. Lord has it from an American on the spot that all classes of the population want a plebiscite. Now Mr. Lord himself is against a plebiscite.

CLEMENCEAU: I've nothing to add to what I have said. I persist in thinking the plebiscite a mistake. Since I'm alone in this, I must bow; none the less I continue to believe that we are headed for grave difficulties in Upper Silesia and that a prompt settlement would have been better.

WILSON: Here is the scheme for defining the powers of the commission on the plebiscite.

[The scheme is adopted.]

CLEMENCEAU: Is occupation provided for?

WILSON: Yes.

CLEMENCEAU: Is the evacuation of the German troops stipulated?

WILSON: Yes.

CLEMENCEAU: What interval shall we set for the plebiscite?

LLOYD GEORGE: The committee will make a proposal at the end of the year.

CLEMENCEAU: Who are the troops of occupation?

LLOYD GEORGE: I think we'll all have to participate. I'd still prefer that it was the Americans.

WILSON: I'll consult my military authorities.

CLEMENCEAU: Who'll pay the expenses of the occupation?

ORLANDO: The country who'll get Upper Silesia.

They resumed on the morning of June 14th.

WILSON: We have decided to have recourse to the plebiscite to deprive Germany of the slightest pretext for irredentist action in the future. Besides, the Germans realize that the population is Polish in majority but they deny its wish to be joined to Poland. Mr. Paderewski has marked out two zones—the mining region to the east, where the result of the plebiscite seems to him not doubtful, and the farming region to the west, where the result is doubtful. This must be taken into consideration. Accordingly we have decided:

1. That the plebiscite shall be held by commune [township, parish].

2. That it shall be put off for several months in order that German pressure may be eliminated.

3. That the German troops shall immediately evacuate Upper Silesia.

PADEREWSKI: I can't pretend that this is not a cruel blow, for we had been promised Upper Silesia. If the plebiscite turned out unfavorable to us it would be the peasants, the workingmen, who would suffer. As to the period of waiting which you have provided, it will create an unwelcome tension. The plebiscite should not be put off longer than six months at the most. Our delegation accepts your decision with the respect it has for you, but not without profound regret.

WILSON: Your words move me deeply; I've gone through many doubts and scruples of conscience.

CLEMENCEAU: You know that my opinion has never changed.

LLOYD GEORGE: I was myself much moved by the statements of Mr. Paderewski. We have reflected a long while, but I am certain that Poland has nothing to fear in the mining region from the plebiscite.

WILSON: An American who went there tells me that union with Poland is desired by everybody and that the result will be favorable.

DMOVSKI: I am convinced that taken altogether the plebiscite will give good results. I know the German argument well. They declare that the population does not want to be Polish. I realize that fifty years ago it was no longer Polish save in speech, but during the past half century there has been a great awakening. This might now create difficulties if districts which in 1919 might hesitate to vote for Poland should rise up against German rule later. What would the Great Powers do?

WILSON: To deal with such questions is one of the essential offices of the League of Nations.

LLOYD GEORGE: Quite so; we can't settle everything at once, but there'll be permanent machinery for adjustment.

DMOVSKI: What have you decided about the evacuation of Upper Silesia by German troops?

WILSON: It will take place at once after the signature.

DMOVSKI: What have you decided about the German officials?

WILSON: The commission has full power to drive them out.

DMOVSKI: The commission in its work would have to be aided equally by the German and the Polish element.

WILSON: The commission will have discretionary powers.

[Mr. Paderewski and Mr. Dmovski retire.]

LLOYD GEORGE: All the partisans of Poland asked that the plebiscite be put off, and here's the Polish delegation asking that it take place as soon as possible.

WILSON: I should have supposed that an interval of from one to two years was a guaranty for Poland.

CLEMENCEAU: Possibly; but Mr. Paderewski tells you that the intervening period runs the danger of driving everybody crazy.

WILSON: We must take what he said into consideration and adopt a plan that allows at need an abridgment of the interval before the plebiscite. I suggest we say from six to eighteen months. [Adopted.]

So Mr. Lloyd George had his way, and a plebiscite in Upper Silesia was provided for, accordingly, by Article 88 of the Treaty of Versailles, as follows:

Article 88: ''In the portion of Upper Silesia included within the boundaries described below, the *inhabitants* will be called upon to indicate by a vote whether they wish to be attached to Germany or to Poland. . . . Germany hereby renounces in favor of Poland all rights and title over the portion of Upper Silesia lying beyond the frontier line fixed by the Principal Allied and Associated Powers as the result of the plebiscite.''

Section 4 of the annex to this article specifies and limits very precisely who the qualified voters are to be.

a. All persons of either sex who have completed their 20th year.

b. Who were *born* in Upper Silesia or were *domiciled* there by January 1st, 1919.

c. Or who had *lost* their domicile by being *expelled* by the German authorities.

Clause c enlarges the definition of "inhabitants" by including the banished inhabitants; *they* can come back; but not Germans born there and emigrated voluntarily. To have meant that *all* persons born in Upper Silesia should vote after completing their 20th year, and then to add an annex describing which persons should vote there would have been a manifest absurdity.

One would suppose this pretty clear; but the Germans who had emigrated from Schleswig were allowed to return and vote in violation of provisions virtually similar to these. The same provisions, virtually, applied to Allenstein and Marienwerder in East Prussia (see Article 95), and the treaty was violated in the same way. When it came to Upper Silesia the precedent thus established was claimed by Germany and conceded by the Allies. Germany asserted that Section 4 of the Annex *destroyed* the meaning of "inhabitants" in Article 88.

This grows more inconceivable when you find, in Section 5, that "regard will be paid to the wishes of the *inhabitants* as shown by the vote"—nothing said about emigrated Germans; that the report of the commission computes the number of voters as 1,900,000—which is the number of inhabitants of Upper Silesia in 1910, according to the Prussian census—no question of emigrants here; and that the German note of May 1919 confines itself to requesting that the right to vote be granted to "any German subject aged 20 years complete and living in the plebiscite territory *at least a year before the conclusion of the peace.*" No question of emigrants here. This request, as the reader will notice, was granted by clause b of the annex, fixing January 1st, 1919. What followed is more inconceivable still.

In the summer of 1920, the Allies allowed that emigrated Germans should vote in Upper Silesia. In the autumn, Monsieur G. Leygues obtained the concession that at least these Germans should not vote on the same day as the inhabitants. In January 1921, at the Paris conference, this concession was renounced by France. In March the plebiscite took place, and Germans to the number of 190,000 entered and intimidated the voters. This election failed utterly in its object, which was to register the true aspirations of the inhabitants. From March until August—again in violation of Article 88, which sets one month after the vote as the term in which frontiers and administration are to be settled—nothing is settled; then the Supreme Council passed the mess it had made to the League of Nations. Then the League of Nations by its decision awarded Poland more than was, according to German ideas, satisfactory.

At this the German Cabinet resigned office and took it again the next day, like something in a comic opera, while the Berlin papers were remarking, ''We must help accelerate the Polish process of decay,'' and that Germany was no longer bound by the Peace Treaty because ''*it has been grossly violated again!*'' Soon the League of Nations confessed itself at a loss, not very unnaturally. What could it do? It had been founded upon a theory of human nature rather than on a condition, and consequently rested on sand, which we must hope may slowly change to rock. Meanwhile, we usually supply sailboats today with auxiliary power. The suggestion of power, during all this passing back and forth of responsibility, came from quite another source. General Ludendorff, in a speech he made at Koenigsberg, indicated his way of settling the question of Upper Silesia.

''I entertain no doubt,'' he said, ''that the destiny of our country will be decided sooner or later by a battle for that land to our east. When the hour comes remember what won us our victory at Tannenberg—the will of our leaders, our faith in those leaders, our discipline and courage in the face of death. The greater our country's need the more closely shall we rally round the black, white, and red flag of Prussia. We are proud of our beloved Prussia; we are, and we wish to be, Prussians.''

Great applause followed these words, the audience gave the general an ovation. A counter demonstration by socialists was promptly suppressed.

In May 1922, Poland and Germany agreed to abide for fifteen years by the decision of the League of Nations. Will this be another scrap of paper?

The Treaty of Versailles had had but few readers. During our presidential campaign in 1920 many friends of the League of Nations reproached me for being a Republican. Not one of these friends had read the treaty; most of them had never even seen the outside of it. Yet, perfectly ignorant of its many provisions, unwise and hastily prepared, they wished it ratified. I hope that I have made clear the story of Upper Silesia. First, early in 1919, it is to be given outright to Poland; next, a string is tied to this gift by a plebiscite, at which shall vote only native-born and residents naturalized before January 1st, 1919, and residents exiled by Germany; next, contrary to this signed agreement, German emigrants are to vote; next, these are to vote on a different day from the inhabitants; next, they are to vote on the same day; finally, 190,000 of them enter and vote on the same day, and the election is an intimidation and not free, precisely as Clemenceau told Lloyd George it would be and Lloyd George told Clemenceau he was sure it wouldn't.

Would not a sticking to the treaty have been simpler? This is not a case of posterity *interpreting* the vague language of a document it did not write; it is the departure by the stipulators from their own specific stipulations. Many a set of politicians have gone back on a treaty which their predecessors signed; but never until now have we seen a set of politicians going back within two years on what they have signed themselves; and this irresponsible levity about a solemn agreement not only belittles the Allies and encourages Germany in her plan of revenge but it insults and impairs the sense of honor of the entire civilized world.

APPENDIX B

Foch Speaks His Mind

On November 7th, 1920, eighteen months to a day after the Treaty of Versailles was delivered to the Germans, Marshal Foch was on his way to Amiens to decorate the graves of the Australians who had defended the city for three years, and saved it in 1918, and had left fifty thousand dead on French soil.

Perhaps it was because he was in the same private car in which the Germans had signed the Armistice almost exactly two years before, that his companion, M. Jules Sauerwein, a writer for *Le Matin*, found him in a mood, at first slightly reluctant but finally almost without reserve, to talk about the Armistice. He broke his silence about this and also about two other matters of historic interest, namely, the circumstances in which he was made commander-in-chief of the Allied armies after the disaster to the 5th British army in the great spring drive of 1918, and the tardiness as well as the character of the peace treaty.

No observer can look at the face of Foch, especially at his eyes, without perceiving that his is a nature of perfect loyalty and also that whatever animation may pass over the surface, he is deeply and finally sad. This comes not alone from the personal bereavement that he suffered in the war; it is due also, and possibly even more, to the undoing of his work by the politicians, which he foresaw but which he was powerless to prevent.

When the world read his reasons for granting an armistice at the time they were published—the sparing of human life, since all was gained without further bloodshed—they seemed adequate. Very few could have known then that the Armistice was forced upon him against his conviction, and that loyalty alone prompted him not only to assent openly but also openly to support the step taken. What he would have done had he known that no peace would be signed until the following June, no one can be sure, probably not even he.

To lay the calamity of the Armistice wholly at Mr. Wilson's door is probably not any more correct than to leave out his influence altogether. Several causes would seem to have combined, and were alleged then, and later. It was said that the British army, after its tremendous and exhausting pursuit, could have gone no further then; that all the armies had marched so far in advance of their bases of supply as to make further progress at that time, or until the spring, impossible; that every bridge and other link of communication had been destroyed by the retreating Germans, so that necessary repairs both in front and in the rear would have delayed an invasion of Germany until spring, giving Germany time to entrench herself formidably; and, finally, that Mr. Wilson, whose 14 points had helped to allay in January a growing socialistic opposition to carrying on the war in 1918, had by his notes to Max of Baden in October again revived this opposition to an extent so widespread that it had to be reckoned with. These reasons, if true, must have seemed strong in November 1918. A complete answer to them, however, is to be found in the plan for the Lorraine offensive to have been launched on November 14th. In the light of that, any threat to withdraw the American troops would have been by itself enough to have forced the Armistice; and if such a threat was in fact made, Mr. Wilson's figure will stand almost as prominent in history as that of the Kaiser.

Much controversy surrounds the delay in uniting all the armies under the command of Foch after this had been urged in high quarters. The conversation between him and Sauerwein throws some light upon this, but not enough. Foch begins by expressing weariness of repeating the story of the Armistice, but as he warms to it, occasionally dropping into colloquialisms for which it is not easy to find English equivalents, his opinion of the slump from victory to failure is revealed, as well as his unhappiness.

"What is an armistice? It is a suspension of arms, a cessation of hostilities, which has for its object the discussion of peace by putting the governments which have consented to it in a situation such that they can impose the peace on which they have decided.

"Has the Armistice which I signed on the 11th of November, 1918, fulfilled its object?

"Yes, since on the 28th of June, after seven months of

negotiations, Germany accepted all the conditions of the
Allies. I had said to M. Clemenceau, the President of the
Council, 'Here is my Armistice; you can make any peace you
please, I am in a position to enforce it.' If the peace has not
been good, is it my fault? I did my work; it was for the
politicians to do theirs.

"I had been thinking the peace over for a long while. By
September 1918 I was writing to M. Clemenceau. I said to
him: 'The end of the war approaches. Send me a member of
our foreign ministry to inform me of the conditions of peace
which you are preparing in order that our armies may occupy
all the regions which should serve as a guaranty for the
execution of the treaty which you will make.'

"M. Clemenceau replied: 'That is no business of yours.'
"'Do you wish me to tell you about the Armistice? It has
been told so often! Very well; I'll tell you that when I saw
them entering this car, Erzberger and the two others, accompanied by a naval officer whose name I have completely
forgotten, I had a moment of emotion. I said to myself,
'Here is Germany. Very well, since it is coming to me, I
will treat it as it deserves. It is beaten. I will be stiff, cold,
but without rancor or rudeness.'

"'I had reached Rethonde at six in the evening, where my
train was put on a siding. Next morning a train arrived
very slowly, pushed from behind. It was the German train.
They laid a footbridge between the two trains because it
was very muddy. An instant later Weygand entered and
told me that the German plenipotentiaries were at hand.
Erzberger comes first, and presents the others in a fairly in-
distinct voice. It's translated. I say: 'Gentlemen, have you
your credentials? We'll examine their validity.' They show
me papers signed by Max of Baden. We consider them satisfactory. I turn to Erzberger and say to him: 'What do you
desire of me?' 'We have come,' he answers, 'to receive communications of the conditions on which you wish to make the
Armistice.'

"'I answer: 'I have no communication to make to you. If
you have any request to present to me, make it.' And he
gives some more explanations. I say to him: 'Do you ask
for an armistice?' He answers me: 'We ask it.' I reply:
'Then I will inform you through my intermediary upon

what conditions the allied governments consent to grant the Armistice.'

"We sit down in the next car where my officers were. Admiral Wemyss at my right, Weygand at my left, and opposite me Erzberger, between Oberdorf and Winterfeldt. Weygand read them the conditions, which were translated piece by piece.

"I saw them collapse. Winterfeldt was very pale. I even think he was crying. After the reading, I add at once: 'Gentlemen, I leave this text with you; you have 72 hours to answer in. During that time you can present me comments of detail.'

"Then Erzberger became piteous. 'Monsieur le maréchal, I pray you will not wait for 72 hours. Stop the hostilities today. Our armies are the prey of anarchy; bolshevism threatens them; this bolshevism may spread over Germany, over all central Europe, and threaten even France herself.'

"I don't budge. I reply: 'I don't know what condition your armies are in; I only know the state of my own. Not only can I not stop the offensive, but I will give the order to push it with redoubled energy.'

"Then Winterfeldt takes it up. He had notes in front of him and he had carefully got up his case.

"'It is necessary,' said he to me, 'that our chiefs-of-staff should confer and talk over together all the details of execution. How can they? How can they communicate if the hostilities continue? I request you to stop the hostilities.'

"I answered him: 'These technical discussions will be entirely in order in 72 hours. From now until then hostilities will continue.'

"They withdrew. As for me, I send an order to all the Allied armies, a last call to the courage and energy of all. All the commanders-in-chief returned me an enthusiastic answer: 'Count on us, we shall not stop.'

"I skip the three following days. The Germans attempted submersion, submersion by means of notes. Weygand received them and transmitted them to me."

Here the marshal with a smile of kindness and recognition interrupted himself to speak of his colleagues.

"They are," he said to me, "crack-a-jacks. Ah, how well they know their business! And when there was talk of sending Weygand to Poland, and somebody said that he had never been in command, I said: 'Don't worry, he'll know what to do.'

"On the evening of the 10th I remind the Germans that they must sign the next day. They receive a long message from Hindenburg telling them to sign; but the revolution breaks out in Berlin, and I tell them: 'Who do you represent now?' They show me a telegram from President Ebert, a cipher telegram which was signed '606.' I don't know why. This telegram satisfied their authority.

"During the night of the 10th I didn't sleep much.

"I was resting between midnight and one o'clock, and then the Germans arrived. I allowed them 5,000 mitrailleuses, and some camions. That was all. At 5.15 they signed in heavy, furious handwriting. At seven o'clock I left for Paris.

"At nine I was with M. Clemenceau. He was not particularly amiable. He was growling. He asked me if I had yielded to the Germans . . . but no matter about that . . . I told him that at eleven o'clock the cannon must be fired to announce the end of hostilities. He wanted it to be at four in the afternoon at the moment he should mount the tribune in the Chamber of Deputies. I told him that the Allied armies had been advised since the night by my order; that at eleven o'clock the last shot would be fired, and the whole world would know it.

"On this M. Barthou, M. Neil, and others entered his study and backed me up. He consented to have the cannon fired at eleven o'clock.

"I said to him: 'My work is done. Yours begins.'"

SAUERWEIN: But was it really over, your work? After beating Germany wasn't it your duty to give advice as to the peace?

FOCH: I don't know if it was my duty, or rather I believe it was, and that's what I understood; but I never was given the right.

"I often saw M. Clemenceau and I sent him three written notes. But let me tell you the end which will explain the beginning to you. The peace which they proposed to sign— I spoke to you about it at the time—seemed bad to me. I summed it up thus: neither frontiers nor pledges.

"For the security of France the frontier of the Rhine was

needed, a military frontier, you understand, not a political
one. For the reparations due France I demanded the occupation of the left bank of the Rhine until the full compliance
with the treaty was consummated, because in my opinion
that was the only way to secure those reparations.

"In the month of April, the 7th, I think, I was allowed to
be heard at the council of ministers. I had vainly asked to be
heard by the French delegation. They refused me. I recall
that council of ministers. I came there with M. Jules Cambon
and Tardieu. I asked at first if they kept no minutes. It
appears that this was not the custom. Then, as I had committed my remarks to paper, I gave a copy to each minister
and then began to speak and develop my theme: no guaranties, no security.

"M. Poincaré supported me, he alone, I must acknowledge
it. After that they begged me to retire. Going out, I said
to M. Tardieu before M. Cambon:

"'Some day there will be a High Court to judge us, because France will never understand how we came to make a
failure out of victory. On that day I want to present myself with a tranquil conscience and my papers in order.'

"I made one more attempt. It was at the full session of
the 6th of May, when they gave to the Allied powers the
treaty which had been finished during the night. The Portuguese, and others whom I don't recall, protested. Then I got
up and developed my theme once more. They listened, nobody said a word, and the session rose.

"While they were taking tea in the adjoining room I found
M. Clemenceau and said:

"'I had the honor to ask a question, and I should be glad
of an answer.'

"Then I saw him talk animatedly a moment with M. Wilson and M. Lloyd George. Then he came back to me and
declared:

"'Our answer is, that there is no answer.'

"I replied:

"'Monsieur the President, I am asking myself if I will
accompany you tomorrow to Versailles. I find myself facing
a case of conscience, the gravest that I have ever known in
my existence. I repudiate that treaty, and I do not wish
to participate in the responsibility by sitting beside you.'

"He was not pleased, and urged me to come. In the evening he sent M. John Dupuy to me, who held a long discourse with real emotion. Then I said to myself: 'The Allied governments are going to present themselves before Germany to impose a treaty upon her. Is it possible for them to present themselves without their armies, without the chief of their armies? I haven't the right. It would be to weaken them in the presence of the enemy.'

"At Versailles I found myself by M. Klotz. When the ceremony of delivery was over, I said: 'Monsieur Minister of the Finances of the French Republic, with such a treaty you can present yourself at the bank of the German Empire and you will be paid in fake money.' M. Klotz replied acrimoniously, 'That is not my custom.'

" 'It will be your custom,' I retorted.

"And those are the people," concluded Marshal Foch, looking sadly at his pipe, "those are the people to whom I said:

" 'Make what peace you wish, I'll take care that it's performed.' "

SAUERWEIN: It looks as if the head of our government did not love you to excess.

FOCH: What can you do? I don't know if he liked me, but he did not show it. I recall a council of war in London, the 14th of March, 1918. I had been nominated commander-in-chief of the reserve army, which didn't exist much. At that meeting I asked the English to contribute effectives to this army.

"Marshal Haig declared to me, in the name of the English Government, which was principally represented by Mr. Lloyd George, that it was impossible. I was going to answer sharply when—

" 'Be quiet,' said M. Clemenceau vigorously to me, 'I'm speaking in the name of the French Government, and I declare that I accept Marshal Haig's answer.' "

Here, writes M. Sauerwein, Foch smiled, and that violent incident seems to have left not the slightest bitterness.

"I said to myself," continued Foch, "wait. Tomorrow I'll say something. And next day when the council was on the point of separating, I spoke, and I was not cut short this time. I declared that a formidable offensive was preparing, and I added that I knew what allied battles were. I've taken part at the Marne and in Italy. Here is what the liaisons ought to be (I said) and here is the way to play team-work, those are the precautions to be taken, &c., &c. I assure you (I said to them) that nothing is ready to resist the offensive and that it may be a disaster.

"'They were impressed all the same. And a few days afterwards at Compiègne and Doullens they remembered me. [This was when Gough's army had been defeated.]

"'At Doullens there were Lord Milner, Marshal Haig, M. Poincaré, M. Clemenceau, M. Loucheur, and General Pétain. I was not satisfied. From what I could learn, General Pétain was getting ready to retire on Paris, General Haig to the west. It was the open door for Germany—it was defeat.

"'Marshal Haig, supported by Lord Milner, said there must be a responsible head and unity of command. I was proposed.

"'We can,' said Clemenceau, 'give to Marshal Foch the command of the armies operating round Amiens.'

"'Marshal Haig was the one who opposed this and declared that there was only one sensible solution, which was to give me the command of the armies on the west front. M. Clemenceau bowed, and it was decided.

"'At lunch, which followed, M. Clemenceau said to me:

"'Well, you have it, the place you wanted!'

"'I lost patience a little; I answered:

"'What, Mr. President! You give me a lost battle and you ask me to retrieve it. I accept, and you've the idea that you've made me a present? It requires my entire self-effacement to accept in such circumstances.'"

POSTSCRIPT

Eight Years After

TO the pages of the above Appendix, Time can do nothing: they record the intimately spoken words of world figures about world subjects during hours of world crisis: their dramatic interest remains, their historic interest has but increased: here are Woodrow Wilson, Lloyd George, Clemenceau, Foch, and Paderewski, all in moments of deep and controversial emotion—and each of these remarkable men draws the main outlines of his own character.

To my own pages, Time has brought a few corrections, and much verification. What is expressed in the title of the book and elaborated in Chapter twenty-eight, grows more true each year.

OWEN WISTER.

Long House, April 23, 1928.